NEVER FORGET THE TRUTH

TRUTH BOOK THREE

F. D. ADKINS

F. D. Adkins

*"For with God
nothing shall
be impossible."
Luke 1:37 KJV*

F. D. ADKINS LLC

To my Heavenly Father,
Who tells me I can
When I say I can't.
"For with God nothing shall be impossible." Luke 1:37 KJV

NEVER FORGET THE TRUTH

A CHRISTIAN THRILLER

Truth Book Three

CHAPTER ONE

E motions wage war inside me, battling for control of my body. Fear of failure paralyzes my muscles, while anger and frustration at not being able to enjoy what should be the happiest time of my life force blood through my body in violent pulses. With trembling hands, I grip the handle of my Glock nine-millimeter pistol so hard that my white knuckles ache. *He's here. I know he's here.* Sweat beads erupt on my forehead and run down my face. *Or maybe it's tears,* I think. At this point, it doesn't matter. Both sweat and tears reflect the turmoil tearing away at me.

Swallowing the lump in my throat, I move my left hand from the gun and rest it on the bathroom doorknob. I pause for a second, take a shallow breath, and hold it as I try to absorb the words running through my head. *Never Forget... be not afraid... for the Lord thy God is with thee whithersoever thou goest.* In an attempt to make no sound,

I twist the knob in slow motion and crack the door open an inch at a time until I can peek through. *I knew it.* My chest tightens, and a sharp pain stabs through my sternum as my eyes peer across the room and fall on the open bedroom door. *The door was closed. I am positive that I closed it.*

With a quiet step, I shift to the side of the bathroom door and press the front of my body against the wall. *Three. Two. One.* I fling my right foot out and kick the bathroom door open. Keeping my torso shielded behind the wall, I lean around the casing just enough to scour the room. *Nothing. Maybe he's under the bed.*

I press my lips together and still my breathing as I clutch the handle of the gun in my right hand and steady it with my left. With the tip of my nine-millimeter pointed at the bottom of the bed skirt, I pad toward it with soft steps, wishing I could quieten the sound of my pounding heart. A glimpse of movement in my peripheral vision sends my reflexes into action. In a swift motion, I swing my arm around and aim at the door.

"Ellie, no. It's me!"

"Get back," I almost yell. "He's in here." Panic floods through every syllable.

"Ellie," Steve takes a step into the room, "put the gun down. No one is in here."

"He's here. Please get back." My voice cracks. I swallow and try to think fast. I need to convince Steve to listen to me. "I heard something, and the door was open. I know I closed the door, Steve." My words quaver with hysteria, and I start to talk faster. "I pushed on it and counted to seven to make sure it latched. It was closed."

"Yes, it was." Steve takes another step. The dark skin on his face is tinted red with alarm. "But I opened it. The noise you heard was me trying to find my phone charger." He glances around the room. "I thought I might have left it in here last night."

I look at him through narrowed eyes and scratch my head. "Didn't you tell me that you and Spencer were going to the store before breakfast?"

"We were, but then I decided to wait because I think I'm going to need a few more things to finish the room." Steve lets out a long sigh as he runs his hand in a fast swoop through his dark brown hair. "Would you please put that gun down?"

"Oh," I say aloud as I realize that I still have the gun aimed out in front of me. I drop my arm to my side and let the tears pool in my eyes. "I'm sorry," I mouth the words because I can't seem to get any sound to come out.

Steve's strong, muscular arms drape around me, and he pulls my head into his chest. He strokes my brown hair and tucks a loose twig behind my ear. "Ellie, honey, I know that nightmare still haunts you, but he can't take our baby. He's dead. Why can't you accept that? Agent Morgan has reassured you, and you even did your own research." He pulls back and gazes down at me with soft eyes. The same dark brown eyes that drew me in when I woke up in the training facility. "Try putting your personal feelings aside and look at it from a professional standpoint. You work for the FBI, and you've seen the evidence. He received the death penalty. Uncle Dukakis even witnessed his execution, and you have been to his gravesite. If that's not enough, he was fingerprinted at the prison, and not just his thumb, but all his fingers. Ellie, the fingerprints all matched and identified him as Dennis Denali. We have a lot of things to fear right now with the outbreak of crime and the uprising against the government, but my father is not one of them. And, besides that, with all the security features we have added, this house is like a fortress."

"I'm aware of all of our alarms and robots and cameras and lasers and high-tech surveillance gadgets, but if he wants in here, nothing will stop him." I drag my feet over to the bed and drop onto the mattress. I squeeze my eyes closed and try to put my thoughts in order, but I can't decipher which ones make sense and which ones don't.

"You're right. Maybe it's just pregnancy hormones," I croak out. "I know I have obsessive-compulsive disorder, but I have always been able to distinguish the obsessive thoughts from the rational ones. I mean, I sometimes lack control over my compulsive rituals, but in my mind, I have recognized that it was an obsessive thought triggering my compulsions." Tears stream down my cheeks and drip from my face. I swipe both hands beneath my eyes and wipe them away. "But not this time. Even though I've seen the proof, right now, the danger is so real in my mind. I'm scared, Steve. I'm so scared. I'm going to be a mother. A mother is supposed to protect her child." I roll my eyes up at him. "What if I can't protect my baby?"

Steve sits on the bed next to me and scratches his fingertips across my back in a gentle motion. "Okay, let's think this through like you would any other obsessive thought. First," he pauses, "I'm not going to say it. You are." He stares into my eyes with a smile spread across his face.

I return his stare, remembering the words he wrote on the note the day we met. "Never forget. 'Be not afraid...for the Lord thy God is with thee whithersoever thou goest.'"

"That's right." He pulls my head over onto his shoulder. "Ellie, God has never let you down. Let Him carry this worry. This baby is His creation, another one of His masterpieces. And He already knows everything that's going to happen in this child's life. Your stress is not going to change that."

I nod without lifting my head.

"Second, I think it's safe to say that no mother is better qualified to protect her child than you. You work for the FBI, and I've seen your fighting skills. It wasn't that long ago that you rendered two strong men unconscious with a kick to the head." He gapes at the floor and lets out a heavy breath. "But, Ellie, I have to be honest. No, my father is not an issue, but your job is. You are seven, almost eight months pregnant. With the rebellion going on in this country against authority, anyone associated with the government or law enforcement has a target on their back. As your husband, I'm supposed to protect you, and I've installed every security feature imaginable on this house, and some that aren't even imaginable. But I can't keep you safe when you leave here. Will you please take early leave? Please."

"Hmmm. Aren't you contradicting yourself?" I ask.

"I'm sure that's how it sounds, but no, I'm not. Choosing to leave this house and go into a federal building is no different than jumping off a bridge. The danger out there is real. Law enforcement has no control, and they are outnumbered. Yes, God is in control, but you shouldn't intentionally put yourself in danger."

I use my hands and push myself up off of the bed. "It's not like I am out in the midst of the chaos. Since I'm pregnant, the bureau will only let me work inside the office. I like my job. Please try and understand. It gives my mind something to focus on, and I need that." I look down at my protruding belly. "I've already had to give up my morning run, and I can't even go for a walk outside because it isn't safe." I notice the frown lines on my husband's face and a thought stops me for a second. *If our roles were reversed, how would I feel?* My shoulders slump because I know I wouldn't feel any different than he does. "Alright, I'll think about it." I reach out my hand and smile, thankful that God has given me a husband who really does love me the way the Bible says a husband should love his wife. "And now that we have concluded that our former president is not hiding under our bed, let's go and get some coffee and toast. I'm starving."

"Sounds good," Steve agrees and rises to his feet. "Herb has the coffee ready, and I want to show you some paint samples for the baby's room."

I lean over the bed and use my hands to smooth the wrinkles in the bedspread where we were sitting.

As we walk toward the door, Steve places his hand on my stomach. "He is rambunctious this morning. Are you sure you should have coffee?"

"Fine. I'll have water." I blow a puff of air out of my mouth.

"We do have decaf, you know."

"No, thanks." I roll my eyes up. "That sort of defeats the point of having a cup of morning coffee."

"Hey, is your mom still having everyone over for dinner tonight?" Steve asks, picking up a stack of paint samples off the table in the hallway.

"Yes. She says we are doing some wedding planning, but my gut tells me she is up to something else. I'm just not sure what."

"As long as she is cooking, she can be plotting anything she wants," he mumbles. "I wonder what she's making for dessert. Ooooh... I hope it's coconut cake with extra icing."

I can't help but laugh. "You know she always makes banana pudding for Spencer." I stop at the kitchen door and shake my head.

Waves is standing in the center of the kitchen with his metal hands covering his eyes. His red mohawk quivers as he counts. "Seven... Eight... Nine... Ten... Ready or not, here I come." He drops his hands. "Oh, Good morning." His robotic voice always has a cheerful tone. "Spencer and I are playing hide and seek. And let me tell you, that little monkey is a whiz at this game. I can never find him, but as soon as he finishes counting, it seems he has already located me."

"That's because you won't stop singing," Herb drones with sarcasm.

Waves pauses and then wheels toward the door. "Row, row, row your boat gently down the stream. Merrily, merrily, merrily...."

Herb's black toupee bounces as he shakes his head. "He could at least learn a new song." He places two cups of coffee on the table.

"Thanks, Herb, but I'm going to have water. Too much caffeine is not good for the baby." I sit down in the chair, wondering why I find it necessary to use polite manners with Herb, Claude, and Waves. After all, they're robots. But they have such human personalities, and they are so kind and respectful when they speak. *Of course, that's because they are programmed that way.* After we stopped Dr. Eckert's plan to stimulate mass murder across the country, Waves and Claude became part of our household too. Steve has made a few programming tweaks for added security, but for the most part, their individual personality traits are still the same.

Herb wipes his metal fingertips on his apron and leans over toward me. "No worries, Mrs. Ellie," he lowers his volume, "your coffee hasn't contained caffeine since you notified me of your condition. You have decaf with two splashes of sugar-free caramel." He raises back up and straightens his red bowtie. "But I will get you some water too."

Steve sits in the chair next to me and spreads out the paint samples. Spencer bounces up seemingly out of nowhere and leaps into his chair on the other side of the table. He lays an apple, a banana, and an orange in front of him and grabs our hands.

"I'm with him." I lay my hand on top of Steve's. "Let's say the blessing first. I'm hungry."

Steve flips his hand over and squeezes mine. "Father, we thank you for keeping us safe and for providing for our needs. And we thank you for blessing us with this child, Lord. We ask that you would please calm Ellie's fears and keep her and our son safe. Help her to be able to enjoy this blessed time in her life. And Lord, we pray for our country. We pray that the fighting and the violence would stop, that these people would turn from the revenge they seek, and that they would put their trust and faith in you. Father, we lift your name and give you all the praise. In Jesus' Holy name. Amen."

I lift my eyes and touch the rim of my coffee mug to my lips.

"I thought you weren't having coffee." Steve glares at me.

"Well, I was recently informed that I've been drinking decaf for months without knowing it, so why stop now?" I take a bite of my peanut butter toast and move my eyes over the array of paint options spread on the wooden tabletop. "This is a lot of colors to choose from," I utter through a mouth full of toast.

"I wanted you to see all of the options."

I glance over and try to read Steve's expression. The look on his face tells me that he already has a favorite. "So, which one do you like?"

He twists his mouth to the side as if he's considering all the choices. "The norm is usually blue for boys, but I'm really drawn to this one." He slides a paint card from the stack and hands it to me.

"It's bright." I notice the words printed in the lower corner, *Canary Yellow*. "I like it. It reminds me of the sun. And babies love bright colors. Let's go with that one." I reach for my coffee and freeze. "Uh oh. What time is it?

"Seven-thirty," Steve answers. "Why? I thought you were off today."

"I am, but..." I slide back from the table.

"You haven't checked your seven o'clock text from Jillian."

"No. And she is probably on her way over here by now," I say, worrying about her coming out by herself with all of this pandemonium going on.

"Just eat. You probably left your phone in the bathroom. I'll go look for it." Steve pats my back and heads out of the room.

I hold the warm coffee mug in my hands, thinking about how I must get a bit of my OCD from my mother. My sister, Eileen, disappeared almost four years ago. That's when my mother's compulsive texts started. Even though we found Eileen and have endured much greater trials since then, my mother still sends a text precisely at seven o'clock, noon, three o'clock in the afternoon, and nine o'clock at night before bed to make sure I'm okay. And it's always the same text.

> *Please text back that you are okay and always know Mom loves you.*

Steve darts back into the kitchen and hands the vibrating phone to me.

"Oh, no. Twelve texts and a missed call." I swipe the screen and type a reply as fast as I can.

> *So, so sorry. I didn't realize the time. Everything is great! I love you too! Can't wait for dinner tonight.*

As soon as I hit send, the phone jingles. "Mom. I'm sorry," I answer, hoping my apology will smooth things over. "I texted you just now."

"Ellie, did you read my texts?" Mom spouts through the phone, and I can hear the tears hiding behind her choked words.

I swallow hard afraid to know what's wrong. "I was in a hurry to let you know I was okay. What is it? You sound like something's wrong?"

"Eileen." Mom sniffles. "She's been in a car accident. Your father and I are on our way to the hospital. It's that new big one outside of Arlington. The woman who called said that she didn't have any information about her condition. Apparently, the hospital is slammed with all of this rioting and craziness, and the woman's job is contacting a relative and scaring them to death when someone is brought in."

"It'll be okay, Mom. Let me know if you hear anything else. Steve and I are on our way."

CHAPTER TWO

"She has to be okay. Please, please, let her be okay." I squeeze my eyes closed and grip the edge of the seat as Steve whips the car into the hospital parking lot. *I can't lose her again.* It's as if I'm living the day Eileen disappeared all over again. Her car was found abandoned on the side of the road, and for two years, we searched for her with no idea or leads as to what could have happened. That's when I got the letter from President Denali saying he had chosen me to be a part of his special crime unit, Soldiers Against Crime. Of course, that turned out to be a lie. He had really chosen me to be a part of his personal army that would repopulate the earth after he dropped poison on the rest of humanity. I was taken to his special training facility where he was erasing the memories of his trainees in order to eliminate any knowledge of God. He actually believed that he could create a world where he was the supreme leader and faith in

God wouldn't exist. But it was no coincidence that I was chosen for his army and had to go to that training facility because that's where I found Eileen. President Denali had frozen my little sister in a tube because he couldn't make her forget her Heavenly Father.

I shake off the horrors flooding into my mind, reminding myself that I also met my husband in that facility, so my going there was part of God's plan. With that thought, I go back to sending up prayers to God, begging Him to take care of Eileen.

"Wait to get out until I come around to your side of the car and make sure you have quick access to your gun." Steve veers into the first parking space available. Out of the corner of my eye, I glimpse Steve watching a group of young men huddled around a truck a few rows over. "I hope you brought your badge. That's our ticket to getting through the metal detector with a weapon."

I wipe the moisture from my cheeks with my fingertips. "Yeah, I have it. The gun is in my holster under my jacket, and my badge is in my purse."

In a second, Steve is already around the car, opening my door. I take hold of the grab handle to help pull myself up and out. With Steve's arm around my shoulders, we stride to the emergency entrance and stop in front of the glass sliding doors, but they don't automatically open as they would have before all the commotion started.

A guard stands on the other side and his voice comes through a small speaker mounted on the wall. "Hello. Place your thumbs on the identification pad one at a time, and I'll need to know your reason for entering the building today."

Steve presses his thumb to the pad first. "We're here to check on my wife's sister, Eileen Hatcher. She was in an automobile accident."

I guess the last name on the screen catches the guard by surprise because his face turns a pasty white, and he starts to stutter.

"S-Steve D-D-Denali...Denali is your last name?" His pitch rises in question.

"Yes, sir. That's correct. And this is my wife, Ellie." Steve motions toward me.

I reach over and press my thumb to the pad, but the guard keeps his eyes plastered on Steve.

"Must be rough having the same last name as the scumbag president that wanted to kill us all," the man says, raising one eyebrow.

"The name is no big deal," Steve replies. "What's rough is knowing that scumbag was my father."

The guard's eyes widen so much that I don't know how he keeps them in their sockets.

"But on the upside, I have no memory of him." Steve continues to rant. "He was such a loving father that he erased my memory."

"Th-that's t-t-terr-ible," the guard sputters out, and then he drops his focus back to the screen. "Federal Bureau of Investigation, huh?"

"Yes, sir." I clear my throat and wipe another tear from my face. "Please, I need to know how my sister is."

He looks at me with questioning eyes. "I am assuming since you're a federal agent, you are armed."

"Yes, sir." I nod.

"Step quickly through when the door slides open," he instructs.

The doors slide but only halfway. Steve places his hand on the small of my back, giving me a gentle nudge. As soon as we're clear of the doors, they slide closed, and a large, walk-through metal detector stands in front of us.

"Mrs. Denali, place your weapon on the tray." The guard pushes a small metal basket toward me. "You can pick it up after you pass through."

"What about my purse?"

"Just hold it," he replies.

I follow his instructions without taking my eyes off my gun and grab it the second I step out of the detector. Steve comes through the detector right behind me.

"It appears that your sister is still in the emergency room." He points to another door. "At the end of the hall is the waiting area."

"Thank you," I blurt out and take off down the hall before Steve has a chance to speak. I don't turn around, but I can hear his shoes clomping against the hard tile floor right behind me.

"Why won't they tell us anything? If they aren't going to let us see her, the least they could do is tell me if my baby is alright." Mom's tear-filled voice echoes through the door before I even cross the threshold. "It's so frustrating. I don't know anybody who works here."

"Mom," I say as soon as I enter the room. Her short brown hair with streaks of gray is curled and sprayed so every strand stays in place, but her puffy eyes are swollen and bloodshot.

Mom leaps from the chair next to Dad and yanks me into a hug. "Ellie, they won't tell us how she is. They keep saying they don't know. I'm scared. How can they not know?" Mom rattles off between short, strained breaths.

"Mom, you have to calm down. Let me go talk to them." I kiss her cheek and move toward the receptionist counter that is enclosed behind solid glass. A small metal circle is embedded in the center with small holes to speak through. I stare through the glass, and an older woman with black-dyed hair pinned in a bun on top of her head looks up at me. "Yes, I'm Ellie Denali. Do you have any information on my sister, Eileen Hatcher, yet?"

As I finish my question, a younger brunette woman in scrubs steps up. The older woman starts to answer, but the younger woman cuts her off. "Oh, the doctor just finished up with Ms. Hatcher. You guys can come back and see her. I'll meet you at that door." She nods to a wooden door off to the side of the little window.

I breathe a sigh of relief even though I still don't know her condition. But I can't imagine they would allow us to all go back if it was serious. "Thank you so much," I say to the woman as I turn and motion for Steve, Mom, and Dad.

We follow the nurse to a small examining room. Eileen is lying on a gurney-type bed with wires hooked to her arm and chest. I'm not even sure when or how Mom got past me, but I blink, and she is standing beside Eileen.

"Baby, what happened? Are you okay? Is anything broken?" Mom's questions come out so fast that I'm not sure Eileen knows which one to answer first.

Eileen parts her mouth to speak, but before she gets a word out, the door opens, and a man with a stethoscope around his neck sticks his head in.

"Eileen, the nurse will bring your discharge papers in a few minutes," he informs in an overly friendly tone.

"Thanks, Ted," Eileen replies with a slight smile on her face.

"Oh, is this your family?" The man steps into the room. He's probably in his late twenties and has dark hair and hazel eyes.

"Yes." Eileen sits up and points to each of us as she introduces us. "This is my mom, Jillian, my dad, Tom, my sister, Ellie, and her husband, Steve."

"It's nice to meet you all," the man remarks. "I'm Dr. Flynn." He extends his hand to my dad. "But call me Ted, please."

Dad shakes Ted's hand. "So, Ted, I assume my daughter is okay since I heard you say discharge papers."

Ted continues to shake everyone's hands... but mine. I tuck myself back in the corner and give a little wave. I don't like to touch people's hands. I sort of have an issue with germs. I'm not as bad as I used to be because now it doesn't bother me to hold hands with my family and my closest friends when we pray. But considering we're in a hospital and the man is a doctor, that means extra germs from my obsessive-compulsive point of view.

"Yes," Ted confirms, "she's going to be fine. I'm guessing she may be pretty sore for a few days, and she will most likely have some bruising. But nothing serious to worry about." He steps toward the door. "I hate to run, but I have another patient waiting. I'll see you guys tonight though. Eileen, take it easy today."

"I will. Thanks, Ted," Eileen says with a glow on her face that speaks the opposite of someone who has just been in an automobile accident.

The doctor tosses his hand up in a wave and exits the room. Mom, Dad, Steve, and I all cast our eyes on Eileen at the same time.

"Sis," I scratch my head, searching for the right way to word my question.

"Eileen," Dad interjects before I put my thought together, "what was that man talking about?"

"He was explaining that I might have some bruising because of the airbag—"

"Not that part, Eileen." Dad rolls his eyes. "The part about seeing us tonight."

"Oh," Eileen cracks a smile, "Ted asked me to dinner tonight, but I told him I couldn't because my mom was preparing this big dinner at our house. We kept talking, and we sort of hit it off. So, I invited him to join us."

"So, let me get this straight," I glare down at my sister, "while we are racing to the hospital in fits of tears worried to death if you are okay, you are making goo-goo eyes at the doctor and planning a date."

Mom claps her hands together. "Well, I think it's wonderful. Because of that horrible President Denali, Eileen missed out on a lot of dates."

That's true, I think to myself and shrug. *She was sixteen when she disappeared, the time when most girls start to date. She spent two years of her life frozen in a tube. And, on top of that, she lost all of her childhood memories. It's taken quite a while for her to put her life back together.* "Mom's right. I'm sorry, Eileen. Ted seems nice. I'm glad you invited him to dinner."

"Now, sweetheart," Mom pats Eileen's hand, "are you okay? Tell us what happened."

"Well, I thought that if I went out early in the morning, the troublemakers might still be sleeping, and it would be safer." Eileen covers her face with her hands. "Oh, this is embarrassing."

"What, honey? What happened?" Mom presses.

"You guys know that I'm a bit of a slow driver. I guess the man behind me got impatient because he tried to pass me. As he got right beside me, a car came flying over the hill. I knew he was going to get hit head-on if I didn't get out of the way, but a guardrail hugged the shoulder of the road." Water pools in the corners of Eileen's eyes. "I had nowhere to go, so I slammed on my brakes to let him over in front of me." Her face stiffens as if she is experiencing the accident all over again. "It all happened so fast. He veered over into the side of my car. The impact forced me off the road, and my car flipped over the guard rail and landed on its top."

Both of Mom's hands fly up to her chest as she gasps. "Your car was upside down. It's a miracle that you're alright. What about the man who ran you off the road?"

Eileen lifts her shoulders. "I guess he's fine. He didn't stop."

"He ran you off the road and left." Dad raises his voice. "The police didn't catch him?"

"The officer took my description of his car," Eileen says in a carefree tone, "but he said with all the crime taking place, a hit and run wasn't a top priority. He even noted that if he hadn't been driving past, an officer probably wouldn't have been sent to the scene."

I shake my head in disbelief that the situation in our country has come to this. "What was so important that you needed to go out anyway? You shouldn't be going anywhere alone right now."

"Coconut."

I narrow my eyes. *Did Eileen say coconut? She risked her life for coconut.* "Coconut?" I repeat in question.

"Yes, we were out, and I wanted to make a cake. Last time you guys were over for dinner, I heard Steve say he really liked Mom's coconut cake, so I was going to make one for tonight," Eileen explains.

Steve drops his head. "Great. Now it's my fault."

The door swings open, and a nurse steps in holding a computerized tablet. "Eileen Hatcher?"

"Yes, Ma'am," Eileen answers.

"I'm here to take care of your discharge paperwork." The nurse moves over to the side of the bed.

I lean over and kiss Eileen's head. "This room is kind of small for all of us to stay here. Steve and I will see you tonight."

Eileen reaches up and pats my belly. "Thanks for coming to check on me. I love you."

"I love you too, sis."

"Take it easy today, Eileen. I'm going to let you take a rain check on that cake." Steve looks over his shoulder and smiles as we exit the room.

Steve takes my hand as we walk side by side through the waiting room and back into the main hall toward the exit.

"I don't know if it's strange or sad."

Steve tilts his head. "What's strange or sad?"

"The emergency room is overloaded with patients, but the waiting room for family and friends is practically empty," I remark in a solemn tone.

"People are afraid to go anywhere." Steve squeezes my hand, and his feet stop moving.

"We should wait," we both say at almost the same time and then smile at each other.

"Great minds think alike," Steve utters as we walk back into the waiting room.

I don't break stride and give Steve a chance to lead. The ache in my lower back draws me to the first chair I see. Without touching the armrests, I ease myself onto the seat, tucking my purse in beside me, and clasp my hands together on top of my round stomach. Steve takes the seat next to me and leans his head back against the wall.

I try to block my growing irritation, but it's eating at me that this man is going to get away with running my little sister off of the road. I get my mouth half-open to vent to Steve, but his eyes are closed. *I guess you can catch a five-minute nap anywhere.*

I turn my focus to the door and watch for Eileen, Mom, and Dad to come out. *Thank you, Lord. Thank you for letting Eileen be okay.* I still can't wrap my mind around the fact that her car flipped upside down on the other side of a guard rail, and she only has a few bruises from the airbag.

A few moments pass and the door swings open. Dad holds it as a nurse pushes Eileen through in a wheelchair and then he and Mom follow.

"Ellie, Steve," Eileen's face lights up, "I thought you left."

Steve jumps at the sound of her voice and speaks up. "We only made it a few steps down the hall. Ellie and I decided that we should wait and walk out with you guys."

The nurse pushes Eileen down the hall to the main door where the guard is stationed. "Alright, here we are. I'm sorry, but under the circumstances, this is as far as I am allowed to escort you." Her lips turn slightly down, and her shoulders slump. "Funny, it used to be the opposite. We were required to get you to your car." She exhales with a defeated groan. "Oh, how times have changed. Do you need the wheelchair, Eileen?"

"No, I'm fine. You didn't have to push me this far," Eileen stands and rests her hand on the nurse's shoulder, "but thank you. I appreciate your kindness."

The nurse caps her hand over Eileen's. "That's what I'm here for. I hope you feel better." She spins the wheelchair around toward the waiting area. "Stay safe," she says over her shoulder and then moves back down the hall.

"Alright, Baby Girl," Mom wraps her arm around Eileen's waist as if she is helping her along, "let's get you home so you can rest."

"I saw your car when we pulled in. You're not parked that far from us," Steve says, glancing at Mom as the guard slides the doors partially open, and we step outside.

The freezing winter air hits me in the face and rushes up my nose. Usually, I whine about being cold, but right now the weather is the least of my worries.

Dad twists his head, scouring the parking lot with his eyes. "Ah, could be worse. At least it's daylight."

The hair on my neck stands at attention and prickles run down my spine. I hug my arms around my body and slide my hand under my jacket until my fingers touch the handle of my gun. The men from earlier are gone, and no one seems to be around, but for some reason, I have this eerie feeling. Chills cover my body, and it has nothing to do with the low temperature. *If it's daylight and the sun is shining, why is the sky so dim? And why does everything seem so still? The wind is blowing, but the leaves aren't even swaying.*

Watching and listening, I step off the sidewalk with Steve hovering close to me. I notice Dad holding his hands out, moving right behind Mom and Eileen like he is shielding them, and his eyes are still darting from side to side. Maybe I'm imagining it, but even the white hair seems to be standing on end on top of his head. *I guess I'm not the only one feeling a bit uneasy.*

Mom points at her white Criss Cross sports utility vehicle. "Oh, look. We are only three spaces down from you."

"Listen," Dad urges in a low, firm voice, "we'll see each other tonight. Let's not tarry out here. Everybody, get in the vehicles."

"I agree." I veer toward our little hydrogen fuel car with Steve so close that I can feel the warm air brushing by the side of my face when he exhales. He opens the passenger door for me, and right before he closes the door, a scream slices through the air. *Mom. No!* I shout in anger to myself. *Why didn't we watch until they were in their car?*

Steve's body shifts back and forth. I can tell he doesn't know whether to take off toward the sound of my mom's scream or wait for me to get out of the car. He waits, but not for long because I leap out with my nine-millimeter in my hand and my heavy heart trailing behind me.

As I round the back of the car, my heels dig in, and I stop dead.

Two young men are backing away from Mom's car, making no effort to hide their appearance. One has pale skin and short blonde hair that is perfectly combed. The other one has dark, tousled, shoulder-length hair with darker skin. Both are wearing jeans. The man with the blonde hair has one arm clamped around Eileen's neck and is pressing a gun to her head with the other. Eileen's face is hardened, but with a gun to her head, she obviously isn't fighting. On the contrary, her entire body is limp. She is making him pull every ounce of her weight along with him. The man with dark hair has his gun trained on Mom and Dad.

"If you love your daughter, you better close your mouth, lady," the dark-haired man yells, stopping with his aim pointed directly at Mom.

An immediate silence fills the air. Somehow, Steve steps in front of me without making a sound. I ease the gun behind my back. There's nothing I can do. The man has a gun to my baby sister's temple. Silent tears gush down my face as I watch the two men shuffle backward across the lot, dragging Eileen with her feet bouncing across the pavement.

"I think they're headed for that red pickup truck on the end," I whisper to Steve in a barely audible voice. "We have to get the tag number... What on earth?"

Another well-dressed man in khakis and a polo shirt steps out from between two cars right behind the blonde-haired man who is dragging Eileen and thrusts the barrel of a pistol into the back of his head. The dark-haired man must catch the movement in his peripheral vision because he pivots with his weapon, whipping his arm in the direction of the newcomer.

Without thought, I react. The second that the dark-haired man's aim is off of my mom, I fire. The deafening boom from the shot echoes through the air. The man's gun ricochets across the pavement, and he falls to the ground with his left hand clasped around his right wrist.

The blond-haired man loosens his grip on Eileen, but he doesn't drop his gun. Instead, he twists his body in a hard motion, swinging his weapon around with him toward the newcomer behind him. Another gunshot sounds, this time from the newcomer's weapon, and the blond-haired man's body slaps the pavement.

The guard rushes out of the hospital with his gun drawn and aimed somewhat toward the dark-haired man. The guard's hand is trembling so badly that I'm not sure he should be aiming the gun at all, but he manages to get to the dark-haired man and subdue him. However, considering the man is flailing around on the ground, covering a bullet hole through his hand, he doesn't exactly put up much of a fight.

"Is that Ted?" Steve mutters in disbelief as the newcomer escorts Eileen back across the lot.

"I wish I could say it was good to see you all again, but I would rather our next encounter had been in a more pleasant situation like dinner tonight." Ted lets go of Eileen, and Mom pulls her into a hug.

"Talk about perfect timing. How...? What were you doing...?" I can't seem to get my question out.

Ted nods. "No doubt, it was pretty impeccable timing. I just got off of my shift and was heading home."

Eileen wriggles loose from Mom's embrace. "Thank you, Ted."

"No worries. Now, go get some rest. I'm going to watch all of you get in your car, and I will see you tonight... that is, if you're still having a dinner party after all of the drama today... and if I'm still invited after," he pauses as he glances over his shoulder at the man's body on the ground and then turns his focus back to us, "shooting someone."

Mom lets out a deep sigh and smiles. "Oh, you are definitely invited. I don't even want to think about what could have happened if you hadn't been getting in your car."

I pause, looking at the man that I shot through the hand. The guard is with him, but I know I'll need to wait and take care of a report.

Ted darts his eyes between me and the man the guard has cuffed on the ground. "That was an amazing shot. Do you target practice or what?"

"I work for the FBI. I need to do a report." My words drag out, expressing my unhappiness about having to stay there.

"It's not safe here, especially in your condition. Call it in on your way home. I'll wait here as a witness and answer any questions. Chances are there are no officers available to come anyway." He twitches his head toward the guard escorting the man to the emergency entrance. "Besides, protocol says we have to take him into the hospital for treatment."

It disgusts me to admit it, but Ted is right. I have seen firsthand the number of calls that go without a response from authorities. There are too many to handle. I haven't mentioned it to Steve or my family because it's too horrible for my mind to comprehend. But instead of adding law enforcement, a new department has been created, a cleanup crew that drives around and recovers the deceased bodies like the man lying on the pavement that Ted shot. I bite my lips together until I can push back the tears. "Thanks, I appreciate it. I'll make the call from the car before we leave. I want to make sure they know you did what you had to do," I say, peering across the lot at the unmoving blond-haired man lying in a pool of blood.

"Come on. Let's get out of this parking lot before something else happens," Dad urges.

"I'll see you tonight." Eileen casts a smile over her shoulder as she climbs into Mom's SUV. "And thanks for saving my life."

Steve wraps his arm around my shoulder and guides me back to the car. As we walk, I whisper a silent prayer thanking God for Eileen's safety and another for the blonde-haired man's family. Ted did what he had to do. If he hadn't, it could've been my baby sister. But still, someone out there loves that man, and someone is going to be grieving when he doesn't come home.

CHAPTER THREE

S pencer sits on my lap, rubbing his small hand across my stomach. He is fascinated that my stomach has gotten so big so fast. And when he feels the baby kick, the biggest, toothiest smile covers his face, and he claps his hands in excitement. I think it's like a game to him. However, riding with him on my lap isn't all that comfortable anymore. This hydrogen fuel Hydromax isn't that big, and my ginormous belly fills up what space there is. At least, it's a bit roomier than the little Volkswagen, but that 'bug' is still my favorite. Too bad we can't find gasoline so we can drive it. I'm afraid it is going to sit and ruin. Anyway, I don't have the heart to make Spencer get in the back. He has always demanded the front seat, and since we have always let him have it, this has become the official seating arrangement. We rescued him when we were all in President Denali's facility. Like Eileen, he was frozen in a tube too. It doesn't seem fair to punish him because of my discomfort. He's already going to have a lot of adjusting to do when the baby comes.

Steve pulls the car around to the back of my parents' house, and we go up the steps to the screen door. I stare at the swing gently swaying on the porch and imagine rocking back and forth with my baby boy in my arms. Spencer taps on the door from his position on Steve's shoulders.

The blinds crack apart in the window, and after a few seconds of heavy clatter, Dad pulls the door open. The smell of pot roast and cornbread makes my mouth water before I even step inside the house. My mom was raised in the Deep South, so she's a master of Southern cooking.

Steve helps Dad get the heavy-duty bar bolted back in place. After the day Eileen had, I can understand why he feels the need to barricade the door, but more people are coming. He's going to work himself to death if he keeps taking that huge steel bar on and off. My eyes drop to my stomach, and I realize that it doesn't matter to Dad if he has to lift that heavy bar a trillion times. He'll do whatever it takes to keep us safe. I know he has made some questionable decisions in the past, but he made those decisions with the best of intentions. He thought he was doing what was best for us.

A rumble in my stomach yanks me from my thoughts. "Oh, Mom, that smells delicious. I'm starving." I walk over to the counter, sucking in deep breaths hoping that if I inhale hard enough, I will be able to taste it. "What can I do to help?"

Mom's lips curve into a proud grin. "It would help a lot if someone could sample it and make sure it has enough seasoning."

"My dream job," I say with a laugh.

Mom eases closer, and as she hands me a spoon, she tucks my hair behind my ear. "After you test my cooking, would you go talk to Eileen?" Mom speaks so low that I have to read her lips. "I'm worried about her."

I pause to listen. "Is that the piano?"

"Umm-hmm." Mom gives me that 'see what I mean' look.

Eileen only plays piano when she is upset. I suppose it's a stress release like running is for me.

"I'll go talk to her." I stick the spoonful of roast in my mouth. "That is so good. I hope the baby doesn't come out thinking I can cook like this." I'm dying to take another bite, but I know I need to talk to Eileen. Everyone will be here soon.

I lay the spoon in the sink, and as I head out of the kitchen, Mom is holding Spencer and telling him in a baby-talk voice about the banana pudding she made for dessert.

I waddle down the hall toward the den, and the sound of the piano gets louder. *Oh my... 'Fur Elise.' Eileen only plays that when ultimate depression has set in.* I stop in the doorway and lean against the casing. She and I look almost identical, but our talents are a different story. My sister has such a gift for music. As for me, let's just say that my elementary school music teacher wouldn't even let me play the triangle.

I stare in awe, smitten by the sound. I wish that she didn't have to be upset to want to play because I love to listen to her.

Eileen must catch sight of me out of the corner of her eye because she stops playing and looks up. "Ellie, I didn't know you were here already."

"We decided to come a little early. I thought Mom might need some help." I drop down beside her on the piano stool. "Want to talk about what's bothering you?"

"I'm fine," Eileen says as she taps middle C with her index finger.

I roll my eyes at her. "Sis, you were playing 'Fur Elise.' We all know that means you're upset about something."

"Note to self. Pick a new song." Eileen lays her head on my shoulder. "Ellie, I could've been killed twice today. All these questions keep racing through my mind."

"Like what?" I ask.

"Why wasn't I? Is God trying to send me a message or even a warning? Have I done something wrong?"

"Well, are you aware of anything that you are doing wrong?"

"No," she whimpers.

"Eileen, because something bad happens to you, that doesn't mean God is punishing you for doing something wrong. We live in a sinful world, and being a Christian doesn't exclude us from facing troubles and tribulations. But the good news is that, as Christians, we don't have to go through those dark times alone. We have God to carry us through them. Remember Romans 8:28. 'And we know that all things work together for good to them that love God, to them who are called according to His purpose.' Sis, an evil man put us in that training facility, erased people's memories, used cryogenics to freeze some of those people, including you, because he couldn't separate them from God, and then more evildoers forced us to go back there a second time. God wasn't punishing us. He let us go there because we were part of His plan to stop that evil. And look at all the other positives God worked from it. Gerald and Teresa accepted Christ. I met Steve, and we got married. Alice is one of my closest friends, and she's engaged to Gerald, who she met there. You and Teresa have become best friends, and on top of all that, now you know what God wants you to do with your life."

"Don't forget Spencer," Eileen adds with a smile.

"No," I lightly tap Eileen with my elbow, "we certainly can't forget Spencer. That little monkey has added sunshine to all of our lives. But I am thankful he sleeps in his own room now. I couldn't imagine all of us squeezing in that bed with this belly."

Eileen turns her head away and giggles.

"I'm glad you're feeling better. What's so funny?" I prod.

"I'm sorry." Her giggle bursts into a hysterical laugh. "This image popped into my head."

"What image?"

She is laughing so hard she can barely catch her breath. "The image of you, my obsessive-compulsive germaphobe sister, giving that monkey mouth-to-mouth resuscitation."

"Laugh if you will, but my mouth-to-mouth resuscitation saved his life."

She stops laughing and throws her arms around my neck. "Thank you, Ellie."

"For what?" A tear runs down my cheek as I return my sister's embrace.

"For making me feel better... For always being there. And even though I can't remember anything before that training facility, I know you've always been there." She sniffles, and her back quivers beneath my hand. "Ellie, how do you do it? After all that you've been through, you have it all together. You're so strong no matter what. I want to be strong, but inside I just want to curl up, pull a blanket over my head, and cry."

I can't help but let out a chuckle at her statement. "Sis, I'm the furthest thing from having it together, and there are plenty of times that I do curl up and cry, blanket and all. But then, I remind myself that is exactly what the enemy wants me to do. He wants to bring me so far down that I can't focus on anything God has planned for me." My own words filter in my ears, and I realize that my obsession with Dennis Denali has been paralyzing me. "Would you believe this morning that I had my gun aimed at my bed because I thought my deceased father-in-law was hiding under it?"

"You still think President Denali is alive?" Eileen questions.

"Yes, but I know it isn't rational. There's more than enough proof that it was actually him who was executed." I sigh. "I'm letting my fear get the best of me."

Eileen lifts her head. "I don't want you to be afraid or sad, but it's nice to know that I'm not the only one who feels crushed to the ground sometimes."

"Sorry to interrupt," Steve says from the doorway. "Your mom told me to let you guys know that all the guests are here." He turns and disappears back down the hall.

Eileen stands and helps pull me to my feet. As we walk to the door, I drape my arm around her shoulder, which is a little awkward since she is taller than me.

"Ellie," Eileen stops and turns her eyes toward me, "Teresa is a close friend, and I don't know what I would do without her, but you're my best friend. You and I have a connection that I can't explain."

I smile back at her. "I can. We're sisters!"

CHAPTER FOUR

I never thought we would have enough people in this house to fill Mom's humongous dining table, but tonight, we have to pull up two extra folding chairs. When Steve and I got married, Mom gave us her smaller table. She said she needed a larger one now that Steve and Spencer were part of the family, and eventually, she knew there would be grandchildren too. However, I never imagined she meant a table that seated ten. It's a bit oversized for the room, but it fits perfectly with Mom's antique farmhouse décor. The dark-stained wooden top has a hand-scraped appearance, and the turned legs are about seven or eight inches in diameter. Three chairs line each side with two seats on each end.

Steve nudges my leg under the table and rolls his eyes at me with one side of his mouth slightly turned up. I know he is getting a kick out of Mom's name tags on the table assigning seats, and I'm sure he is thinking the same thing that I am. *Mom is playing matchmaker.* Mom has strategically placed Dukakis and Steve's mother, Cynthia, beside each other at the end. I shift my eyes to meet his with the same sly grin.

Usually, when we have dinners, Mom hints, but everybody tends to split into men on one end and women on the other. This time, she made sure they were sitting together. She and Dad are at the other end of the table with Steve, Me, Eileen, and Ted on one side and Gerald, Alice, Teresa, and Spencer on the other.

"Alright," Gerald rubs his stomach, "let's say the blessing. This smells so good that I can't contain myself any longer." He wipes his mouth with his hand. "My mouth is watering so much that I think I'm drooling." Gerald looks pretty much the same as he did when I first met him, except his stocky build has gotten a little stockier. He still has his brown hair in a military-style cut. I guess the short hair makes wearing the hair net easier when he is working in the kitchen.

"Oh, Gerald," Mom laughs, "you are just trying to make me feel good. But let's do connect our hearts in prayer. We have so much to be thankful for today. Dukakis, would you do the honors?"

We clutch onto each other's hands, unifying ourselves.

"Dear Heavenly Father, as we gather here around this table, we praise you. We praise you for allowing us this time of fellowship together in the midst of the storm going on around us. We praise you for protecting Eileen today. Lord, we know you must have special plans for her, and we ask that you guide her and help her in the path you have destined for her life. Lord, we pray that same prayer for the rest of us, that you would help us to shine for you in this time of darkness and chaos. Father, we thank you for this meal and the provisions that you have blessed us with. In everything, we give you all the thanks, praise, and glory. In Jesus' holy name, we pray. Amen."

"Amen," we all say somewhat in unison.

"Gerald, why don't you get us started and dip yours first," Mom slides the pot roast toward Gerald on her left, "since you are drooling and all."

"Let me at it." Gerald grabs the ladle. "I'm not shy."

Mom's grin grows larger as she watches the excitement build on Gerald's face with every spoonful that he dumps on his plate. "Oh." Mom turns her eyes back to the group. "I wanted to thank our first-time guest, Ted, for so graciously helping set the table and pour the drinks."

Ted tosses his hand lightly in the air. "It was the least I could do. I appreciate the invite and you including me in this meal with your family." He scratches his head. "To be honest, I'm not sure of the last time I had a home-cooked meal."

"Well, then, you're in luck because I made enough to feed an army, so you eat up."

"How's the restaurant doing, Gerald?" Dad probes. "I'm guessing not a lot of people are risking their lives to go out and eat."

"No, I've actually had to shut down the dining room. With the risk so high, I can't afford to pay the insurance premium," Gerald explains as he puts the ladle back in the dish and slides it to Alice. "We're only filling delivery orders and catering to businesses for lunch, so employees won't have to leave their workplace. I got connected with a network of other restaurants in the area on that new social media platform, BridgNect. Since all of us are trying to stay afloat, we're working together and splitting up the catering jobs in hopes that we can keep from going under until this is over."

"That's great." Teresa leans her head in and looks across Alice at Gerald. "Instead of competing, businesses are working together to help each other. With all of the negative media, it's nice to hear something positive in all this."

Gerald tries to smile, but his cheeks are full. He swallows hard. "Yeah, there are still a lot of good people out there. The problem is the bad ones are overtaking the country."

"The aftershocks," I mumble to myself.

Alice must have read my lips because her eyes meet mine across the table, and she mouths the words, "I think you're right. His plan is still in progress."

"So, Ted, you're a doctor in the ER?" Dukakis spurs the conversation. "I bet you are staying busy."

Ted sighs. "Oh, man. It's unbelievable. I can't even remember the last time I've been able to take a break, much less get a bite to eat during my shift."

"What are they doing about all of the patients that come in? I'm sure you're seeing a lot of serious injuries," Dad chimes in on the conversation from the other end of the table. "There can't be enough room in the hospital to keep them all."

Ted's forehead wrinkles. "I probably shouldn't say too much, but it is what it is. We've been ordered to only admit serious cases that have a significant chance of survival with medical care. Everyone else is either sent home or," Ted drops his head and lowers his voice, "given something to end their pain."

Mom gasps. "You mean... permanently?"

Ted shifts his head up and down in a quick, subtle jerk. "When I went to medical school, I thought I could make a difference. I thought I would be that doctor who took the time to listen to patients and figure out what was wrong when others couldn't. I thought... I could save lives. I never imagined that I would be carrying a gun and picking and choosing who I thought had a chance to live."

Cynthia grips the edge of the tabletop with both hands. "I have finally accepted that Dennis is dead, but this path of destruction all leads back to him. He is responsible for this." She squeezes her eyes closed. "I wish the American people would wake up and see that they are not rebelling against a corrupt government. They are turning away from God exactly like that horrible ex-husband of mine wanted. When Dennis Denali was president, he was willing to destroy society to create a world without God, and the people who are destroying our society right now are no different than him."

"Well said, Cynthia." Dukakis pats her hand. "Well said."

Alice buries her face in her hands. The ends of her long blonde hair almost dip into her plate. "Why does all of this have to be happening right before our wedding day? No one is going to come."

Gerald puts his fork down and puts his arm around Alice's shoulder. "Alice, sweetheart, you know how much I love you, and how much I want to marry you, but if you want to postpone, I understand."

Alice reaches up to her shoulder and clutches Gerald's hand. "No. Cynthia's right. This is exactly what President Denali and Dr. Eckert or Mordecai Crawley or whoever wanted," she spouts through gritted teeth. "They all may be dead, but they are not ruining my day from their graves." She straightens her back with that determination Alice is known for. "Even if it is just the two of us, Gerald, we are getting married on February fourth, and that is final."

"Alright then." Mom dabs her mouth with her napkin. "The wedding is only three weeks away, so let's get to making the final plans. After all, that's why we are having this dinner tonight."

"I think it's highly possible I may need to have some extra alterations to my dress. It seems that I may have gained a bit more weight than the seamstress allowed for," I say, biting my lips together, hoping no one panics at the lack of time left.

"Don't worry, dear," Mom cracks a grin. "I already called her. We're supposed to meet her tomorrow. And speaking of dresses, have you had your final fitting yet, Alice?"

"Yes. I went down this morning, and it's perfect." A wide grin spreads on her face. "Oh, let me show you the photo." Alice pulls out her phone, and Gerald stretches his neck to peer over her shoulder. "Would you stop it? You're not allowed to see." She gently shoves his shoulder.

"What's up with that rule anyway?" Gerald complains.

"It's tradition," Alice answers, glaring at him.

Alice passes the phone around to the girls because in all honesty, I don't think the guys are that interested, except Gerald, of course.

Mom takes the phone first, and after she lets out a squeal that could break glass, she touches her hand to her chest. "Oh, Alice. The dress is beautiful, and I don't think you could've chosen anything that suits you more." She casts her eyes on Gerald. "Gerald, you are going to be blown away... absolutely blown away."

Gerald reaches over, and as he strokes the side of Alice's face, he tucks a twig of her long hair behind her ear. "I already am. I have to be the luckiest man in the world."

Alice's cheeks fill with a rosy-red glow.

Mom passes the phone to me, and I realize why Mom squealed. In the photo, Alice is wearing a plain white satin sleeveless gown that is perfectly fitted to her petite frame. The high neckline is trimmed in rhinestones that match the sparkle in her diamond helix piercings. As I hand the phone off to Eileen, I move my eyes around the table, mesmerized by God's work. In the midst of so much evil, God brought together a group of people and turned them into an inseparable Christian family who is always there to help and support each other no matter what.

"Dukakis, your turn." Mom pulls out a notebook with a checklist and a pair of reading glasses. She places them on her face as she interrogates Dukakis about his part. "Is the church good to go?"

Dukakis sighs.

"Dukakis." Mom raises her eyebrows and glares through the glasses resting on the end of her nose. "I do not like the sound of that sigh."

"Relax, Jillian. I'm doing my best. It's all set for now, but some of the congregation is concerned about safety. So... we only need to sign a two-part waiver, and everybody will be happy."

"What are the two parts?" Mom inquires.

"First, Jillian, they want us to agree that if anyone is injured, the church won't be held responsible, and second, if any of our guests become violent and injuries occur or damage is done to the property, we are responsible for any and all costs." Dukakis shrugs. "That's all.

Our church has never worried about those details before, but really, it's pretty standard even if all of this craziness wasn't going on."

"I agree." Mom pushes the glasses back up with her index finger and then marks a check on her list. "That's no big deal." She runs her finger down the page. "Gerald, do you have enough employees willing to help out for the rehearsal dinner Friday night and then for the reception after the wedding Saturday?"

"Are you kidding?" Gerald puts his hand up to cover his full mouth. "Everyone volunteered."

A buzzer wails from somewhere under the table.

"What's that?" Dad scoots his chair back.

The same alarming noise sounds on the other side of the table.

Ted pulls out his phone. "It's one of those emergency alert messages."

I look over, and Teresa is swiping the screen on her phone. A few seconds later, it's like surround sound with everyone's phone pulsing out the alert signal.

Dad pushes up from the table. "I think we had better move to the living room and turn on the television."

Without a word, the rest of us rise to our feet and follow him. That is all but Spencer, who sits frozen with his eyes locked on the bowl of banana pudding.

"Oh, no. We can't leave him in here alone with that." Steve turns back and lifts Spencer from his chair.

Dad flips through the channels, and every station is airing the same breaking news alert. He stops on the National News Network. A reporter sits behind a desk with a disturbing image of the Capitol Building in Washington D. C. filling the background. The building is surrounded by mobs of people. Many are carrying flaming torches, and some even have visible rifles. Military personnel have a blockade set up guarding the building.

My heart sputters. My legs tremble. Only a single thought runs through my mind. *This is the world my baby will be born into.*

As Dad turns up the volume, Steve's hand presses against my back, and I feel the pressure of his chin resting on top of my head. My knees weaken, and I lean my weight back against him.

"The entire country is in a state of emergency. The United States government is on the brink of nonexistence. At a press conference only moments ago, President Philbert Emerson announced that he is stepping down as head of the executive branch due to threats on his life. For the first time in history, an emergency election has been ordered by Congress. However, one question hovers over them like a dark blanket. Will any qualified candidates step forward to run for office? Earlier last year, several had made public statements indicating intentions to enter the presidential race in the 2052 election, but it seems no one wants to lead the country with a war breaking out within our own boundaries, especially when the government is the primary target of that war.

The situation in the country began to unravel in 2049 when President Dennis Denali was convicted and executed in a villainous plot to destroy humanity and recreate a society in which he would be the supreme leader of a world with no knowledge of God. A heroic and unlikely group stopped his plane only moments before a toxic poison would have been released into the atmosphere. However, as horrid as that sounds, his death sentence was a result of the many lives lost in his so-called Soldiers Against Crime training facility. He had deceived young people into believing he had chosen them to be a member of his elite crime division that would end crime in America. When in actuality, he was erasing their memories in an effort to delete any memory of God. Trainees in which his tactics were unsuccessful were cryonically preserved in hopes that he could remedy the situation later. Many of these trainees were not able to be resuscitated. Thus, a mass murder charge led to his execution.

From there, Americans were then failed again, demolishing any trust left in the federal government when Vice-President Craig Kutchins moved up to replace Dennis Denali. Kutchins fell prey to Dr. Earl Eckert, who at the time was believed to have been an innocent, misled employee in Dennis Denali's training facility. Dr. Eckert had a prior criminal record under another name and was an expert in the area of behavior modification and mind control. Dr. Eckert instigated random violent acts across the country and linked the occurrences to those who had been held in Denali's training facility. Eckert and a member of the President's Council of Advisors on Science and Technology, Dr. Damien Seaver, proceeded to coerce President Kutchins into using this situation to reduce the overpopulation in the country by stimulating subjects to stir riots and enrage large groups of people. Thousands of people were killed. President Kutchins is still awaiting sentencing. However, due to the magnitude of the charges against Dr. Earl Eckert, he has already faced execution. Authorities still have not been able to locate Dr. Damien Seaver." The reporter pauses and then sighs. "Honestly, as I look at the scene around the Capitol Building, I am inclined to believe that Dr. Eckert's plan was a success." He shakes his head. "Anyway, the blows to our government structure just keep coming. President Philbert Emerson, who was appointed as vice-president when Kutchins took office, has decided the risk is too great.

The Speaker of the House, Howard Lucas, will fill the role until a new president is elected by the American people. Due to the dangers involved, no public debates will be held. Any candidate who comes forward will give their stance on the issues via a live online newsfeed. All voting will take place online, so make sure your online voter's registration account is set up and your voter's registration has been authenticated. The election date is set for Tuesday, January 31, 2051, and Inauguration Day will be February 1, 2051."

"I'm going to do it."

All eyes move from the reporter on the television to the source of the voice.

"I'm going to do it," Cynthia declares a bit louder. "I'm running for the presidency."

No one says a word.

Cynthia continues despite the hush and the dropped chins that surround her. "Someone has to take a stand. Dennis Denali tried to remove God from our country, and he has come close to succeeding. For Pete's sake, he even convinced Congress to remove the phrase, 'under God,' from 'The Pledge of Allegiance.'" She extends her lower lip which is glowing with pink lip gloss and blows the brown twigs of hair from her face that fell during her ranting. "Well, enough is enough. It is time for my ex-husband's evil legacy to die. This has to change now." She turns, and her hardened jaw goes slack. She drops her gaze to my stomach, and I watch a tear roll down her cheek. She lowers her voice, "This has to change now because I have a grandson coming into this world."

Dad clicks the off button on the remote control, and as the seconds pass, the silence grows even thicker.

"I'll help," Dukakis blurts out, breaking the monotony of the moment.

Everyone's gaze rotates at once to Dukakis.

He stands with his hands in his pockets, rocking back and forth. "What? She's right. We have no right to complain if we aren't willing to do something to make a change." He turns to Cynthia. "And, in my opinion, there is no better person to lead our country out of this mess."

A hint of pink rises in Cynthia's cheeks, and the corners of her lips curve up. Looking at the floor, she asks, "Do you mean that, Dukakis?"

"Sure, I want to help."

"The part about 'no better person to lead the country.'" She lifts her head with her eyebrows raised in question.

Dukakis stops rocking. "Of course. I wouldn't have said it if I didn't mean it."

"Thank you. It's nice, really nice, to have someone believe in my ability."

"No need to thank me." Dukakis takes his hands from his pocket and uses his fingers to comb over his thinning gray hair. "I call it like I see it."

Mom jogs out of the living room and returns in only a few seconds with her notebook. "This is perfect. Since the wedding plans are all set, and all the items are marked off the list, I have plenty of time to manage your campaign, Cynthia." Mom hesitates and then tones down the excitement in her voice. "That is unless you have someone else in mind."

"Jillian, you are perfect for the job. You are organized, motivated, and most of all," Cynthia taps her high-heeled boot on the engineered wood floor and adds emphasis to her tone, "I trust you."

With Cynthia's comments boosting her ego, Mom thrusts her glasses back onto her face, uses her fingertips to swipe the strands of her short hair off her forehead, and clicks her pen. "Alright, I assume we can count on some sort of help from everyone in this room."

A barrage of words of agreement and affirmation sound off around the room, but I notice Ted doesn't respond. How can anyone blame him, though? He doesn't even know Cynthia.

"That's the spirit," Mom responds with pep. "I thought you would all join the team. Let me write everyone's name down, and then we can divvy up the jobs that need to be done." Mom starts jotting down a list of names in her notebook.

A giggle bursts from Eileen. "I'm sorry, but...," she can't seem to get her laughter under control, "Mom, you have to be the only person left that organizes with pencil and paper." She looks over Mom's shoulder. "And is that cursive? They don't even teach kids to print letters in school anymore much less how to write in cursive."

Mom gives Eileen a stern look. "Hmmm. Mark my words. One day all this mess of technology will stop working, and you'll be thankful that I taught you girls how to write... with a pencil... in your hand... on paper." Mom narrows her eyes and then widens them. "Oh. Speaking of technology, you are our social media expert. Your job will be to work on some strategies and figure out how we can reach the most people there." Mom makes a note without waiting for Eileen to comment. "Alice, obviously the wedding is your primary focus, but could you lend a hand with your computer expertise and help Eileen with those social media alg... algor...?"

"Algorithms?" Alice asks.

"Yes, that's it."

"Of course, Jillian, you don't need to ask." Alice stretches her petite frame taller. "Put me down for whatever needs to be done."

Mom lifts her eyes to the doctor. "Ted, I know you can't contribute much with your schedule, but could you at least spread the word down at the hospital?"

"Sure, I don't usually talk politics at work, especially now," he details, "but I guess I could spread the word about her announcing her candidacy."

Mom stiffens her posture, fixing her stare on him as if she is sure he has more to add.

Ted must become uncomfortable because he starts to fidget. "And I will definitely let them know that she is the one they should vote for."

"Excellent," Mom says in a cheery voice and then writes in her notebook.

"I've got the victory party covered." Gerald winks at Cynthia.

"Jillian," Dad speaks up, "I could make some phone calls to some of my old contacts."

Scribbling more notes on the paper, she says in a monotone voice, "Oh, that would be wonderful." She casts a glance sideways at him. "But most importantly, keep talking and don't disappear."

He twists his mouth to the side and sort of half nods. "I'll try to manage," Dad replies and then cracks a smile.

"Oh, I know who would be glad to help." Dukakis holds up one finger. "Jillian, put down my nephew, Carlton."

"Yes, sir. We'll take all the help we can get." Mom pauses and then parts her lips to continue, but Steve's curiosity already has his mouth in motion.

"Uncle Dukakis," Steve narrows his eyes, "who's Carlton? I've never heard you mention him before."

"Carlton isn't a blood relative of yours. I know you don't remember my wife, Delilah. She died before your memory was erased. But Carlton is her sister's boy... well, actually he's a man now, somewhere around your and Teresa's age, but I still think of him as a little boy. Anyway," Dukakis gets back on topic, "he hosts a podcast for this Christian station on satellite radio."

Teresa steps closer to Dukakis. "Wow. Is it popular?"

"It's not top ranking overall, but it's held the number one spot in Christian podcasts for the last six months."

No way. "'Armed and Ready'... That's your nephew?" I ask with wide eyes and a bit of excitement in my tone.

"Yeah, that's it," Dukakis answers. "Have you listened to it?"

"I never miss it." I realize I'm shouting and lower my voice. "He isn't afraid to confront today's issues with the Bible, and he always uses the scripture in the correct context."

"Woo-hoo. Carlton has just moved to the top of the list." Mom is almost bouncing up and down with joy. "Do you think he'll help?"

"Are you kidding? He'll be ecstatic about helping a candidate who's putting God first in her campaign." Dukakis pulls out his phone and types on the screen.

A clatter from the direction of the kitchen, followed by broken glass, causes a hush to fall over the room. Steve spins and sidesteps in front of me with his arms extended as if it is now an automatic instinct to shield me. Dad pulls a gun from his waistband and strides to the doorway.

I rise to my tiptoes so Steve can hear my whisper. "Where's Spencer?"

His shoulders droop. "The banana pudding," he mumbles and then speaks louder. "It's okay. Spencer must have slipped out when I wasn't watching."

I slide past Steve. "Help your mom plan. I'll clean it up."

When I walk into the kitchen, Dad's chin is almost touching his chest. His pale skin is whiter than normal, and his arms are hanging limp at his side with the gun still clutched in his right hand.

Spencer is sitting on the floor with his hands covering his eyes. Smeared banana pudding is matted in the fur close to his mouth, and the pudding in his hair seems to be all that's left of the dessert. The antique milk glass bowl that had held the pudding is now lying in shards on the tiles around him. Spencer spreads two of his little skinny fingers apart as if I can't see him peeping to assess my level of anger.

Dad rolls his eyes and fixes them on me. "What are we going to do? Your mother is going to have a heart attack. That belonged to her grandmother."

Spencer must understand because he whimpers and closes his fingers back together.

Oh no. I swallow hard as I squat and carefully pick up the large pieces. "Why does it have to be something irreplaceable?" I hold up a jagged chunk of the milk glass with raised dots molded into it. "Maybe we could glue it."

"I think she would notice." Dad lowers himself next to me and opens a plastic bag for me to drop the large shards into. "Ellie, you're going to get cut. Let me get the broom." Dad rises, and in a moment, he's back, holding out a small hand broom with a dustpan attached. I swipe the small slivers into a pile.

"Please, be careful, Ellie," Dad warns in a quiet, but serious tone.

"I'm fine, Dad. I'm using the broom."

"No, that's not what I mean." He gurgles, clearing his throat, and then continues keeping his volume low. "I'm talking about Dennis Denali. Please don't ever let your guard down."

"But, Daddy, he's dead. I've come to terms with the fact that I've been acting irrationally, and I'm sorry that I've upset you with it."

Dad lifts his finger, and with a slight tug on my cheek, he turns my head to face him. "Ellie, I don't think you're acting irrationally, and you haven't upset me. My gut tells me he is alive, and I know yours does too."

I move the broom in slow motion, letting the bristles catch the tiny slivers as I let his words sink in for a second. *No. I can't go on living in fear of that man.* "Daddy, he has to be dead. The fingerprints prove it was really him that was put to death. I have to move on with my life. I can't let that evil man consume my thoughts anymore."

"Baby girl, I don't want you to have to worry about him, but it's also my job to protect you." Dad pinches the bridge of his nose and squeezes his eyes closed. "Do you recall that morning at the hotel when I showed up acting like an idiot?"

I can't help but giggle. "You mean when you disappeared, and then when you came back, you thought Mom had run off with Dukakis. But they had actually come to rescue us from the facility?"

He gives a curt nod keeping his expression serious. "You have a good memory." He blows out a deep breath. "That morning in the hotel, I was in the middle of trying to tell you all something that I had remembered when we were interrupted by that news report."

I stop sweeping and stare at the floor sorting through the details of the night we spent in that disgusting room. I've tried my best to block that experience from my mind. It was so nasty that Dukakis had to go to the store and buy some sleeping bags to spread on top of the mattresses, so we wouldn't have to touch the bedding.

As if I'm in a trance, the grout lines between the tiles on the floor get fuzzy, and the image of the room fills my mind. I haven't forgotten about Dad knocking on the door the next morning, and the shock on his face when we were all there, not just Mom and Dukakis...but then what? ... oh... I do remember...Dad was sitting on the edge of the bed, rocking back and forth... then the news report... all those people had been killed.

I twist my head and let my eyes meet Dad's. "Why did you never go back and finish telling us if it was important?"

"Everything was so chaotic, and more people were going to die if we didn't do something. My story kind of lost priority." Dad gazes back at me, unblinking with knitted brows. "Besides, at the time, it was only a weird, unwarranted hunch. But after everything played out, more pieces of my memory created a bigger puzzle. I've desperately been trying to work it, but too many pieces are still missing."

"Dad, what are you talking about?"

"That morning at the hotel, I was going to tell you all that I had remembered Dennis Denali saying that he could never be destroyed. Craig Kutchins had never been the type to act on his own, and I couldn't accept the fact that even as president he would issue an executive order without it being someone else's idea. I kept thinking the whole mess sounded like Denali. But then, Dr. Eckert came into play, and I decided that my hunch was unwarranted and had to be wrong. So, I tried to put it out of my head."

I look at Dad, wishing his words made no sense, but unfortunately, I know exactly what he means. "You tried, but you couldn't. That's what I've been struggling with. I've seen the proof, but..."

"But the knot in your stomach is still there," he finishes for me, "just like the knot in mine."

"Yeah," I shake my head, "but Dad, when I stop and make myself think it through, I realize that, of course, he thought he couldn't be destroyed. He wanted to take the place of God."

"I agree, but there's one more thing." Dad swallows hard. "After he said that he could never be destroyed, he mumbled something else that I never quite made out. I've wondered about it all these years, but I really didn't think it was important. At least not until Eckert and Kutchins went down. Then, it started keeping me awake at night. I couldn't get any peace, and my stomach stayed balled up. But no matter how hard I tried, all I could remember was incoherent sounds."

"Dad," I twist my mouth to the side, trying to choose words that won't hurt his feelings, "if you didn't understand what he said then, what made you think you could figure it out years later?"

"I'm still not finished." He glances toward the hall and then back at me. "After Eckert got the death penalty, I finally started to sleep again, for a few nights anyway, until I had a nightmare. I dreamed that I was back in that office with President Denali, sitting across from him, listening to him rant and rave. He said he could never be destroyed. And then he mumbled those words, those same words that I had never been able to figure out, but this time I heard him loud and clear. He said, 'Damien will make sure of that.'"

Breathe, Ellie. Breathe. The small broom falls from my hand. "A-a-as i-i-in Doctor D-D-Damien S-Seaver?"

"I don't know for sure, but I can't imagine what other Damien it could be."

"But...," I massage my forehead with my fingertips, "Agent Morgan said he could find no such person."

"I know, and I have tried and tried too—"

"Tom. Is everything okay?" Mom's voice grows louder as the sound of her feet taps down the hallway toward the kitchen.

Dad pulls a folded white envelope from his pocket. "Here, put this somewhere safe. Read it when you're alone, and don't tell anyone. We won't be able to catch him if he gets spooked. Besides, no one would believe us anyway. It seems the authorities have tunnel vision and can't see outside the box."

I don't have time to hesitate or ask questions or even address his comment about the authorities since I'm an agent with the FBI. I grab the envelope, tuck it underneath the giant elastic panel on the front of my pants that stretches to cover my belly, and snatch the broom back up off the floor. *The floor looks clean. Seven more swipes to be sure. One. Two. Three. Four. Five. Six. Seven.* I lift the dustpan and empty it into the plastic bag.

"Oh, dear." Mom's hand flies to cover her mouth as her eyes catch sight of Spencer and the bag full of broken glass. "Tom, your grandmother's antique bowl," Mom says with a hint of despair.

Dad scratches his head and peers up at Mom. "I thought that was your grandmother's antique bowl."

"No." Mom shakes her head. "Don't you remember your mother giving it to us as a wedding gift?"

Dad gazes back down at the pile of shards in the bag. "Well, at this point, it doesn't really matter. It was only a bowl anyway. What's so special about a bowl?"

Mom opens her mouth as if she is about to argue the family heirloom issue, but she stops herself before any sound comes out. Instead, she leans down and picks up the bag. "Here, Ellie. Let me help you up." She grabs my hand and tugs me to my feet.

Steve steps up behind me as everyone else files into the room. "It appears that we may need to get someone home." He kneels beside Spencer, who is now curled in a ball on the floor.

"Jillian," Cynthia pulls Mom into a hug, "Dukakis and I have to get going. Carlton is so excited that he wants to meet with me tonight.

He said he's going to do a special podcast to let me announce my candidacy."

Mom claps her hands. "Oh, make sure you call and tell me all about your meeting."

"Sure thing." Cynthia steps back. "And listen, I can't thank you enough for managing my campaign. You have no idea how much it means to me."

"It was nice to meet all of you." Ted waves his hand as he walks through the kitchen toward the door. He stops beside Mom. "Mrs. Hatcher, thank you for dinner. It was absolutely delicious."

"I'm glad you could join us," Mom replies. "Do you have to leave so soon?"

"I'm afraid so. My shift starts in a couple of hours." He glances back at Eileen, who is right behind him. "But, if it's okay, I'll stop by tomorrow and check on Eileen."

One side of Eileen's mouth curves up. "Do all of your patients get house calls?"

Ted winks at her. "Only the ones I find interesting."

Steve nudges up to Mom's side and manages to get one arm loose from Spencer for a quick hug. I slide in behind him and kiss Mom on the cheek.

"Ellie, don't you forget to text me the second you get home," Mom orders.

"Yes, ma'am." I crack a smile. Even though my baby isn't even here yet, I already understand my mom's worry.

Alice and Gerald slip in, taking turns hugging Mom, thanking her for dinner and for helping with the wedding plans.

After all of the goodbyes are said, I follow Steve to the door as he cradles Spencer in his arms. The poor little monkey has his hands pressed tight against his stomach. Everyone else treks behind me.

With fierce grunting and straining noises, Dad tugs on the steel bar, shimmying it side to side, trying to wiggle it from the brackets holding it to the door frame. The bar slips free, and Dad almost falls backward but goes down on one knee instead. He blows out a deep breath and uses the bar to push himself up. As he turns around, his shoulders are slumped, and he looks a bit defeated. "I hope everyone has a weapon—" Before Dad finishes his statement, Spencer's mouth opens, and partially digested banana pudding projects like a missile straight at Dad's face. Dad stands unmoving with droplets dripping from his eyelashes, and I notice his hands clenched into fists. After a second, he swipes his fingers across his eyes and drops his head. "It appears that Spencer is armed," he utters in a somber, dry tone. "Does everyone else have protection before you go out?"

Slow nods and a few mm-hmms fill the room, with the exception of Gerald, who speaks up.

"I forgot my gun at home this morning, but I grabbed a rolling pin as I left the restaurant."

"A rolling pin?" Dad mutters.

"Yeah. It's a French rolling pin, about two feet long, solid wood." Gerald stretches his stance taller and lifts his chin as he explains. "It'll do the trick."

Alice must see the frown lines forming on Dad's face. "We rode together, Mr. Hatcher. I have my revolver."

Mom hands Dad a towel, and he steps to the side as we all pad past him with soft steps.

"Sorry, Dad." I pat his shoulder. "I love you."

CHAPTER FIVE

The ride home was quiet. After ridding himself of the banana pudding, Spencer used my stomach for a pillow and slept the whole way. And I could tell by the strained look on Steve's face that he was preoccupied with his mother's decision to run for president. As we pull up the driveway, I want to say something to erase the worry written in the lines on his crinkled forehead, but exhaustion seems to have turned my brain into a hard sponge unable to absorb any information, and everywhere I search for something to say, I find an empty hole. On top of that, a nagging ache is tormenting my back, and no matter which way I twist or turn, I can't seem to alleviate the discomfort.

Steve pulls the Hydromax into the new attached garage. After the door closes, we sit in the car until Steve sends a signal to Claude with his phone getting an all-clear. When Claude signals back, we climb out of the car, or in my case right now, roll out of the car. Even though we are in the garage, Steve still has to press his thumb to the pad... and hold his eye in front of the iris scanner... and wave his hand in front of the palm vein scanner... and then type in a ten-digit code. Carrying in groceries is a complete nightmare, but Steve says keeping our baby safe is his top priority. I'm surprised he hasn't designed something that takes a blood sample.

I kick off my shoes right before we walk through the door. Steve stops to double-check that all the security features are reset. With one hand applying pressure to my back and the image of myself lying in bed driving every step, I drag my feet toward the hall that leads to the bedroom.

"I'll be there in a minute," Steve calls after me. "I'm going to check the rest of the security system and get Spencer to his bed."

Herb wheels into the room as I move into the hall. "No worries. I will take Spencer. It is time for me to turn in myself." He simulates a yawn with his hinged mouth and lifts his metal hand to stifle it.

As I pass through the bedroom, I grab my pajama shirt from the drawer and almost make it to the bathroom when a sharp pain shoots from my aching back and spiderwebs through the muscles in my stomach. Doubling over, I press on my belly and shuffle to the side of the bed. Through my shirt, I feel the edges of the envelope. *I almost forgot.*

When the pain subsides, I lower myself onto the side of the bed and slide the envelope from the panel of my pants. Flipping it around, I stare at it for a minute and then insert my index finger under the flap, ripping the corner. The piercing pain squeezes around my belly again like claws stretching around from behind me. The cramping paralyzes me, pulling my upper body over my knees. I stretch out my hand, thrust the envelope into the top drawer of my nightstand, and let my body fall over onto my pillow.

I lie on the bed curled in a ball as the cramp dissipates again, but as the stomach pain eases, the ache in my back only gets worse. *Pajamas.*

I still have my clothes on that I have worn out of the house. I'm getting germs on the bed. My throat tightens at the thought, and I struggle to take a deep breath. *It will only take a second to change clothes. I can do this.* I suck another deep breath trying to fill my lungs and use my arms to push myself to a sitting position and then to my feet. *I can do all things through Christ which strengtheneth me.* With my pajama shirt wadded in my hand, I glide my sock feet across the floor and into the bathroom.

My body is desperately begging to sit down, but the knowledge that I have not yet washed my hands repeats in my head like a message on a scrolling sign. *It will only take a minute. If I wash my hands, I'll feel better.* Using the back of my hand, I flip the handle up on the faucet and then extend my fingers under the automatic soap dispenser. A few drops of soap fall into my hand, and I begin my handwashing ritual. As I rub and the bubbles lather, I count to seven over and over seven times. When I utter the last seven in my mind, I turn off the water and dry my hands, letting the pain in my back help me fight the urge to repeat the process.

Pajamas. Hurry and put on the pajamas. The sooner I get them on, the sooner I can lie down. I give myself a pep talk, trying to remind myself of the reward at the end because I know I'm going to have to use my back muscles to change my shirt.

A minute later, the task is accomplished, and I scurry toward my goal.

Steve walks through the bedroom door as I exit the bathroom. "Ellie, you look a little pale."

"I'm fine. I just need to get off my fee...," my last word drags out through gritted teeth as I wrap my arms around my torso and hunch over.

"Ellie!" In a second, Steve is beside me with his arm around me. "Ellie, what is it? Is it the baby?"

Pressing my eyelids closed, I squeeze his hand as he guides me to the edge of the mattress. "It's okay. I'm fine now."

"No. I don't think you're fine." Steve's hand is trembling inside my grip. "You shouldn't be having that kind of pain. We have to get you to the hospital."

"My mother is an emergency room nurse. Just call her."

"Fine," Steve sighs. "Herb!" Steve yells loud enough to be heard on another planet. "Could you bring me my phone?"

In less than ten seconds, Herb appears in the doorway with his long metal fingers wrapped around Steve's phone. His other metal hand flings to his chest. "Oh, dear. What's wrong with Ellie?" He wheels over to Steve and extends his hand.

"She's having a bit of pain," Steve replies, taking the device from Herb's hand. "I'm going to call her mother and see what she recommends."

Claude wheels into the room in time to catch Steve's explanation.

"Oh, maybe I can help. If you remember," Claude taps his forehead, "I do have a zettabyte of memory." He moves his mouth into a square grin, shifting the hand-drawn freckles on his cheeks. I probably have the whole worldwide web stored up here. Now tell me what's going on."

Steve rolls his eyes. "Search away, Claude. I'm going to call Jillian."

Claude continues to interrogate me. "How far along are you, Ellie?"

"Seven and a half months."

"And where are you hurting?"

I close my eyes. "My back aches, and my stomach cramps sporadically."

"I see." Claude begins to make beeping noises, and then his head spins around shaking his short, red, curly hair. "Oh, yes." He points one finger up in the air. "I've got it. I have found the answer."

"Which is...?" I stare at him, waiting for his reply.

"Call your doctor immediately and go to the emergency room." Claude's tone is full of pride, and he stretches his neck taller as if he has found a cure for a new disease.

Even in my discomfort, it's hard to stifle the giggle building inside at the sight of his excitement. "Thank you, Claude," I say, admiring his enthusiasm.

"Glad I could be of assistance. Let me know if there is anything else I can do to help." Claude turns toward the door, and his rotating conveyor belt-type feet carry him out of the room.

Steve steps back up beside me as he taps the screen on the phone. "Your mother said to call your doctor and go to the emergency room. I called Doctor Lannigan's after-hours number. Surprisingly, he answered, but he's out of town. He said to go to the large emergency room in Arlington. That is the only place accepting walk-ins."

I nod in defeat. I know he's right. Something could be wrong. But I can't help but think about having to get dressed again and how badly I want to curl up on this bed and not have to move my back.

All of a sudden, my thoughts realign inside my brain, and panic pulses through my veins. *Something could be wrong, or... or I could be going into labor. It's way too soon. I can't go into labor now. Oh... oh... Lord, please! Please let the baby be okay.* A rush of adrenaline overpowers the pain. "My clothes are in the bathroom."

Steve darts across the room and comes back with my pants. "I'll help you slip these on. Your shirt is fine. Oh, your mom wanted to meet us there, but I told her not to. It's too dangerous. So, she made me promise to call her the second we knew something."

"That's good. After this morning in the parking lot, they definitely don't need to be out after dark... which reminds me. I need my purse and my gun."

"I'll get them," he says, helping me from the bed. "Let's go."

"Ellie, please try to relax."

I hear Steve's words, but his voice seems so far away. I can't process what he's saying over the buzzing alarm echoing in my head and vibrating through my body. Since I arrived in the emergency room, I have had an ultrasound, an IV inserted into my arm, and three vials of blood drawn. However, for the last hour, nothing has happened. I have sat here on this tiny bed in this miniature room with wires running from my stomach, leading to a monitor next to me that is recording the baby's heartbeat and how often he moves. I keep asking what's going on, but no one will tell me anything. The nurses just keep saying that the doctor will be in shortly. Meanwhile, every muscle in my body is frozen stiff, and my eyes are glued to the monitor, watching every beat of my son's heart. *Father, please protect this baby. I know I need to relax, but I'm so scared. Please let my baby be okay.* A drip falls from my cheek, and I clutch the blanket under me tighter.

"Ellie," Steve whispers as he wipes beneath my eyes with the tips of his fingers, "try taking a few deep breaths. His heartbeat is strong." Steve points to the screen. "If the baby were in trouble, this room would be crawling with doctors and nurses, and I would have been kicked out to the waiting room." He touches my chin and gently turns my head toward him. "I love you, Ellie. It's you I'm worried about right now."

The perfect rhythmic sound of the baby's heartbeat and Steve's words intertwine in my mind. I close my eyes and let all of the air escape from my lungs. "I love you too." I lift my gaze to meet his. "I know I have to relax, but I can't make the panic stop. The baby isn't even here yet, and I already can't protect him."

Steve leans over and kisses my forehead. "Give -it -to -God. You are doing your best."

The door swings open.

"We meet again." Ted smiles as he pushes the door closed.

"It's been nice getting to know you, but I wish our encounters wouldn't continue to involve a hospital," Steve replies as he shakes Ted's hand. "I hope you have good news."

"Well, it looks like someone wanted to have the baby a little early." Ted taps on the screen of his tablet. "No worries, though. The nurse has noted that you have not dilated at all. We've been giving you a new medication through your IV that interrupts preterm labor if administered early enough. Previous medications like tocolytics only delayed the process for a few days, but this drug is usually effective in stopping labor completely, especially if neither your body nor the baby is ready. And the ultrasound shows that the baby hasn't turned. If you add in the fact that your cervix isn't opening yet, I think it's a safe assumption that your preterm labor is stress-induced. Thankfully, you didn't waste any time getting to the hospital, and the contractions have stopped for now, which is a good thing considering you're only a hair over thirty-five weeks."

"So, how long will this medication delay the labor?" I ask as I open and close my hands, counting to seven in the back of my mind.

Ted leans back against the counter and crosses one leg over the other. "Hopefully, for a few more weeks. Full term is forty weeks, but ideally, you want to make it until at least thirty-seven weeks."

"Her obstetrician is Doctor Lannigan. Can you forward everything to him? He's out of town, but I guess she needs to see him as soon as he's back," Steve says, rubbing his chin.

"You had put all of his information on the check-in forms, so the hospital will automatically send the records to him. However, I actually spoke with him a bit ago. Since he's your doctor and this is his field of expertise, I wanted to coordinate with him about a plan of action. I don't know about other things going on in your life, but I was able to relate to him your eventful morning with Eileen's car accident and the men in the parking lot. Dr. Lannigan agrees that your early labor is a result of anxiety and stress." Ted lays the tablet on the steel countertop and steeples his fingers together. "I know you're not going to like this, but Dr. Lannigan and I both believe that bed rest for the remainder of your pregnancy is the only option. Like I said before, at minimum, we don't want you to deliver before thirty-seven weeks."

I press my hands together and drop my head, touching my forehead to my fingertips. "What exactly do you mean by bed rest?"

"No work... no leaving the house. Eh," he shrugs, "for your own safety, you shouldn't be leaving the house in this mess anyway. But no cooking, cleaning... definitely no lifting. Essentially, lie down most of the time. It's okay to get up to go to the bathroom, take a quick shower, or get a glass of water, but I don't want you on your feet for more than ten minutes at a time."

"So, can I go home now?" I ask in a tone filled with desperation. After all, I have a phobia of germs, and this is the second time I've been here today.

"Normally, we would keep you overnight, but considering the lack of space... yes, you can go home. The nurse will come by in a few and remove the IV. Dr. Lannigan won't be back in his office until Friday. He wants to see you first thing at eight o'clock. But I don't want you going that long without the baby's vitals being checked, and I prefer you not to leave the house, so I'll drop by your place tomorrow and make sure everything is still normal." Ted uncrosses his legs and pushes himself up from his leaning position on the counter. "I have to get moving to the next room. Take care and stay off your feet."

Steve steps up and shakes Ted's hand again. "Thanks, Ted. I really appreciate you taking care of Ellie and the baby."

"No problem. That's my job." Ted grabs the doorknob. "And besides, we're friends now. I'm even on your mom's campaign staff."

Steve laughs and nods. "I don't think you were given much of a choice."

"Ah, I'm not much of a political person, but I'm glad to help. It's nice to be part of something that's going to make a difference." Ted walks out, closing the door behind him.

I squeeze my hands into fists, trying to hold in the tears, but streams trickle down my cheeks anyway. Steve doesn't say anything. He just takes my hand and holds it between both of his.

I close my eyes and lift my head toward Heaven. *Father, thank you for taking care of this baby. Thank you for not letting him come too early and for giving him a strong heartbeat. But Lord, I'm going to need help with this. My OCD gets out of control when I sit and think, and you know I have to stay busy and how active I am. Help me, Lord. Please help me to deal with this. Help me not to do anything that will hurt this baby. Help me not to let my obsessive thoughts get out of control.* I sigh, letting a breath escape from my mouth. *Lord, I can't do this alone. But I know I can do anything with You. Please carry me and keep my son safe and healthy.* In a low voice, keeping my eyes closed, I whisper Philippians 4:13 to myself, absorbing the power of the words. "I can do all things through Christ which strengtheneth me. I can do all things through Christ which strengtheneth me. I can do all things through Christ which strengtheneth me. I can do all things through Christ which strengtheneth me. I can do all things through Christ which strengtheneth me. I can do all things through Christ which strengtheneth me. I can do all things through Christ which strengtheneth me."

Chapter Six

I should be at work right now, doing my part in the office to help
with the shortage of law enforcement. I know I had promised Steve
I would think about taking early leave. However, I didn't think that
meant I would be sedentary.

On the upside, I did sleep much later than usual today. But that's
because we didn't arrive home from the hospital until almost three in
the morning, and I think something that they gave me at the hospital
must have made me drowsy because I slept hard for a solid eight hours.
I'm usually an early riser, so under normal circumstances, I would be
upset with myself for sleeping until eleven o'clock. But considering my
current situation, I'm not complaining. If I had sat here awake all that
time, my every thought would have been consumed with worry that
my labor might start again. At least that took a few hours off the time

I have been awake today trying to keep my mind busy, which at this point has only been three hours, but it seems like so much longer.

When I woke up, Spencer was on the bed next to me with his little hand on my stomach. He started making his little monkey noises and pointing at my stomach. I think he was trying to tell me that the baby had been kicking. I hadn't felt it though, or I guess, paid attention, is a better choice of words. The baby is so active now that I don't notice it so much anymore.

Once Spencer had toned down his excitement, I lowered myself to the floor and kneeled by the bed. I had a lot to talk to God about. Then, I made a brief trip to the bathroom to freshen up. When I crawled back into bed, I sent Mom a quick text to let her know everything was okay. Steve had called her before we left the hospital and filled her in, so she knew not to panic when I didn't text her at seven o'clock this morning, but I knew she would still be going crazy with worry until she heard from me.

I guess Steve must have heard me stirring because he came in and kissed me good morning. He said he had some work to do. I was a little disappointed that he wasn't going to sit with me because I had hoped he would help me keep my mind busy. But I reminded myself that I couldn't be selfish. He has been trying his best to get ahead so he can have a few weeks off with the baby. On top of that, word has gotten out about his unique security designs. With security and safety being a major threat to everyone right now, companies are practically begging to be at the top of his list.

After that, Herb served me breakfast in bed. I thought the silver platter and the cloth napkin were a bit much since I only had a toasted bagel with peanut butter and a cup of orange juice. Herb has repeatedly told me since the beginning of my pregnancy that drinking orange juice is important because of the folic acid and vitamin C. He hovers over me worse than a mother. I tried to eat as slowly as possible to take up more time, but one can only drag out eating a bagel and drinking a glass of juice for so long.

Since I hadn't done my morning devotion yet, I took out my black leather Bible that my mother gave me when I was ten years old. It is the red-letter King James Version with my name embossed in gold in the lower corner. Anyway, I flipped open to 1 Peter, chapter five, and read for a while, stopping after each verse to soak in the message, but I kept going back to verses six and seven. *'Casting all your care upon him; for he careth for you. Be sober, be vigilant; because your adversary the devil, as a roaring lion, walketh about, seeking whom he may devour.'*

I have read those verses so many times before, but today they spoke to me in a whole new way. The message in verse six, appearing right next to the message in verse seven, filled me with awe. I literally sat staring at the page for several minutes because it was as if God was talking directly to me. *Actually, He was.* He had to be because there is no other explanation for me reading those verses today and the tingling sensation in my chest as I absorbed the words. This worry that is trying to rule my mind... I'm supposed to give it all to God. *Verse six.* The devil knows that my obsessive-compulsive nature is a weakness, and he is like a 'roaring lion' looking for the opportunity to attack. I know my weakness. I know the devil's tactics. I have to be on guard. *Verse seven.* I read those verses over and over and over and over because I knew there was a deeper connection. *How do I guard when I can't control my thoughts?* Then, it hit me. *My thoughts are obsessive worries. Cast each one to God.* I closed my Bible and placed it back on the nightstand.

I fluffed my pillow and leaned back against the headboard... and here I am.

Now what? I glance at the clock on the wall. *It's only two o'clock.* I clutch my hands together on top of my stomach and close my eyes, trying to keep my mind empty of all thoughts. *The envelope.* My eyes pop open, and I shift my focus to the top drawer of my nightstand. *I should see what is in the envelope.* I push myself up on my elbow. *No. I am in the house. Steve has made this house an impenetrable fortress. I am safe. Opening that envelope will only create stress.* I lean back on the pillow, fighting the curiosity gnawing at my insides and making every effort to block the image of the envelope that is now etched into the front of my brain.

In the midst of my preoccupation, my phone startles me. Every nerve in my body twitches in response to the sudden break in silence. I fill my lungs with air to calm myself and reach for the phone. *Mom.* "Hey, Mom."

"Ellie, are you okay?"

"Yes, I'm fine." I sigh with exasperation. "Just not used to having to sit and do nothing."

Mom laughs. "Most people would love to have orders to sit and do nothing," she pauses, and her voice takes on a serious tone, "but I know it's hard for you. Try to think of it as resting up for the baby, because trust me, before long, rest will be something you only daydream about."

"I know... but, Mom, when I sit still, it's so much harder to battle the obsessive thoughts."

"So, when you can't sleep, use your brain for something else. Read your Bible, read a book, watch those old comedy reruns you love, work a puzzle..."

"Oh, I didn't think about puzzles. I love puzzles."

"Well, you are in luck." She emphasizes every word as her excitement escalates through the phone. "Someone gave me this five-thousand-piece puzzle of 'The Last Supper' for Christmas last year, and it's still in the shrink wrap. I'm coming over in a few hours to check you out myself, so I'll bring it. Do you need anything else?"

"Mom, I don't want you going out when it's not necessary. Remember the incident in the parking lot of the hospital? It's dangerous."

"Ellie, nothing is going to stop me from coming to see my baby girl. I am sure the hospital checked you thoroughly, but I will not rest until I have looked you over myself. Besides, I'm driving from my garage to your house without stopping. I'll be fine."

"I know better than to argue with you." I giggle. "I would never win. At least make Dad come with you."

"I will if he gets home before I leave. You haven't heard from him today, have you?" Her voice cracks on the last word.

"No, why? Where is he?"

"I don't know. He was gone when I got up this morning. I found a note by the coffee kettle saying he was going to get some security supplies. I thought he would be home by now. I tried calling, but his phone must be dead, as usual, because it goes straight to voicemail. I tell him and tell him to keep that thing charged, but he never does. I don't even know why he bothers carrying it with him." Mom groans. "Aaaah, I'm sure he will be home soon."

"Well, text me before you leave so I can time you."

"Okay. It's a little after two now. I'll probably leave here about four-thirty, so I can get back home before dark... and we have that new nine o'clock curfew that starts today."

"Curfew?" My pitch rises in surprise. "What curfew?"

"You haven't heard the news today?"

"No. The only time I have even held my phone today was to text you. What happened?" Panic starts to rise in my chest.

"Before you left here last night, you saw what was happening around the Capitol Building in Washington. They showed pictures of the National Mall on television this morning, and a lot more are floating around on the internet. I couldn't believe it. The Washington Monument and the Lincoln Memorial are covered in graffiti. The Capitol Building was burned to the ground along with the Smithsonian and several other museums." I can almost feel the heat from Mom's rising anger through the line. "Words cannot describe the images that were shown... pieces of history and beautiful architecture ruined. I just don't understand."

I don't even know what to say. *The Capitol Building... all of that history destroyed. Why?* A tear beads in the corner of my eye. *What is this solving? And a nine o'clock curfew for the entire country... has that ever happened? No, it couldn't have. Not that early.*

"Ellie, are you still there?"

"Yeah. S-sorry, Mom. I was processing."

"Oh, what is wrong with me? I shouldn't have told you about all that. You don't need to be upset."

"No, no. I'm not upset, and I would have found out in a bit anyway when I picked up my phone. I know I'm not supposed to be stressed, but at the same time, I'm not a fragile porcelain doll. I do work for the FBI." I hesitate, still thinking, and then continue. "But I'm trying to figure out why a nationwide curfew, especially that early if all this happened in Washington?"

"I guess when what was happening in Washington got wind, the idea spread, or for all I know it could have already been some sort of organized plot. But rioting broke out in the capital city of every state across the country. Looting, arson, rape, murder... the destruction went far beyond structures..."

Mom is still talking, but her words become static, and I only hear Alice reading the phases on the timetable sent from Dr. Seaver to Dr. Eckert.

> *There are four phases... Phase one has today's date, July 2, and is titled, 'The Exposition: Setting the Scene.' Phase two, dated July 3, is titled, 'Rising Action.' And phase three, dated July 4, is 'The Grand Finale'....*

I remember she stopped, and someone in the van asked about phase four.

She continued reading, but we didn't know what it meant.

> *The date reads July fifth with a plus sign after it, and it's titled, 'Aftershocks.'*

Now we know, I think to myself. *We might have stopped phases two and three, but phase four is in motion.* I give my head a quick shake, pulling my thoughts back to Mom, who is still talking. I notice that her anger has faded, and now she is sniffling.

"Ellie, you know the verse...Romans 8:28, 'And we know that all things work together for good to them that love God, to them who are the called according to his purpose.' I have already been on my knees this morning thanking God because I have no doubts that your bed rest is a gift from God. You and your baby are home safe. That job of yours can't call you in and put you in danger. God has a plan, and he's going to help you through this. Just trust Him, Ellie. Just trust Him."

"I do, Mom. I do with my whole heart." I swallow hard, thinking about how hard it is to let go of my fear. "But I have trouble giving Him the worry. I guess I'm a control freak. No, I know I'm a control freak."

"Ellie, I'm pretty sure that it is safe to say that everyone except Jesus Himself struggles with giving fear and worry to God. We simply have to remember we're a work in progress and to keep on trying." Mom sighs. "Okay, dear, I'm going to find that puzzle and make sure I have everything in my medical bag to check your blood pressure and listen to the baby. I'll text you before I leave. Try to rest. I love you, baby girl."

"Okay, Mom. I'll see you soon. Love you too."

I lay the phone on the nightstand and reach for the top drawer. *Do I really want to open the can of worms that could be in that envelope?* I sit there with my eyes fixed in a trance on the drawer, my hand frozen on the handle. *Dad gave no indication what was inside. What if I don't open it, and the information could have saved someone's life?* I slide the drawer open a millimeter. *If that were the case, Dad would have done something about it. It's probably a wild goose chase, which he does seem to go on. And I'm not in a situation where I can take off on a wild goose chase.* I push the drawer closed. *But maybe it's...*

"Ellie, I have a surprise."

I turn and find Steve standing in the doorway wearing overalls, a toolbelt, and a train conductor's hat. I lift my eyebrows. "Are we going to fix a train and then go for a ride, or are we just worried that the train will break down?"

"Ha-ha." He lifts his eyebrows and lowers his head, pretending to glower at me. "Do you think you are up for a short walk?"

"If that's the surprise, it couldn't be a better one. I've been longing to go for a walk." I push myself up off the bed, and Steve jogs across the room to help me. "Thank you, but it's okay. I can get up."

"Well, don't get too excited about that walk. We're only walking through the house."

"Better than lying here." I nod. "I'll take it."

He puts one arm around my waist and his other hand under my elbow. I should probably tell him all that isn't necessary, but I like his arm around me. We walk out of the master bedroom and a few steps down the hall to the next room that he has kept off-limits from me for the past few months.

"Okay, cover your eyes." A child-like excitement gushes through his tone, and his ear-to-ear toothy grin is like a flashing neon sign advertising his pride about whatever is behind the door.

I giggle as I lift my hands and cap them over my eyes.

"Keep them covered. I'll tell you when."

The doorknob rattles, followed by a faint creak of the door opening.

"Take a step." He guides me with both of his arms around me. "Okay, you can look."

I lower my hands..., and... I – am – speechless. I can feel my mouth hanging open, but I can't form any words. I spin in a circle, pressing my hand to my chest, taking it all in or at least trying to take in every detail. There is so much. The entire room is painted a bright, almost neon yellow, even the ceiling, and somehow, he has raised it in the middle to form a tray ceiling. In the center of the raised tray is a three-foot circle flush-mounted light with rays painted around it in orange and red blended streaks. The lower part of the ceiling that forms the perimeter has a train track running around the room through a diorama of mountains, trees, bridges over glittering streams, and a town with a train station. The floor has large squares of carpet, each in a different color. A white bassinet with a handmade wooden rocking chair next to it sits in front of an apple tree painted up one corner with branches spreading onto the adjacent walls. On the opposite wall is a painted mural of the Ark. The front of the wooden vessel is lifted on a wave, and the windows all have a different animal peeking out. Well, all but one window. One has a giraffe with its whole neck extended through it and a speech bubble next to its mouth that reads, NEVER FORGET! JESUS LOVES YOU!

I keep turning, and when my eyes fall on the final wall, my hands fling up to cover the gasp flying from my mouth. The cream-colored wardrobe that I saw at the antique store stands in the center with its two giant doors on the front, two large deep drawers on the bottom, and four intricate hand-carved lion's paw feet forming the base. I can't hold it in anymore. My happiness explodes in the form of waterfalls from my eyes. Windshield wipers couldn't swipe them away as fast as they are falling. "H-h-how? Wh-wh-when?" I'm not sure if I am supposed to be, and since I can't see my feet, I'm not sure. But I think I'm jumping up and down.

"I hope those are rivers of joy flowing down your cheeks."

I move my body in a slow circle. "This is... I don't know how to describe it. No words that come to my mind even come close to explaining how magnificent this is. I can't fathom how long... how much work this took. You raised the ceiling." I tilt my head back and peer at the sun in the middle of the tray. "How on earth did you raise the ceiling in the middle?"

"Well, the roof was all stick built or hand framed, not trusses. So, I did a bit of bracing until I could reframe with the recess a foot higher," Steve says as he takes off his tool belt. "But you haven't experienced the action of the room yet." He steps to the door and yells, "Spencer!"

I lift the neck of my t-shirt and use the fabric to dry my face.

"Ok, so first, notice the bassinet has wheels that flip down." He points to these tiny castors attached to the rocking feet. "I know you will want it in our room at night to start with, but during the day, this room is closer to the main part of the house."

"Oh, I can roll it wherever I want it."

"Yep." His eyes sparkle with excitement.

Spencer scampers into the room and jumps into the bassinet.

"Alright, buddy, show her how it works."

Spencer lies down and lightly whimpers. The bassinet rocks in slow motion, and classical music plays in a low tone. As Spencer's volume rises, the bassinet rocks faster, the music gets louder, and the sun begins to change colors, dancing with the beat.

"Our son is going to love this. I love this."

"Okay, Spencer. You can stop crying." Steve unrolls a sleeping bag in the middle of the floor and spreads it out. "Come on." He takes my hand. "You've been on your feet too long." He holds my arms and lowers me onto the sleeping bag. "I know it isn't the most comfortable, but I want you to see it from the baby's perspective. He gets on the floor with me and slides a pillow over for me to rest my head on.

"We're lying down?" I question.

"Yes. The baby will be lying down looking up."

"Oh, okay." I wiggle around until my head is comfortable on the cushion. "Wow, this ceiling is beautiful."

Steve lies back beside me, tilting his head in, so it touches mine, and clutches my hand. The train begins to move and builds speed around the track. I follow it with my eyes through the mountains and over the bridge. It travels through a tunnel into the town where it stops for a few seconds at the train station. The whistle blows, and it takes off again. My chest tingles, and I'm like a leaf floating through the air, too light for anything to bring it down to the ground. "This is amazing." I reach across my body with my other hand and rub my fingers across his arm. "I can't believe you did all this. I feel like I'm in a fairy tale."

"Do you think the baby will like it?" he asks in a quiet voice with a serious edge.

"Are you kidding? He's going to love it. I'm actually thinking of moving our bed in here. I can't remember the last time I felt this relaxed."

"Really?" Steve lifts his head and narrows his eyes as if he's trying to read my thoughts. "Maybe I should set up the bed in here until the baby comes. You need to stay relaxed."

I shake my head and let out a light cackle. "You know you would have to stay in here with me all the time though because the fairy tale only exists with the handsome prince."

He leans over and brushes his lips across mine.

"Well, this is a bit awkward." Herb's voice filters through the room.

Steve looks up, and I lift my upper body on my elbow and turn my gaze toward the door. Herb has his metal fingers over his eyes.

"Herb, for Pete's sake, uncover your face," Steve huffs and rolls his eyes. "Is something wrong?"

Herb lowers his hands, but the red centers in his dark brown eyes are aimed at the ceiling. "I didn't mean to intrude on a personal moment, but a gentleman is at the door. He insists that you were expecting him today, but you always inform me ahead of time when guests are going to be dropping by. Herb swipes his hands across his apron. I mean I haven't even a speck of tea made. Anyhow, he refers to himself as Ted and insists that he is a doctor. But he is dressed in street clothes and has a weapon of mass destruction strapped to his body."

"A weapon of mass destruction?" Steve leaps to his feet.

"Yes, sir. He has a revolver in a holster under his shirt. The scanner at the door immediately picked it up."

"First off," Steve glares at him, "a revolver is not a weapon of mass destruction."

The red centers in Herb's eyes glow. "It most certainly is. It has the potential to kill six people."

"Fine." Steve breathes out. "Second, I apologize that I forgot to let you know, but Ted is the doctor who saw Ellie in the emergency room. He said he would come by and check on her. Where is he now?"

"He is still outside." Herb shakes his head. "You didn't think I would let him in with a gun, did you?"

Steve tilts his head in a gesture of understanding. "Point made. You did good, Herb. I'll take it from here." Steve walks out of the room and turns down the hall in the direction of the front door.

"By the way, Herb," I push to my knees, trying to get to my feet, and Herb extends his hand, giving me a gentle pull, "Mom is coming in a little while."

"Oh, splendid. I'll go make tea." Herb wheels full speed from the room.

I follow him out at a much slower speed and head toward the sound of a conversation in the living room that keeps mentioning my name.

"Ellie," Ted says as soon as I'm in sight, "what are you doing on your feet? You should be lying down."

"It's okay. I'm only on my feet to walk in here," I say in a sarcastic tone and then crack a grin. "Besides, if I remember correctly, you said I could be on my feet for up to ten minutes."

"Alright, you got me. But, please, come and have a seat." He points to one of the armchairs. I notice he does a double take at the old Bible lying in the middle of the coffee table, but he doesn't comment. "How are you doing? Any more back pain or contractions?"

"No. I feel great," I reply, gripping the arms on the chair to sturdy myself as I sit. "Crazy, I know, as big as my stomach is, but I don't even have any discomfort in my back. To be honest, if it weren't for the clumsiness from my awkward body size and shape, I could go for a jog."

He opens a black leather bag on the coffee table and pulls out a stethoscope and sphygmomanometer. "Hmmm. We might want to keep an eye on this new energy level. Obstetrics is obviously not my specialty, but I have heard that women can get a burst of energy before they go into labor. They call it nesting." He presses the end of the stethoscope to my chest, and then I lean forward, and he presses it against my back. My arms are small, and the cuff on his sphygmomanometer is large, so it wraps around several times. I worry that it won't tighten enough, but he gets a reading the first time. "Blood pressure 125 over 82. Not bad." He proceeds to check my pulse with his fingers against my wrist, and without a word, he squats beside the chair and places the end of the stethoscope on my stomach, shifting it several times before he seems content. "Heartbeat is strong. No worries there." With his fingertips, he pushes lightly around on my belly. "Hmm." Pursing his lips together, he pushes on all the same spots again. "I'm not positive," he remarks with hesitation as he stands, "and it has been less than twenty-four hours since the ultrasound, but I believe the baby has turned. If that's the case, Ellie, you need to be on strict bed rest. At least, until Dr. Lannigan can make it back and examine you himself."

"I'm supposed to see him Friday morning, right?" I know that's what he told me, but I ask anyway to confirm.

"I'm not sure now. He called earlier today to see if you had been released to go home." Ted talks as he puts his stethoscope and sphygmomanometer back in his bag. "In consideration of last night's events, airlines have suspended all flights until safety protocols have been reviewed by the TSA. Since today is Tuesday, he said he still hopes everything will get back up and moving so he can be back by Friday, but it's out of his control."

Herb speeds out of the kitchen. "Driveway alarm sounded," he mutters as he whizzes past us to the front door. "Probably Jillian," he shouts back over his shoulder.

A couple of minutes later, footsteps pad onto the porch, and the buzz of the scanner fills the room with a light vibrating noise.

"So that thing at the door lets you know in a few seconds if someone is armed?" Ted probes, pointing toward the door.

"Actually, it tells us in less than half a second. The rest of the humming is only a distraction to the person at the door.

"Wow." Ted's eyes widen. "That's impressive for home security."

Herb opens the door, and Mom teeters in with both arms full of bags.

I twist around in the chair. "Mom, I thought you weren't coming until five o'clock."

"Ellie, honey, it's almost five-thirty. And I texted you before I left the house."

*My phone...*I drop my head. *It's on the nightstand in the bedroom.*

Mom sets the bags on the floor behind the sofa. "Hey there, Steve. Dr. Ted, it's good to see you again. I didn't expect you to be here. Are you checking on my baby and my grandson?"

"Yes, Ma'am, and it's good to see you again too."

"Well, Doc, is everything okay?" Mom steps behind the chair and kisses the top of my head.

"All her vitals are perfect. The baby's heartbeat is strong. I am a bit concerned with her burst of energy, and it feels like the baby has turned now. I told her she probably needs to adhere to strict bed rest," Ted explains, picking up his black medical bag.

"I realize you're referring to nesting, but Ellie has always been energetic. I don't know if I would categorize her energy level as nesting, but you're the doctor." Mom leans over my shoulder. "Ellie, are you having any more pain?"

"No, I'm perfectly fine." I tilt my head back and look up at her. "I think it's the baby's position that has Dr. Ted the most concerned."

"Well, babies change position a lot, but sometime around now, they usually turn head-down," she mumbles low, almost as if to herself. Then a bit louder, she asks, "What position is the baby in?"

"It's head-down, but I found it odd that it changed so quickly. I guess as a mother, you are more experienced in this area than me. I'm more accustomed to trauma, but my gut is still sending off warning signals." He puts down the bag and rubs his fingers across my stomach again.

I can't help but set the record straight. "Mom's knowledge isn't only from having children. She has been a nurse for over thirty-five years."

"Oh, wow. How did I miss that bit of information at dinner last night?" He taps Mom's shoulder.

"Now, Ted. You go with your gut. I'm only a nurse. I don't have a Ph. D."

"In this case, Mrs. Hatcher, I believe your experience trumps my education." He twists his mouth to the side and scratches his chin. "I tell you what, Ellie. Since you aren't in any pain or discomfort, and you're having no contractions, keep doing what you've been doing today. Bed rest... and on your feet no more than ten minutes at a time." He widens his eyes, and his gaze pierces mine. "Most important is no stress. I'll check in with you tomorrow."

"Yes, Doctor."

Mom gasps. "Oh, look. It's almost six o'clock."

"What's at six o'clock?" Steve questions.

"Oh, my goodness. Have none of you checked your phones?" Mom walks around the chair. "Dukakis sent out a group text to the campaign staff. Carlton is airing a special podcast for Cynthia to announce her candidacy."

"I was so preoccupied with the nursery that I honestly don't even know where I left my phone." Steve pats the pockets of his overalls and twitches his shoulders. "Oh, well. I will look for it later. Let's go in the kitchen and see if we can find it on the television."

"I have to get going." Ted shakes Steve's hand. "Hopefully, I can pick it up on XM. I have to be at the hospital early tonight." He hurries to the door. "Take it easy, Ellie. Goodnight, Mrs. Hatcher." He opens the door and waves to Mom as he goes out.

"Here, sweetheart," Mom takes my hand and places her other hand under my elbow, "let me help you."

I push off the armrest with my other hand. "Is Dad still not home yet?"

"No, but don't worry yourself. I'm sure he will be home soon. I got to thinking about that note he left," Mom explains as we walk into the kitchen. "If he was going for security supplies, he has probably spent the day on a wild goose chase. He didn't say exactly what he was looking for, but I can't imagine him being able to find any items related to safety or security right now. According to the news, most gun shops are shutting down because their shelves are empty, and they can't get any stock to fill them."

Steve pulls a chair out for me at the kitchen table and then holds one for Mom.

"Thank you. What a gentleman!" Mom exclaims. "You sure don't see many men treating women like ladies anymore."

Steve grabs the remote and pulls out another chair as Spencer bounces up and takes the fourth seat at the table.

Steve types "Armed and Ready" into the search bar, and the station picks up just as the podcast is beginning. A young man's face fills the screen. He has short dark brown hair with natural curls that stick out in multiple directions on top of his head.

> "Hello, I am Carlton Clearwater, and welcome to a special edition of my podcast 'Armed and Ready.' I have a special guest here today with a big announcement."

Carlton pauses as if he hasn't rehearsed what to say and is thinking.

> "I'll be honest. I have been beyond discouraged with our political system for quite a few years now. But my faith has never been in mankind. My faith is in God. That being said, I believe that God has gifted some to be leaders, and after a long heartfelt discussion with her,

my gut tells me this is the case with my guest today. Yes, she was married to the former president, Dennis Denali, and she was also one of his victims. Her husband faked her death in a horrible car accident and used her as a subject in his cryonics experiments. It is hard to believe, but this woman lost years of her life as she stood frozen in a human-sized test tube. Cynthia Denali understands betrayal. While most of us only heard about it, she experienced the evil side of Dennis Denali firsthand. I ask that you give her your attention for a few moments and listen to what she has to say. I think she may be the answer we have been praying for."

The camera view backs away, showing Cynthia in the seat next to Carlton.

"Thank you, for that astounding introduction, Mr. Clearwater."

The camera zooms in on Cynthia. She is quiet for a moment, and I wonder if she's saying a silent prayer in her mind. She smiles and begins to speak.

"When John Winthrop boarded the Arabella with the Puritans and headed for America, he made a reference to the book of Matthew in the Bible, Matthew 5:14 to be exact. John Winthrop's vision was for the Puritans to arrive in the new world and shine like a 'city on a hill,' setting an example for the world.

In 1774, The First Continental Congress opened in
prayer. Our Declaration of Independence dated July 4,
1776, and written by our founding fathers declares, 'a
firm reliance on the protection of divine Providence.' In
a speech, regarding the Declaration of Independence,
delivered by one of those founding fathers, Samuel
Adams, remarks, 'We have this day restored the Sov-
ereign, to whom alone men ought to be obedient. He
reigns in Heaven, and with a propitious eye beholds
His subjects assuming that freedom of thought and
dignity of self-direction which He bestowed on them.
From the rising to the setting sun, may His kingdom
come.' Many argue that there is no mention of God in
The Constitution of the United States. I suppose that
depends if one views Article VII as part of the document because, within the date, it clearly has the words
'the Year of our Lord.' There are reported sightings on
record of George Washington kneeling in prayer. And
as president, George Washington issued a Thanksgiving Proclamation, recommending that Americans set
aside November 26, 1789, as a day to give thanks to the
Almighty God. Now, because of its grand significance
as I look at our country at this moment and time, I
cannot help but ponder the truth behind the words of
former President Ronald Reagan, 'If we ever forget that
we're one nation under God, then we will be a nation
gone under.'

When my former husband took office, he led Congress
to remove the phrase "under God" from our pledge of
allegiance. Then he proceeded to try to remove God
from the world by destroying humanity and repopu-

lating with a society that would follow him as supreme ruler.

Fellow Americans, look around. Look at what is happening in our country. I see a country that is letting my former husband's plot succeed from his grave. I see a society that is aspiring to be no better than him. So, now, ask me why I am choosing this platform to speak to you. Why am I choosing this podcast with a Christ-following audience to announce my candidacy? Because fellow Americans, God is the cornerstone of my campaign and the foundation on which I plan to rebuild our country. Now, ladies and gentlemen, I am not suggesting in any way that our religious freedom be infringed upon. Our forefathers fought for our freedom of religion. And it is each person's individual choice to accept Christ's sacrifice and his free gift of salvation. However, the roots of our country sprouted and grew from people with a faith in God, and even though Christianity was not imposed upon Americans, it was very much a part of the beginnings of our country. Let me add to that statement by saying that God was definitely not forced to be excluded from our culture. I believe that I have more than proven that in my opening remarks. If I am elected president, I plan to take us back to our roots. Because, the way I see it, we only have two choices. We can continue on the same path as flesh-eating bacteria gnawing and eating our country alive, destroying ourselves from the inside out, or we can make a change. We can go back to the beginning and put respect for God back in our country. The Bible, God's Word to us, states in Isaiah 60:12 King James Version, 'For the nation and kingdom that will not serve thee shall perish; yea, those nations shall be utterly wasted.' And then in Psalm 33:12, 'Blessed is the nation whose God is the Lord; and the people whom he hath chosen for his own inheritance.' Please, I am asking that you join me in my efforts, and together, let's save the United States of America. Let's put our nation back under God. Thank you."

Carlton returns to the screen, but I don't hear his voice. And I no longer hear the doubts in my head about Cynthia being president. Of course, it was never Cynthia or her ability that I doubted. It was the negative effects that would surround our family. But God created each of us for a purpose. And now I realize that this may very well be Cynthia's.

CHAPTER SEVEN

I jolt awake, my heart scampering in my chest. I don't know why. I wasn't dreaming, or at least I don't remember it. I push myself up and swing my legs off the side of the bed. Sitting on the edge, I wrap my arms around myself and rub the raised, tingling goosebumps covering my arms. My airway tightens, and the tingling spreads over my entire body. Darkness fills the room, and the only sound is Steve breathing as he sleeps on the bed beside me. *What is it? Why am I on the verge of a panic attack? Lord, please help me calm down.*

I touch my stomach as the baby shifts from one side to the other. *The baby's fine,* I reassure myself and let out a silent sigh of relief. Unfortunately, that does not put a damper on the state of alarm my body is in. I open my mouth halfway and take in a slow breath. I don't want to wake Steve, so I exhale as quietly as I can.

Daddy. I throw my hand over my mouth to stifle my gasp. *That's it. I fell asleep before I called to see if he made it home.* I reach for my phone on the nightstand, noticing the time illuminated in red. *Three o'clock. What am I thinking? I can't call in the middle of the night. And besides, the light from the screen will wake Steve.* Clutching the phone in my hand, I lower myself back down on my pillow and tuck my legs under the blanket. *Something's wrong. Mom would have called to tell me if he made it home... I would have heard the phone ring. She didn't call because she didn't want to upset me. I should have known something wasn't right. He wouldn't be gone all day and all evening over security supplies... did he really think he would find ammunition anywhere?* Gritting my teeth, I squeeze my eyelids together as tight as I can as if I can squeeze the troubling thoughts out of my head, but instead, the hailstorm of worry pummeling down on my brain only gains strength. *Why would he go out in this chaos... alone? He saw what happened in the parking lot of the hospital. Something bad has happened to him. He's been shot and left for dead. I have to find him. Kate. I'll call Kate. She will help me.* A chill runs down my spine, and my body quivers with a hard jerk. *Ellie, stop. Fight it. You are letting the obsessive thoughts take over,* I scold myself. *Armor. Put on your armor. Use the sword of the spirit. 'Yea, though I walk through the valley of the shadow of death, I will fear no evil: for thou art with me; thy rod and thy staff they comfort me.'* The tension in my muscles takes over, and I grip the phone tighter in my right hand and twist the sheet around my left, grasping it with all my might. *'Fear thou not; for I am with thee: be not dismayed; for I am thy God: I will strengthen thee; yea, I will help thee; yea, I will uphold thee with the right hand of my righteousness.' 'Come unto me, all ye that labour and are heavy laden, and I will give you rest.'* My heart rate slows, and my hand loosens from the sheet. I lift my head and rub my face across my pillow, drying off the streams flowing from my eyes. Nestling my head back in the pillow, I will myself to keep the bad thoughts out. That means I have to fill my mind with good thoughts. *'Amazing Grace, how sweet the sound! That saved a wretch like me!'* The words echo in my head as I sing them in my mind. *'I once was lost, but...'*

A squeal echoes outside the door. My heart somersaults, and I plummet off the bed onto the hard floor. Thankfully, I land on my knees and elbows, and my baby takes no impact other than maybe the lack of blood flow when my heart stopped for a second.

"What happened?" Steve yells. "Ellie?" The glow of his lamp suddenly filters across the bed, and in an instant, he is standing over me. "Oh. Oh no! Are you hurt?" He drops to the floor beside me, but I am already pushing myself to my feet.

"I'm fine," I say, trying to catch my breath so I can tell him about the squeal.

"Ellie, you're not fine. I'm calling an ambul...," he stops midsentence. "Never mind. We'll never get an ambulance. I'll drive you." He turns toward the dresser and then turns back. "Come on, you can wear your pajamas."

"Will you listen?" I blurt out in an effort to get his attention. "Someone squealed. It came from down the hall."

Steve droops his shoulders. "Ellie, you must have had another nightmare."

"It was not a nightmare. I was awake," I sputter as I lean over to grab my pistol from the drawer.

"Listen," he argues. "Nothing but silence. Everything is fine. You just think you were awake. Whatever you heard was in your dream. It wasn't the nightmare about my father, was it?"

Another squeal reverberates from somewhere on the other side of the bedroom door, but this time it doesn't stop. The wail drags on, rising and falling in pitch like a bad song stuck in my head.

I grip the handle of the gun with both hands. "I guess we are both having the same nightmare," I mutter under my breath.

Steve darts around the bed, pulls his .45 caliber from his side table, and dashes to the door, pushing himself in front of me. "Stay close behind me." He opens the bedroom door and steps into the dark hallway in the direction of the shrieking cry.

"The nursery," he whispers.

"Is that music?" I ask in a low whisper. "That sounds like Spencer."

"He can't get out of his room without Herb knowing." Steve pauses for half a second with his hand on the knob and then flings open the door. He shifts the aim of the gun around the room, and with a loud, exasperated sigh, he drops the gun to his side.

"Told you it sounded like Spencer." I put my hand over my mouth to hold in my giggle. The bassinet is rocking at full speed, and the sunlight is dancing on the ceiling to the music. However, the music is only faintly playing, not loud like earlier.

"The baby is going to cry on purpose, isn't he?" Steve utters as he stares at the bassinet with a look of disbelief covering his face.

"Probably," I answer. "My mom says babies learn quickly."

Steve lowers his head and extends his hand beneath the base of the bassinet. "A wire must have come loose. The volume of the music should be increasing in proportion to the volume of Spencer's voice."

"Oh, thank goodness." Herb speeds into the room.

"Herb, how did Spencer get out of his room? You are programmed to wake up if he as much as breathes too loud," Steve rants.

"Well, I had a slight security situation. I wear many hats around here you know." Herb picks Spencer up out of the bassinet and moves back toward the door with no further explanation.

"Security situation. Herb, stop!" Steve's voice rises. "What are you talking about?"

"One of the motion body heat detector alarms halfway up the drive was set off. Claude and I went to check it out." Herb looks back over his shoulder. "I apologize for Spencer. He was fast asleep when I left his room."

The blood drains from Steve's face, and his tone changes from frustration to concern. "No...Herb, it's okay. You did the right thing. What happened with the alarm? D-did you find what set it off?"

"The body heat sensor was activated, so whatever it was, it definitely was not a leaf or a tree limb. Claude is still outside checking. I stayed inside to guard the doors and watch the monitors. But then, I realized Spencer was missing, and with the alarm issue, I was so frightened, I thought my motherboard was going to overheat."

"Herb, I want you and Spencer to stay in here with Ellie. Lock this door, and don't open it for any reason." Steve's jerky hand motions make his worry obvious. He stretches his leg in a giant stride to the doorway just as Claude rounds the corner, and they smack right into each other. The metal tip of the gun clanks against Claude's metal torso, but luckily, the gun doesn't fire. Something big flies from Claude's hand, landing with a thud on the hardwood floor in the hallway.

"Pardon me." Claude bounces backward, spins around, and scoops something off the floor. He spins back around holding a humongous rat by the tail. "Herb, I found our trespasser."

"An opossum," Herb's mechanical voice wavers with excitement. "What a coincidence! I was searching for a fun new recipe in my database yesterday morning, and would you believe I came across this mouth-watering photo of roast 'possum with sweet potatoes? Apparently, 'possum was a delicacy during The Great Depression era."

"This is not The Great Depression era, and we are not eating that," Steve grumbles.

"Hmph." Herb grunts. "Have you seen the news? I would say that we are in a greatly depressing era."

Steve shakes his head and glares at the 'possum still dangling by its tail from Claude's hand. "Why did you bring it inside? What if it gets loose in here? You know 'possums pretend to be dead."

"Oh, he's not dead," Claude asserts. "He is sleeping. I shot him with a tranquilizer dart."

"Take him back outside," Steve huffs, pinching the bridge of his nose. "And Herb, Jillian wants to work on Cynthia's campaign here, so Ellie won't have to travel to her house. It will be a small gathering here tomorrow evening... well, at this point, I guess I should say later today. Jillian is bringing a salad and dessert, and Gerald and Alice are bringing a couple of side dishes. Could you please prepare a main dish," Steve's voice deepens, "something besides 'possum," he rolls his eyes toward Herb and then continues in a normal tone, "that would feed ... umm... thirteen or fourteen people?"

"Very well," Herb wheels toward the hall with Spencer cradled in his arms, "but you should have seen the picture of that roast 'possum. It would be the perfect centerpiece for a potluck."

"Ugh. I have to see what's wrong with this music before I can sleep. It's eating at me."

"Oh." Herb's voice filters from the hallway. "About that. Spencer was playing in there last night, and that blaring classical music was fraying my wires. I couldn't handle another minute of it, so I adjusted the volume setting."

"Herb!" Steve yells.

"What? Sorry, I was not programmed to enjoy classical music," he murmurs in an undertone with sarcasm, but his computerized voice still reverberates into the room. Then in a loud voice, he yells back, "Couldn't you make it play hip-hop or reggae?"

Steve gets on his knees, lays the gun next to him on the floor, and peers under the bassinet. "Research shows listening to classical music raises your baby's IQ."

"I hate to interrupt this argument that you are having with a robot that you programmed," the worries about Dad start flooding back in, "but what is this about a gathering? When did you talk to my mom?"

"Oh, I was going to tell you. Your phone was ringing last night, and I answered it before it woke you." He grabs his gun and pushes back to his feet. "Apparently, the response to the podcast last night was overwhelming. Right after my mother's speech, tons of Christian organizations started contacting Carlton, announcing their support and wanting to know what they could do to help with the campaign. So, anyway, Jill—"

"Sorry," I reach up with my left hand and rub my left temple, "but I need to know something else first. Did she say anything about Dad? I've been lying awake in a panic worrying."

"Yeah," Steve's forehead crinkles, "he's fine. He texted your mom after she got home. He had to get a hotel because he drove all the way to Richmond for some kind of coating that would make car windows bulletproof. When he got there, they were sold out, and he didn't have time to get back home before the curfew. She said he should be home in time to come with her to the campaign organizer at four."

"Bulletproof coating?" I utter aloud, but inside I am questioning why I still have this horrible panic in my stomach.

"Yes, they used to make this polycarbonate material that you layered onto the existing glass. Now I think it's some type of glaze that chemically melds with the glass. But I would have thought that any chances of finding that available in a store would have vanished when this whole mess started. You know... I wonder if I could fabricate somethi..."

My mouth stretches in a wide yawn. "Honey, could you worry about this bassinet and bulletproof coatings later, or at least think about it lying in our bed? I'm exhausted."

"What's wrong with me? I completely forgot," he says, tucking the gun in his pajama pants. "You have been on your feet way over ten minutes."

As I pad back to the bedroom with one of Steve's hands touching the small of my back and his other hand gently nestling my elbow, my anxiety settles, my muscles relax, and my heartbeat changes from a pounding drum to a soft lullaby. It's as if his love for me travels from his fingertips like an electric current to my brain, illuminating a message that I know, but for some reason, have trouble remembering sometimes. '*And we know that all things work together for good to them*

that love God, to them who are the called according to his purpose.'
The words of Romans 8:28 remind me of meeting Steve in President
Denali's training facility. As horrible as it was to be in that place, I
would never have met the man of my dreams if I hadn't been there.

Steve holds my arm until I sit on the side of the bed. I place my
gun back in the drawer of the nightstand and then let my body sink
into the mattress.

"I wish you would've woken me up," Steve says as he climbs into
bed.

"What? Why?"

"I don't want you lying here worrying yourself to death while I'm
sleeping." He clicks off the lamp. "From now on," he reaches over and
clutches my hand, "wake me up so we can worry together."

Thank you, Lord, for letting me go to that facility. Exhaustion pulls
my eyelids closed, and my mind finally shuts down.

Chapter Eight

"Ellie," Steve calls as he steps into the doorway, "what is Kate's cell number?"

"Oh, don't worry. I have already notified the office about my medical leave. I called Tanner first thing this morning." I look up. "I know being a supervisory agent, trying to make sure all the important cases are covered, has to be stressful right now, but he could have been a little more friendly."

Steve leans against the door. "I take it that he wasn't happy."

"Not at all, and he didn't use any tact in communicating his unhappiness either. He said now he would have to take another agent from the field to cover the computer casework."

"You can't help that you have to take leave," Steve reassures me.

"I know that, and Tanner does too. I guess he was just letting off steam."

"Anyway, do you have Kate's number? I still need to talk to her."
He pushes off of the door casing, straightening his stance.

I give him a curious look and then grab my phone from the nightstand. "Is something wrong?" I swipe the screen, taking a quick note
that it is eleven fifty-nine, and... there's her text.

> *Please text back that you are okay and always
> know Mom loves you.*

I tap a quick text back, so I don't forget.

> *I am great. Love you too. Please be careful. See
> you in a few hours.*

I click back to Kate's info and share her contact information with
Steve's phone.

"I don't think so," he replies with his eyes making contact with
everything in the room except me.

Pursing my lips together, I stare at him with an unblinking gaze,
waiting for him to elaborate. He doesn't.

In a swift movement, he slides his phone from his pocket, and his
eyes dart from the wall to the screen. "Great. You sent it to me. Thanks,
Honey." And he disappears down the hall.

That's weird. I wonder why he wouldn't tell me. I twitch my shoulders shaking it off and turn my attention back to the book on my lap.
*Four down. An animal native to the Sahara. Five letters... starts with
'a' and ends with 'x'. Hmmm... Something's wrong. What was he not
telling me?* I lay my crossword puzzle to the side, and blowing out
a loud, frustrated breath, I toss the blanket back. "I'm allowed ten
minutes," I mumble under my breath. "Besides, I'm thirsty anyway."

I slide my feet into my giraffe print slippers that Mom got me for
Christmas and trudge down the hall toward the kitchen... *where did
he go? Probably in the den... a.k.a. Steve's invention emporium.*

As I near the entrance to the den, his voice carries into the hall.
"Thanks, Kate. I appreciate it. Oh, and you can probably reach him
easier than I can. Could you let Agent Morgan know that we would

love to have him come too?... Anytime between four and five. We are starting early so everyone can get home before the curfew. ...Great, hope to see you this evening."

I breathe a sigh of relief. *What was I thinking? Nothing's wrong... he's campaigning for his mother.* I pad on into the kitchen to get something to drink.

"Mrs. Ellie, what are you doing up?" Herb is standing in front of the stove, glowering at me with his hands on his hips.

"Relax, Herb. I only came to get something to drink."

He wipes his metal fingertips on his white apron. "I could have brought it to you."

"I'm allowed ten minutes at a time, and you have other things to do besides wait on me. I know you must be overwhelmed with getting ready for the campaign party." I pull a glass from the cupboard.

"Oh, dear." Herb rushes over to my side. "Mrs. Ellie, you should not be reaching that high." He takes the glass from my hand. "Sit at the table, and I will squeeze you some fresh orange juice."

I drop my head, realizing there's no need to argue. Steve has programmed him to wait on me hand and foot. I shuffle over and drop into one of the wooden dining chairs. I'm curious about this fresh juice. I thought he had been getting it from a jug.

Herb takes out a couple of oranges and rolls them on the counter. Then, he slices each one in half. In a swiping motion, like he is dusting off his hands, he rubs them against each other, and then he picks up one of the halves in his right hand. I expect him to hold it over the glass and squeeze it. Instead, he holds it over the glass and crushes it in his grip. With wide eyes, I watch as he opens his hand and drops the peel that now looks like a wadded tissue into the composter.

Herb continues with the other three halves and zips over to the table with a full glass of juice. "Okie dokie, here is your daily dose of folic acid and vitamin C." He is back in front of the stove in a flash.

I lift the glass to my lips and take a sip. *This is so refreshing. I can't believe I thought it came from a plastic jug.* "I feel really bad. I should be helping you get everything ready. What did you decide to make?"

"No worries, Mrs. Ellie. Your main concern is making sure the baby is healthy," he casts a glance at me over his shoulder, "and keeping him in your tummy until his lungs are well-developed." He turns and opens the oven door. "I decided to keep it simple. I am making pork tenderloin with garlic and butter and a honey apple glazed ham." He uses the baster and squeezes the hot liquid over the ham.

I finish the glass of juice and carry it to the sink. "Thanks for the juice, Herb," I smile at him, "and the company. This whole bed rest thing leaves me a bit lonely with more than a bit too much time to think. But I suppose I better go lie down since it won't be long until I'll need to get ready for our party or meeting or whatever this thing is that we are having." I crinkle my eyebrows, realizing that I'm still not sure of the purpose of this get-together.

At least, my mind is at ease now, and I can go back to my puzzle. I fluff my pillow, propping it against the headboard, pick up my puzzle book, and locate where I left off. *Four down. Animal native to the Sahara.* I take the pencil and fill in the remaining letters to make the word 'addax'. *Next one. Five across.* I scan the page to find the small number five. *There... seven letters... third letter is 'c'... ends in 'e'...* As I read the clue, the letter President Denali sent to me drifts into my mind, the one that was nothing more than a bare-faced lie. The letter stated that because of my astounding work ethic in the criminal justice program, he had chosen me to be a part of his new special crime unit. He even referred to my being chosen as a 'high honor'. *Lies... all lies. He chose me alright... to be a pawn in his evil demented plot to destroy humanity. He was going to erase my memory... try to make me forget God.* A tear drips from the corner of my eye. Alice, Gerald, and I were fortunate. We still have our memories... but Eileen, Steve, and Teresa can't remember anything before Denali's training facility. I can't help but smile though. *He couldn't make them forget God.* Steve had a whole notebook of Bible verses that he had written down from memory.

I look back down at my book and pencil in the letters 'd-e-c-e-i-v-e' for five down. *Denali wasn't the only one who tried to deceive us.* President Kutchins ordered us all back to the facility because Dr. Eckert had led everyone to believe something could be wrong with our brains. Come to find out Dr. Eckert wanted to use his mind control tricks to turn us into violent puppets that would instigate mass murder and reduce the population.

I lean my head back and cover my face with my hands, trying to block out the bad memories. But instead of blocking out the memories, his evil face creeps in, hovering, growing until his image crowds and pushes all of my other thoughts aside, and then the nightmare... the terror that I have managed to hide as a repressed memory somewhere deep in the folds and crevices of my brain... my greatest fear brought to the surface... replays like I am watching a high-definition video in my mind.

The roar of crashing waves fills my ears as the skin on my heels melts away, leaving raw flesh.

"I told you there is no place to run," his deep voice fumes as he drags my body across the scorching sand.

I gaze up at the blue sky and the wispy clouds that feather across it like random brush strokes in a painting. Then it disappears. The burning sand, the blue sky, and the bright sun all fade. Now my feet bounce over roots and rocks, and I am encompassed in a canopy of green.

He shows no mercy as his hard hands squeeze around my wrists. A door creaks open. He lifts my body and drops me into the chair. "Eat," he orders. "And show a little more respect. Without me, you die."

I lift my head and stare straight into the face of pure evil, but I am not afraid. "You...you don't give me life. 'He that hath the Son hath life; and he that hath not the Son of God hath not life.' That's from God's Word... 1 John 5:12."

*His feet pound against the dirt as he trudges back to the door. "Eat,"
he hisses.*

"I will eat for his sake, not yours." I take an orange from the bowl.

*He stops with his hand on the door and glares at me over his shoulder.
"At least, we agree on something." He turns back, and the door slams
behind him.*

My phone chimes, yanking me from the terror in my mind. With
a clenched jaw, I lift my head, too angry from the memory of the
nightmare to even wipe the tears from my face, and reach for my
phone. *Kate.* I swallow hard and take a deep breath, hoping my voice
doesn't tremble, but then my finger is shaking so badly that I try to hit
the button three times before I make contact to answer the call.

"H-Hello."

"Ellie? You okay?" Kate's concern flows through the line.

A quick shallow breath in. "Oh. Hi, Kate. Everything's fine. Well,
other than I miss work."

"I know. I was disappointed when I found out you would be out
for a while. But taking care of yourself and the baby is most important.
Speaking of taking care of yourself, I hope I didn't cause you to have
to get up to answer your phone."

"No," I assure her, "it's right here by the bed. So, what are you up
to?"

"Well, I'm sorry to bother you when you're resting. I tried Steve's
phone, but he didn't answer. And I wanted to pass along this information as quickly as I could."

"No worries. I'm thankful to be conversing with someone." I
laugh. "I can pass along the info."

"Well, I couldn't trace the location of your dad's phone, or rather,
I'm still working on it."

My upper body springs up, and I toss my legs off the side of the
bed. *Steve called her about my dad.* A sharp twinge stabs through my
chest as my heart sinks into my stomach.

"It's not on, so it'll take a bit more time." Kate continues to explain. "However, the two texts that came to your mom's phone did not come from your dad. The texts came from two separate phones that pinged off of two different towers on opposite sides of Washington D.C. The texts were most likely sent from burner phones, and I would almost guarantee if we search—"

"They are in a trash can or lying on the side of the road," I finish for her.

"That's my guess."

"Kate, something is terribly wrong," my voice quavers, and the bitter taste of stomach acid fills my mouth. I no longer try to hide my hysteria, and desperation echoes in the rush of speech flooding through my lips. "I know the department has to be throwing loads of work at you, but please, you have to help me find him."

"Ellie, you know I'll help you. But before we jump to conclusions, let's examine every angle." She pauses. "Has your dad ever been known to carry a burner phone? I'm not sure why he would have the need to. I'm only saying that it's a possibility that he was the one using burner phones to send the texts and not someone else."

As much as I'm sure that's not the case, I have to answer her honestly. "I don't know about recently, but when we escaped the facility... the second time... Dad and Mom both had burner phones. And now that you ask, I remember Mom saying that Dad insisted they have two on hand all the time." The line goes quiet for a few seconds, so I continue. "Kate, something has happened to my dad. I feel it. I woke up in the middle of the night, almost having a panic attack with worry. Help me, Kate. Please."

"Ellie, I already told you I would help, but I hope you know that with the chaos going on, we aren't going to be able to get any other manpower on this." Kate's voice softens. "Listen, you don't need to be upset or stressed right now. I don't have children, but I've heard that pregnancy hormones can cause women to be more emotional which could explain the intensity of your gut feeling. Until we prove otherwise, I want you to keep telling yourself that your dad most likely sent those texts from his own burner phone. Why? I don't know. But it doesn't make sense that someone else would harm your dad and take the time to send your mother fake messages."

She's right. I'm overreacting. What would be the purpose of someone else pretending to be Dad and sending Mom texts? But where is he, and why would he send her texts from a burner phone?

"Ellie?"

"Ye—" I only get half a response out when a thought slams into my head so hard that I'm left in a daze. *The envelope. That has to be it. He has a history of acting on his own or going off on wild goose chases without telling anybody. He's trying to find Denali or prove he's alive or find Damien or... oh, it doesn't matter. If that's what he's doing and if he isn't hurt or worse, he is in imminent danger.*

"Ellie?" Kate says louder.

I snap out of my daze. "Yeah, I'm here."

"Look, I'm at work. I have to run, but I'm coming over in a bit to help with Cynthia's campaign. We'll talk then."

"Okay, but Kate, let's not say anything to my mom just yet. She's been through too much already. She shouldn't have to deal with the thought of losing him or any one of us again. Let's try to find something out for sure first."

"I get that. I don't think she knows that Steve called me, so I won't even let on that I know your dad is gone."

"Thanks, Kate. I'll see you soon."

I lower the phone with my eyes fixed on the drawer of my nightstand, and it's as if my state of consciousness drifts outside of my body. A low buzz hums in my ears, and every muscle in my body goes limp. Some sort of defense mechanism must kick in because I feel nothing. No sadness... no fear... no panic... only numbness as if none of this is real... like I'm watching a horror movie... or reading a fiction novel. *But this is good. If I'm going to find Dad, I have to treat it like a case at work... as an outsider with no personal connection. I'll only find him if*

I look at the evidence from an objective standpoint without my emotions taking over. I suck in a deep breath and thrust out my hand toward the drawer.

"Ellie, did I hear you on the phone? Was that your mom?" Steve comes around the bed from the doorway.

I look over my shoulder and pull my hand back.

"No." I turn my eyes toward the floor. "It was Kate. She tried your phone, but you didn't answer."

He plops down on the bed beside me. "I'm sorry. I didn't want to upset you," he mumbles in a barely audible tone. Then he raises his volume a bit. "Your mom doesn't know I called her. I don't even know why I did."

I tilt my head up a little and roll my eyes so I can see his face, which appears to be absent of any blood flow. "Because you had the same gut feeling I have had, and you couldn't sit around and do nothing."

"Yeah, I guess that sums it up." He puts his hand on my knee. "What did she say?"

"The texts didn't come from Dad's phone. They most likely came from a burner phone through one of those apps where you can make a text look like it's coming from a different number."

"S-so," Steve's voice cracks, "where is your dad?"

"Good question. His phone is off, which will make it harder to track, and that is if she is even able to track it at all."

"Ellie, I'm sorry. I'm sorry that your dad is missing, and I'm sorry that I didn't tell you why I was calling Kate," he rattles off so fast that his words trip over each other.

I turn my head as I lay my hand on top of his, and I gaze into his deep, dark brown eyes. "It's okay. I know you're worried about me being under stress and what it could do to the baby." I squeeze his hand. "I'm thankful that you cared enough to call her."

He nods. "How long will it take her to track him if his phone is off?"

"Considering the state of the nation and that she's trying to help us on top of her already overwhelming workload, I have no idea. She had to hang up, but I could tell by her voice that she will do everything that she possibly can. She's coming over for the campaign planning. She said we would talk more then, but I insisted that she not say anything in front of Mom."

"Hopefully, between the wedding and the campaign, Jillian's mind will stay occupied."

I place my free hand on my stomach and peer over at the nightstand.

"Ellie, are you okay?" He leans around me as if he's trying to figure out what I'm looking at.

"I need to tell you something. I know you disagree, but please hear me out because I think it might have something to do with Dad's disappearance."

He crinkles his forehead with his mouth agape. "You know I'll hear you out... but this doesn't sound good. You're scaring me, Ellie. What is it?"

I take a deep breath and push down on my stomach in an effort to dislodge the baby from my rib cage. "Here goes." I sigh. "The other night when Spencer ate the pudding and broke the dish, Dad was in the kitchen with me. He was worried and told me to keep my guard up." I fix my eyes on Steve to catch his reaction to my next statement. "Dad said that despite all the proof and regardless of what everyone else thinks, his gut was telling him Dennis Denali is still alive."

"But Ellie...," Steve shakes his head, "my father can't possibly have survived—"

"Wait. I'm not finished." I lift my eyebrows. "You said you would hear me out, remember?"

"Yes, I'm sorry. Continue."

I take another shallow breath. The baby is putting so much pressure under my ribs that I can't seem to fill my lungs with air. "Dad went on to explain that he had heard Denali tell him in his office that he could never be destroyed. Of course, Cynthia has stated that she'd heard Denali say that as well. But here is the part that got my attention." I cough to clear my throat. "Dad said that right after Denali's claim that he could never be destroyed, he mumbled something else, but Dad never made out what it was. Anyway, to summarize, after Eckert got the death penalty, Dad had a dream about the day he was in that office with President Denali, and he heard the words loud and clear. President Denali said that he could never be destroyed. Damien would make sure of that."

Steve's face looks like he's wearing those glasses with eyes that pop out on springs. "As in Damien Seaver... the Damien Seaver that Agent Morgan can't find, and therefore, we have assumed that he does not exist. That Damien?"

"I'm not sure. It would be a bit of a coincidence if there were another Damien, but Dad said he had tried to find Damien Seaver too with no luck."

Steve pinches the bridge of his nose. "What is it with you and your family and these nightmares that contain grand epiphanies?"

"Excuse me." Heat rises in my face.

"I don't even have dreams," he continues as he squeezes his eyes closed. "Maybe when my father had my memory erased, it did something to my head, and I'm not capable of dreaming. Uuuuughhh!" He throws his head back and lets out a wail of frustration.

"Steve," I say in a calm tone.

"Sorry, I'm a little frustrated, a lot confused, and..." his expression softens.

"Worried?" I prod.

He gives a slight nod that I almost need a magnifying glass to see.

"Well, don't let your emotions carry you into a spiral yet. I'm still not finished."

He takes a deep breath and rolls his eyes.

"Mom was coming into the kitchen, so he didn't get finished with what he was telling me. He hurriedly slipped me an envelope, instructed me to read it when I was alone, and told me not to tell anyone because no one would believe us anyway and we couldn't catch Denali if he got spooked."

"Oh no... your dad has gone out searching for my fath— President Denali," Steve whines and closes his eyes. "I am so afraid to ask, but what's in the envelope?"

"I don't know. I never opened it."

"What? Why?" his voice escalates in surprise.

"Well, not long after we got home, you took me to the hospital. And then, I was forbidden to be stressed about anything, so I figured it was best if I waited because whatever was inside could upset me and bring back all of those obsessive thoughts about him being alive and trying to kidnap the baby and..." I gasp, out of breath.

He wraps his arm around me and pulls me closer. "I'm proud of you. I don't think I would have been able to contain my curiosity."

"I wouldn't be proud of me yet if I were you." I tilt my head and rest it on Steve's shoulder. "We have to open it."

"Because you think it might help us find your dad?" His question comes out as more of a monotone statement.

"Yes, and I'm afraid, if we aren't too late already, we may not have time to waste."

He swipes the hair from my eyes and pulls it behind my shoulder. "Where's the envelope?"

I lift my head and reach for the knob on the front of the night-stand. "I stuck it in here before we went to the hospital." I slip the envelope out of the drawer. Clutching it in both hands, I stare at it for a few seconds. *I don't get it. What could possibly be in here that everyone else would have overlooked?* I flip the envelope over, tear the sealed flap open all the way across, and slide out a tri-folded piece of white paper that has a lot of smaller papers tucked inside of it. Sliding over a few inches, I twist sideways and lay the paper on the bed between Steve and me, so I don't drop its contents on the floor.

Neither of us speaks, and our breathing is minimal as I carefully flip open the folded paper. A photo of President Denali as a young man is on the top. He is in the photo with another young man with long, dark hair, perfectly parted on the right side with a large, raised mole protruding out right below his hairline. Both of them are wearing dark sunglasses and matching dark red blazers with the same emblem. Because of the angle, I can't make out the letters on the emblem.

"Maybe the jackets represent a fraternity or club or something?" I hand the photo to Steve. "Do you know anything about your dad when he was in college?"

He casts his eyes sideways at me. "You're kidding, right? I don't know anything that happened when I was in college." He sighs. "I don't even remember going to college."

"Sorry. I didn't mean to be insensitive. I thought maybe you had asked Cynthia or Dukakis about him." I pick up a news article printed off of the internet, and my eyes burn at the sight of the headline.

"U.S. SENATOR DENNIS DENALI'S WIFE KILLED IN HORRIFIC ACCIDENT"

"I know you didn't mean any harm. I guess one would think I would have tried to find out about his past, or for that matter, my past, but I really have no desire to know anything about my father. If I didn't think it might help us find your dad, I wouldn't look at any of this stuff about my father now."

"I honestly can't say that I blame you," I reply in a dry voice, not meaning to seem unsympathetic, but the article has me entranced. *Why would Dad have this in here?* Not wanting to take the time to read the article word for word, I scan the page looking for something important. Steve leans in, looking at the page in my hand.

Cynthia Denali... wife of Senator Dennis Denali... killed in early morning crash... on her way to

Wallenhearth Law Office where she is a senior
partner... pickup truck crossed yellow line coming
around curve, forcing Cynthia Denali's SUV off
the road. SUV hit guard rail... rolled down embankment... caught fire... The driver of the pickup
fled scene. A witness reported passing a black
pickup driving at an excessive speed just prior to
seeing the flames erupt off of the embankment.
The witness was unable to obtain a license plate
number but did see a decal in the back window of
the pickup with the letters NAC...Authorities have
not apprehended the driver and will not release
any information as to whether they have even
identified the suspect.

I stare at the paper, wondering why the question had never crossed my mind before. *Who's charred remains were found in the SUV?* I shrug. *Still, how does this article have anything to do with Dennis Denali being alive now?*

"Am I missing something?" Steve scratches his head.

"I don't think so, or at least, I don't see anything that helps."

"Then why are you still staring at the page and chewing on your lip like you do when you are solving a puzzle."

"I was just curious as to the remains found in the SUV. Clearly, they were not your mother's, so who was killed in the accident?" I tilt my head and look up at Steve.

"How am I supposed to know? I wonder if the authorities have even thought to go back and reopen the case since Cynthia is obviously alive," Steve remarks, picking up a group photo.

I stretch my neck, straining to see. "Wow, that club, or whatever it is, has a lot of members, and they're all wearing those red jackets like your father and that other guy in the first photo."

"I bet it's a fraternity," Steve speculates, turning the photo where I can examine it.

I scan the names in extra small print at the bottom.

"I think that's my father." Steve uses his pinky finger to point to a guy in the second row.

"Yeah, I see his name. Row two. Dennis Denali." I continue to scan the names. *Row three... no names I recognize... Row four... nope... Row five... no... wait... yes.* "Here we go. Mordy Crawley. He should be the fifth one from the end." Steve and I bump heads, trying to move our eyes closer to the photo. "Sorry." I rub his temple where we collided and then look back to the picture.

"That's him," Steve asserts with certainty. "My father has known our dear ol' Dr. Eckert for a long time."

"Definitely," I agree. "This guy is a slightly younger version of the man in the photo Alice had in the van when Teresa recognized him." As the statement leaves my mouth, a thought hits me like a bolt of lightning striking a metal pole. "It was a clone," I say, thinking back to Dr. Mordecai Crawley committing suicide after getting caught illegally and unethically experimenting with cloning and then turning up years later as Dr. Earl Eckert working in President Denali's training facility.

"What?" Steve asks.

"In the accident... I bet it was a clone of your mother."

His brow furrows, and his expression freezes for a few seconds. "As bizarre as it sounds, it seems the most logical explanation, especially considering what we know of Crawley and Eckert."

I reach down between us and snatch the snapshot of the two men back up.

Steve glances over. "Hmm. Is there any writing on the back? That's my father, but who is the other guy in the photo?"

I flip it over. "No, nothing. They both have on those red jackets. Do you see this guy in the group photo? His shoulder-length black hair shouldn't be hard to spot."

A moment passes as Steve gawks at the group photo. "I don't see anyone in this group with long hair. They all have short-cuts, perfectly groomed."

"Weird. No idea why Dad has this in here." I toss it on the stack that we have already looked at and pick up the next, which appears to be quite a lengthy article with no photo. My eyes widen at the sight of the title.

"UNIVERSITY DISBANDS FRATERNITY AFTER MULTIPLE 'CULT' ALLEGATIONS"

Without a word, I slide close to Steve so we can both skim the article that covers the entire front and back of the page.

> Fahrenhall University announced today that, due to the number of allegations and complaints, the latest fraternity to organize on their campus, Nu Alpha Kosmos, has been ordered by the administration to disband. The fraternity has been under investigation for several months after numerous new recruits to the fraternity reported being forced to repeat a daily chant giving praise to the fraternity leader and were warned if they were caught having affiliations with any religious group, there would be serious consequences. After being sanctioned and placed on probation, complaints continued. The Board of Directors for the university stated that this fraternity was not under a national charter, and therefore, the college administration had full authority to disband the organization, and by unanimous vote of the board of directors, had exercised that authority. In a recent interview, the president of the university,

Dr. J. Collingsworth, stated, "Fahrenhall University is renowned for outstanding academia, and our graduate program is ranked top in the nation. We will not tolerate any group that brings negative publicity, and we certainly will not tolerate any organization that could be labeled or recognized as a cult."

Apparently, Nu Alpha Kosmos was organized by a group of students with a mutual interest and a common goal of 'making the world a better place to live.' Only a few of the members have been willing to speak to the press, all of whom denied knowledge of any required chant praising their president, Damon Sivers. None of the recruits who filed the complaints or made the accusations have come forward to speak with the press on the issue, and the university is required to keep their identity confidential.

According to a university spokesperson, it was Sivers who presented the proposal along with a petition displaying several hundred signatures asking permission to organize the fraternity. The spokesperson said all documentation had been in order, thoroughly detailing the purpose of the fraternity, the community service requirements of each member, and the motto of the organization, 'A Better Future, A New World, It all starts here. Nu Alpha Kosmos comes together to make change appear.'

Reliable sources speculate that the college may have larger problems depending on how long ago these complaints were filed with the administration. Authorities are refusing to comment, but they are also not denying that Aiden Carraban, the young man who has been missing for two months now after attending a church revival with his girl-friend, was a member of this fraternity, especially since family members have publicly confirmed Mr. Carraban's affiliation with Nu Alpha Kosmos on social media and voiced their concerns about the group.

Our reporters have tried to reach Sivers to get a statement, but at this time, we have not been able to locate him. Rumors are circulating that he may have withdrawn as a student at Fahrenhall.

Steve and I both turn our heads at the same time, letting our eyes meet.

"Damon Sivers." Goosebumps pop up on my arms as I say the name.

"Sounds sort of familiar, doesn't it?" Steve remarks in a monotone voice.

I lower the article still absorbing the words, trying to figure out what it means, or what my dad thinks it means.

"My brain is starting to hurt," Steve complains, picking up another page from the stack. "It would have been easier if we had dumped a ten-thousand-piece jigsaw puzzle out on the bed. At least, we would have known the pieces were supposed to fit together." He peers down at the page. "Oh, brother," he drawls out and tilts the paper toward me.

"Person of Interest in Murder Case Attended Fahrenhall University Under False Identity"

Police are still searching for a person of interest in the death of Aiden Carraban. The charred remains of a twenty-one-year-old male were discovered two weeks ago by hikers in a wooded area not far from the church where Carraban had attended a revival the night he disappeared. Due to the nature of the investigation, authorities will offer no further details surrounding Carraban's cause of death.

However, after threatening reports involving a new fraternity at Fahrenhall University in which Carraban was apparently a member, authorities have been trying to locate the fraternity president, Damon Sivers, for questioning. At a press conference earlier today, the chief of police requested the public's help. He stated that Damon Sivers was attending Fahrenhall University under an alias and had provided the university with false identification and forged credentials. The chief is asking that if anyone has any information on Sivers' real identity or his whereabouts, they will please come forward.

"Ahem!"

The sound from the doorway makes us both jump, and Steve drops the paper onto the floor.

"Sorry to interrupt," Herb says, still standing in the hallway. "I thought you might need a reminder that our guests will be arriving shortly, and I also need to know where you would like the buffet to be set up. I have run through some calculations assessing the amount of space needed for our array of dishes in relation to the number of guests that will be accessing our buffet, and I recommend utilizing the countertops in the kitchen for the buffet and the den/office as our banquet hall. I think we can slide a few of the inventions to the side and bring in the two large folding tables from the garage for a dining table."

"Yeah, Herb," Steve reaches down for the paper that fell to the floor, "whatever you think. It doesn't matter."

"Very well. I will take care of the setup." He turns back down the hall, but in a loud voice, he utters, "Chop. Chop. I cannot take care of a buffet and entertain guests."

I bundle the pages up and fold them back inside the outer piece of paper. "There are only a couple of things left. We can look at those later tonight," I say, putting the envelope back in the drawer.

"I don't see the hurry. Nothing in there is going to help us find your dad," Steve mumbles as he stretches with his arms over his head, and then he blows out a deep breath. "Do you need some help getting ready?"

"No, I get ten minutes on my feet. Remember?"

He smiles. "Umm Hmm. Like you have ever gotten ready in ten minutes before."

I laugh and tap his arm with my fist as I trudge to the bathroom.

"Okay, then. I'm going to move the stuff in my office for the tables." He glances back at the clock. "I'll be back in ten minutes to help you."

CHAPTER NINE

Chaos rings in my ears, sending a steady ache crawling and spreading like a spider web through my shoulders, up my neck, and over the top of my head. As much as I love all these people, our house is not meant to accommodate this number of guests. After all, this is an old farmhouse. When we happened upon this place after our first escape from Denali's facility, it looked like it should have been torn down a long time ago. The paint was almost gone from the clapboard siding, and well, I wondered if it was even safe to enter. But we did, and when I saw the dusty Bible inside on the coffee table, I knew God had led us here. President Denali had not allowed any outside reading material in the facility, meaning no Bibles. I remember picking up the Bible off the coffee table and hugging it to my chest.

I turn and peer through the cluster of people, letting my gaze fall on that same Bible on that same coffee table. I had to keep that exactly as it was. Anyway, Steve bought the house and surprised me when we returned from our honeymoon. He had completely renovated the house, and we now have a garage, but in the grand scheme, it is still a small farmhouse that is now filled with way too many people talking at the same time. And to top it off, we are only ten minutes into the evening, and all of the guests have not yet arrived. We're still waiting for Carlton, Kate, and Agent Morgan. Nonchalantly, I press my fingers to my temples and attempt to rub away the headache that is forming. *I'm sure when we sit down to eat, the noise will die down,* I tell myself as the pain intensifies.

Herb speeds by wiping his hands on his apron. "I do believe the rest of our guests are coming up the drive now. Could someone keep a check on Spencer? He is eyeing the orange creamsicle cake, and I am certain I saw a drip of saliva escape from his little monkey lips."

"Oh, my. I got him covered, Herb." Mom's voice echoes over the top of everyone else's in the room. "We don't want another banana pudding incident."

Poor Mom. Keeping busy has always been her defense mechanism. When Eileen disappeared and Dad stopped talking, she worked non-stop. *I guess this wedding and campaign couldn't have come at a better time. Hopefully, that will keep her mind off of Dad's disappearance.*

Alice and Eileen sidle up to the bench where I'm seated at the entrance to the hall.

"There you are." Eileen sits down next to me. "What are you doing over here by yourself?"

Alice sits down on the other side of me. "I noticed you rubbing your temples. I'm guessing you are trying to escape the noise?" she raises the pitch of her voice in question.

"Oh, no. I hope it doesn't look like I am being rude." I put my hand to my chest.

"No, no." Eileen brushes my hair behind my shoulder. "Everyone knows you are on bed rest. We were only worried."

"Thanks, but it's nothing to be concerned about." I smile. "Just the lack of sleep last night and the beginnings of a tension headache."

"Are you sure you don't want me to go get Ted?" Eileen narrows her eyes as if she does not believe that I'm okay.

"No," I pat her knee, "and you girls don't have to sit here and babysit me. I know you have dates to attend to."

"Well, I'm still not sure I consider Ted a date, and besides," Eileen holds her side and giggles, "Mom is filling him in on some campaign duties that she has assigned to him."

I bite my lips together to suppress the laugh that is trying to escape.

"Hey," Alice leans back and crosses her arms, "I have a few moments out of Gerald's sight, and I would love to catch up with my best friend."

"Out of his sight?" *That doesn't sound like Alice.* "Is everything okay between you two?"

Alice heaves a sigh. "Everything is wonderful. I guess my wording sounded bad. You know Gerald is the love of my life. It's just..."

"Just what?" Eileen chimes in.

"I know the world has gone mad, and it is frightening." Alice rolls her eyes toward the ceiling. "But the closer we get to the wedding, the more protective Gerald gets."

"Ah, that's sweet," Eileen says with a puppy dog expression. "He's afraid of losing you."

"I know that," Alice whines, "but I need to get work done. And if Gerald has to be at the restaurant, he insists I be there with him. If I go to the restroom, he waits outside the door. When he is not at the restaurant, he comes to my apartment and stares at me while I try to work. I can't decipher computer code with someone three inches from my face. And last night, he stayed up all night in his car outside of my apartment," Alice makes quotations with her fingers, "to keep an eye out."

Eileen's puppy dog face has disappeared. Now her eyes are bulging from their sockets. "Okay, I concur. He is going a wee bit overboard. I was planning a bridal shower. Do you think you will be able to come?"

"Are you kidding?" Alice's face lights up. "No way would I miss it. How long have you been planning this?"

"Since you set a definite date. Did you really think we weren't going to have you one? A bridal shower is kind of a 'must' for a bride," Eileen says in a sarcastic tone. "Of course, I am rethinking the entertainment now."

"What entertainment?" I crinkle my forehead in confusion.

"Since you are on bed rest, and it's not exactly safe to have it out somewhere, I found this really old movie called *Runaway Bride*, but now I'm not so sure that is the best movie choice." She cracks a grin as she looks at Alice.

"Oh, please." Alice leans her head back and gently taps it against the wall. "Nothing would keep me from marrying Gerald. I just wish he would lighten up a little."

"Hey, you girls want to see the nursery?" I ask, suddenly remembering no one has seen it.

"The nursery... you have it finished?" Eileen looks at me as if I have kept something from her.

"Steve surprised me with it yesterday. You won't believe it."

"We've seen the rest of the house. I doubt the nursery will be a shocker. But yes, you know we're dying to see it." Alice gets to her feet. "Are you feeling up to it though?"

"I'm fine," I say and then lower my voice to a whisper, "but we'll have to sneak past Herb and all the other people who think I'm not even supposed to stand up."

"There's the most beautiful woman I have ever laid eyes on," Ted peers at Eileen around the door frame. "I was wondering where you disappeared to."

"Sorry, I didn't mean to abandon you." Eileen steps toward the door. "Ellie was showing us the nursery."

Ted's mouth falls open as his eyes scan the room. "Wow."

"Yeah, really," Eileen adds. "This room will be the envy of every baby in the world."

Ted whistles. "Adults too. I would love to have this room."

Gerald rounds the corner. "Alice, I was worri... whoa." His entire body jerks when he notices the nursery. "Unbelievable. That man never ceases to amaze me. Is there anything he can't do?"

I grin from ear to ear. "No, I'm pretty sure there isn't. Hopefully, our son will be just like him."

"Well, the saying goes, 'like father, like son.'" Ted steps into the room. "Eileen, I actually came in here because your mother is looking for you."

"Oh, okay. Let's go see what she wants." Eileen disappears down the hall with Ted behind her.

"Are you coming, Alice?" Gerald says in a respectful but expectant voice.

"I'll be along in a minute. I want to finish talking to Ellie."

Gerald pauses as if he is considering waiting for her, but then he turns with his head hanging low and trudges from the room.

"Alice," I put my arm around her shoulder, "you should talk to him. Tell him how you feel."

"I know, and I will. But, while no one else is around, I wanted to ask about your dad. Your mom was telling me that he went out of town and hasn't made it home yet. The way he was barring the door the other night, it's hard for me to imagine him leaving your mom and Eileen alone in the house overnight. Is everything okay?"

I open my mouth to explain, but Kate rounds the corner.

"Kate, I didn't know you were here yet."

She walks over and pulls me into a hug and then does the same to Alice. As she steps back, her head moves side to side and then up to the ceiling. "Lucky kid," she mutters and turns to face me. "I know you don't want me to say anything in front of your mom, but...," she stops with her lips parted, casting me a glance that I'm certain means she is awaiting my approval to speak in front of Alice.

"It's okay. I was actually about to fill Alice in."

"I figured... but making sure." Kate continues in a low voice. "I was able to locate your dad's phone." She lifts a clear bag from her purse. "It was in the bushes at the end of your parents' driveway."

"I don't understand. How could his phone be that close? He left in his car. Has anyone found his car?" *This makes no sense.* My throat constricts as panic rises, and I'm so confused that my brain cannot even create a crazy, obsessive thought.

"Ellie," she drops the bag back into her purse, "I won't stop looking for your dad until we find him, but I think we need to look at the evidence. I checked the phone for prints. Only your dad's fingerprints are on it. Then, we have to look at where we found the phone and the fact that we know your dad had a history of keeping a burner phone."

"So, am I reading between the lines correctly in assuming those texts your mom told me about did not come from your dad's phone?" Alice interjects.

I blink back the water in my eyes and nod.

"But your mom doesn't know that they didn't come from his phone," Alice hesitates, "and I'm guessing she doesn't know that someone could make a text appear to come from another phone." Alice's voice trails off as she wraps her arm around me.

"Look, Kate," I add a confident edge to my voice even though my stomach is trembling from uncertainty, "I know how the situation appears, and I'm aware of my dad's history. But I also know that my dad would not leave my mom and my sister in that house overnight alone right now. His character would never allow him to do that. My gut tells me he's in trouble."

"Kate, you said that you already checked his phone for prints. Do you need it for anything else?" Alice asks in her take-charge voice.

"No, why?" Kate questions.

"Could I take it and search through it? Maybe there's something stored on it that could give us a clue where he is?"

"Sure, if that's okay with Ellie." Kate pulls it back out of her shoulder bag. "Honestly, I don't know of anyone else I would trust more to search through it."

"Yes, Alice," I plead, "and thank you. I didn't want to burden you before your wedding with all of this, but you're a computer genius. If something is there, you're the only one who would find it."

Alice takes the plastic bag with the phone and slides it into the pocket of her slacks.

"Ellie," Steve's tone sounds a little upset as he strides into the room, "I'm quite sure you have been on your feet for more than ten minutes."

"We were just about to help her to the living room," Alice relates with a grin.

"Thank you." He cracks a smile at Alice through his hardened face. "I'm glad you girls got some time to talk though. That probably helped her a lot more than bed rest."

"We did have a lot to talk about," Kate adds.

"You all always have a lot to talk about," Steve smirks. "Where is Agent Morgan? Did you tell him to come?"

"I tried his cell a few times, but he never answered," Kate replies. "I'm sure their department is as busy as ours, so I can understand why. But I did leave him a message."

"Well, I'm sure he got it." Steve takes my hand. "Come on. We're about to eat."

It took a bit for everyone to get their food and get seated. On our way to the kitchen, Steve took a brief moment to introduce Carlton to Kate, Alice, and me since we were hiding in the nursery when he arrived. After that, Dukakis led the blessing of the food, and then everyone insisted that I go through the buffet line first, so I could go and sit. Steve helped me with my plate. Even though I could have carried it myself, I let him because I knew it was an act of love.

However, I do wish I had gotten a video of Steve's face when he saw the pork tenderloin. Herb had arranged it with steamed sweet potatoes surrounding it on a fake silver platter positioned on the kitchen island, so it appeared to be the centerpiece of the buffet. As soon as Steve laid eyes on the meat, his hand flew to his mouth, his shoulders drew up, and his face turned a shade of red that I'd never seen on him before. It took a minute for me to trace his gaze and figure out what had him so upset, but when it did, I was laughing so hard that my side started to cramp. To sum up, my laughter without immediate explanation did not help the redness on his face. Of course, once I could talk and got the words out explaining that it was pork tenderloin and not roast 'possum, he was laughing too. In retrospect, considering the conversation last night, in addition to the size and shape of the meat almost perfectly matching the torso of our little security breach, if I had not been in the kitchen when Herb was preparing it, I would probably have thought the same.

The house is much quieter now that everyone's mouths are full of food. Steve and Herb were able to fit the two long folding tables in the den, a.k.a. Steve's office, end to end, and we have all managed to squeeze in around them.

"So, Carlton," Mom's voice breaks through the chewing noises filling the room, "tell us about the podcast and all these calls you've been getting in support of Cynthia."

Carlton takes a sip of water and leans back in his chair. "It's overwhelming. That's the only word I can think of. As soon as we went off the air yesterday, emails and messages on social media started pouring in by the hundreds." He rubs his hand across his head as if he is trying to tame the wild curls. "I knew the special podcast making her first announcement to a Christian audience, especially given her stance on the issues affecting our country, would get her some support. But considering people's feelings about anyone associated with the government right now, I never imagined this kind of response."

"I could see this kind of response." Dukakis lays his fork down on his plate. "People may be distrusting of the government, but at the same time, they know things cannot continue like this. People don't want to be confined to their homes in order to stay safe, and now their freedom is being infringed upon with this nine o'clock curfew. How long do you think Americans are going to tolerate that?"

"Well, from messages I've received, I'm guessing that almost every church in the country has last night's podcast on their website as well as posted on every social media platform." Carlton scoops up a sweet potato on his fork.

"Alice and I have been working on Cynthia's personal platforms," Eileen interjects. "I added the link to last night's podcast to the feed on all of her existing social media profiles, plus created an account for her with a group forum on that new one, BridgNect. People are already collaborating within the forum and coming up with their own ideas to campaign for her."

"That's great, Eileen. I bet that's where a lot of my feedback has stemmed from," Carlton comments. "Do you know a lot about this new Bridgnect? I don't have an account on there yet, but I hear it's the latest craze in social media."

"I don't have an account yet either, but it's growing fast." Eileen waves her fork, gesturing with her hands as she explains. "The algorithm is more relaxed, so posts with external links get shown to a larger audience. You definitely need to get an account. 'Armed and Ready' is a phenomenal podcast that needs to be accessible on every avenue possible."

"If you have the time, I would appreciate your help in setting it up." Carlton takes a drink of water as he focuses on Eileen.

Eileen smiles. "Sure. I'd be happy to."

Ted's jaw appears to harden as he glares across the table at Carlton.

Alice must notice the animosity building because she speaks up, taking over the campaign discussion. "I'm glad the social media aspect of the campaign is well underway. Cynthia and I have been working together, and I have her campaign website up and running." Alice lets out a giggle. "I think Cynthia is sick of me already. It took us a while over the phone to enter all of her ideas and her stance on the issues. But I think it's important that her website be the one place that contains all the information about Cynthia, the issues, and her reasoning for running with no political party affiliation or backing."

Gerald swallows hard. "She is telling the truth. I sat right beside her at the restaurant. I think they were on the phone for two hours. Of course, I enjoyed every minute. My Alice is something else with those computers. It's going to be so nice having her working at the restaurant, taking care of all that computer security stuff. Nothing is safe anymore on those things, and I'm technologically challenged. If it does not cut, chop, mix, or cook food, I know nothing about it."

"Gerald, what are you talking about?" Alice's voice quavers. "W-we haven't discussed me working at the restaurant."

"Oh." Gerald's face goes blank. "Well, I assumed that since we were getting married, you would be there at the restaurant beside me."

"Of course, I want to be there beside you all the time, and I would love to take care of any computer issues you have. But, at the same time, I feel like God has gifted me with this ability to understand computer code and technology for a reason. And I was going to talk to you about it later, but since the topic has come up," Alice lays her napkin on the table, "this morning, I received a job offer that I can't turn down."

"Why?" Gerald still looks confused. "Why can't you turn it down?" he asks with his brows knitted together.

Alice closes her eyes and lowers her voice. "Because of this job... I could make a difference in the world... maybe save some lives... and prevent families from going through unnecessary pain because one day they wake up and their child is missing." She opens her eyes. "That's why. I know this is what God has prepared me for."

The corners of Gerald's lips curve down, and his head drops. The only sound in the room is Spencer shoveling orange cake into his mouth. I can't help it. I have to break the monotony and take the focus off of Gerald.

"Wow, Alice, this sounds like a really big deal. What exactly is it you will be doing?" I take a bite of the tenderloin as I wait for her to answer.

"Human trafficking. I know this has been a problem for a long time, but the news has been so focused on all of the violence that I hadn't realized how many more teenage girls have disappeared in the last few months that are all believed to be victims of trafficking. In the last three months, more teenage girls have gone missing than in the last five years. And, of course, it's not just limited to teenage girls. The number of younger children has also risen dramatically."

"So, you would be doing what?" I ask, still a bit confused.

"I have been instructed to keep most of the details confidential, but I can say that I would be tracking the computer activity of quite a long list of names on a log that authorities have deemed as suspects."

"I don't know a lot about computers, but I have seen you in action." Dukakis slides his chair away from the table. "If anyone on that list has typed one incriminating word into their computer, then they might as well go ahead and confess because you'll find it."

Alice's cheeks glow a rosy shade of pink. "I appreciate the boost of confidence, but I think you're exaggerating a tiny bit." She holds her thumb and the tip of her index finger close together to gesture a smidgen.

"I'm telling the truth, and you know it," he says laughing. "Now if you'll excuse me a minute, I have to go find a piece of that cake Spencer has." He casts a glance at Spencer's plate. "I mean, had."

Herb flies past the door, almost running Dukakis over. "Another guest is coming up onto the porch. I hope the food is still warm." He spins around and heads back toward the kitchen. "Claude, get the door. I have to warm the food."

A moment later, Agent Morgan steps into the room.

"Agent Morgan," Steve stands and extends his hand, "glad you could make it."

Everyone around the table gives a wave and a greeting.

"Sorry, I'm late. Work is a bit... well, it's ultimate pandemonium." Agent Morgan looks around the room as he speaks.

"I can't imagine why," Steve remarks. "But no worries, we have plenty of food left. The buffet is set up in the kitchen."

"Oh, thank you. I'm starving. But I want to congratulate our future president first," he says loud enough for everyone to hear. He steps around Steve and walks to the far side of the table where Cynthia is seated.

"I appreciate the congrats, but it's a little early to prepare an acceptance speech." She stands and touches his shoulder in sort of a distant hug.

As Cynthia sits back down, Agent Morgan lowers himself into Dukakis's seat. "Well, I want you to know that you have my support. It's so nice to finally have someone running for office who has the backbone to make a change in this country and isn't all talk. Just let me know what I can do to help."

Dukakis strides back in with his cake and rounds the table, not even noticing Agent Morgan until he is next to his chair. "Oh, Agent Morgan, I didn't know you were here. It's good to see you." Dukakis switches his plate to his left hand so he can shake hands with his right.

Agent Morgan stands. "I finally managed to escape from Homeland Security so I could celebrate with this stunning lady who is about to be our next president."

I notice more color floods into Dukakis's face at Agent Morgan's comment.

"Oh, I bet I stole your seat." Agent Morgan steps aside.

"No, it's fine," Dukakis continues in a friendly, sincere voice. "I can sit in that open seat at the end."

"I'm going to get a plate anyway. I'll grab that empty seat when I come back." Agent Morgan pats Dukakis on the back and heads off into the kitchen.

"Alright," Mom slides on her reading glasses, "we need to get back to the agenda of this gathering before curfew kicks in." Pushing her plate aside, she opens her notebook and clicks her pen.

And as the pen clicks, so does my brain. My mom's voice fades away, becoming only background noise, and my vision blurs. I'm left with an image of my dad and the contents of that envelope swirling through my mind like leaves caught in the wind. I almost get focused on one of the pages, but then it gets caught back up in the breeze and takes off again. And I move on to another.

I may be on bed rest. But luckily, I don't need to stand to use a computer because I have some investigating to do. And I do still work for the FBI.

Damon Sivers, who are you, and where did you go?

CHAPTER TEN

I jerk awake in a state of confusion to the sound of a wailing siren. My insides tremble in shock as my body leaps from deep sleep into full-blown panic.

"What's happening?" Steve springs upright. "Ellie, are you okay?"

"I'm fine... I think," I answer in a mumble.

The lamp flicks on. "Siren. Where's the siren coming from?"

"I-I don't know."

"Ellie," Steve points to my nightstand, "it's your phone. What did you do to your ringtone?"

"Oh. I forgot I changed it. I was bored yesterday," I say with one hand stifling my yawn as I reach for the phone with the other. *Gerald.* "Why would Gerald call at six o'clock in the morning?" I tap the screen and manage to utter, "Hello," through another yawn.

"Ellie, have you talked to Alice?" Gerald almost screams into the phone.

"No. Why?"

"She's gone. Ellie, Alice is missing." He screams even louder.

"Gerald. Calm down. It's six o'clock in the morning. She's probably sleeping," I blurt out before his words sink in. "Wait. Why would you think she's missing?"

Audible tears crash through the earpiece. "I walked her to the door of her apartment last night," he sniffles, "and waited until she got inside. I even double-checked to make sure the door was locked before I walked away. My stomach knotted up when I got in the car. Her apartment complex always gives me the heebie-jeebies, so I decided to sleep in the car. I kept thinking I could never live with myself if I left and something happened to her. And now look, something has happened to her. Ellie, how could I have let something happen to the woman I love... my future wife? Ellie," his voice cracks as he talks faster, "I can't live without her."

His breaking sobs are so loud that I have to hold the phone a few inches from my ear. "Gerald, if you were in the parking lot all night, how can Alice be gone? Maybe she just isn't answering the door," I suggest.

"No, that's it. I did leave. A little after five, I couldn't get comfortable, so I went to the restaurant to get some pear pastries with cream cheese drizzle. They are Alice's favorite. I was going to surprise her. But she wouldn't answer the door, and her phone went straight to voicemail. I was scared, so I unlocked the door and went inside. She's gone. Ellie, she's gone."

I finally shake the cobwebs from my mind. Steve has moved over and is sitting right next to me on the edge of the bed. I don't even need to put the phone on speaker. Gerald's panicked tone is so loud that it is reverberating off of the walls in normal mode.

"Gerald, was the door ajar, or was there any sign of forced entry?" I ask, trying to remain rational and approach the situation from a professional standpoint. If something is wrong, I can't help her if I panic.

"No. I opened it with my thumbprint... and all that other stuff Steve added."

I start to speak, but Gerald puffs and continues. "I know you think because this door has all of this security, no one could have gotten in. But let me tell you, if someone wants to do something illegal, they will find a way. A bunch of electronic gadgets is not going to stop them."

"I agree, Gerald. I'm going to call Kate, but I have to ask you these things first because she will ask me." I let out a shallow breath. "What about her car?"

"It's not here."

"Her car is not there, and there are no signs that anyone tried to break in." I look over at Steve. He rolls his eyes the second I glance in his direction. "Gerald, I know you're scared of losing Alice, but I need you to stop, take a deep breath, and think this through. Her car is not in the parking lot. Don't you think it's more than a big possibility that she left while you were picking up the pastries?"

"Her phone is going straight to voicemail. I know Alice. Something is wrong." His words run together, and with the deeper edge in his voice, I am pretty sure he is speaking through gritted teeth. "She's your best friend. If you won't help me, I'll find her myself."

"Gerald, wait. Don't hang up. Of course, I'm going to help you. She is my best friend, and I would do anything for her." I pause, searching my brain for the correct wording. "I'm only trying to look at this from every aspect. I can't stand the thought of you being this upset if Alice only went to the store or something."

Silence flows from the other end of the line.

"Gerald?" I swallow hard, wondering if he's angry with me. "Gerald, are you there?"

"Yes," he mutters so low I barely hear him. "I'm sorry. You are in no condition to be burdened with this. I shouldn't have called." He sighs into the phone. "Alice would be furious with me if she knew I upset you."

"Gerald," I turn, letting my eyes burn into Steve's, "stay right there. Steve and I will be there in a few minutes."

Steve's mouth falls open, but he doesn't say anything... yet.

"Ellie, no," Gerald argues, but his voice cracks and is gravelly from crying. "You're supposed to be on bed rest. Stay home. I'll wait here. If she isn't back soon, I will find her."

"Listen to me. Alice is my best friend... and so are you. I won't be on my feet. We'll figure this out together. I'll try to call her on the way, and you let me know if you hear from her. See you in a few." I start to hang up, but just in case, I add, "Oh... and Gerald, don't touch anything, okay?"

"Okay." His voice trembles. "Thanks, Ellie."

I tap the end button and brace myself for Steve's sermon about how I'm not supposed to be stressed out.

"Just sit there and stay off your feet." He stands and steps toward the closet. "I'll get your clothes."

"Thanks," I reply in shock that he isn't putting up a fight about going.

He returns in a minute wearing jeans and carrying a pair of black stretchy leggings and a red long-sleeved t-shirt. "Are these okay?" He holds them up.

"Perfect." I smile and take the clothes from his hands. "So, why aren't you arguing with me about going?"

"Well, I want to argue. But they're our friends. And I know if it were one of us, either of them would be here in a heartbeat. I have to wonder though," he says as he walks around the bed and pulls open his nightstand drawer, "Alice seemed a little irritated at dinner when Gerald assumed she was going to work at the restaurant. Maybe she isn't answering his call on purpose." Steve takes out his gun and tucks it into his jeans.

"I'm sort of thinking the same thing. I think Gerald has been a bit smothery lately."

Steve comes back around the bed. "You mean like sleeping in his car outside her apartment."

"Yes, but on the other hand, Alice is head over heels in love with Gerald. Unless her signal was blocked, she would have answered." I tap Alice's photo on my phone and hold it to my ear.

"Hello, you have reached Alice's alter ego. Leave a message, and I'll have the real Alice call you back."

I lift my head and gaze up at Steve, trying to hide the moisture that I'm afraid is glistening in my eyes. "Straight to voicemail. It doesn't even ring."

"Come on." He takes my hand. "Let's go." He forces a fake smile as he pulls me up.

I grab my badge and gun from my nightstand, and then he guides me like an old woman out the door.

Steve gives a signal and turns into the parking lot of the apartment complex. It doesn't have a gate or a guard or anything. One would think they would have added one, but I suppose it may be difficult to find someone to work security nowadays. Steve finds a spot not far from Gerald's car, and as he shifts into park, my muscles tense. It's a quarter until seven, and the sky is lightening. But this creeping darkness looms around me like a shadow hovering over my shoulder, and it's sending all of my senses into high alert. *Relax.* I remember what Gerald said on the phone about Alice's apartment complex giving him the heebie-jeebies. *It's Gerald's words getting inside my head.* I take a deep breath and remind myself that I have been to Alice's apartment complex so many times I can't even count them and never felt the least bit uneasy. Nevertheless, I pull my jacket around me and keep my hand on the grip of my nine-millimeter.

Steve comes around and helps me from the car. The parking lot appears to be vacant of life, but I still keep my finger above the trigger. We trudge up the steps to Alice's apartment on the second floor, and Gerald must be watching for us because he swings the door open the second we arrive.

We walk inside, and as soon as Gerald gets the door secured, he pulls me in a hug first, and then Steve. "I'm so sorry to have called and got you out in this mess. Ellie, I don't know what to think. Nothing is out of place. No sign of a struggle. And after I've had a few minutes to collect my thoughts, I'm more confused than ever. Her car is gone," he runs his fingers through his short brown hair that is pressed flat on one side, "but it's not like Alice to go anywhere without telling me." He lowers himself onto the sofa and buries his face in his hands. "Of course, she hadn't told me about her new job, had she?"

"Gerald," Steve pauses as he takes a seat next to him, "maybe her leaving was last minute. Maybe it has something to do with this new job, and she didn't have a heads up that she would be going out so early."

"Maybe." Gerald leans back and rests his head on the back of the couch.

"I'm going to take a look around," I say, peering back through the apartment. "Maybe I'll see something that gives a clue where she went."

I waddle along in slow motion, scouring the room with my eyes. The kitchen countertops are spotless, with nothing out of sorts, and no notes stuck anywhere. But if she had an appointment, it would be on the calendar stored in her phone. *Her desk. It's in her bedroom.*

I stop in the doorway of her bedroom and take in the sight of her perfectly made bed. *She knew she was leaving. She had time to make the bed.* Feeling a little more at peace, I walk over to the desk in the corner. The desk is clean except for the bag with Dad's phone and her closed laptop. I slide open one of the desk drawers, but then a twinge of guilt forces me to close it right back. *What am I doing? I have no right to be violating Alice's privacy. She obviously left on purpose.*

"Ellie," Steve calls from the living room. "It's okay. Alice just texted."

I hurry to the living room. Instead of a slow wobble, I put one hand in the curve of my back for support and speed wobble. "Where is...," my words trail off at the sight of Gerald's face. Streaks of tears are shimmering on his red cheeks. "What's wrong?" I ask in a low voice.

"Alice texted that she needed some space to think. She said she wanted to see her mom and that she was on her way to visit her at the nursing home." Gerald wipes one side of his face with the back of his hand.

"In Tennessee?" I blurt out in a shocked tone. It's hard to fathom that she would be traveling that far alone right now.

"Doesn't make sense, does it? I guess she is having serious second thoughts about marrying me," he mumbles with his eyes fixed on the wall.

"Did she say anything else?" I ease over and sit on the coffee table so that I am directly in front of Gerald.

"She told me not to worry. She would be back soon." Pools stand in the bottoms of his eyes, and his shoulders quiver. "Not worry? How can I not worry?" he almost shouts.

With my elbows on my knees, I lean toward him and speak softly. "Gerald, I know Alice loves you. I think that she is feeling overwhelmed." I put my hand on his knee. "See, most girls dream of their wedding day. With people afraid to leave home, and now the early curfew, I think she might be concerned about the big church wedding she envisioned. The other night at my parents' house, Alice seemed a bit stressed and concerned that no one would show up. And don't take this personally, but it seems that you may have been going a small fragment overboard in trying to protect her. I could see how she might have been feeling a little smothered."

Gerald drops his head and fidgets with his hands. "I was upset about the job thing, especially since she hadn't talked to me about it. I told her on the way home that I preferred she work at the restaurant with me. She was angry... well as angry as Alice can get." He slumps his shoulders and lowers his head farther. "That's why I went to get the pastries. I was going to apologize. I had no right. God gave Alice her talent for a reason, and I have no right to interfere with what God is calling her to do. I guess I was afraid I wouldn't be able to protect her. It sounds like she would be tracking some very dangerous people." He bites his bottom lip. "No. That's not it. Alice is a strong woman. I guess I hadn't even realized it until now... now that I might lose her anyway, but I think I was afraid of what happened to my parents."

"I've never heard you mention your parents. What happened?" Steve asks.

"They got a divorce when I was younger. I spent most of my childhood with my grandma. She's the one who taught me to cook. Mom and Dad both had careers with long hours. Dad was in pharmaceutical sales, so he traveled a lot. Mom was an accountant. Grandma said they were apart so much that they didn't know how to be together. So, they went separate ways, and I went with grandma."

"Gerald, you realize you and Alice are not your parents." I lower my head a bit and try to look up at his hidden face.

"Yeah," he whispers.

"You even said yourself that Alice never went anywhere without telling you?" Steve's pitch goes up on the last word, forming a question.

Gerald doesn't say anything, so Steve continues. "And I can't think of a time that Ellie and I have dropped by your restaurant to eat that Alice hasn't been there." Steve grunts, clearing his throat. "I have to be honest. I'm not crazy about Ellie's line of work. But it's what Ellie feels is the path God has prepared her for. God created each of us for a purpose... His purpose. And who am I to interfere with that? But, other than our jobs, Ellie and I do everything together." Steve scoots to the edge of the couch and twists toward Gerald. "You and Alice are like that too. You two are always together. And most importantly, you are both Christians. You both put God first in your lives, which means you will put God first in your marriage. And I believe a marriage with God up front and center is a marriage built on a rock. It will stand strong through any storm that comes its way."

Gerald looks up and cracks a smile. "You're right. Thank you." But then his face goes blank, and the corners of his lips curve down. "I wish I could talk to her. I need to tell her how sorry I am. I need to tell her how special she is, and that I'm proud of her. I know God has bigger plans for her than to stand beside me in a restaurant all day. The woman is a walking computer." His eyes widen. "Obviously, God has an important job for her. He gave her a photographic memory." He pauses. "I have to go to the nursing home."

"Gerald, why don't you give her a couple of hours," I suggest. "I'm sure by then she will answer her phone. And she hasn't seen her mom in a while. Spending some time together might do them both good."

"Okay," he agrees in a tone that shouts he really does not agree.

"But," I add, "I promise I'll keep calling her until she answers so we know she's safe."

Steve stands. "Alright mother-to-be, I need to get you home so you can rest."

He helps me up from the coffee table, and I almost fall.

Gerald jumps up and grabs my other arm. "Oh no," he yells. "Are you in labor? What's happening?"

"I'm fine," I say as I snicker at his reaction. "My legs went to sleep. Sitting on that hard table cut off my circulation. But I think I'm good now."

We plod toward the door when I remember Dad's phone. *Maybe I could find something on it since Alice is going to be gone for a while.* "Hold up. I'll be right back. I need to get something. I hurry to the bedroom, pick up the bag with the phone, and drop it in my purse. "I'm ready now," I rattle off, moving back through the living room.

"A penny for your thoughts."

I remove my hands from my face and turn my head in slow motion toward Steve's voice at the door.

"Sorry, I guess that saying is outdated. With inflation, it probably should say 'a hundred-dollar bill for your thoughts.'" He crawls up onto the bed and sits next to me. "I don't like that stressed look on your face, especially when you are not supposed to be under any stress. Why is your face blood-red and your hands shaking?"

I lean my head back on the headboard and stare at the ceiling. "Well, let's see. Alice still isn't answering her phone. However, I did just get off the phone with Mom who is no longer buying into these random texts she is getting from Dad because every time she calls him, the phone goes straight to voicemail. Except she's not worried that something has happened. She suspects he's up to something or involved in something that he shouldn't be and is not answering her calls on purpose. On top of that," I touch the top of my closed laptop, "I did a little bit of research before that lengthy call with Mom and discovered that not only was Aidan Carraban's murder case never solved, but Damon Sivers was never found either."

"Whoa, that's a lot." Steve rubs his chin. "Let's take one thing at a time. First, do you know the name of the nursing home Alice's mother is at or the town that it's located in?"

"No, neither. I only know it's somewhere near Knoxville."

"Ugh. Without a smaller radius, we would be playing the lottery trying to call around." He is silent for a few seconds. "I know she's covered up, and I hate to bother her, but I don't like Alice traveling all that way by herself. Let's call Kate and have her track Alice's phone."

"Funny, I was thinking the same thing. I hate to add something else to her plate, but Kate will understand."

"Okay, that takes care of your first issue. We'll call her in a second. Now, as for your mom, I know she would never upset you or stress you out intentionally, so I am betting her worrying is probably a whole lot worse than she is letting on to you."

I nod. "I'm sure. I was hoping that the campaign and the wedding would keep her mind occupied, but when your husband leaves and won't answer your calls... well that scenario pretty much says it all."

"Wow." Steve whistles. "With everything going on, I hadn't even absorbed what she must be going through until you spelled it out just now. Maybe I should go get her and bring her here. We could talk campaigns and weddings."

"That's a good idea. Let's wait a bit though. She and Eileen are baking a cake for Carlton to thank him for all his help with the campaign. Apparently, he's coming over so Eileen can help him set up that BridgNect account."

"Oh," Steve taps his forehead, "I forgot Eileen is there with her." He rolls his eyes toward me. "Well, maybe Carlton being there will keep her mind busy."

"I hope so. If Dad doesn't show up soon, we're going to have to tell her about the texts and the burner phone."

Steve shrugs. "Anyway, continuing on. Why are you stressing yourself by looking for this Damon Sivers? If he has been missing all these years, I doubt he has anything to do with your dad's disappearance."

I slide open the drawer beside the bed and take out the envelope. "I checked out the other things in this envelope too. There are two other papers that we didn't look at earlier. One is an article that interviews a few students about Nu Alpha Kosmos, and guess who one of the students is that was interviewed?"

"You're not letting this go, are you?"

"No, I'm not. My dad is missing," I answer in exasperation.

"I'm sorry." He gently touches his fingertips to my face and brushes them down my cheek. "So, what did my dear old dad have to say in the interview?"

"In a nutshell, he stated that he was new to the fraternity. He joined because he believed the group was about creating a better world through service to the community. And that he personally had no knowledge of any chant or praise for the leader nor any rules that would dictate or control his religious habits." Narrowing my eyes, I continue, "And this part is pretty weird." I skim the page for the line I'm looking for. "Here it is. He says, 'Why would anyone who wants to be part of this group need that stipulation? Our purpose has nothing to do with higher powers. We are about loving our world and the things in it. And as far as a ritual, the only chanting I have witnessed at meetings is the recitation of our motto. A Better Future, A New World, It all starts here. Nu Alpha Kosmos comes together to make change appear.'"

Steve narrows his eyes back at me. "What's weird about it?"

"He is referencing scripture," I say, dragging out the words for emphasis.

With his forehead crinkled, he gives me a quizzical stare. "I must have missed that part. Let me see it."

He takes the paper from my hand, and I point to the lines with the reference.

He reads, mumbling the words under his breath. "Our purpose has nothing to do with higher powers. We are about loving our world and the things in it." Steve sits with his mouth agape for a minute. "You're right." He glares over the top of the paper, letting his eyes burn into mine. "1 John 2:15 says, 'Love not the world, neither the things that are in the world. If any man love the world, the love of the Father is not in him.' My father's comment would have been overlooked at the time this was written, but clearly, he is stating the group's stance on Christianity." He drops his gaze back to the paper. "Maybe it's because I know what my father was capable of, but I can feel his hatred through his words in this article... and what scares me... what really eats at me... is that he knows the Bible." Steve's jaw hardens, and with his free hand, he squeezes the edge of the mattress. "Inside, a part of me wanted to believe that if he had known about God or had been taught about God when he was younger, there's no way he could have planned what he did. But he knew. Ellie, if he knew that verse, he must have known what Jesus did for him."

I wrap my arm around his back, and as I lay my head on his shoulder, I glimpse a tear in the corner of his eye. I swallow, pushing down my own tears at the sight of his pain. I wish I could think of something to say that would ease the hurt and help heal the wounds left on his heart by his dad. But no words seem right, so we just sit in silence for a few minutes.

After a bit, Steve blows a puff of air out of his mouth, making his cheeks expand, and I notice he releases his death grip on the bedding.

"We need to take all this stress and worry to God. The worry about my dad, Alice and Gerald, your mom and her campaign, our baby being born in the middle of this chaos." I slip off the bed onto my knees on the floor. "Let's cast our cares on him, together."

"'If two of you shall agree on earth as touching any thing that they shall ask, it shall be done for them of my Father which is in heaven.'" He kneels in front of me and takes my hands in his. "Matthew 18:19. That verse was in my notebook... well, it is in my notebook." He peeps over the bed at the blue spiral notebook underneath the Bible on his side table.

Steve pulls my hands close to his chest and lowers his head. "Dear Heavenly Father, thank you. Thank you for keeping us safe, for letting Ellie and the baby be healthy, and thank you that we can be here together talking to you. Lord, the burdens are mounting, and we need you. Please help Ellie with all of this stress and protect her and my son. Please be with Tom and Alice as they are out in the midst of the evils being committed, and we ask that you keep a charge of angels around them protecting them. We lift Alice and Gerald to you and ask if their marriage is your will for their lives, that you would heal their relationship. And I pray for my mother's campaign. I admit I have had my fears about this, but Lord, if this is your purpose in her life, then please guide her and protect her."

He is silent for a moment, so I take my turn. "Father, I thank you that we can come to you and that you will carry all of this worry. Please take care of my daddy. I have a feeling that he's out there trying to find some bad people, and I'm really scared that he is in trouble. Lord, please comfort my mother. She has been through so much already. And Alice, this is not like Alice to take off. Whatever is in her heart or her mind and wherever she is, please take care of her. And if it is your will, allow this to bring Gerald and Alice closer together. I pray for Cynthia, that you will guide her in this campaign, protect her, and show her the way. And last but not least, take care of my son and my husband. Please keep them in your embrace, safe from all harm. We praise you, Father. All these things we pray in the Holy and Precious name of Jesus. Amen."

"Amen." Steve lifts his head and kisses my forehead. "I am curious. What's on the other sheet of paper?"

I lift my head, confused for a second. "Oh... in the envelope."

Steve stands and pulls me to my feet.

Sitting back on the side of the bed, I slide the paper from the stack. "I'm not sure. It's a list of addresses. No names. No explanations or notations. Only addresses." I turn the list toward him and twist my mouth to the side.

"You are not going to any of these places."

"I wasn't planning to." I smile. "But I am going to research them. A few are scattered across the country, but most of them are in the states surrounding Washington."

"Research is acceptable, but you need a small break from the stressors. I'm going to call Kate about Alice's phone, and then we are going to the nursery."

"No arguments. I love the nursery, but why?" I raise one eyebrow as he walks over to the armoire.

He opens one of the doors and pulls out a wide-brim yellow hat with a black band. He turns around placing it on his head. "Because I made a promise to a certain little monkey that we would watch *Curious George* with him."

I cover my mouth and bite my lip.

"Laugh if you want. The hat is important to him." He smirks at me.

"Where did you even get that?" I prod.

"It was on a table at the antique store when Spencer and I went to pick up the wardrobe for the nursery. Spencer wouldn't leave the store without it." Steve faces the mirror above the dresser and touches the brim of the hat. "Despite what you think of it, I kind of like it."

"I'm only ribbing you. It does have a unique distinguished style."

"I'm not sure if that was a compliment or not, but I'm glad the hat makes you smile. Anyway, come on. I know you're anxious to find something that will help find your dad, but you need a break. So, one episode, okay."

"I don't know. I don't have a costume," I reply in a serious tone and then burst out laughing. I press my lips together until I have it under control. "Sorry. I couldn't help it." I pick up my phone. "Get Spencer, and I'll be there in a minute. I want to call Kate."

I grab a few extra pillows from the hall closet on my way back to the bedroom. As much as I needed the break and as good as it felt to laugh, I'm anxious to check out that list of addresses. If Dad is in trouble, the clock is ticking. Speaking of the clock ticking, I hope it doesn't take Kate too long to track Alice. Kate texted a couple of minutes after I called her and said Alice's phone was off. Of course, I had already suspected Alice had powered it off because it wasn't even ringing before her voicemail came on. So, like Dad's phone, she said it would take her a bit longer.

I prop the extra pillows against the headboard so I can sit up without most of my back and neck resting against the hard, rigid wood.

"Herb said you hadn't had your juice today," Steve says, carrying a large glass of orange juice into the room. He sits it on my nightstand, and then crawls across and props up on the bed beside me. "You're not doing this alone." He picks up the page of addresses.

As I open my laptop, Herb's mechanical voice echoes through the house. "Communication... all I ask for is a little communication. Couldn't someone have told me we were expecting guests?"

"Guests? Were we expecting company?" I question, surprised that he hasn't said anything about it.

Steve swings his legs over the side of the bed. "I wasn't aware of anyone coming by. I'll go and check it out."

My phone vibrates. "Oh. I hope this is Kate," I say as I look at the screen. "What? How?"

Steve stops halfway across the room. "What's wrong?"

"Kate said that she tracked Alice's phone... to our address."

"Oh, thank goodness." He exhales with a loud sigh. "That must be her at the door."

CHAPTER ELEVEN

With the weight of the worry about Alice lifted from my shoulders, my body moves faster than it has in a while. Anxious to
see her face, I scoot past Steve in the hall and round the corner into the
living room, three strides ahead of him.

I freeze with my mouth open to greet Alice. *Where is she?* Herb is
holding the door open as Cynthia and Dukakis step inside.

"Oh, hi," I say in a dry tone, peering past them in search of Alice.
Realizing my dry tone, I try to smooth over my rudeness and add an
edge of excitement to my voice. "I didn't know you guys were stopping
by, but I'm so glad you did. I can use some company. This bed rest
thing has me feeling so isolated." I give them each a quick peck on
the cheek and a speedy embrace, keeping my eyes on the door as Herb
closes it behind them. "Oh, Herb. Keep it open for Alice," I blurt out.

His red eyes illuminate as he pulls the door back open and sticks his head out. "Alice isn't out here. Were we expecting her?"

"What?" I choke out, squeezing by Herb so I can look for myself. "She has to be here."

Steve's hand touches my shoulder as he peeps over me at the empty porch. "She's not here, Ellie. Kate must have made a mistake. Come, sit on the couch. I'll send her a quick text and have her run the location again." Steve pulls his phone from his trouser pocket. "Are you sure you gave her the right phone number to track?"

I blink to shield the tears that are trying to escape. "I'm positive. I texted her Alice's contact info stored in my phone."

"What's going on?" Dukakis's voice echoes with worry.

Cynthia takes my arm. "Come sit on the couch, sweetheart. Tell us what's happening." She holds my elbow and helps me lower myself onto the couch, which I'm grateful for because my knees are quivering, and my legs are like noodles trying to hold up my body. She takes a seat next to me and wraps her arm around my shoulder. She and I have become close since she accepted Jesus as her Savior. Not that we had problems or anything before that, but now we seem to have this connection. I can talk to her about anything.

"Dad's still missing," I blubber, unable to contain my tears. "And now Alice has taken off, apparently to visit her mother at a nursing home in Tennessee, but she isn't answering her phone."

"Actually, it appears that Alice has her phone turned off," Steve adds as he taps a text on his screen. "We're concerned about her safety traveling that far alone."

Cynthia pulls a tissue from her handbag with her other hand and dabs my eyes. "Now listen to me. I know you're worried, and I can understand why. But this worry is not going to help anything. On the contrary, it's only going to hurt you and the baby." She lays the tissue on her lap and squeezes my hand. "Ellie, you know the scripture. You study it daily. So, you know the Bible tells us not to worry. How about Matthew 6:27? Hmmm. Say it with me."

With my eyes closed, I repeat along with her, "'Which of you by taking thought can add one cubit unto his stature?'"

"And you are aware of what that verse means?" She speaks in a soothing and reassuring voice.

"My worry is not going to change the outcome," I answer, keeping my eyes closed.

"That's right." She lets go of my hand and wipes my eyes with the tissue again.

"Ellie," Dukakis sits in the armchair facing the couch on the other side of the coffee table, "instead of thinking the worst, try approaching the situation from the other direction. Let's start with your dad. I'm guessing that you are letting your thoughts run rampant with every bad scenario possible. But, as much as I love your father, we know he has a history of taking matters into his own hands, and he's probably off chasing a whim somewhere. As for Alice, maybe there is no signal wherever she is, or an even more probable scenario is that she is visiting her mother and doesn't want to be interrupted."

"Uncle Dukakis is right, Ellie. We shouldn't be worrying when we don't even know if there is anything to worry about." Steve drops into the other armchair.

I nod in agreement, but in reality, it's a lot easier to say I shouldn't worry than it is not to worry. I pull in a deep breath through my mouth, filling my lungs with air, and then slowly let it escape. "Let's talk about the campaign. How is it going?"

"Unbelievably well," Cynthia answers. "I would have never imagined in a trillion years that this many people would be coming forward and publicly announcing their support. I am in awe. I was prepared to be shunned and ridiculed. But God... that's all I can say... But God stepped in, and He does amazing things. This is His doing, not mine."

Steve leans forward with his elbow on his knees. He clutches his hands together, and the protruding vessels on his forehead make his tension evident.

"Son, is something wrong?" Cynthia twists her body a bit to face Steve. "Oh, dear. It's the campaign, isn't it? I should have asked if you and Teresa were okay with me running for president. I didn't even think about how this might affect you."

"No, Mom, that's not it. I mean, honestly, I was a little concerned about the campaign at first, but now, I'm confident that this has always been part of God's plan for you."

"Okay, Son, if that's not it, then what's bothering you?" Cynthia prods in a mothering tone.

"I need to ask you some questions." Steve lowers his head and clasps his hands on the side of his face. "I don't want to. I have no desire to know anything further about my father," he sighs, "but I have no choice."

"Why?" Cynthia's posture stiffens, and her eyes narrow. But in a split second, her shoulders relax. "I'm sorry. I didn't intend to sound snappy. I can understand that you have questions about your father, especially since you have no recollection of him before he erased your memory. But what's this about you having no choice?"

"I think for the sake of your campaign, it's best to keep your knowledge limited. Right now, it's nothing but a few puzzle pieces that may or may not belong to a puzzle at all. It was given to Ellie in confidence, so until we know that it belongs to a real puzzle, we have to honor that confidence. And, just in case anything does come to light, you honestly know nothing."

"Well, as curious as I am, that is very honorable of you." Cynthia leans back on the couch and tosses her hands in the air. "So, fire away. What do you want to know?"

"When did you meet him?"

"In college." She pauses and closes her eyes as if she's picturing the scene in her mind. "I was in the bookstore purchasing the access card for my Constitutional Law textbook, and as I stood in line to pay, I kept feeling someone gawking over my shoulder. And I say 'felt' because I could actually feel warm air from someone's breath on the back of my neck. Of course, I was appalled, so I turned around, planning to explain the importance of personal space. However, when I laid eyes on Dennis, I could no longer remember why I had turned around. Something about him..." She opens her eyes. "Well, I might as well not sugarcoat it. I melted. It wasn't so much his dark, flawless skin, his defined cheekbones, his dark brown eyes dotted with gold specks, his perfect white teeth that glistened as he smiled, or his broad shoulders in that red fraternity blazer as it was the confident, intelligent aura that radiated from him before he even spoke. I stood speechless. I imagine my mouth was hanging half-open. But Dennis didn't have any problem with words. He was laying it on thick with his smooth talking from the second his lips parted."

"Dennis always did have a way with words," Dukakis remarks. "I believe he could have gotten rich selling snow suits at a beach stand in Maui."

Cynthia nods in agreement and continues. "I remember he commented on the access card I was purchasing. He said he was intrigued by a woman interested in law and asked about my major. When I told him that I was pre-law, he didn't hesitate to use flattery. He said he wasn't so sure that law would be the right field for a woman like me because he was certain that my beauty would be such a distraction in the courtroom that no one would get a fair trial. He went on to tell me that he was also pre-law and had taken Constitutional Law the previous semester. Then he asked me to dinner at some new French restaurant that he had been wanting to try. He said that it would give us the opportunity to discuss the elements of the course, and in addition, he was interested in hearing my thoughts on the process for amending the Constitution. I declined his invitation, but he didn't accept 'no' that easily. It seemed almost as if every time I would blink, I would bump into him on campus, and since I had never seen him before the day in the bookstore, it was obvious he was stalking me."

"Wait." Steve holds up his hand. "I'm confused. If he made you melt, why did you turn down a date with him?"

"Because as dreamy as he was, he was not part of my short-term or long-term plans. I had my life and my career mapped out in detail. I had already been hurt by love, and I had no intention of repeating that pain. My sights were on the presidency. But let me point out that I thought I was a Christian. Maybe a better wording would be to say I called myself a Christian because I had been raised in a Christian home. But unfortunately, back then, my reasons for wanting to be the head of the executive branch were selfish and only for personal gain. I had no thoughts of helping the American people or bettering our country. And I certainly had no plans to make God a part of it." She gives her head a quick shake. "Anyway, Dennis kept pressing until I finally had dinner with him, and the next thing I knew, we had completed our undergraduate studies, and I had agreed to marry him before we started the grad program."

"I know the strength of your faith now, but I'm curious. You said you were raised in a Christian home," I hesitate, wondering if I am crossing some sort of line with my questioning, "and you considered yourself a Christian in college. When did you abandon your faith?"

"Oh, Ellie, I don't know that I ever had a personal relationship with Jesus when I was young. My parents were devout Christians. They taught me about God, read the scriptures to me and with me, and took me to church. The word Christian had always been a part of my vocabulary. I had recited a prayer with the preacher one Sunday morning when I was five or six years old and stood in front of the church. But the truth is, I hadn't felt anything... no change... no new desire to be more like Jesus. I never had this hunger to read my Bible, and that list of fruit Paul gives in Galatians, I had none of that. As I got to know Dennis, I don't think I ever even asked him about his religious beliefs. I knew he didn't go to church, and it didn't bother me that he didn't." Cynthia leans forward, uncrossing her legs and crossing them back with the opposite leg on top. Holding up one finger, she continues. "But not long after we were engaged, I started to notice that he never came to my parents' house, and then it became obvious that he was going out of his way not to associate with them. So, a few weeks before our wedding, I decided I had to know what his problem was with my family. When I asked him, he said that he did not like being forced to take part in something he didn't agree with. Dennis explained that his parents had tried to push being born again on him when he was a child, but he knew better. And nothing irritated him more than being forced to pray or stand and wait to eat while everyone else did."

"Mama was sure Dennis would come back," Dukakis mumbles, "but after he went to college, that was it."

"What do you mean 'that was it'?" Steve asks, tilting his head toward his uncle.

"He never came around... never even called," Dukakis's voice is hoarse and crackly from emotion. "Mama was heartbroken. She would hide her pain and tears, but her eyes were always red and swollen."

"I never met any of his family except for Dukakis." Cynthia gazes at Dukakis with questioning eyes. "And, Dukakis, I didn't meet you until our wedding. I didn't even know Dennis had a brother."

Dukakis clasps his hands together. "Well, that's sort of ironic because Dennis didn't know his brother was at his wedding. Do you remember how tongue-tied he got when I came up and introduced myself to you at the reception? All his buddies were watching, so he couldn't pull one of his tantrums. I gave him a big hug and congratulated him."

"You weren't invited?" In shock, the words slip right out of my mouth.

"Invited? Huh. Dennis never invited me to anything. He tried his best to pretend I didn't exist." Dukakis chuckles. "But I didn't care. I was determined to show him how much his family loved him in spite of how he treated us."

"Is that why you would show up at our house... without warning?" Cynthia prods.

"A surprise visit was the only way I could see Dennis."

"Mom," Steve slips into the conversation, "did you not question why you didn't meet his family?"

"When I asked, he told me his family wanted nothing to do with him, and he managed to add an edge of pain in his voice that broke my heart. From then on, I didn't want to bring up a painful topic, so I never pried or asked any more questions. Besides, it's not unusual for families to have problems."

"Please don't take this the wrong way. I'm not giving you the third degree. I'm just trying to understand." Steve strokes the stubble on his chin. "If I followed the story correctly, at that point in your life, you believed you were saved, and you referred to yourself as a Christian. So, if you knew my father's stance on Christianity, why did you still want to marry him?"

"I suppose you're referring to the scripture about being unequally yoked. Like I said before, I didn't read my Bible, I was all about myself, and I was blinded by love for a man who had no idea what love was. And as strange as it sounds, this man who was offended by anything to do with God knew the Bible well enough to use it to drag me into his Godless world. And the woman who almost aced the bar exam was stupid enough to believe every word he said." She looked up as tears pooled in the bottom of her eyelids. "I am not proud of who I was back then."

"My father used the Bible to turn you away from God? How could he possibly do that?"

"Steve, your Uncle Dukakis wasn't exaggerating when he said Dennis could get rich selling snowsuits on the beach in Maui. He chose random verses and used them out of context, and he chose the ones that he thought would eat at me the most. For example, he once asked me, 'If you're a Christian, are you not supposed to follow God's instructions in the Bible?' Of course, my answer was yes. It seemed like an easy question. Then he remarked, 'I guess you have to revere me as your Lord.'" Cynthia coughs as if she choked on her last words. "Now I was in love. But since I still had my grand aspirations and was very much an independent woman, I was taken aback by this comment. I asked him what on earth he was talking about. I hadn't read my Bible in a while, but I knew it didn't say anything about Dennis Denali being revered as anyone's Lord. With a smirk on his face, he quoted Ephesians 5:22. 'Wives, submit unto your own husbands, as unto the Lord.'"

"But," Steve says, shaking his head.

"I know, Son, I know now. But take note, your father chose verses that he knew would attack my weakest link." Cynthia lowers her voice. "I went to a junior college for my first two years. My family didn't have the money to pay for my college and getting the prerequisites at a two-year college saved a lot of money in loans. Anyway, during my freshman year, I met a young man who I was sure was 'the one'. He was a knight in shining armor in the beginning. He said all the right things, feeding me all the words I needed to hear. And then, after a few months, the newness wore off, and he started making comments, hurtful comments, to make me feel inferior. I wasn't thin enough... I wasn't athletic enough... not only was I a woman, but I wasn't smart enough to make it in law school," she sniffles.

Emotion is etched and woven into her words, and as puddles collect in my eyes, I rest my hand on her forearm.

Cynthia continues, "Eventually, it got to me. I fell into depression and almost quit school altogether. Then, one day, I saw him out with another girl. Come to find out, there were several other girls. And he had done the same to all of them. Making us all feel inferior gave him some sort of weird high. The depression left, and I was left bitter and determined that no man would ever have that sort of control over me again. Dennis never knew that was what drove my independent, no one will stand in my way, attitude that I put forth. But he did know that I would not stand for my independence to be infringed upon. Little did I realize, that was exactly what Dennis had been doing all along." She pauses and straightens her posture. "But back to the topic before I got off on that tangent. Dennis quoted Ephesians 5:22, yet he made no mention of the verse before it, where all Christians should submit to each other. Ephesians 5:21 says, 'submitting yourselves one to another in the fear of God.' And he certainly never brought up Ephesians 5:25 which states, 'husbands, love your wives, even as Christ also loved the church, and gave himself for it.' He chose one verse, manipulated the words of it, and relished in the fact that he was driving me away from God with it. He got inside my head and convinced me that I could not have a career or dreams or do anything on my goal sheet and still be a follower of God. And soon, I was so caught up in our worldly life that I never even thought about God anymore."

I notice Dukakis staring at the old, tattered Bible on the coffee table, and then, with a twinkle in his eye, he shifts his gaze to Cynthia. "But God."

"What?" Cynthia squirms but then cracks a smile back at him.

"Dennis tried to rip you from your Father's arms. But God... But God didn't give up on you. Dennis almost killed you... But God stepped in and saved you." Dukakis slides to the edge of the armchair. "'But as for you, ye thought evil against me; but God meant it unto good, to bring to pass, as it is this day, to save much people alive.' Remember Joseph? In the book of Genesis, his brothers sought to destroy him. But God... God had big plans for Joseph. And just like Joseph ended up saving so many lives during the famine, I believe God has big plans for you to save the people of our country."

"He's right, Cynthia." I pat her knee. "Steve and I both were concerned about this election and the persecution that you would have to endure being the widow of Dennis Denali. But Proverbs 19:21 says, 'There are many devices in a man's heart; nevertheless the counsel of the Lord, that shall stand.'"

Herb rolls into the living room with a tray filled with cups and a teapot. "Sorry for the delay, folks. I had to brew a new pot."

"Oh, Herb. You didn't need to go to all that trouble on our account." Cynthia touches his metal arm as he places the tray on the table.

"Are you kidding?" Herb raises the pitch of his mechanical voice, adding drama. "I cannot have the future president of the United States in our home and not serve tea." He fills all of the cups except for one. "And Mrs. Ellie, since tea has caffeine, I took the pleasure of squeezing you another glass of juice."

"Thank you, Herb." I take the teacup filled with juice, wishing it was caramel coffee.

"Herb. You're the best. Thank you." Dukakis takes a giant gulp from his teacup.

Herb strolls back to the kitchen, and Steve glances over Cynthia's head at me. I'm not sure why he's giving me a strange look, but I have to ask Cynthia and Dukakis one last question.

"The fraternity that Dennis was in... do either of you know anything about it?" I cast my eyes back and forth from Cynthia to Dukakis.

"As I said, Dennis and I weren't close. Well, we were as kids, but he started distancing himself his senior year of high school, and then when he left and went off to college, I no longer existed to him. But he was my big brother, and I secretly kept up with what he was doing. I drove down to the college a few times and followed everything he did on social media. During his freshman year, he joined this fraternity. However, when I read about it, I thought it sounded more like a club than a fraternity. It involved something about making the world better and doing community service. A lot of water has passed under the bridge since then, but if I remember correctly, that fraternity didn't stick around too long. I believe there were some complaints, and the school shut it down."

Cynthia shrugs, "I didn't transfer to Fahrenhall until my junior year, which is when I met Dennis. I wasn't aware that the fraternity had been closed down. He wore that red blazer all the time and went to meetings somewhere off campus." She scratches her head. "I wondered why they didn't have a fraternity house."

"Alright then," Steve turns toward his uncle, "the question goes to you then, Uncle Dukakis. Do you remember the leader of the fraternity before it disassembled?"

Dukakis's eyes widen. "Oh, yeah. I forgot about that. Some college kid disappeared, and weeks or maybe months later, they found him murdered. The guy who started the fraternity was a suspect, and he took off. I don't think they ever found him," he mumbles, tapping his fingers on the side table by his chair. "What was his name?" He keeps tapping his fingers. "Getting older is so frustrating. Why can't I remember?"

Herb darts back into the living room. "Sorry to interrupt, but we have a slight problem."

Steve jumps to his feet. "What kind of problem?"

He squeezes his eyes closed and shakes his head. "A hide-and-seek game has gone bad."

"Oh, no. You all lost Spencer." Steve takes a giant step and opens his mouth to yell.

"Spencer's fine. Well, he is a little upset, but he is having a bowl of ice cream to calm his nerves. Waves is the one who is not fine. He wedged himself between the washer and dryer, and now he can't get out." Herb clutches his apron in his hands. "Every time Claude and I try to pull him out, there is a horrible metal grinding sound."

Steve tilts his head back and exhales. "Did you try to move the washer or the dryer?"

"Claude," Herb screams as he does a one-eighty and sails back into the kitchen.

"Damon... Damon Sivers... that's it." Dukakis slaps the table. "I knew it was in my brain somewhere."

"Dukakis," Cynthia frowns, "what did you say his name was?"

"D-D-." The excitement drains from his face, and his voice becomes low and serious. "Damon Sivers." He grunts and swallows hard. "It, uh, sounds a bit like Damien Seaver, doesn't it?"

"There, there, now. The important thing is that nothing crucial was damaged." Herb pats Waves on the back as they both roll into the living room.

Waves has a blanket wrapped around his shoulders, and his red mohawk is shaking as he trembles. "Nothing crucial was damaged? Do you not see my face?" Waves whines.

"Oh, that is only superficial. Besides, I'm sure the scratches will buff right out," Herb consoles and then pivots his head toward Steve with a hard jerk. His eyes light up, and he enunciates in a hard, rigid tone, "Mr. Steve, would you please tell him the scratches will buff out."

Steve grabs a handful of his own hair and looks as if he might pull it out in frustration. But instead, he lets his hand fall to his side, and he steps over to Waves, who is still visibly shaking all over. Steve touches the scuff marks on Waves' cheek. "I can grind away the marks and polish it out. It will be as good as new."

"Weally?" Waves asks in a computerized puppy-dog voice.

"Yes, really. And if you're still not happy, I have another cheek plate in my office."

Waves' mouth spreads open. "Row, row, row your boat gently down the stream. Merrily, merrily, merrily..."

"Oh, brother." Herb points Waves back to the kitchen. "Come on. I have to put the washer and dryer back. Claude had to go check the cameras."

Steve's phone chimes. Still standing from Herb's scare, he slides his phone from his pocket. As he gawks at the screen, creases form and cover his forehead.

"Is that Kate?" I wiggle, trying to scoot to the edge so I can stand.

"Yeah. She ran the trace again." He lifts his head and peers at me. "She says that it still shows Alice's phone is here."

Chapter Twelve

"I don't understand. Alice isn't here. Why is the location of her phone showing that she is?" I press my hands to the side of my head.

"Maybe she's somewhere on the property," Cynthia suggests. "Never mind. Steve has the perimeter monitored with more security than Alcatraz. If she was here, you would know it."

Heat rushes to my face, and my chest tingles from the fluttering beat of my heart.

"Ellie, honey, you need to relax." Cynthia lifts my hair off of my neck. "There has to be a rational explanation, and we can't figure it out if we have to take you to the hospital." Her eyes suddenly lock on Dukakis.

His face is blanched, and he is sitting on the edge of the armchair seat, staring straight ahead. Under his breath, he keeps repeating, "Da-

mon Sivers... Damien Seaver... Damon Sivers... Damien Seaver..." The
issue with the phone hasn't seemed to sink in, so I'm quite certain that
he hasn't heard a word of the conversation.

Spencer scampers into the room wearing the yellow hat. He stops
in front of Dukakis, takes the hat off, and holds it up, but Dukakis
doesn't appear to notice him.

With a drooping head, Spencer whimpers and darts out of the
room.

"Dukakis," Cynthia calls out, "are you okay?"

Dukakis doesn't respond, not even a flinch.

Steve reaches out his hand and takes a step toward him.

Cynthia lets my hair fall. "Dukakis," she raises her voice.

He snaps from his trance and casts his eyes up at Steve. "Damien
Seaver. He's a real person."

"We still don't know that for certain. The names are similar, and
Mordy Crawley was part of that group too. He could have fabricated
the name, Damien Seaver," Steve answers. "But right now, we have to
figure out what's going on with Alice. She could be in danger."

Spencer scurries back, carrying something with an orange wrapper in his hands. He leaps onto Dukakis's lap, almost knocking the
breath out of him, and thrusts the package into Dukakis's hand.

"What...?" Dukakis looks in his hand, and his mouth spreads
into an ear-to-ear toothy grin. "Spencer, you are something else. How
about we share this?" He rips open the wrapper and gives Spencer one
of the peanut butter cups, and he takes the other. Spencer tosses the
yellow hat on top of Dukakis's head and shoves the peanut butter cup
in his mouth at the same time.

"Okay, it seems Dukakis is going to be alright, so back to Alice,"
Cynthia sighs, and then her eyes widen. "Are you sure she didn't forget
her phone here at dinner last night?"

"I'm sure because Gerald got a text from her this morn..." I lose
track of what I'm saying as a strange thought slaps into my head and
pushes everything else aside. *No.* I rationalize. *Too much of a coinci-*

dence. I narrow my eyes as I roll the thought over in my brain. *There is no way the two can be related. That is, unless she found something on Dad's phone.* I suck in a hard breath, and my hand flings to my mouth. "Steve, you didn't tell her about the text she sent Gerald, did you?"

"No, and I really don't think..." He pauses, shaking his head. "It would be a bit odd for that text to have been sent from another phone too. One situation has nothing to do with the other."

"Are we talking about Tom's disappearance again?" Dukakis asks as he bounces Spencer on his knee.

"Dad has sent Mom several texts that appear to have come from his phone, but they didn't. Instead, the texts were sent from a burner phone. So, we know he's up to something. The question is whether he's in danger and someone is pretending to be him, or is Dad the one sending the messages from his own burner phone? Do you remember when you and Mom rescued us from the facility, and Mom had the burner phone?" I lift one eyebrow, waiting for his response.

"Yeah. She said that Tom always kept a burner phone on hand."

I straighten my back, hoping the baby will reposition himself. "But don't say anything. My Mom doesn't know that the texts didn't come from Dad's phone. We don't want to upset her more until we know there is something to be upset about." I turn my attention back to Steve. "Look, there's a chance the two could be connected. A slim chance, but it's still a chance." I pull on the armrest and rock back and forth, shifting my weight in an effort to escape the low plush couch cushion that I'm trapped in. "My phone is in the bedroom. I need to call Kate."

"My phone is right here." Steve lifts his phone. "I'll call her, but why do you think there's a chance Alice and your dad's disappearance are connected."

I grunt, still tugging on the arm of the couch. Failing at my attempt to get up, I take a breath and continue explaining. "I forgot to tell you with everything going on, but Kate talked to me last night in the nursery. She found Dad's phone in the bushes at the end of my parents' driveway. Alice took the phone to see if she could find anything on it that would help." I finally get to my feet. "It struck me a second ago that maybe she found something and went to check it out." I plod toward the bedroom.

"Ellie, where are you going? I told you I would call her," Steve yells after me.

"I'm going to get Dad's phone. I grabbed it from Alice's bedroom when we were at her apartment this morning."

I snatch the bag from my purse on the dresser and hurry back to the living room. I start to take a seat back on the couch but decide on the firmer armchair next to Dukakis instead.

"Kate didn't answer, but I left her a voicemail and sent her a text," Steve says as his phone chimes. "Oh. This is her. Umm. She says she's in a meeting. She will check the text to Gerald as soon as she is finished." Steve pauses. "Oh, duh, I forgot to send her Gerald's number." He taps the screen.

"Thanks, Honey. I'm sure she will do it as soon as she can." I pull open the zipper bag and slide out the phone. "Oh, no." I have no idea if I say the words to myself or out loud. I swallow hard and press my lips together, fighting the acid pushing up and burning my esophagus like lava about to spew from a volcano.

"Ellie." Dukakis sits Spencer on the floor and touches my shoulder.

"Th-Th-This i-i-is n-not D-Daddy's phone." I lift my flooded eyes. "It's Alice's."

Chapter Thirteen

"So...," Steve narrows his eyes at me, "you picked up Alice's phone in her apartment thinking it was your dad's. I still see no reason to hit the panic button, Ellie."

"Oh, I think there is," I rattle off. "One, Alice couldn't have texted from her phone if she left it in her apartment. And two, why would she have placed her phone into the bag that Kate gave me Dad's phone in... unless she was trying to give us a clue that something was wrong." *Seven deep breaths. In... out. In... out. In... out. In... out. In... out. In... out. In... out.*

"Cynthia," Dukakis stares straight ahead, "I need to go home and look for something. Do you have time to go with me?"

"Umm. I'm not sure. What time is it now?"

"One o'clock," Steve answers, looking at his phone.

"Maybe. How long will it take? I have to be in my home office at five-thirty." Cynthia stands and picks up her handbag as her eyes focus on Steve. "Eileen has posted a live event on BridgNect. I am doing a brief speech and then a Q & A session with viewers. Eileen believes it will help me make a personal connection if I'm answering real questions from real voters. And even though I'll only have time to answer a handful of them, she said it would give me a better idea of what the American citizens are thinking and what they're most concerned about. Then I can address those issues in future speeches."

"That's a great idea, Mom." Steve tries to sound interested and supportive, but I can tell that he's overwhelmed and torn between keeping me calm, worrying about Dukakis's pale face, and encouraging his mother. "People like to feel important, and if you're taking the time to personally interact with them, it will make a big difference."

"Alright," Dukakis hugs me as he rattles on to Cynthia about the plan, "we'll run by my house first since it's on the way to yours. It shouldn't take long."

"Please be careful," I say to them both as I hug Cynthia over the top of my belly.

"Don't worry about us. We're in Dukakis's van. With that new wrap and those decals of his, people steer clear."

"What new wrap?" I was so caught up in looking for Alice before that I didn't even notice the van was different. I open the door and step to the edge of the porch.

Steve steps up behind me. "Oh," is all that escapes his mouth.

On the side of the van is a giant decal of a Roman Soldier, and beside him are the words, 'I HAVE ON THE WHOLE ARMOR OF GOD. DO YOU?' The entire hood is a shield that tapers to a point on the front grill between the headlights.

Dukakis and Cynthia wave as they walk toward the van.

"I'm going to stop back by in a while if you don't mind," Dukakis yells while he holds the passenger door for Cynthia. "That is if I find what I'm looking for."

"Sure." Steve waves. "And the van looks good, Uncle. Maybe it will encourage some others to put on their armor."

"That's the plan." Dukakis smiles and circles to the driver's side.

We walk back inside, and Steve secures the front door.

"Ellie, I had a thought," he says, turning toward me.

"What?"

"Don't act so surprised. I do have thoughts sometimes," he remarks with a smirk.

"That wasn't a tone of surprise. It was a tone of hope. I'm hoping this thought is going to find my dad or Alice."

"Oh," he mumbles. "It's not that great of a thought."

"Could you please share it anyway?" I prod.

"Well, I know a person's phone is sort of personal, and I don't want to invade her space. But maybe the name of the nursing home and the phone number are stored in her contacts, and we could find it and call. If she isn't there or hasn't been to see her mother today, then we would know Alice is in trouble because I've never known her to lie about anything."

I pick up the phone off the table. "You're brilliant. And I don't think it's an invasion of privacy if the person is missing and could be in danger."

Steve twists his mouth to the side. "I forgot about the password. I'm sure it's complex with Alice's computer knowledge."

"No worries." I power on Alice's phone, type in her password, and scroll through the contacts.

"You know her password?"

"It's the date of the wedding, of course," I answer, shaking my head. "I bet this is it, 'My Vacation Home Assisted Living.'" I start to press the call button, but my brain draws a blank. "OOOOh," I growl. "What's her mother's name?" I tap the side of my head. "Jane, that's it."

Steve taps the side of his head. "I can't believe that worked for you."

I can't help but giggle.

His lips curve up. "Glad I could make you smile."

I hit the call button and put the phone to my ear.

"My Vacation Home Assisted Living. Please listen to the entire message as the menu options have changed."

I pull the phone away, tap '0', and hold it back to my ear.

"Please hold while your call is transferred to the operator."

A real person's voice comes on the line. A woman with a professional and friendly tone greets, "Thank you for calling My Vacation Home Assisted Living. How may I direct your call?"

"Yes, I'm trying to reach the mother of one of my friends. Her name is Jane Jacobs."

"Oh, I know Jane. She is the sweetest woman. I'm sorry, but she doesn't hear well enough to talk on the phone. Is there something that I can help with or a message that I can pass along to her?"

"Well, actually, I'm looking for my friend. Alice was supposed to be coming to see her mother today, but I haven't been able to reach her. Under the circumstances, I'm concerned and was hoping to confirm that she was there or had been there today."

"Well, security is extremely tight, so the log will reflect any visitors. Give me a moment to check that for you. I'm going to place you on a brief hold."

Country music fills the line, and a moment later, she returns.

"I'm sorry. Jane hasn't had any visitors in quite a while. However, I did learn that her daughter uses a special app that shows captions on the screen to talk to her mother every Sunday at one o'clock, and a nurse is always present in case Jane needs help. The nurse on duty day this past Sunday noted that Jane spoke with her daughter for about a half-hour."

I blink back the tears. "Thanks for the help."

"No problem. And Ma'am," the woman's voice softens, "I'll be praying that you find your friend."

"I would appreciate that. Thanks again." I lower the phone.

Waves bounces into the living room with a scarf wrapped around his face, covering the scratches, and Spencer riding on his shoulders. Spencer sneezes as Waves' mohawk tickles his nose.

"Since our guests are gone, could we repair my face now?" Waves' words are muffled through the scarf.

"We sort of have a lot going on right this minute. We'll have to do it later," Steve answers.

"Okey dokey," Waves utters, dropping his head as he moves back to the kitchen.

"Aaah. He is so pitiful. Go take care of him. It won't take you long," I say, looking toward the kitchen. "I'll try Kate again, and then I'm going to try to research those addresses."

"Ellie, you know Waves is a computer, right? He's not a real person."

"I know, but he has been through so much with us that he feels like a member of our family. So, please."

"Oh, alright," he concedes. "But lie down and try not to worry."

I drop onto the bed, thankful for a moment to let the tears fall without everyone panicking about my stress level. I've been holding it in for so long that water bursts from my eyes like heavy rain from a dark storm cloud. Holding my pillow to my chest, I curl up on my side and let it all out.

After a couple of minutes, the cloud is empty, and I push myself up. Sitting on the side of the bed, I pull in a deep breath through my mouth, look up, and whisper, "'In my distress, I called upon the Lord, and cried unto my God: he heard my voice out of his temple, and my cry came before him, even into his ears.'" I love Psalm 18:6. It reminds me that God hears my cry... a little voice in a big world filled with a cacophony of voices all sounding at the same time... and God still hears me.

With my mind reset, I grab my phone and dial Kate.

Only half of a ring resonates before she answers, and her panicked voice penetrates my ear. "I got Steve's message and just finished tracing that text. Ellie, it came from a burner phone," she rattles off without even saying hello. She hesitates, but before I gather my words, she continues, "I don't want to worry you, but let's face it. She took your dad's phone last night, and the fact that all these texts are coming from burner phones may not be a coincidence."

"It's definitely not a coincidence, Kate. When we were at Alice's apartment this morning, I picked up the bag with Dad's phone that you had given Alice last night. I thought maybe I could find something on it since she was visiting her mother. But a little bit ago, I realized it is Alice's phone in the bag, not Dad's. That is the reason the location of Alice's phone keeps showing my address. Alice put her phone in the bag."

"Why would she put her phone in the bag?" Kate questions. "That doesn't make sense."

"You have to know Alice. She is always thinking, and she would know if I discovered her phone in the bag, I would know something was wrong," I spout off so fast that I have to gasp for a breath before I can keep going. "Steve had the idea to find the number for the nursing home in Alice's contacts. I phoned them, and her mother hasn't had any visitors, much less Alice. Their records appear to be thorough too because they had noted that Alice spoke to her mother via an online video closed captioned app on Sunday at one o'clock."

"Do you know where your dad's phone is?" Kate asks.

"No. It could be at her apartment. I thought I had it in the bag, so I didn't look anywhere else. How long will it take you to track it?" *Because we know it's powered off,* I think but don't say it out loud.

"I don't know. The system is so overloaded, but I'm working on it as we speak." Her voice is tense but professional. "Ellie, is there anything else you haven't told me? At this point, I need to know everything."

"Yes, but please keep this part between you and me for now." I pause, hoping I'm not making a mistake by telling her, especially when Dad instructed me to keep it a secret. "The last time I saw Dad, he said that he still believed Dennis Denali was alive. He gave me an envelope and told me to look inside but not tell anyone about it. It's mostly old articles and photos of President Denali during his college years, but there's also a sheet of paper with addresses jotted down on it. A few are widespread, but most are in the states surrounding Washington D.C." I pull open the drawer and take out the envelope. "I was getting ready to research them online."

"Ellie," she interrupts, "you know Dennis Denali is dead, right? Please tell me you are not buying into this and getting worked up."

"I know what I've been told, and I've seen the proof."

"Then why is your tone filled with doubt?" she presses me.

"My gut is shouting otherwise."

"I have the location," she changes the subject. "The dot is showing right behind Alice's apartment complex. Is there a dumpster back there or anything?"

"Probably. I don't think I've ever been behind her building."

"It doesn't matter. We know something's wrong, and as much as I believe Dennis Denali is dead," she sighs, "those addresses are all we have to go on. Can you send me a picture of the paper?"

"I'll do it now. Let me know if you find anything."

"You know I will. And don't worry. We'll find them." Her words reassure, but her voice echoes the opposite.

"Thank you. I don't know what I would do without you right now. Keep me posted," I say and lower the phone.

I lay the sheet on the bed and snap a picture. Then I hit send and grab my computer. *The first one is in Fairfax. I'll start there.* I pull up the search engine and type '1218 Fei—.'

"Ellie!" Steve yells as he rounds the door casing into the room. His eyes are glistening with moisture. "We have to get to the hospital. My mother's been shot."

"Shot?" I leap to my feet.

"I don't know anything else. Dukakis was hysterical, and I couldn't get any other details out of him except that the ambulance took her to the hospital here in Fairfax because it was closer." His voice cracks. "That's enough to tell me it's bad. They've been taking everyone to the big hospital in Arlington." We rush down the hall toward the garage. "The EMT must not have thought she could make it to Arlington."

I don't say anything. I can't say anything. My mouth is so dry that my tongue feels like a cotton ball inside my mouth. It takes every ounce of my willpower not to gag. *My dad... Alice... now Cynthia...* I slide into the passenger seat, tightening my arms around my stomach, but the shaking only gets worse. My face scrunches as I squeeze my eyes closed. *Lord, I'm scared. Please help!* With my arms still embracing my torso, I rub the sides of my stomach. A verse from my morning Bible study floats into my mind, overtaking my thoughts. I let it fill my head and let my inner voice recite it. *'And He arose, and rebuked the wind, and said unto the sea, Peace, be still. And the wind ceased, and there was a great calm.' Mark 4:39. Amazing. All he had to do was speak, and the raging waters calmed.* I exhale, letting the air escape through my mouth in a slow and steady stream. *No storm is too great. He is at the helm. I need to let Him steer.*

CHAPTER FOURTEEN

I hold my breath as Steve whips the car into the hospital parking lot, and then I let it out when the car lands back on all four wheels. His knuckles have been white from his death grip on the steering wheel ever since we left home.

"Ellie, I didn't think. Did you happen to grab your gun and badge?" He swings into a parking space and thrusts out his hand to hold me back as he slams on the brakes.

"Yes. They're in my purse."

"Get your gun. I'll come around and help you out."

I didn't even hear him open his car door, but he is already slamming it behind him. I pull the gun from my purse and slide it in the holster inside my jacket. When Steve opens the door, I need both hands, but as soon as I'm out of the car, I put my hand back inside my jacket and grip my gun.

Steve and I both keep our eyes peeled, but it's still daylight, and no one seems to be lurking. *Yeah. That's what we thought when Eileen was attacked.*

We don't have to go through the same red tape as the hospital in Arlington when we saw Eileen. Dukakis is standing inside the door by the guard, watching for us, and the doors slide open the second we approach.

Before he says a word, Dukakis throws his arms around Steve and pulls him into a tight hug. His eyes are swollen and puffy. "The doctor is with her now. They won't tell me anything since I'm not immediate family." His shoulders jerk and twitch as he hiccups with each sob.

Steve pulls back. "Which way is the E. R. desk?"

Dukakis points through a set of glass doors. Steve takes off, and Dukakis and I follow.

"Where is Teresa?" I ask, wondering why she isn't here yet.

"I couldn't reach her. I left her a voicemail and sent her multiple texts. Last night at dinner, she was talking about this major exam she had to study for. Maybe she turned off her phone so she could focus." Dukakis stops in front of an empty couch that we can all three fit on and gestures for me to sit.

I don't respond. I keep my eyes peeled on Steve, watching for his reaction as he speaks to the nurse at the counter. But he doesn't have a reaction. He just nods and heads back toward me and Dukakis.

"They don't have an update yet, but they'll let us know as soon as they have any information. Here, Ellie," he takes my hand, "you need to sit." He turns to Dukakis. "Uncle, you need to sit too."

"Let Ellie sit. I want to kneel and pray." Dukakis drops to his knees by the end of the sofa.

"Let's pray together," I suggest with my hand on the wooden arm of the sofa, already lowering to one knee.

"Sit on the couch. We'll kneel beside you." Dukakis pats the seat.

"No, I want to kneel. That's the least I can do," I insist, placing my other knee on the floor.

Steve drops next to me, and the three of us connect arms in a huddle.

"Father, we kneel before you, thankful that we can come to you with our burdens. And right now, with connected hearts, we bring you a heavy load." Dukakis leans in, gently letting his head touch ours. "Lord, we ask if it's your will that you would heal Cynthia's wounds and allow us to have more time with her, allow Steve to make new memories with her, and allow her grandson the chance to discover what a wonderful grandmother he has. Lord, we leave this in your hands. In Jesus' Holy Name."

"Lord," Steve speaks in a sullen tone, "I-I don't have any memories of my mother when I was a child, and I admit I was a little distant and hesitant at getting to know her at first. But you didn't give up on me, and you didn't give up on her. You heard our prayers and chased after her heart until she accepted you and your love. I know it's selfish, but I want my son to know her, and I want to know her better. Father, if you're ready for my mother to come and be with you, then we will be thankful that she will never hurt again. We'll be thankful because we know we'll see her again. But we ask if it is your will that you would leave her here with us and let us enjoy being with her just a while longer. In Jesus' Name."

"Dear Lord, thank you for the privilege to come to you and talk to you and spend time with You. Lord, I thank you for the time that we've had with Cynthia and the blessing that she has been in our lives. We are thankful that we know she is one of your children. But Lord, my husband has lost his earthly father, and he doesn't have a lot of moments built up in his memory of his mom yet, and our son hasn't gotten the chance to meet her. So, we ask if it is according to your plan, that you would heal her and let her be okay. In Jesus' Name, we ask. Amen."

"Amen." Dukakis and Steve utter a little out of sync.

Steve and Dukakis each take one of my hands and help me up. I sit on one end of the sofa, and Dukakis takes the other. Steve stands, or rather, walks in circles, nervously fidgeting with his fingers.

After a few minutes of twisting my head side to side, watching Steve pace back and forth in front of us, my stomach begins to churn. "Steve, honey, please come and sit with me. Dukakis hasn't even gotten to tell us what happened."

That gets his attention, and he drops onto the couch between me and Dukakis. We both stare at Dukakis, waiting for him to give us details.

Dukakis looks down at his trembling hands. "We had already gone by my house, and I was taking her home so she could get ready for her live speech thing. We were sitting at a stoplight laughing. She had been ribbing me about being a hoarder ever since she had seen the basement of my house." A tear drips from his chin. "I was laughing instead of paying attention. A truck flew up out of nowhere and passed by so fast. I only heard a small pop. I didn't know what it was or that anything had even happened until the truck was already out of sight." He bites his bottom lip and turns his face away as his shoulders and back quiver and quake.

I can tell from Steve's expression that he feels guilty for pressing Dukakis, but I can also understand his need to know.

"Uncle Dukakis," Steve whispers, placing his hand on his uncle's back, "it's not your fault. You didn't do anything wrong." After a mix between a sigh and a groan, he continues, "Please, I need you to tell me. Where did the bullet hit her?"

"In the back of her shoulder, I think. There was so much blood... so much blood," he mutters under his breath. He uses his hands to wipe his eyes and turns back to face us. "The EMT said it exited through her chest. I'm sorry, I'm so sorry."

"Don't apologize. This is not your fault," Steve reassures him.

"She was with me in my van. I know the world that we're living in, and I let my guard down."

"You're human, Dukakis." Steve leans forward with his face in his hands. "Even if you had seen the truck coming, you would have had no idea they were planning to fire a bullet, and in the split second that it appeared and sped away, what could you have done? You're not the one who shot her, so stop blaming yourself."

"The only woman I felt...," Dukakis trails off, and he squeezes his eyes closed.

"The only woman... what?" I ask.

"Nothing, it's nothing. I didn't mean to say it out loud."

I swallow, knowing I'm about to step beyond acceptable boundaries into what is known as interfering in people's personal lives. "Have you told her?"

"What?" His head jerks toward me.

"Have you told her how you feel?" I repeat.

Now Steve is staring at me too. "What are you talking about, Ellie?"

"Look, Dukakis. Only you know your feelings, and they are certainly only yours to share. But, if you care about someone, and you don't tell them, how are they supposed to know? And that person might feel the same way about you."

"And that person might not," Dukakis adds.

"True, but either way, you know. And besides," I lower my voice, "you may never get another chance."

A minute or two passes as we sit in silence. I guess it's rude, but my eyes are glued to the nurse behind the desk, hoping that at any second, she is going to pop up with good news.

"I can't answer for my mother, but in my eyes, she would never find a better man to share her life with."

Steve's response is a bit delayed, but it puts a smile on Dukakis's face, all the same.

"Well, I was sort of hoping we could go on a real date first before we start sharing the rest of our lives together," Dukakis remarks, getting a chuckle from all three of us. "But," he switches back to a serious tone, "thank you. That means a lot." He looks at Steve. "Do you really think I should tell her?"

"Yes, I definitely do."

Dukakis peers down at his hands, twiddling his thumbs. "I-I can't explain it. After I lost Delilah, I thought that was it. She was the one, and I would never have the desire to spend time with anyone else. And I haven't until Cynthia came back into our lives." His Adam's apple bobbles as he swallows hard. "It's nice, you know, to have someone to spend time with. Cynthia makes me laugh, and I'm so relaxed around her. But, in a way, I feel guilty, like I'm not being loyal to Delilah."

"Uncle Dukakis, I'm going to be honest. I don't know how I would feel in your position. I couldn't imagine my life without Ellie. But Delilah has been gone a long time, and I don't think God wants you to spend the rest of your life alone. You and my mother are both Christians. I don't see anything wrong with taking it slow. Go on a few dates and then follow where God leads you two."

"Mr. Denali." A man in green scrubs with a surgical hair net covering his head and a mask pulled below his chin stands beside the nurse behind the desk. The nurse is pointing in our direction.

Steve is on his feet, striding toward the desk before the man finishes 'Denali,' and Dukakis is right on his heels. A rush of adrenaline pushes me up from the sofa, and in a few seconds, I am following close behind them."

"Are you Cynthia Denali's next of kin?" the man asks Steve as I approach.

"Yes, I am. I'm her son, Steve. Well, I have a sister, but she isn't here."

"Your mother had a very close call, but she's going to be fine. Luckily, the bullet exited intact, barely missing the top of her right lung. We'll be moving her to a room in a few hours, but I want to monitor her here for a while longer."

"Can we see her?" Dukakis blurts out.

"Of course. She's a little groggy from the pain meds, but she is awake." He presses his lips together and touches his hand to his chin. "Mmm. I know crimes at this point are pretty much going unpunished since the number of violators far outweighs the amount of law enforcement officers. However, I understand that Mrs. Denali is running for president. This could have been a random act, or it might not have been. We don't have enough security to monitor every room, so I suggest someone stay with her at all times."

"Oh. Don't you worry about that. She will not be left alone," Dukakis asserts in a firm tone.

"Good." He moves around the desk to a door the same height as the desk and pulls it open. "Come on this way."

Steve waits for me to go first, and with his hand on my back, we follow the doctor. As we walk, I thank God over and over that Steve still has his mother, and my son will still have the chance to know his grandmother," one corner of my mouth curves up, "and maybe the president of the United States.

As the doctor stops in front of a door, I notice a pump of hand sanitizer out of my peripheral vision hanging on the wall. I help myself and quickly rub as I count to seven, seven times in my mind.

"Mrs. Denali is in the procedure room." The doctor places his hand on the door handle, which makes me want to offer him some hand sanitizer. He turns toward us. "It is a smidgen larger than the examination rooms. She can stay in here unless we need it. Of course, as I said, we will be moving her to a private room in a few hours anyway." He swings the door open. "Mrs. Denali, you have guests."

The doctor steps to the side to let us enter. "It was nice to meet you all. The nurses are monitoring her and will be in every few minutes, but let the nurses know if she has any problems."

"Thanks, Doctor," Steve says as he gestures for me to go inside.

Cynthia is lying on one of those small gurney size beds with an oxygen mask covering her face, an IV running to her wrist, a wire taped to the end of one of her fingers, a blood pressure cuff on her arm, and lots of other wires, straying in every direction going to and from various monitors.

"Cynthia," I half-prop myself on the side of the gurney and touch her arm, "praise the Lord you are okay."

"God is good." She reaches over with her other hand and pats the top of mine. "Now, will you please tell me why you're not at home with your feet up?"

Steve steps up to the other side. "That's pretty self-explanatory, isn't it?" He leans over the bed and kisses the top of her head. "You really scared us."

"Well, it was no trip to the doughnut shop for me either," she says, smiling.

Steve shakes his head. "Well, I learned something today."

"What's that?" The skin on her forehead stretches as she widens her eyes with curiosity.

"That I better make sure and tell you I love you every time I see you. You seem to have a lot of close calls."

"That's true." Cynthia bobs her head in agreement. "I've been frozen and brought back, been killed by brain shocks and resuscitated, and now I can add being shot to my list."

Dukakis rubs her foot as he stands at the bottom of the bed. "I don't think you can count this time. You didn't actually die."

"Thanks to you." Her cheeks glow pink.

"Me?" Dukakis's posture stiffens in shock. "No thanks to me. I didn't do a very good job of protecting you."

"There's nothing you could have done about me being shot, Dukakis. But you did save my life?" Cynthia grips the rail on the side and grits her teeth.

Laughing must be pulling at her wound, I speculate.

"The authorities came in the back door and questioned me. Apparently, since I'm running for president, this case takes priority." She rolls her eyes as she speaks. "I told them that was pathetic, and that my shooting was no different than anyone else's. But they still made me give a statement detailing what I remembered. The detective said that if I had not been twisted around and leaning forward, I would have been shot in the head. And—," she drags the word out, "I wouldn't have been twisted around and leaning forward if I hadn't been laughing at you for being a hoarder."

"My hoarding saved your life," Dukakis comments in a dry tone.

"It certainly did, so please, continue to hoard." She waves her hand in a circle.

"Glad I was able to help." He pretends to tip his hat since he isn't wearing one.

"Cynthia, I have to ask. How on earth can every hair on your head be in place and perfectly curled under after being shot and lying in a hospital for several hours?" I stroke a twig of her brown hair.

"Oh, I use this ultra-hold spray. Dennis hated my hair curled under, so I make sure it doesn't move."

"I glance at Dukakis. His eyes are locked on Cynthia, and as he looks at her, his face glows." I move my focus to Steve and clear my throat, hoping he catches the hint. "Cynthia, now that we know you're okay, I'm going to see if the vending machine has apple juice."

"After you find the vending machine, go home and rest," she orders.

"There's a chair right there in the corner," I retort. "I'll be back in a minute." I peer at Steve over my shoulder who apparently did not get the subliminal memo I was sending, and once I catch his attention, I shift my eyes hard toward Dukakis.

"Oh." He jumps as the epiphany seems to hit him. "Ellie, you can't go out there by yourself. I'll come with you. We'll be right back, Mom."

"You guys take your time." Dukakis eases around the side of the bed and takes her hand. "I'll keep a close eye on her until you get back." He drops his gaze to Cynthia. "Actually, I won't be leaving at all. I'll be here until they send you home," he says to her.

I pull my hand up inside my shirt sleeve and use it to open the door, so I don't have to touch the handle. "Agent Morgan," I utter, leaving my mouth half-open. Of all people, I didn't expect him to be standing there when I opened the door.

"Ellie, Steve, is she okay? I came as soon as I heard."

"Y-Yes, she's going to be fine." The tone of Steve's reply reflects as much surprise as my mouth, which is still hanging open.

Agent Morgan drops his shoulders and touches his fingers to his sternum. "What a relief. I was so worried. I've watched her speeches over and over. This country needs that woman." He leans to the side, trying to look past Steve. "Is she awake? Is it okay if I say hello?"

"Yeah, sure." Steve steps back into the room, holding the door open, and I go back in too. My fake trip for juice does no good if Dukakis doesn't get to talk to Cynthia.

"There's our future president looking as beautiful as ever." Agent Morgan strides up to the opposite side of the bed from Dukakis. "Thank goodness you're alright, Cynthia. I was worried sick."

"Thanks, Allen. That is sweet of you to be so concerned." She reaches up, dragging the IV tube, and pats his shoulder. "But how did you even hear about it?"

"I've been tied up with cases most of the day, but when I walked in the office a bit ago, the shooting was the buzz of the entire office. You are a candidate in the presidential election, you know. And the one that everyone I've talked to is supporting. Anyway," his voice softens, "when I heard, my heart hit the ground."

"That's great news," Dukakis remarks. "Cynthia, people all over are supporting you and pushing for you to win. Of course, if it's God's plan for you to be president, nothing in this world can stop it. 'There are many devices in a man's heart; nevertheless the counsel of the Lord, that shall stand.' We seem to recite that verse a lot in this family, but it's true."

"Do you really think God has been preparing me for this?" she asks in a tone that pleads for reassurance as her eyes focus on Dukakis for the answer.

"If this isn't part of His plan, then we are doomed," Agent Morgan rattles off.

But Dukakis looks back into Cynthia's eyes, and I'm pretty sure that he doesn't mean to interrupt Agent Morgan because I don't think he even knows Agent Morgan is speaking. "Cynthia, when we were at the Hatchers' house the other night, and you said you were going to run, I knew there was no one better. If anyone can turn this country around, it is you. But then, when I heard you on Carlton's program, tears filled my eyes, and I actually cried." He lifts his eyebrows and lowers his head. "And let me say I don't cry very much, but when I do, it is usually because I have felt the power of God moving. Yes, everything you have been through, the way He brought you back to Him, Ellie's constant nightmares that turned out to be your rescue... I believe those were all pieces of the puzzle. And with each piece, He molded you and filled you with the passion and energy that I heard in your speech the other night. Only God knows tomorrow and what He has in store for us, but I believe with my whole heart, this is part of His purpose for you." A lopsided grin forms on his face. "And I say part, because you also have a grandson on the way, and I believe He intends for you to be an amazing grandmother too."

A flush creeps up into Cynthia's face, and she flutters her lashes as a tear drops from the corner of her eye. "Thank you," she mouths not seeming to be able to get sound to come out.

"Don't thank me." He swallows and finishes in a raspy voice. "I'm only calling it as I see it." Coughing, he looks over at me. "And Ellie, between Steve's nursery and the spoiling that Cynthia is going to be dishing out, you're going to have your hands full."

We all laugh except for Steve.

"I don't get it. What's wrong with the nursery?" His forehead puckers as his eyes search each of our faces.

We laugh even harder, which makes Steve scowl and narrow his eyes.

"Hem." Agent Morgan gets Cynthia's attention. "If you'll excuse me for a few minutes, I'm going to talk to the hospital administration and let them know I will be guarding your room tonight, and when I go to work tomorrow, I'll have an agent to take my place."

"Allen, I appreciate the offer, but no, thank you."

"Cynthia, you need security. This was probably not a random act," Agent Morgan argues.

"It doesn't matter. I'm not going to accept an agent protecting me when innocent people are being killed left and right in the streets because there aren't enough law enforcement officers. I'm in a hospital with security, and Dukakis has already said he would stay right here until they release me."

He smiles and puts his hand on her shoulder. "You are one of a kind, Cynthia Denali. Is there anything I can get for you before I go?"

"No, and I do appreciate the offer, Allen, but it wouldn't be right for me to have added security when those poor people out there trying to get to work and earn a living don't have any."

He nods. "Call me if there's anything I can do. Meanwhile, I'll be campaigning for you."

"That, you can do," Cynthia affirms with a big nod. "And you can take Ellie and Steve out with you. Ellie needs to be at home off of her feet."

"But Mom..." Steve stops mid-sentence, glancing at my stomach. "Yeah, you're right. I love you, Mom. After Ellie rests, we'll be back."

"I love you, too, Son."

I step up and give her the best hug I can. The railing on the bed and my big belly create an obstacle. "Love you, Cynthia."

"Love you, too. Now get home and take care of my grandson."

Steve has his arms around my waist as we walk down the hall behind Agent Morgan, who hasn't said a word and seems to be walking extremely slowly. My phone dings in my purse, and I slip it out, hoping it's Kate with some good news, or at least, some information. But instead, it's an alert email from work. I know I'm on medical leave, but I need to stay up to date, so I tap the screen and open it.

> *It is with deepest sympathy and regret that we inform you of the untimely death of one of our own. Special Agent Kate Matthews was tragically killed in an explosion earlier today. Agent Matthews is believed to have been investigating an anonymous tip involving illegal activity at a local warehouse. We will notify you of the arrangements as soon as they are made available to us.*

The phone bounces off the tile floor. My mouth is open, but I don't know if I'm screaming.

CHAPTER FIFTEEN

"Ellie!" Steve's arms wrap around my torso, catching me before I hit the floor.

"Please wake me up." I press my eyelids together. *This is just another nightmare. It isn't real. Calm down. This isn't real.*

Steve drops to the floor and pulls me to him.

With my face buried in his chest, I jerk all over, wailing with sobs. "Please." I gasp hard for air. "Wake me up."

"You're not asleep, Ellie." Steve's voice is filled with desperation. "Please, honey, you have to tell me what is wrong."

Footsteps approach all around me.

"Sir, is she okay? How can we help?" a woman asks somewhere above me.

"I don't know," he mutters in response.

I push my head harder into his chest, letting the sound of his heart block out the panicked voices.

Steve swipes the hair from my face and leans over me with his mouth close to my ear. "Please, what is it?" he whispers. "You're scaring me. I don't know what to do."

"M-M-My ph-phone," I hiccup the words between the violent shakes of my body.

"Her phone... where's Ellie's phone?" Steve almost shouts.

"Right here." Agent Morgan must be on the floor right beside us. "She dropped it when she fell."

Steve's left hand lets go of me. He must be reaching for the phone.

His heartbeat pounds harder and faster against my cheek. His left hand is back, and he pulls me closer. He doesn't say anything to anyone. He only mumbles under his breath. "God, what is happening? Please help."

It's my fault... my fault that she's dead. That warehouse had to be one of the addresses I gave her. I'm sorry, Kate. I'm so sorry. I ball my hands into fists and pull my arms in tight. *I'm so sorry.*

"Sir, we have a gurney. We'll take her and check her out when she's ready." It sounds like the doctor who saw Cynthia.

"I'm not sure what's going on," Agent Morgan replies. "Let's give them a minute."

The voices around me keep multiplying, getting louder and louder.

"Oh, no. Mom, it's Ellie." Feet pound against the tile.

Eileen? Mom?

"Agent Morgan," Mom yells, "what's wrong with Ellie?" Her voice echoes through the hospital.

The rhythm of running feet clacking on the floor gets closer. In a few seconds, Eileen drops behind me, and her arms drape around my back. "What happened? Why aren't the doctors checking her?" Eileen asks in a fast but calm tone.

"I don't know," Agent Morgan answers. "I really don't know. No one is saying anything."

"Steve?" Eileen's pitch rises in desperation.

The pressure from Steve's chin resting on the top of my head lifts. "Kate," he chokes out. "Kate, uh." His hands grip me even tighter. "K-Kate was killed. E-E-Ellie got a m-message on her phone f-from w-work."

The cacophony of voices ceases as if a switch has been flipped off. Heavy silence surrounds me except for a loud gasp from my mother and a whisper, "No," from Agent Morgan followed by a thud that sounds like he crumples the rest of the way to the floor.

Another hand touches my back, and a faint voice filters to my ear... someone uttering a prayer... *Carlton.*

I listen as he prays for peace and strength and healing... for family and friends. I listen as he thanks God that we will be able to see Kate again. And then I listen as a voice inside me starts to speak. *'Have I not commanded thee? Be strong and of a good courage; be not afraid, neither be thou dismayed: for the Lord thy God is with thee whithersoever thou goest.'* With my face hidden in Steve's chest, I blink to clear the pools of water away. *I am commanded to be strong. Dad and Alice need me to be strong. I can do all things through Christ which strengtheneth me. I can do all things through Christ which strengtheneth me. I can do all things through Christ which strengtheneth me. I can do all things through Christ which strengtheneth me. I can do all things through Christ which strengtheneth me. I can do all things through Christ which strengtheneth me. I can do all things through Christ which strengtheneth me.* After I repeat the verse seven times, I'm ready... armed and ready.

"Amen," I say after him as I lift my head and wipe my eyes.

Eileen pulls my hair back, and Steve gazes into my eyes with worry etched in lines all over his face.

"I'm sorry. I'm okay now. Can we go home?" I ask, trying not to let myself give back into the tears.

Steve stands and grabs a hold of both of my hands to pull me up. As I rise to my feet, I fix my eyes on Agent Morgan sitting on the floor. He's looking straight ahead with an icy stare on his face and his lips pressed tightly together, forming a thin line. I can't tell if he's hurting or angry, but I suppose it could be a mix of the two. Because now that I think about it, I'm hurting and angry... *angry with myself for sending her that list of addresses.*

Suddenly, Agent Morgan leaps to his feet. His cheeks are blanched and pasty. "I need to get out of here. I'm going to be sick," Agent Morgan mumbles and takes off down the hall.

I watch, wondering for a few seconds if we should go after him, but maybe he needs space. When he's out of sight, I turn and hug Eileen. Carlton pats my shoulder as I do, and I notice his other hand is resting on Eileen's shoulder. I have no brain cells left to put any thought into it, so I turn and hug Mom. Before I escape her embrace, Ted's voice reverberates, approaching from down the hall.

"What is my second favorite patient doing on her feet? I would say my favorite, but we know who my favorite is." As the comment leaves his mouth, he casts his eyes on Eileen, and I notice a slight grimace form on his face at the sight of Carlton. He turns his focus back to me and continues to talk. "Ellie, I know you're worried about Cynthia, but you need to be at home resting."

"I'm going," I mumble with my head down not ready to get into a discussion about Kate. Then I remember that we're at the hospital in Fairfax. "Wait, what are you doing here? You don't work at this hospital."

"I called him," Mom answers for him, "to tell him about Cynthia."

I nod and take a step when I realize Steve has stopped.

"Jillian, I want you and Eileen to come and stay at our house tonight," Steve says, not giving a choice. "Actually, pack lots of stuff because you two are staying until Tom gets back."

At the mention of Dad, Mom's eyes get watery. I know Steve didn't mean to upset her, but she's going to have to face it sooner or later. We don't know where Dad is or when he will be back. And she and Eileen can't stay at that house alone.

Mom doesn't answer, but her head jerks in a quick nod.

"I'm holding you to it. We'll be expecting you," Steve affirms and then turns, taking my arm. We make our way to the exit.

As my eyes fall on the glass doors, my muscles tighten. Darkness is already taking over.

"Do you have your hands on it?" Steve asks.

"Mm-hm." With my hand under my jacket, I tighten my grip and loosely rest my finger on the trigger.

"Steve. Ellie. Wait!"

My heart jumps at the sound of someone yelling. Steve must have startled too because his arm that's around my body twitches.

Dukakis runs up behind us.

Steve twists around. "I thought that you weren't going to leave Mom."

"Oh, I'm not. Jillian, Eileen, and Carlton are in there with her. Cynthia is still determined to do that live speech on BridgNect, so Eileen is helping her." He sucks in like he's out of breath. "They told us about Kate," he chokes out and presses his lips together. "I-I -uh I'm sorry. Ellie, I know you were close to her. I can't seem to wrap my mind around it. She's so young... too young," he mumbles, shaking his head. "Anyway, Cynthia insisted that I try to catch you and give you the box."

"Box?" I widen my eyes.

"That's what I went to my house to look for earlier. When my parents died, there was a box of Dennis's things in the basement that my mother had kept. I've never opened it, but I'm sure it has to be things from his childhood since he never came back home after he left for college. Of course, this leads me to doubt that there is anything about Sivers in there unless he had somehow met him before college, and that's not likely. But it's all we have of Dennis's, so it's worth a try."

"Where is the box?" Steve asks.

"In my van."

"I figured they kept it for evidence or something." Steve gives me a questioning look.

"Nah. They gave it a quick going over at the scene and told me I would have to take it because they had no way to get it towed right now. The detective said they had cars sitting on the side of the road all over the place, and any wrecker service that did have drivers willing to come out and work was covered up."

"Where are you parked?" Steve stares through the glass doors. At what, I don't know because the sky is completely dark now.

"I was in such a hurry I don't think I'm even in a parking space. I guess I better move it into a space." Dukakis shrugs. "Of course, what are they going to do... have it towed?"

"We're parked right out here. Pull your van over to our car. Once we load the box, you can pull the van into our spot as we leave," Steve details his plan and lifts his leg to step toward the door. "Dukakis, do you have a weapon?"

"Sure do. But don't worry about me. I'm not afraid. As Paul said in Philippians, 'For to me to live is Christ, and to die is gain.'"

The guard hits the button, and we step through the sliding doors. The walkway beneath the awning is well-illuminated, but as I scour the lot, only a few dots of light from the scattered poles give any break under the starless, cloud-covered sky. And, of course, as we step off the walk, I notice our car is nowhere near one of the dots. Thankfully, Dukakis was right. His van is parked right by the ambulance entrance next to the walk, and for the safety of the EMTs and the patients who are being unloaded, that area is lit as bright as an airport runway.

As I slip into the passenger seat, I give my gun to Steve. He closes my door, the back pops open, and I look over my shoulder just in time to see a huge cardboard box slide into the back. Two seconds later, the driver's door opens, and in a blink, we're backing out of the space. I pump some sanitizer from the bottle I keep in the door and rub my hands while I count.

Neither of us speaks for a bit. My thoughts won't leave Kate, and sitting in the quiet, dark car, I can't hold back the water gathering in my eyes. I pull my phone from my purse and click on the local news app. Even though I expect it, the sight of the headline burns my eyes.

"FBI AGENT KILLED IN EXPLOSION OUTSIDE LOCAL WAREHOUSE"

"What are you looking at?"

I notice Steve in my peripheral vision, leaning and trying to glance at my phone as he drives.

"An article about the explosion on the local news site." I read aloud so Steve will focus on the road.

"Authorities have confirmed that at least one person has been killed in an explosion earlier today outside what should have been a vacant warehouse. The warehouse is part of a small industrial park that is located just off Feint Road on the outskirts of Fairfax. That particular business park has not been active in quite some time. The few factories that had been part of the park were closed down years ago because of failure to comply with pollution regulations in a rural area.

At this time, it is uncertain if there were other fatalities from the explosion, and no other details are being released. However, there has been some speculation that the agent was investigating a possible drug ring operating out of the warehouse."

I use my shirt to dab the corners of my eyes. Even though I used sanitizer, I still don't want to touch my face. Knowing that Feint Road must be on that list of addresses, I pull up the photo on my phone that I sent to Kate. I read the first line and drop my head. The whispers start up again, but in my head, they sound like screams. *You did this to her, Ellie. You did this.* I bite my lips together until I can taste blood. *Be strong, Ellie,* I say to myself in a roar, battling the whispering screams. *You have to be strong for the baby. You have to be strong for Dad and Alice. God commands you to be strong.*

"Ellie." Steve reaches over and rests his hand on top of mine. "Are you okay? Do I need to take you back to the hospital?"

"I don't need to go to the hospital, but I'm not fine," I utter through clenched teeth. "Kate... it's my fault. I'm the reason she's dead."

"Ellie," he speaks softly as if he is speaking to a child, "that's your OCD talking. You have been with me all day. Thinking you had anything to do with Kate's death is not rational."

The condescending tone in his voice brings a rush of heat to my face. *He doesn't understand. He is trying to help,* I remind myself. I squeeze my eyelids together as hard as I can. "I sent her the list of addresses right before we left for the hospital. The warehouse where she was killed," I swallow, almost gagging because my mouth is so dry, "it's the first address."

A minute of silence passes as he stares straight ahead at the road through the windshield. "A couple of things..." His eyes dart toward me and then back to the road. "One. This is absolutely in no way your fault at all." His tone is so reassuring that more guilt pierces through my chest for letting my anger rise at his earlier tone.

I interject before he gets to the second thing. "How do you figure? If I hadn't given her the address, she could not have gone there. Hence, my fault."

"Okay, answer this question. When you gave Kate the list, did you in any way ask her to go to those addresses and check them out, especially alone?" He casts me another glance.

"No. I blabbed to her about the envelope and the addresses. She tracked Dad's phone, and the location showed somewhere behind Alice's apartment. Then, she asked me to send her the addresses because she said the list was the only thing that we had to go on right now in looking for them. That should have been my bright red flag that she planned to personally go check the places out, at least the ones close by."

"Ellie, you did not ask her to go there, nor did you think that she planned to. And on top of that, the address of the warehouse being on your dad's list could be a coincidence." He hesitates. "Come to think of it, the news article did not give a specific address. It said a warehouse in a business park off Feint Road. Your dad's list was detailed. What was the address on his list?"

"1218 Feint Road."

"I know it's a stretch, but she could have been there investigating something else. Before you jump to conclusions, look up 1218 Feint Road on the internet. You don't even know that the address on Tom's list is a warehouse... or even a business for that matter."

I pull up the search engine on my phone.

"But that brings me to the second thing," Steve continues as he turns into our driveway. "It doesn't add up."

"What doesn't add up?" I ask typing in *1218 Feint Rd, Fairfax, VA*.

"Her going there alone. Think about it. You're going out to investigate a warehouse. You have no idea what's there or what's going on there. Would you ever go alone, without backup, and without telling anyone where or why you're going?"

"I know what you're saying. If she were following normal protocol, she wouldn't have been there in that situation. But under the circumstances, no agents would have been available to go with her. If you add to that, her knowing Alice and being worried about Alice's safety, then yes, her going there alone makes perfect sense. And," I turn the map on my phone toward him, "I can't get a clear view because of all the trees, and it looks small, but 1218 Feint Road is definitely an old industrial building."

He twists his mouth to the side and half nods as he drives the car into the garage. "It's still not your fault. You didn't ask her to go there, and even if you had, you had nothing to do with the explosion."

I tap the screen on my phone.

"Who are you calling? Can't it wait until we get inside?" Steve closes the garage door behind us.

"I'm calling Tanner."

"This late?" he questions.

"It's not that late. It's only six-thirty, and besides, it wouldn't matter if it was the middle of the night. I have information about Kate's death that is pertinent to the investigation, and since he is our supervisory agent, I'm sure he is heading up the case. We're safe inside the garage. Please, give me a minute. I want to get this over with."

"Ellie, that map shows large buildings lining that entire block. That might not have been the warehouse she went to," Steve persists.

"I'm not taking that chance. And maybe if their investigation is going in the right direction, it will help locate Alice and Dad."

Chapter Sixteen

I study my swollen, puffy face in the mirror, wondering if it looks that way from all the tears I've shed today or if I've gained weight in my face too. I puff out my cheeks and blow a gust of air out of my mouth. *I came in here to get out of those germ-covered clothes I had on at the hospital, not stare at myself in the mirror.* I reach over and put my hand under the automatic soap dispenser for the fourth time. *Ellie, you have to stop.* I scold myself. *Your hands are going to get raw again.* I rub, letting the soap lather as I count to seven, seven times, and then rinse.

Steve is sitting on his side of the bed facing the wall when I walk out of the bathroom.

"What are you doing?" I ask because it's unusual to see him sitting still.

"I tried to call Teresa, but she still isn't answering. It seems like a long time to be studying. You would think she would be breaking for dinner." He glances at the clock by the bed. "It's seven o'clock," he grumbles. "Oh, well. I guess there's a reason she has straight A's."

I plop down on my side of the bed and lean back against the headboard. "We need to stand behind her and offer her as much encouragement as we can. She spent a few years believing her name was Dr. Joanne Fleming. I think her self-esteem took a hit when she found out that her Ph.D. was fake, and she didn't even have a high school diploma. Teresa wants to prove to herself that she could be a doctor if she wanted."

"But she could be a doctor if she wanted. Teresa could do anything she sets her mind to," Steve argues with almost a hint of anger in his tone. "And Dr. Fleming wasn't a real person. Dad fabricated a character that he wanted Teresa to be. She has to focus on who God wants her to be... not my father"

"And she is. She's going to be a clinical psychologist. Teresa is an amazing person and way smarter than your father's fictitious Dr. Fleming. I'm only saying that her working and studying so hard is her way of proving it to herself."

He shrugs. "Yeah, I understand. I really do. I'm still trying to figure out where I learned to program those robots."

"It doesn't matter. You have a gift for technology, and a natural artistic vision for designing and integrating ideas that no one else could even come close to imagining." I tap the back of my head against the headboard.

Steve lifts one leg at a time onto the bed and leans back beside me. "You seemed pretty upset about your conversation with Tanner. From what I heard of your end of the call, I take it he wouldn't hear anything you had to say."

"Let's see. He yelled because I called Kate and took up her time when they have real cases to attend to, and he emphasized the word 'real.' He informed me that as a federal agent, I should have known to call and file missing person's reports about Alice and Dad with the local police instead of hounding the Federal Bureau of Investigation."

"Like that would do any good," Steve utters as he rolls his eyes.

"That's what I told him. Anyway, he held to the same story that the news site said was speculation"

"The anonymous tip about a drug operation?"

"Yes, except he added the possibility of illegal weapons too. According to Tanner, Kate had a report on her desk detailing an anonymous tip to that address, and she had handwritten at the top, 'meet at 3:15.'"

"Who was she meeting?"

"No idea. Her phone was destroyed in the explosion, and they're still working to get a list of calls and texts that were made from her number."

"So, it was a coincidence about the address. See, you were blaming yourself for nothing."

I press my lips together for a second. "No, it wasn't a coincidence. Don't you see? That report was fake. Kate was covering herself, so if anything came up, she had documentation proving she had a reason to be at that warehouse. The part I'm not sure of is whether or not she was actually meeting someone there."

"Oh." Steve's head slightly bobbles up and down. "Now that part of the phone conversation makes sense. Is that when you got a little heated and told him that you weren't crazy."

"I think so. It doesn't matter. He thinks I'm crazy, and most likely I won't have a job to go back to after the baby is born." I pinch the bridge of my nose. "The funny part is that he thinks I am out of my mind, and I didn't even get to the part about Dad's addresses having to do with President Denali still being alive."

"Now what?" He reaches over and pats my thigh.

"I have to call Gerald and tell him about Alice and her phone," I sigh, "and the text coming from a burner phone, and that she hasn't been to see her mother. How do I do that and not tell him about the envelope and Dad's phone?" My voice wavers in and out. "What are we going to do? Kate was killed because of that list of addresses. We don't have time to waste. We have to find Dad and Alice. And, obviously, Tanner is going to be no help."

"I already tried to call Gerald. I didn't want you to have to deal with telling him, but he isn't answering either. I'm not sure why people carry phones if they aren't going to answer. I left him a message to call me back. At least, we have until then to figure out how to tell him." Steve taps his chin and twists his mouth to the side as if he is deep in thought. "Ellie," he continues to tap his chin, "Agent Morgan appeared to be pretty shaken up when he left the hospital, so I don't know whether to call now or give him a bit longer, but at this point, our only option is to call him."

"I doubt he will believe us either, but you're right. He's our only option." I swipe the hair from my eyes and turn my face toward Steve. "Speaking of Agent Morgan, is it just me, or have you noticed a drastic change in his behavior toward your mother?"

"You mean since the whole running for president thing started." Steve forces a laugh. "Yeah, he's made it pretty obvious. Maybe he has a thing for women in politics. I think Mom made it clear where she stood though. At least, her eyes did anyway. Every time she looked at Dukakis, her eyes sparkled. I've never seen her that way." He pauses and rolls his eyes to the ceiling. "Of course, I don't have any memories of her around that many men, now do I? Thanks, Dad!" he yells in frustration.

A heavy silence settles between us.

I roll to my side and lay my head on his shoulder. "I'm scared... really scared. I can't keep pretending everything is okay." I lift my eyes to meet his. "Kate is dead, and something bad has happened to Dad and Alice," I utter through quivering lips. "It's all connected, and I don't know what to do or where to start." I pop straight up. "The box. Where's the box?"

"Oh. I left it in the living room. I'll get it." He rocks backward and then up to his feet and freezes.

"What's wrong?" I ask with my nerves on edge.

"Is that Reggae?" He narrows his eyes and scrunches his forehead.

Blocking the chaos of turmoil flying around in my brain, I tilt my ear toward the door. "Yes. Yes, I believe it is." I twist around, push myself off the bed, and follow Steve into the hall.

We step through the nursery door, and my chin drops. Herb is whipping his hand back and forth at warp speed, rocking the bassinet so fast that it's only a blur. Waves is standing in the middle under the flashing light, bopping his head to the beat, and Spencer is flying around the perimeter of the room with his arms above his head, gripping onto the engine of the train as his body dangles.

At the sight of Steve, Herb stops rocking, the music ceases, and the train comes to an abrupt halt. Spencer loses his grip, and with the law of inertia in play, he doesn't stop but continues his path through the air until he grasps onto a handful of Steve's hair to stop himself. With a wad of Steve's hair that is no longer attached to Steve's head, Spencer smacks into the wall and falls to the floor with a thud. He squeals but bounces to his feet.

"Did you hear a beep? The oven must be ready." Herb wheels toward the door, scooping Spencer up in his arms as he passes. "Come on, Spencer. Let's get the pizza in the oven. Mr. Steve and Mrs. Ellie haven't had dinner yet."

Waves follows, still bopping his head to music that's no longer playing.

Steve doesn't move. He stands rigid with his hands balled into fists at his sides. His face lacks expression, and his lips are pressed in a straight line.

I inch closer and touch my fingers to his head. "Are you okay?"

He rolls his eyes to meet mine. "That pizza better have sausage," he grumbles through gritted teeth.

I drop my hand and step into the center of the room. Slowly my body turns in a circle, and I let my mind drift. As I detach from my surroundings, the present fades, and I am suddenly watching the last few days as if I'm a character in a movie.

Steve rests his hand on my shoulder. "Ellie," he utters.

"How?" I mumble. "This can't be real. Three nights ago, I sat on the kitchen floor with my dad, and last night I stood in this very spot talking to Alice and Kate. Now Kate is gone, and as hard as I try to push it from my mind, I wonder if the same is true for Dad and Alice. All in a matter of three days." My gaze falls on the words painted on the wall. *NEVER FORGET! JESUS LOVES YOU!* "It reminds me of the verse, umm, I think it's James 4:14. 'Whereas ye know not what shall be on the morrow. For what is your life? It is even a vapour that appeareth for a little time and then vanisheth away.'" I gulp, stifling the wail that is building inside me. "We're all running around in fear. The government is even ordering us to be home by nine o'clock. Why? Dukakis was right when he quoted Paul in his letter to the Philippians. 'For me to live is Christ, and to die is gain.' No matter what happens, no matter how much pain and grief pierces my heart, I lift my hands in praise because I know all their names are written in the 'Lamb's Book of Life.'"

Steve spins on his heels and strides to the door.

"Where are you going?" I ask, wondering why he's walking out in the middle of our conversation.

Without looking back, he answers, "To get that list of addresses and call Agent Morgan. We're going to find Tom and Alice."

I nod and drag my feet to the rocking chair in the corner. With one hand on the armrest, I let the heaviness of my tired body pull me down into it. I press my head against the back of the chair and close my eyes. *Lord, please give me strength.*

A few minutes later, Steve trudges back into the room and drops the box in the middle of the floor. "I really have no interest in going through my father's childhood mementos," he says, plopping down next to the box.

"Did you talk to Agent Morgan?"

"Yes. It didn't go as well as I had hoped. He was a bit upset at first. I think his exact words were, 'I cannot believe that we are rehashing that nonsense about Dennis Denali being alive.'" Steve flips the cardboard flap open. "But because Kate was involved, he's going to investigate the addresses on Tom's list."

"Honestly, it sounds like it went better than I expected. At least he's helping." I slide out of the chair and scoot across the floor beside Steve. "I wish the chances of finding something helpful in this box were a little more promising." I reach in and pull out a tattered teddy bear with one eye. "I just don't see how anything from his childhood could possibly help."

"We have a guest coming down the drive," Herb calls from the living room.

As if it's choreographed, we roll up on our knees and stand at the same time.

"Ellie, you don't have to get up. I'll see who it is."

"It's probably Mom and Eileen already. I'll come and sit in the living room."

"I wouldn't think that they would have had time to go home and get their things." He shrugs. "But I don't know who else it could be," he says, letting me go out of the room in front of him.

Herb is holding the door as I step into the living room.

"Ted, I didn't know you were stopping by. Are you here to check up on me?" I notice the black bag in his hand as I lower myself into the armchair. I don't want him to fuss at me for being on my feet.

Before Ted gets a chance to answer, Herb interjects as he secures the front door back. "Well, not to worry, with the number of unexpected guests lately, I have decided it is best to keep a fresh pot of tea brewing at all times. I will be right back with a speck of tea." Herb speeds off toward the kitchen.

"I really don't need a cup of tea," Ted whispers, "but I'm afraid if I say no, it may upset him."

"Yeah, you probably should just take the tea." Steve laughs as he shakes Ted's hand.

"And to answer your question, Ellie," Ted turns his focus back to me, "yes, I did stop by to check up on you. Your stress level at the hospital had me concerned, so I wanted to check your blood pressure and make sure you weren't having any contractions."

"Well, I can't tell you that I'm not upset. One of my closest friends was killed today. But I'm not having any pain or contractions, and physically, I feel fine."

Steve steps up behind the armchair where I'm sitting and puts his hands on my shoulders.

"I'm sorry about your friend. It's hard losing someone you're close to," Ted says, looking away as if his thoughts are somewhere else. "And I'm glad you're feeling okay, but if you don't mind, I'd still like to check your vitals since I'm here."

I nod, brushing the hair from my face. "I would appreciate it. It's nice of you to keep dropping by, especially since I have no idea when Dr. Lannigan is going to be back."

Ted wraps the blood pressure cuff around my arm and pushes the button. "That's good. One twenty-two over eighty-one." He drops it back in the bag and grabs his stethoscope.

Herb appears through the doorway carrying his silver tray with teacups and the teapot. "The tea is served." He places the tray on the coffee table.

I notice one cup is already filled with orange juice. *I think I'm going to turn into an orange.*

Spencer comes up behind him with his little fingers wrapped around the handles of the sugar bowl and sets it on the table by the teacups.

"Thank you, Spencer," Herb says as he pours two cups of tea. "You are always such a great help."

Spencer takes the lid from the sugar bowl and dumps sugar into each of the cups, including the juice. When he finishes, he shakes the container upside down and then looks inside it to make sure it is empty.

Herb's mechanical mouth curves down into a frown. "I suppose, unless you plan to eat your tea with a spoon, I will get some fresh cups."

For some reason, I have this huge craving for something sweet. "Thanks. I'll just take my juice with a spoon."

Steve and Ted stare at me with wide eyes as I lift the cup.

"What?" I stare back. "I wouldn't want to hurt Spencer's feelings now, would I?"

"Ted," Steve moves over and takes a seat on the sofa, "I'm concerned about her lack of sleep, and after today, I'm afraid it's going to get worse." He glares at me again. "After that juice, probably much, much worse," he mumbles in a low voice.

"I can imagine that she'll have difficulty sleeping tonight." Ted places the bell of the stethoscope on my stomach, moving it in various locations. He lifts it then continues talking. "I had nightmares for a solid month after my dad died. To tell the truth, I still have them sometimes."

"It sounds like you were close to your father. That must have been...," Steve pauses and changes his wording, "that must be hard. I don't have any memories of my father, but I know how close Ellie is to her father and the special bond that they share. How long ago did you lose him?"

"About ten years ago. I was sixteen." Ted's hands tremble as he places the stethoscope back in his bag and pulls the zipper closed. "He was hit head-on by a drunk driver on his way home from my high school football game."

"You played football?" I ask, thinking he may not want to talk about his dad.

"Not after that night." Ted clears his throat and blinks. "Ellie, you need to sleep. Once the baby comes, you're going to wish you were better rested. Doxylamine tablets are safe during pregnancy, and they're available over the counter. But I actually take them myself sometimes after long shifts at the hospital, especially if things have not gone well... if you know what I mean. Let me look. I may have some in my car." He picks up his bag and steps toward the door.

Sleep without nightmares does sound good. "Are you sure the medicine won't hurt the baby?"

"I'm positive." He stops and twists his head toward me with a smile. His lips part as if he is going to speak, but then he draws his mouth closed, turns back around, and continues his trek to the door.

Steve follows him. "I'll walk you out and see if you have the tablets."

Ted pauses again still facing the door. "I have a confession to make. Checking your vitals is not the main reason I stopped." He looks over his shoulder. "I was hoping Eileen would be here. I heard you tell Jillian at the hospital that you wanted them to spend the night." He places his hand over his face, rubbing his eyes. "I sort of acted like a jerk when I saw her and Carlton together. I tried to call her and apologize, but she won't answer."

"I'm sure she'll call you back," I reassure, wondering what he must have said to her that would keep her from talking to him. "She's probably busy getting her things together."

"Well, when you see her, will you tell her I'm sorry?" He drops his head. "I had no right to get upset. I felt a little threatened, I guess. I've never met anyone like Eileen, and when I saw Carlton with his hand on her shoulder, I suddenly had this fear that I wouldn't get a chance to know her better."

"You're right. My sister is one of a kind. And I wouldn't worry. I think Carlton was only being supportive in lieu of the circumstances."

"Thanks," Ted nods.

"We'll tell her you stopped by looking for her," Steve adds as he follows him out the door.

Without waiting for Steve to return, I push to my feet and rush down the hall to the nursery. I'm anxious to eliminate this box as anything that can help.

"Ellie."

That was quick. "In the baby's room," I yell back.

Steve appears in the doorway with a box of tablets.

"Did you run to and from his car? I didn't expect you to be back inside so fast," I say, folding the flaps of the box back, pressing on the creases to keep them out of the way.

"No, I didn't run." Steve shakes his head and walks toward me. "It's dark outside, and he had to get to work. Take one of these."

"Not yet. Mom and Eileen aren't even here yet, I want to look through this box, and," I close my eyes as my hands start to tremble, "how am I supposed to go to sleep when I know Dad and Alice are in trouble? I have sat around, ignoring the situation too long, pretending there was a logical explanation." My voice fades in and out as the tears build in my eyes. "I'm done sitting around doing nothing."

"Okay. Then, I'm helping. But first, I'm going to call Jillian because it's eight o'clock, and they should've been here."

I nod and wipe my tears as he pulls his phone from his pocket, taps the screen, and sticks it to his ear.

"Great." He pulls the phone away, taps the screen again, and returns it to his ear. His shoulders fall as he drops his hand with the phone to his side. "Neither your mom nor Eileen are answering. I better go look for them. Let me grab my gun, and I'll be back in a few minutes. Let me know if you hear from either of them."

"I'll go with you."

"No, it's late, and I don't want you in any danger." He walks over and kisses the top of my head. "Besides, you need to look through the box and research those addresses online."

I freeze, weighing the argument in my mind. *I don't want him going alone... But I do need to be working on finding Dad and Alice... But what if Mom and Eileen are in danger?... What if Steve gets hurt?...* I clutch the sides of my head.

"Ellie, work on the box and the addresses, please, in here where you and our son are safe." His phone jingles in his hand. "Oh. Praise the Lord. It's your mom." He lifts it to the side of his face. "Jillian, I was just about to come looking for you... Oh... Why don't I come and get you?... Surely ten minutes won't matter... I don't like it, but okay... Love you too... I'll tell her... Okay. Bye." He lowers the phone, inhales, and lets it out in a long groan.

I stare at him, waiting for him to fill in the gaps since I only heard his part of the conversation.

"Jillian and Eileen are home. Carlton followed them from the hospital to make sure they made it safely. That's why they didn't answer a while ago. He was waiting on the porch while they got the door secured with that giant metal bar. I'm a little confused. I hope that doesn't mean that she hasn't been barring the door all this time. But anyway, she said it was too late to come, and she felt safer there than traveling here at night." He takes another deep breath. "And if I come to get them, we wouldn't make it back here by curfew. She said to tell you she loves you, and she and Eileen will come over in the morning."

Spencer scampers in, clutching a checkered tablecloth with Herb rolling along behind him with a pan of pizza and paper plates.

"I realize it's later than normal, but you need to eat," Herb says as Spencer unfolds the cloth and spreads it on the floor. When Spencer is finished, Herb places the pizza in the center and the two plates on the edge.

Claude speeds in the door carrying a tray with two huge, clear glass mugs full of chocolate milk. "I hope chocolate milk is satisfactory. I don't normally do kitchen duty, but I have been informed that we are working to smooth over an unfortunate incident that occurred earlier."

"The milk, Claude. Just serve the milk," Herb interrupts.

Spencer picks up the one-eyed teddy bear from the floor and hugs it to his chest. The bear is almost as big as Spencer, and apparently, it has one of those speakers that is activated when its stomach is pressed because when he squeezes the bear, it growls... a loud, frightening, wild animal-attacking kind of growl. Spencer throws the bear across the room and leaps into Herb's arms.

"That is terrible," Herb exclaims. "You can't give a toy like that to a baby. Babies need soothing sounds." He peers at Steve and me as he pats Spencer on the back. "I saw an advertisement for this online parenting class. I'll forward you the details. With a little help, you'll make great parents." He turns and carries Spencer to the door. "Oh," he looks back as he turns a knob on the wall, "we thought you might enjoy your picnic under the stars." He winks and flips off the light switch.

The huge light in the center, painted to look like the sun, goes out, and tiny stars appear, covering the entire inside of the tray ceiling.

"This is beautiful... like we are really outside having a picnic under the stars." I can't help but smile.

Steve slides the box out of the way, giving us more room to stretch out, and then he clutches my hand. "It sort of reminds me of our picnic in the train station when we had that MRE. Remember, it was pepperoni pizza."

"I'll never forget. A picnic with guards marching around us with automatic rifles."

"And we survived." He squeezes my hand and bows his head. "Father, thank you for this time with my wife. Thank you for taking care of us. Please bless this food, and," he pauses, "please help us find Tom and Alice. In Jesus' Name, we pray. Amen." He grabs two slices of pizza and places one on each plate. "It doesn't have sausage." He glares up at me.

I tear a piece off of the crust and pop it in my mouth.

From the hallway, a mechanical voice starts to sing.

"Is that 'Unchained Melody'?" I ask not meaning to talk with my mouth full.

"Well, at least, he has branched out. It's not 'Row, Row, Row, Your Boat.'"

CHAPTER SEVENTEEN

My phone vibrates on the floor next to me. "It must be nine o'clock," I say as I pick it up.

> *Please text back that you are okay and always know Mom loves you.*

I type back.

> *I'm okay. Would feel better if you and Eileen were here. See you tomorrow. Love you too... and tell Eileen I love her.*

"I think you should take those tablets now and get some rest. We can look through this stuff in the morning." Steve looks around at the contents of the box that is now scattered across the carpet of the nursery.

"We just ate that heavy pizza. I have to let that settle a little before I lie down." I roll up on my knees. "Besides, now that we have everything out, I don't think it will take too long. We can pack it back in the box as we go."

Steve picks up a onesie. "Well, start with this. It reminds me of that unitard we had to wear at the facility."

I take the newborn sleeper from his hands. "Oh. It's so cute. It has little frogs on it."

"Note. Our son will never wear anything with frogs. Frogs are bad. They were one of the plagues God placed on the Egyptians."

I shake my head and cackle as I drop the onesie in the box. "Frogs are not bad. They're cute." I snatch up a baby rattle and a small, worn fleece baby blanket with frogs printed all over it.

"Maybe his problems started with the frogs," Steve asserts.

"He was a baby, and there's nothing wrong with frogs. Is that a yearbook?" I glance over, trying to see the book Steve is flipping through.

"I think it's from his ninth-grade year. It's kind of strange that this is the only one in the box."

I shrug. "Maybe he took the rest with him, or they're somewhere else. We only have one box of his things." I pick up a case of magnetic building blocks and a high-tech remote-control airplane. "Hey, look and see if Crawley or Sivers is in there."

"I already did. I don't see them, but they change their names at the drop of a hat. Maybe they went by something else in high school."

"I doubt they had different names back then. I don't think Crawley changed his name until he got into trouble for cloning." I lean over and put the case of blocks in the corner of the box. If I don't start organizing it neatly, we will never be able to fit it all back inside. And besides that, it will eat at me. The plane looks a little on the delicate side, so I place it on top of the blanket.

"Attention passengers, this is your pilot speaking," a staticky voice echoes from the plane.

I must have hit a button.

Steve sticks his head over the top of the box and stares down at it.

"We will be arriving in Paradise soon. No need to buckle up. Seatbelts won't do any good in the triangle. Good luck." The voice stops.

"Was that your father talking?" I ask. "It sounded like a recorded message."

"How should I know?" Steve remarks, turning his attention to a three-ring binder with tattered and torn pages sticking out in different directions. As he picks it up, I notice the cover is black with no label or writing on the outside.

Curiosity overtakes me, or maybe it's hope. I'm not sure which, but the mystery of it draws me over beside him as he opens it. The first page has a picture of an older woman affixed to the top, and a heart has been hand-drawn around it. A printed memorial from a funeral is taped underneath it.

"Who..." I catch myself and let my voice trail off. "Never mind."

Steve rolls his eyes to the side, glaring at me without turning his head.

"Sorry." I smile. "Sometimes, my words come out before I think."

His glare doesn't move. "At least you caught yourself this time," he says, mixing a smile with the smirk on his face.

"It's not just you. I slip up with Eileen too. I know you all don't have memories of anything before that training facility, but I guess I need to work on being 'slow to speak.'" I smile back. I reach over his arm and flip open the printed memorial card. "Janice Denali."

"Huh." Steve points to the fine print under her name. "Look, it lists Dennis and Dukakis Denali as her grandchildren. Janice is my great-grandmother. It appears that she passed away when my dad was a child." His face contorts as he casts his eyes toward the ceiling. "If I did the math right, he would have been about ten or eleven."

I skim the words. "It sounds like she was a woman of astounding faith." I touch my finger to the heart around the photo. "He must have really loved her."

"Hard to imagine, isn't it?" Steve flips the page.

"A news article... 'Local Pastor Arrested and Charged With Driving While Intoxicated.'" I scan through the small words, but it is faded like the printer was almost out of ink. "This happened in California."

Steve shrugs and turns to the next page.

'Church Secretary Embezzles Thousands.' My eyes skitter across the page. "This is in Louisiana." I take my thumb and fan through the notebook. "This whole thing is news articles. Why would he make a scrapbook out of these?"

"If we understood my father's thinking, we wouldn't be sitting here searching for clues. What kind of clues are we expecting to find anyway? None of this is going to help find Tom and Alice." He grasps a whole cluster of pages and turns toward the back. "At least this one has a photo of a Navy assault ship on it."

"Well, I was going with Dukakis's wishful thinking in hopes that we might find something about Sivers or Seaver or whoever he is... or was. But I knew it was a long shot. Dukakis even said it wasn't likely that your father would have known him before college or that fraternity or cult or whatever they were in." I hear my own words as I speak. "This is so confusing." With a long sigh, I look down at the photo. "So, what's up with the boat?"

"It's not a boat. It's a military assault ship, and it disappeared. The last location the satellite picked up showed it about five hundred miles off the coast of Florida, and then it was gone. Search crews found no sign of the ship or the eight hundred and thirty-two crew members on board."

"That's horrible."

Steve closes the notebook. "This is going nowhere. Aside from my great-grandmother's photo, we have a one-eyed teddy bear with anger issues, baby stuff with frogs on it, blocks, a high school yearbook, an airplane headed for paradise, and a scrapbook of random news articles. Can we please go to bed?"

"Yes. Hopefully, we'll hear from Agent Morgan in the morning." I take the notebook from him and put it in the box. "Where are those tablets? That's the only way I'm going to sleep."

"In my pocket. I'll grab you a glass of water." Steve stands and crosses to the door. "Here. Don't forget to close this thing up in the box." He scoops up the bear and tosses it at me as he leaves the room.

I stick out my hand right before it whizzes past my head. Something hard inside the bear hits my fingers, bending them backward. The bear falls to the floor, and I grab my stinging fingers in my other hand. *A light toss would have been sufficient.* Somewhere between a half-bend and a half-squat, I manage to snatch the bear up. *What on earth is in this thing?* I run my hands over it, trying not to set off that angry growl. I fail and nearly jump out of my skin when the ferocious noise catches me off guard. I don't care though because I definitely feel something inside. I flip the bear over in my hands, searching for an opening. A second later, I slide open a zipper hidden amid the tattered fur and pull out a small study Bible and a journal.

Steve ambles back into the room holding a glass of water just as I sit in the rocking chair and flip open the Bible.

"What's that? I thought we were going to bed?" Lines form on his forehead.

"I found them inside the teddy bear that you hurled at me like a major league pitcher. It's your father's Bible and his journal."

"My father had a Bible?"

"Yes, he has even highlighted verses." I hold out the Bible, and he takes it from my hand. Then I turn my gaze down at the words scribbled in marker on the front of the journal.

Property of Dennis Denali
DO NOT TOUCH

Wondering if I should feel guilty for reading his private thoughts, I open the cover to the first entry. The words are printed in messy manuscript, obviously by a child's hand.

I had to stay with grandma and grandpa again today. Dukakis cried again when Mom tried to leave him, so he didn't stay. He always cries. Mom says it's because he's little, and when you're little, you want to stay close to your Mommy.

Grandma and I made sugar cookies, the kind you cut with the shape cutters. It's July, but I still wanted to decorate them like Christmas trees. It's fun to stick the little candies in the dough for the ornaments. But then, it happened again. And this time it was my fault. Because of the cookies, Grandma didn't have dinner ready when Grandpa came in from his meeting at the church. He always quotes that verse in the Bible about a wife submitting to her husband. He told me to go outside to play, but I could still hear him yelling at her. He doesn't know, but I could see him shoving her and hitting her through the window.

When I went inside for dinner, Grandma was locked in the bedroom. Grandpa said she was really sick, but not to tell anyone because she didn't want anyone to feel sorry for her. She was funny like that he said. And then he gave me a scary look, the kind that doesn't need words.

Something inside says I should tell someone, but I don't want Grandma to be mad at me. And I sure don't want Grandpa to be mad either.

I stare down at the page with tear-filled eyes. I know what the boy who wrote this grew up to become, but these words were written by a child, a child too young to have to deal with a secret so big.

And then it occurs to me. *This is where it started. This is where the enemy got his foot in the door.*

As I ponder on my new realization, I float back in time to that day in the kitchen when Dad finally spoke for the first time since Eileen had disappeared. It's as if I am a spectator in the front row, watching the scene play on the big screen.

Teresa had helped Steve, Alice, Eileen, Spencer, and me escape the facility so we could try to stop President Denali's plane from dropping the poison. At that point, she gave us each a folder that contained information about our real identities. The folders weren't that big of a deal for Alice and me because we had not lost our memory. However, Steve discovered in his folder that he was President Denali's son. We went to the White House because we thought that maybe someone would tell Steve where the plane was, but instead, Steve was taken hostage. Then Eileen and I realized after looking through our folders that our father must know about Denali's plan, so Alice, Eileen, Spencer, and I went to my parents' house to talk to him in hopes that he could tell us something that would help us find Steve and stop the plane. After two years of not saying a word, Dad sat on the kitchen floor rocking back and forth, detailing a conversation he had with President Denali as one of his legal advisors.

Goosebumps cover my arms as I hear Dad recalling Denali's words.

> 'Tom Hatcher, you are my personal legal advisor, so I know I can trust you. After all, our contract clearly holds you to the strictest confidentiality. And well, if you ever breathe a word of this, people will think you are crazy, and you will most definitely be locked away to work through the problems with your mental state. I will be using the facility to create what I suppose could be called my own personal army. The people who train there will be responsible for repopulating the Earth. I mean, Tom, you

see how much I have already done to make the United States a better place. But it is still so far from a perfect society. And you want to know what angers me, Tom? I will tell you what angers me. It is all these people who say they are Christians and followers of God. If this many people are Christians, how is the world in the state that it is in? Really, Tom, how can one claim to be a Christian yet curse, get drunk, lie, cheat, and steal like it is no big deal? Where is that Christian fruit I hear about? That is why my army will have no knowledge of God. Once I have a trained army that cannot even remember the God they once were so supposedly devoted to, I will destroy the rest of humanity. Then my followers will multiply, refilling the Earth, and we will have a perfect world.'

Blinking away the moisture blurring my vision, I vanish from my parents' kitchen floor and come back to the present, twisting and turning these new pieces of the puzzle around in my brain, pondering on how they fit. As a little boy, Dennis Denali heard his grandfather, someone he would have respected, claim to be a Christian, and he even heard him quote scripture. But then, young Dennis witnessed this same man hurting his grandmother. That little boy grew into a man still harboring a dark secret, the devil slipped in, and the actions of one man claiming to be a follower of God became a stereotype for all Christians. Over the years, the enemy used that pain and anger to blind Dennis Denali from the truth. I peer up at Steve as he thumbs through his father's Bible. Cynthia said that Dennis quoted that verse about a wife submitting to her husband. It seems that both Dennis and his grandfather forgot to read on because his grandfather certainly didn't exhibit the knowledge that he should be loving Janice 'as Christ also loved the church, and gave Himself for it.' But isn't that one of the devil's tactics?... To pick a verse out of context and use it to lead us into sin? Isn't that how he tried to tempt Jesus... by using scripture? I realize from the story my dad told on his kitchen floor that President Denali never denied the existence of God. But then again, neither does Satan. James 2:19 says, 'Thou believest that there is one God; thou doest well: the devils also believe, and tremble.' President Denali wanted to create a world that didn't know God. *Hmmm. Isn't that exactly what Satan wants?*

"Ellie." I shake from my trance to find Steve gawking at me with wide, worried eyes.

"I'm ready for those tablets," I say as I scoot to the edge of the chair.

"You look... troubled." He hands me the glass of water and two of the pills. "What's in that journal?"

"I only read the first entry." I pop the sleeping pills in my mouth and chase them down with a sip of water. "I think you should read it for yourself." I push up off the chair and place the book in his hands. "I'm going to brush my teeth and say my prayer before these pills kick in." I rock up on my tiptoes as best as I can, let my lips lightly brush his, and leave the room, staggering beneath the weight of my heavy thoughts.

CHAPTER EIGHTEEN

I awaken in darkness. Rough fabric like burlap scratches against my face, and chills cover the bare portions of my arms sticking out of my short-sleeved pajama top. I reach for the blanket, but nothing is there. In a state of half-consciousness, I pat in a circle with my hand, searching for the covers. But instead of soft sheets, my palm strikes something hard. *Mattress... where's the mattress...* My skin snags on a rough sliver, and a splinter stabs into the side of my hand. *Wood... why am I lying on wood?* Alert and in a panic, I glide my hand all around me, touching, feeling, slapping at the air until my fingers collide with a surface. *Boards. Boards are everywhere... surrounding me on four sides. I'm enclosed.* I gasp for air. *Why am I in a box?* In an effort to sit up, I push against the wood beneath me with all my might, but my body is too heavy or it's not responding. Something's wrong. I can't lift myself. *Oh no! The fabric. Something is covering my head... my face...*

I'm smothering. I claw at the fabric trying to rip it. Another gasp for air... my airway is closing... my heartbeat... it's thrumming, drumming, pounding.

"She's waking up. Hurry, we need more sedative before she hurts herself."

Who is that? "Wh-Wh-Who's there?" I stammer.

"You better calm down. Don't forget about the baby. You wouldn't want to go into labor now, would you?" a man warns in a passive, almost sarcastic tone.

That voice. I know that voice. Who is it? "Who are you? What are you doing to me?" I shout through the fabric.

"No need to yell. No one is going to hear."

"Please!" my voice breaks with a sob. "My baby. Please let me go." My words trail off as I tremble in a bag full of tears. "Why are you doing this?"

"You should be more careful who you trust."

My body shakes and heaves.

The voice keeps repeating, echoing in my head, fading a little each time, "careful who you trust... careful who you trust... careful who you trust."

I'm falling. My heart drops, and my elbows and knees smack against the floor. I grunt as the impact knocks all the breath from my lungs. In a panic, I scramble in the darkness to push myself up. I get up to my knees and make another attempt to tear away whatever it is that's covering my face. *Nothing.* I press my fingers against my cheeks. *Nothing. There is nothing on my head.* My eyes fix on the illuminated red numbers of the alarm clock. *Four o'clock. I was dreaming.* I exhale, letting out a soft groan. *Oh. Thank goodness. It was only a nightmare.*

I grab hold of the bedsheet and pull, rolling myself back onto the bed. Out of breath, I lie frozen on my side, clutching the pillow, still trying to absorb that none of the terror was real. *The sleeping pills. That's it. It must have been a side effect of those tablets. I've heard about people having hallucinations after taking sleep meds.*

I let go of the pillow with one hand and glide it across the sheet toward Steve. I don't want to wake him, but if I can get my fingers close enough to touch him, it'll help me relax. Inch by inch I move my fingers farther across the bed. *That's weird.* My arm stretches all the way. "Steve," I whisper. I don't care if I wake him anymore.

He doesn't answer.

"Steve," I say louder. My slowing heart goes back into a frenzy as I pat and then frantically slap all around on his side of the bed. *He's not here.* I swing my feet off the edge of the bed, push up onto my elbow, and click on the lamp. *His pillow is smooth. He hasn't been to bed.*

Adrenaline pumping, I leap from the bed, my heart racing so fast that my skin tingles. "Steve," I yell again, crossing the room to the door. *The journal. Maybe he stayed up reading his father's journal.* My bare feet slap against the wood floor, and as I turn down the hall, my lungs deflate, along with my hope. Not even a faint glow is coming from the baby's room. I trudge on and stop in the doorway. The room is silent and dark. A bit of light trickling down the hall from my bedroom highlights the faint outline of the box sitting in the middle of the floor and that weird teddy bear on the rug next to it... but no Steve.

Breathe. My ribs expand as I fill my lungs. *He wouldn't have left without telling me,* I try to assure myself. *His office. He has to be in there.* I plod out of the room toward the den that he uses for work. The moonlight through the front window gives just enough light to make my way through the living room. As I pass through, I glance at the sofa and into the kitchen, but all of the lights are off. Claude and Waves charge in the laundry room and don't activate until six o'clock unless something sets off an alarm outside. Herb's charging station is in Spencer's room. He is programmed to activate if Spencer moves.

At the sight of Spencer's room ahead, I slow my pace and step with marshmallow feet. The last thing I want is for him to wake up and start bouncing around. He's hyper and rambunctious if he doesn't get a whole night's sleep... more so than usual, which one would think impossible.

I'm not sure why I keep going because I can tell there are no lights on in the den either. Steve keeps the door closed so that Spencer and Waves... well, mostly Waves, will be reminded not to go in and mess with his inventions, but even with the door closed, a trickle of light would illuminate beneath it if he were in there. But since there is nowhere else that he could be, I block out my panic and hold on to wishful thinking as I twist the knob and push.

With my hand still clutching the knob, I stare into the black abyss of a lifeless room with no windows. My knees weaken. And I press my fingers to my temples. *Cynthia. Oh, no. Something has happened with Cynthia.*

I pad back to the bedroom as fast as I can and snatch up my phone. *Why didn't I think to call his phone to start with?* I tap the screen and thrust it to my ear. It rings and then something vibrates. Another ring... another vibration. *No.* I pivot on my heels in slow motion afraid to see what I know is there, but my eyes fall on it anyway. Steve's phone is lying on his nightstand with my name lit up on the screen.

Dukakis. He'll be with Cynthia. Steve was probably in such a hurry to get to the hospital that he forgot his phone.

I tap the screen, my breaths getting shorter and faster, and press it to the side of my face to steady the phone in my shaking hand.

"Hello. This is Dukakis, a sinner redeemed by grace. Leave a message, and I'll call you back."

The hospital. I type into the search bar as fast as I can and hit the call icon.

"First Care Memorial. How may I direct your call?"

"Yes. My name is Ellie Denali. Could you transfer me to Cynthia Denali's room? She is my mother-in-law. I-I'm sorry I don't know the room number," I stumble on my words as I realize that we left before she was moved out of the emergency room into a regular room.

"One moment please." The phone goes silent for a few seconds. "Ma'am. I don't see Cynthia Denali listed as a patient."

"She was brought into the ER yesterday with a gunshot wound. The doctor said they would be moving her, but maybe she's still in urgent care."

"Hold another moment and let me check." Music fills the line this time.

Hurry, please hurry. I rock back and forth on my heels, counting each movement to seven and starting over. I count so many times that I lose track before the operator finally comes back on the line.

"Ma'am. Sorry about the wait. What did you tell me your name was?"

"Ellie. Ellie Denali."

"Thank you. I thought that's what you said, but I had to be sure that Cynthia has you on the list of people we are allowed to disclose information to. And you are listed. She's not in the emergency room either. She was sent home under an outside doctor's care last night."

"Outside doctor? What outside doctor?" I mumble in confusion.

"Let me pull up the records. Oh. Here it is. Doctor Ted Flynn."

"Thank you."

I lower the phone and start to dial Cynthia when the time on the screen stops me. *I can't call her at four-thirty in the morning. She's recovering from a gunshot wound.* I drop the phone to my side. *Lord, help me. I don't know what to do. Would he have gone to Cynthia's house without waking me? The garage.* I jump to my feet and dash out of the room. *Why didn't I think to check if the car was here?*

I race down the hall, and almost trip over my own feet coming to an abrupt halt. The weight of my stomach pulls me forward, and I slam my hand against the wall to stop my fall. *How did I miss that a while ago? Why would that door be cracked?* The moonlight through the window must have shifted. Either that or I wasn't paying attention before because it's obvious now. Of course, why would I have paid attention to it? It's a dirt cellar. We never go down there. *Well, clearly, someone has.*

Opening the door wide enough to peer down into more darkness, I click the flashlight on my phone and shine it around until I find the pull string for the light above the stairs. The one little dim bulb doesn't really help, so I leave my phone light on and run my other hand along the dirt wall to sturdy myself as I ease down the uneven stone steps. The damp, musky smell tickles the inside of my nose, and I pause mid-step and rub it on my sleeve to stifle my sneeze.

At the bottom, the sound of something scurrying makes my heart leap, and I jump back up onto the last step. I shine my light toward the noise, but the critter is gone. Telling myself that it was only a tiny mouse and not a rat, I force my feet to move from the step down to the dirt floor. As I slowly shift the phone around the room, illuminating it bit by bit, the light glitters and bounces off of the few glass jars still sitting on the shelf that lines one of the walls. The home-canned jars of jelly and fruit were here when we discovered this old house. But that's all that was down here then.

As I continue shining the light around the walls, I notice some boxes stacked against the next one. I step closer and realize they contain electrical components and parts. *Oh. That has to be why the door was ajar. Steve is storing some of his work stuff down here, and he must have forgotten to close it.* Shrugging, I turn back toward the stairs to go and check the garage. As the phone rotates with my body, the light dances off something metallic in the back corner of the cellar. With a quick jerk of my hand, I shift the light back to the object. A small square table with metal legs and a brown vinyl top sit in a separate small cavity formed where the stairs take up a portion of the room.

Hmm. That wasn't here before either. Is he working down here now too? Surely not. It's dark down here. The only light is that little bulb dangling over the steps. I hold the light a little higher and take a few steps toward it. The table has a small laptop that I haven't seen before, a flashlight, a black permanent marker, and... *is that a rolling pin?* I take another step and pick up a small clear zipper bag from behind the rolling pin. *I don't understand. Why would this be here?* I move the light closer and flip the bag over and over. *Alice's engagement ring. Dad's credit card case with the white horse.* My mouth falls open as my eyes fix on the indention left by the bullet—the bullet Dad took saving Mom when we were trying to stop President Denali's plane from dropping the poison that would have eventually wiped out humanity.

I use my fingers to move the items inside the bag so I can see.

Eileen's cross necklace. As I stare at it, the image of Eileen at the hospital last night flashes in my head. Acid rises in my throat. *Eileen was wearing the necklace. I saw it when I hugged her.*

I drop the bag as I fling my hand up to cover my mouth. The light from the phone shifts onto the wall above the table. And I scream. My hand over my mouth does no good in suppressing it. The sound reverberates off of the underground walls. *No. Who did this?* I press my hand tighter over my mouth, but I can't hold it. My stomach lurches. Grabbing the edge of the table to keep from falling, I double over, pulling my hair out of the way with my other hand. Tears stream in rivers down my face as my sides heave and jerk.

Wiping my mouth with my sleeve, I lift my eyes back to the wall, staring at what looks like a scene from a movie about a serial killer. Photos are nailed to the dirt wall in a neat row. My muscles freeze in terror, and unblinking, I take in the sight of each one... my dad in the first photo... an 'X' drawn over his face in black marker... Alice in the next one... a black 'X' across her face... then Kate... her face blacked out with marker, scribbled over in large circles like a small child who hasn't yet learned to stay within the lines and has tried to use her face as a coloring book.

My eyes keep moving down the line. Gerald... an 'X' across his face. Eileen... an 'X.' Mom's face... an 'X.' Teresa... 'X.' Dukakis... marked with an 'X.' Cynthia... an 'X.' My photo... I suck in with a loud gasp for air. *My photo. That's me. What's going on?* I breathe in hard, but my airway is closing. With wide eyes, I gape at a photo of

myself... but it's different than the others. There are no markings... no
scribbling... no 'X.'

I glance back down the line of photos. *Dad, Alice, Kate, Gerald,
Eileen, Mom, Teresa, Dukakis, Cynthia, Me... There is no photo of Steve.*

Sweat beads up on my forehead, and chills run down my arms.
None of this makes sense. I scan the table again. In an adrenaline rush
torn between fear and anger, I pluck open the laptop and hit the power
button. A warning message flashes on the screen.

'Thumbprint and Retina Scan Required.
Ten seconds remaining.'

The numbers flash on the screen counting backward.

'Nine.'

'Eight.'

'Seven.'

'Six.'

'Five.'

'Four.'

'Three.'

'Two.'

'One.'

'NAC Security Protection Process Activated.'

What in the world does that mean? I ask myself just as tiny wisps of smoke begin to rise from the cracks between the letters on the keyboard. As more and more smoke seeps out, the keys buckle and warp. And then they bubble up and melt, and within a few seconds, the entire keyboard liquifies. The hot, steaming, black liquid oozes in a stream and runs off the edge of the table onto the floor until the entire computer appears to be nothing more than a greasy spot in the dirt.

I turn and jog up the stairs, catching my big toe on the lip of the stone on the top step. I don't stop, but I'm pretty sure it's bleeding. I dart to the door going into the garage, jerk it open, and breathe a half-sigh of relief. The Hydromax is parked right in front of me. *But where could he be? I've searched the entire...* My lungs deflate, and the urge to retch hits me again. The other side of the garage is empty. The Volkswagen Bug is gone.

The photographs... in our cellar... Steve's photo wasn't there. All the others had an 'X,' I gulp, *except mine.*

I lift my phone and tap on the call button for Gerald. It doesn't ring.

"Hello. This is Gerald. I'm not available..."

I end the call and tap on Eileen. It goes straight to voicemail.

"Sorry, I missed your call..."

I sway and fall against the door casing. *Mom. Please, Mom answer.*

"You have reached Jillian Hatcher. Please leave me a detailed..."

"Teresa," I mumble in desperation.

"Hello. You have reached Teresa. I am not a doctor, but I will still..."

My bottom lip trembles. I flip around, pressing my back to the wall, and close the door.
Dukakis. Come on. Dukakis, pick up.

"Hello. This is Dukakis, a sinner redeemed by grace. Leave..."

I'm dreaming. This is another nightmare. Please let this be a nightmare. I hit the icon for Cynthia.

"Hello. Cynthia Denali cannot take your call at this time. But be assured that I will return..."

Lord, I'm scared. Please help me. Where is Steve? Why would he leave without telling me? I squeeze my eyes closed and press my lips together. My shoulders shake, tapping against the wall behind me. *Herb... Spencer...*

I plow down the hallway, sounding like a squeaky bicycle as a whimper escapes my mouth with each step. No longer afraid of waking Spencer, I burst into his room. Herb doesn't move, and through the soft glow of the nightlight, the blanket on Spencer's bed is flat, too flat for a monkey to be tucked beneath it.

"Spencer," I call out, running my hands over his bed. He's not here. "Spencer," I cry louder. I turn back to Herb. *Why isn't he activating? Spencer's gone.* "Herb." I wave my hands in front of his face and then push on his chest, but he doesn't move.

I sprint to the kitchen, passing through it to the laundry room. "Claude, Waves!"

My hand flicks the switch as soon as I thrust the door open. "Claude... Waves... please."

They both stand like concrete statues without even a twinkle in their robotic eyes. I push on the cord to Claude's charger, but the connection is snug.

My heart falls like an anchor being tossed into the deepest part of the ocean, and my head is being pulled under the water with it. Pressure pushes inside my ears. My vision blurs. I can't breathe. *I'm alone. All alone.* My legs give out beneath me as reality sets in, and I crumple to the floor, shaking as if the fault line in Death Valley has opened and the earth is swallowing me alive.

"No!" I scream in agony. "Lord, why is this happening?" I cry out between my loud wails. *My family... my friends... where are they? What do those pictures mean?* My phone slips from my fingers as I wrap my arms around my torso and collapse onto my side. *Where is Steve? He wouldn't leave me.* My knees pull up as I curl my head down, and my body vibrates against the cold, hard tile floor with every sob. I lie there wallowing in self-pity, my shoulders heaving, my tears flooding onto the floor, my throat burning from the combination of the rising bile from my stomach and the bellows erupting through my lips.

This has to be a nightmare. Wake up. I need to wake up. With my right hand, I dig into my left forearm with my fingernails, pinching and twisting. *Wake up. I have to wake up.*

I yelp in pain. It's not working. I'm still lying on a cold slab in a sea of despair and loneliness, so deep below the surface that the weight of the water is crushing me. *Lord, please help me. I don't want to be alone. Take me too. I don't want to live without Steve... without my family.* I pull my shirt up into my mouth and bite the fabric. *No. I'm overreacting. Steve will be back.* My tears stop. My body trembles from head to toe, but the tears are gone. There is none left. *What am I going to do?*

What are you going to do? You're alone... all alone... all alone. Everyone you love is gone. You're alone. The whispers repeat, getting louder and louder in my mind until they are shouting. *Alone... alone... all ALONE.*

Clenching my hands into fists, I squeeze my eyelids together and clamp my teeth down on my shirt as hard as I can. *Steve wouldn't leave me,* I mutter inside my head, battling against the voice.

Then, where is he? He's not here, is he?

Stop. Stop. I spit the edge of the shirt from my mouth. "Shut up!" I yell, clutching the sides of my face. The baby kicks up into my ribs, turning my yell into a high-pitched shriek and sending my hands down, pressing against my abdomen. *My baby... I have to pull myself together. 'And call upon me in the day of trouble: I will deliver thee, and thou shalt glorify me.'* Psalm 50:15 creeps into my mind and pushes my eyes open. *I'm not alone. All I have to do is call out to Him. He will never leave me nor forsake me.*

Father, I need help. I don't know what's going on. I don't under-stand why this is happening. But I know you're in control, and you will work this out for good. Please give me strength and show me what to do. Please let my family be safe and help me to find them. Please bring Steve back to me. Lord, I know that I'm not supposed to be afraid, but I am. I really am. Please wrap me in your arms. Help me to be brave.

I roll onto all fours and shift up to my knees. *Agent Morgan. Maybe he'll answer. Maybe he can help me locate Steve.* I glide my hand across the floor, twisting back and forth, searching for my phone, which turns out to be underneath me.

My eyes are irritated from crying so hard, and I have to squint to see the screen. I locate Agent Morgan's contact and press the phone to my ear.

It's ringing. That's a good sign.

"Ellie," Agent Morgan answers in a sleepy voice. "What's wrong? Do you know what time it is?"

"Yes. I'm sorry, but I need help. Please, you have to help me," I ramble into the phone.

"Calm down. Tell me what's wrong."

"Steve's missing. Alice is missing. Dad's missing. I've called everyone else, and no one is answering. I think they're all missing too." My voice cuts out as I talk as fast as I can. "And someone has been in our basement."

"Is anyone in the house now?" His voice is filled with alarm.

"No. I don't think so. But the robots aren't even activating, and I can't find Spencer." I realize my statements must seem random and off the wall.

"Just hold tight. I'm on my way." Concern echoes through his tone. "Are you able to watch for me and let me in?"

"Yes. How long will it be?"

The sound of his car starting filters through the line. "Less than fifteen minutes. Ellie. Try to relax. Everything's going to be alright."

"Just please hurry." I put the phone down.

Be strong. God commands me to be strong. 'Have I not commanded thee? Be strong and of a good courage; be not afraid, neither be thou dismayed: for the Lord thy God is with thee whithersoever thou goest.' My posture stiffens as I say Joshua 1:9 in my head. That was the verse on the note Steve gave me the day we met. He had jotted down the verse right after the words... *Never Forget.* I lift my eyes toward the ceiling.

I will never forget. Thank you, Father, for reminding me that I'm not alone. I know you're with me wherever I go. You've always been with me, and you always will be. I am weak, but through you, I am strong. Please carry me, Lord. Carry me through this fire.

I push to my feet with renewed determination, slide my phone into my pajama pants pocket, and walk out of the laundry room repeating Philippians 4:13 out loud, increasing my volume with every recitation. "I can do all things through Christ which strengtheneth me. I can do all things through Christ which strengtheneth me. I can do all things through Christ which strengtheneth me. I can do all things through Christ which strengtheneth me. I can do all things through Christ which strengtheneth me. I can do all things through Christ which strengtheneth me. I CAN DO ALL THINGS THROUGH CHRIST WHICH STRENGTHENETH ME!"

With power in my steps, I stride into the bedroom, round the bed to my nightstand, and clutch my Bible in one hand and my gun in the other. I lift my Bible and press it to my chest, remembering the words written by my mother's hand inside the front cover. "*'Thy Word is a lamp unto my feet, and a light unto my path.' My dearest Ellie, read the words of this book and record them in your heart. Remember, even in the darkness, you are never alone.*" When my mom gave me this Bible, I was a ten-year-old girl afraid of the dark. And here I am, about to be a mother myself, standing in the dark. I squeeze my Bible tighter. *And I am not alone.*

CHAPTER NINETEEN

Through the front window, I stand in the dark living room, watching the lights come up the drive. He must have broken quite a few speed laws getting here. *He said less than fifteen minutes, but it hasn't even been ten.*

I know it has to be Agent Morgan, but to play it safe, I wait and continue looking out the window. I want to be sure it's him before I move to the door because the fact that they weren't in here the second the car turned onto our driveway added confirmation that Claude and Waves aren't functioning.

The car stops in front of the porch steps, and the headlights blink out. The black sedan now blends with the night sky. Apparently, the motion-activated security lights aren't working either. We used to only have two flood lights, one on each end of the house, but after we escaped from the facility the last time and made it back home,

Steve beefed up the security features. Since then, if anyone or anything moves within a hundred feet of the house, the exterior lights up like a spaceship in the middle of an airport runway.

Still clutching my Bible to my chest with my left hand, I take a couple of sidesteps, flip the switch to the porch light with the tip of the gun in my right hand, and slide back to the window. The car door opens, and Agent Morgan's head pops up beside the car. As he closes the door, he appears to be scanning the surroundings. He starts onto the porch, and I get a clear view of his face along with the semi-automatic in his hand.

Leaving the window, I dart to the door and pull it open before he has a chance to ring the bell. "Thanks for coming. I'm sorry for calling in the middle of the night."

He steps inside. "It's okay. I could tell by the tone of your voice that it was an emergency."

I flip on the light as he moves on into the living room. I had left it off before so I could see outside through the window.

Agent Morgan turns to face me with his elbow bent, keeping his gun aimed at the ceiling. "What's this about Steve being missing and the basement?"

I let out a breath, trying to figure out where to begin without rambling. "Steve already told you part of the story on the phone last night... how my dad is missing, and the texts to my mom appear to be coming from my dad's phone, but they're not. And then the same thing happened with Alice. She took off, and Gerald received some texts from her. But when Kate traced them, the messages weren't sent from Alice's phone. Then I gave Kate the addresses in Dad's envelope, and she got killed in that explosion. Well, after Steve talked to you, I took some tablets that the doctor gave me to help me rest. But instead of peaceful sleep, I had a nightmare. When I woke up, Steve wasn't here, and his side of the bed hadn't even been touched." My eyes water as I listen to myself pour out the details, and I battle the urge to burst into tears. "I looked all over the house, thinking he must have stayed up working or fallen asleep somewhere. That's when I discovered the photos on the basement wall." I lift my hand and wipe under my eyes with the knuckle of my index finger.

"Photos?" he mumbles in a questioning tone.

"Individual pictures of Dad, Mom, Alice, Gerald, Kate, Teresa, Eileen, Dukakis, Cynthia, and me are hanging in a row. All of them have marks on their faces except mine, and Kate's photo is scribbled all the way through. There is a bag with items in it that belong to them, such as Alice's engagement ring and Eileen's necklace." Short-winded from my speedy summary, I suck in for air and continue. "The Volkswagen is gone, but we never drive that because gas is so hard to come by. I can't find Spencer anywhere. None of the robots are activating, and the security system doesn't appear to be working." I realize that I am waving the gun in the air, and I lower it to my side.

Agent Morgan's mouth is agape, and his eyes are protruding from his head.

I try to slow my speech, but as Teresa would say 'Time is of the essence.' Nevertheless, I continue at a somewhat lower rate of words per second. "Steve is gone. I know he wouldn't leave, not right now, without telling me. His phone is by his bed. I have tried calling my mom, my sister, Gerald, Teresa, Dukakis, and Cynthia. Their phones don't ring. It goes straight to voicemail like their phones are either off or don't have a signal."

I stop talking, a little concerned because Agent Morgan's facial expression has not changed, and he is not moving.

"Agent Morgan?"

He shifts his eyes down toward the gun at my side.

"Agent Morgan?" I repeat.

"Ellie, first, I think you should let me take your gun. You seem a bit distressed." He reaches toward my hand.

"My gun is fine. And, of course, I'm distressed. My entire family and my best friends are all missing, including my husband." My face burns from the blood rushing to my cheeks.

"All the same, I think it's best if you let me hold it, and you have a seat." He slips it from my hand and guides me to the couch. "Now, if we can back up to the beginning because I'm lost." He tucks my gun in the waistband of his slacks and sits down next to me. "You said Steve told me the story last night, but I didn't talk to Steve. Well, except at the hospital, but—"

"No," I interject, "he called you when we got home. You told him you would check out the addresses because Kate was involved."

"I'm sorry, Ellie. I haven't talked to Steve since we left the hospital. You must have misunderstood."

"I didn't misunderstand." I try to hold in my frustration. "He even said you were a little upset at first because you couldn't believe that we were rehashing the nonsense about Dennis Denali being alive."

"I have no idea what Steve told you, but we didn't speak on the phone last night." He persists as he runs his hand through his dark hair and then smooths it back down.

I stare at his face for a second, not meaning to be rude. I had never noticed the small scar on his forehead before. I look away, hoping he didn't notice.

"Maybe he told you that to calm you down. Were you upset?" he prods in a tone that almost sounds like an interrogation.

"Of course, I was upset." I pinch the bridge of my nose and lower my voice. "I had found out that Kate had been killed, and I was worried about my dad and Alice. But he still wouldn't have lied to me about talking to you."

He lets out an exasperated sigh. "Right now, the point is moot. We need to figure out what's going on." His eyebrows pull together, and his forehead wrinkles. "You were talking a mile a minute but let me see if I can put some of the pieces together." He pauses, tapping his fingers on his chin. "I caught something about your dad having a list of addresses, and then later on, you mentioned rehashing Dennis Denali being alive. So, is it safe to assume your father was doing some detective work on his own?"

"I think that's a safe assumption," I answer.

"Is it also safe to assume that the warehouse where Kate was killed was one of the addresses on the list?" he questions in a matter-of-fact tone.

"I'm fairly certain."

Agent Morgan looks straight ahead and nods. "Alright. In the basement, you saw photos hanging on the wall and a bag of stuff belonging to the people you believe are missing." He turns his head toward me. "Before today, when was the last time you were down there?"

"Probably when we moved in. It's a dark, musky, dirt cellar. Why would we want to go down there?"

"So, you wouldn't know how long the photos have been there?"

I don't answer. I'm not trying to be difficult or rude. I just don't see what difference it makes.

He presses his hands down on his knees and rises to his feet. "I'm going to check it out. Will you be alright for a minute?"

"I'll go with you," I say, wiggling my way off the couch.

He puts his hand under my elbow, steadying me, and at the same time, gives me a boost.

Once I get my footing, I wrap both arms around my Bible and plod toward the hall that passes by the kitchen. "It's this way."

I pull open the door and realize that I left the small light bulb above the steps on.

Agent Morgan peers down at the natural steps carved out of stone that lead into darkness. "This is the only light?"

"Yes. I used the flashlight on my phone before." I slip it from my pants pocket.

He nods and pulls his phone out, swiping the screen with his thumb.

I follow him down the stairs but wait on the bottom step as he trudges over to the table. I don't want to see it again. The image etched in my mind is bad enough.

A moment later, he eases back to the stairs. "Ellie, let me help you back up to the living room. I think we need to talk."

His solemn expression worries me. That and the fact he wants to talk instead of going to look for Steve. "Thanks, but I don't need help." I turn, pressing my shoulder against the wall for stability, and tread up the steps.

Agent Morgan trudges behind me back into the living room, his boots clomping against the floor. Any other time, someone wearing shoes in the house spreading germs on the floor would cause me distress, but right now, my mind is too preoccupied with bigger worries to care.

I don't feel like having to get back up off of that soft couch, so I sit in one of the armchairs. Agent Morgan doesn't bother to take a seat. Instead, he squats beside my chair, slips my phone from my fingers, and lays it on the table. Then he reaches back and takes hold of my hand.

"Ellie," he utters, staring at the floor, "I'm aware that you aren't supposed to be under any stress, but considering what's happening, I don't know how it's avoidable. Sugar coating it is only going to procrastinate the inevitable. I think at this point, the best thing I can do is be honest." He swallows, turning his gaze up toward me. His lips are straight, and the only lines on his face are from age. "Have you considered that maybe Steve is not the person you think he is?"

"What do you mean?" I retort as his question takes me by surprise.

"I know you love him. But I want you to have an open mind and look at all the facts from an objective point of view."

I glare at him through narrowed eyes. "What facts?"

"Well, to begin with, he is missing, and one of your vehicles is gone." He lifts one eyebrow. "It seems pretty clear that he left of his own free will."

"That doesn't mean anything," I state without breaking eye contact. "Both Dad's car and Alice's car are gone. We don't know about the others because we haven't checked."

"I'm not finished. As I said, let's examine all of the facts," he holds up his index finger, "like that Steve is the only person with access to the basement besides you."

"Maybe he was trying to do research and find Dad and Alice without upsetting me," I choke out in a trembling voice.

"Then how do you explain the bag of items?" he counters back.

I don't answer. I don't have an answer.

He continues. "You also stated that the security system isn't working, and neither are the robots... A security system that Steve designed and knows how to disable... And robots that only he knows how to program."

Anger at his insinuation boils inside of me, and I bite my lips together in an effort to keep any words from bubbling out that I might regret. After a few seconds, I try to choose my words with care. "Agent Morgan, I asked you to come and help me. My husband, my family, and my best friends could be in serious danger. You have no right to implicate Steve. He is a Christian man with a strong faith in God. I believe that was evident when his father couldn't force him to forget his faith. Steve had written down a notebook full of verses from the Bible after his memory was erased. On top of that, Steve has more than proven his love and devotion to me. I have no reason to ever doubt him."

He keeps his tone calm and collected and slows his speech as if that's what it takes for me to understand. "I get that you don't want to have doubts about your husband, but, Ellie, you are a professional in law enforcement. You have had in-depth training in assessing a crime scene and examining evidence." He releases my hand and grips the arm of my chair. "So, answer me this. Do you see any other possible explanation?"

"I know my husband. And I know he wouldn't go anywhere in the middle of the night without telling me, and he certainly wouldn't leave me, his pregnant wife," I spout through gritted teeth, "alone sleeping in this house without the security system fully operational."

Agent Morgan pushes to his feet and steps over to the front window. "You're blinded by love. The evidence is as large as a billboard, and it's illuminated with flashing lights right in front of your face. Did you really think he would choose you over his flesh and blood? When you met him, he was working in his father's training facility. He wasn't frozen like the others who didn't forget about God. No, instead, he was working there programming robots that inserted chips into the trainee's heads. Sweetheart, that man has been playing with your mind and toying with your emotions from the beginning."

"Agent Morgan," I stand without even having to push myself up, "I want you to give me my gun, and then I want you to leave. Somehow, I will figure this out myself."

"As an officer sworn to protect, I can't give you your gun, Ellie. You are in no frame of mind to be handling a weapon, and you're not staying here alone. I want you to get some things and come with me. We'll figure it out together."

"Give—me—my—gun," I enunciate. "I have done nothing wrong, and I'm in my own house on my own property... which is where I am staying."

He presses his hand to his forehead. "Why are you being so difficult? Don't you understand? A better future, a new world, it starts here. We have to work together."

I freeze. My heart drums in my ears, and fear pulses through my veins, making my head spin. My muscles go lax, but I tighten my grip. I will not let go of my Bible. *Breathe. In... Out.* I blink, bringing the room back into focus. "Agent Morgan," I say in a low, quavering voice as I let my eyes examine the scar on his head again, "I am not working with anyone who would make false accusations about my husband. Now, please leave."

"You don't have a choice," he says in a firm tone with no emotion.

"Excuse me?" I glance back at the table. My phone is gone.

"You don't have a choice. You either go willingly, or I will have to use force." He takes a step toward me. "And you should know from experience that I'm not afraid to use force."

I ease my foot behind me and creep backward. "Would you really hurt a pregnant woman?"

"I'll do whatever is necessary." He moves a step closer.

"Where's Steve? What have you done to him?" I continue the game of cat and mouse, shifting another foot back.

"Ellie, wake up. Look around you." He extends his arms. "The man of your dreams has been playing you for a fool. You're all alone."

All alone echoes in my ears. Shaking my head, I shift backward again. "No, it's you who has been playing everyone for a fool. A ravening wolf in sheep's clothing. What's your real name? I'm sure it's not Damon or Damien."

"I don't know what you're talking about. You know my name is Allen Morgan. All the stress is making you delusional." He places his gun in his holster. "Come on, and let's get you a few things to take with you. We need to hurry up and get out of here. There's no telling what that husband of yours has planned. This place could be set to explode any minute."

"Dad was right." I stare him dead in the eyes. "You said that you couldn't find anyone by the name of Dr. Damien Seaver. You tried to convince us that he wasn't a real person... that it was Dr. Eckert all along." My shoulders stiffen. "I guess at least part of it wasn't a lie. Dr. Damien Seaver isn't a real person. It's an alias. Tell me, Agent Morgan, how many aliases do you have?"

Lines form in the middle of his forehead as he stares at me.

When he doesn't speak, I keep going. "Allen Morgan, Damon Sivers... how many other identities do you have? You were missing for a long time. You must have a ton of other names?"

"Wow. You have quite the imagination. I think you're in the wrong line of work," he taunts.

"Did you meet Dennis Denali at Fahrenhall University, or did you know him before that?" I continue to prod.

He laughs. "You think I was acquainted with President Denali in college? Now, I know you're delusional."

"A better future, a new world... sounds an awful lot like that fraternity motto. And the scar on your forehead... pretty slick having such a distinguishing mark removed." I swallow, forcing myself to keep my tears at bay. "How about Aiden Carraban? Was he the first person you murdered?" My eyes widen, and I almost gasp at the sudden revelation. "Kate. It was you," I repeat my thoughts out loud. "She never planned to go there alone. It was you that she was supposed to meet at three-fifteen."

His face hardens. "Think you're pretty clever, don't you?"

Snapping myself out of shock, I press on, not letting his change in expression shake me. "No. No. I would have to say you are the clever one. How on earth did you ever get a job working for Homeland Security?"

"You seem to be on a roll. Why don't you tell me?" Sarcasm floods through his tone.

I'm not sure how it comes to me, but I'm already spouting off an explanation before I even process the connected dots in my mind. "The buddy system. Good old President Denali got you the job, didn't he? I bet you didn't even have to work your way up. You started as a supervisory agent."

"Oh, give me a break," he puffs and rolls his eyes. "Don't you think you're reaching just a bit? You work for the Federal Bureau of Investigation. You know first-hand the scrutiny we go through. The interviews, the background checks... our entire lives are looked at under a microscope." He tilts his head and curves up one side of his mouth. "Do you honestly think I could just waltz in and slide into a supervisory position without credentials?"

He has a point, I acknowledge to myself. *But I know I'm right. Come on. Think... think. Don't show weakness now. He can't believe that he's causing me to doubt my theory. How could President Denali have gotten a man with an alias who was wanted for questioning in at least one murder case a management position with Homeland Security? Am I wrong? Is his name really Allen Morgan? Maybe.* I glower at him without batting an eye, keeping up my strong façade. *No. The smug look on his face says I'm on to something.*

"Ellie," he places his left hand on the wall and leans against it, "we need to go."

That's it. The light at the top of the Christmas tree finally illuminates. *President Denali didn't do anything without it aiding his personal agenda.* "President Denali's system that ended identity theft, the genius plan that gained him support from the entire nation... it was never about protecting the American people. He would never do anything to help the citizens that he was planning to kill. It was about giving him the power to change people's identities. Once I entered that facility, he erased my past, changed my birthdate, and gave me a new name with a new birth certificate. My thumbprint suddenly said I was Sarah Sanguine from Greenville, South Carolina. And he made you Allen Morgan with a fake resume hefty enough to put you in the position that he needed you in."

Agent Morgan takes his hand off the wall, straightening his stance and stretching taller. He pushes up his sleeves, and with flaring nostrils, he moves toward me.

"One piece of the puzzle is still missing though," I keep on. "Why did you give up Dr. Eckert? He received the death penalty."

"He didn't follow orders and was no longer needed." He grasps my upper arm in a firm grip.

"Orders?"

He jerks me around, facing away from him, and then pushes me down the hall.

I push back, digging my heels in with as much force as I can to slow my steps, but his weight and strength against mine are no match. My feet slide across the slick wood floor in the hall.

"Eckert was not supposed to put you in any danger or do anything that could harm the baby. The child inside of you is a direct descendant of Dennis Denali. Eckert ignored instructions, hooked you up to that reprimanding thing, and then put you in that room with a maniac programmed to kill."

My muscles tighten, and I lock my legs. "How did you know I was pregnant? I didn't even know I was pregnant." I scrunch up my face in confusion. "And you watched one of your goons slam me down on the kitchen floor and bury his knee in my back. If you knew..."

"I didn't know then," he hisses through bared teeth. "Cy discovered it in his analysis during transport."

"Who's Cy?"

"The generic tin-can-looking robot that inserted the wire in your head." He moves behind me and uses his other hand against my back to thrust me through the bedroom door. "Now, if you intend to have a change of clothes, let's pack a bag." He releases my arm from his grip.

"So, that's why you gave me that disc." My pitch rises, echoing my sudden epiphany. "You wanted me alert in case someone tried to hurt me... for the sake of the baby, of course, not mine."

"I've had enough of your detective work," he barks, pointing to the closet off of the bathroom. "Get a change of clothes... only clothes. Leave the book."

"Are you referring to my Bible? Because it's not just a book. It's God's Holy Word, '...quick and powerful, sharper than any two-edged sword, piercing even to the dividing asunder of soul and spirit, and of the joints and marrow, and is a discerner of the thoughts and intents of the heart.'"

"It's a book," he retorts. "Leave it."

"If it's only a book, why does it bother you if I bring it?" I turn and glower at him.

"If you are the Christ follower you say you are, then I'm sure you are familiar with Psalm 119:11, 'Thy Word have I hid in mine heart...'

If you have done that, you shouldn't need the book," he says with a smirk. "I'm not telling you again. Get your clothes."

"No."

"Pardon me." He rests his hand on the grip of his nine-millimeter.

"You haven't told me where Steve, my family, and my friends are."

"That would be a question for your husband." He slips the gun from the holster. "You saw the evidence in the basement."

A door slams and several sets of footsteps filter from the living room.

"Are you happy, now? Backup has arrived. And sadly, those guys don't have the calm, easy-going disposition that I have," Agent Morgan chuckles. "Various unfortunate events have left them with a bit of a short fuse, especially when they encounter your kind," he adds emphasis to the last part of his sentence.

A middle-aged man, with unkempt, wavy, red hair and a beard, stomps into the room. Scars cover one side of his face. "You didn't show. We figured you needed help." One side of his mouth doesn't move, causing his speech to slur.

"She's being a bit difficult, but nothing I couldn't have handled alone," Agent Morgan replies.

Another man with blonde hair just long enough to pull into a ponytail appears in the doorway. "We need to move. The plane is ready," he sputters out while chomping on a wad of gum. His eyes fall on me, and he strides on into the room past the red-haired man and Agent Morgan. "What's the hold-up? Little lady not cooperating." He yanks my Bible from my hands and tosses it on the bed. "She will now." He jerks my arms behind my back.

I scan the room, looking for anything I could use as a weapon. My heart sinks. *Against three men. I don't have a chance against all three of them.*

"Hold on. I have to get her a change of clothes." Agent Morgan moves toward the closet. "Don't be too rough with her. Remember the purpose of the assignment."

Lord, please help me. Help me to be strong for my son. I know you wouldn't allow me to be in this situation if it wasn't in your plan. Show me what to do. "Why are you doing this? Where are you taking me?" I shout.

The red-haired man grabs a pillow from the bed and pulls off the case. "We don't have time for questions." He caps the pillowcase over my head and starts tying it snugly around my neck.

"What's the purpose of the pillowcase?" Another man's voice says as more footsteps pound toward me.

"If she can't see where she's going, she can't put up as much of a fight."

"Take it off."

Who is that? I know that voice.

"I said to take it off. She doesn't need her oxygen restricted. She's a petite woman, and she's eight months pregnant. Exactly how much of a fight are you expecting?"

Ted. The pillowcase lifts from my head, and his face is right in front of me. "H-H-owww..." I try to question Ted, but the man behind me twists my arms further behind my back. I press my lips together and clench my hands into fists, trying to block the pain, but it feels like my shoulders are going to rip from their sockets any second.

Ted's features harden. "Why are you being so aggressive with her? Hurting a pregnant woman doesn't make the world a better place. Try to remember what our group stands for."

"G-Group. What gr-group?" I stammer as the man still hasn't loosened his grip. "Wh-why are you doing this?"

"New Alpha Cosmos. We are part of a movement to create a new and better world. One without people pretending to be someone they're not," Ted answers in a passive, matter-of-fact tone as he takes the pillowcase away from the red-haired man and drops it to the floor.

"You used my sister," I can't help but yell, and in my anger, I manage to loosen my arms a little.

"You should be happy we're here. We're trying to save your baby," Ted remarks.

"Save my baby?"

"You have to see what's happening. It won't be long before society wipes itself out. Then, we can start over." He shifts his gaze to my stomach. "The leader of our operation says your baby will play a key role in our new society, so we have to get you somewhere safe until he is born." He takes his hand and wipes the sweat from his forehead.

For the first time, I notice this hollow look in his eyes. "Ted, I know you told us that story about your father. I can't imagine how difficult it must have been... and still is for you, but you can't cast the blame on the entire world because of one person's actions."

"It's not just one person. Look at the stats. How many people in this country identify themselves as Christians?" He points to the window. "Then check out what's going on out there." The corners of his lips sag. "Does it look like seventy percent of our population is practicing what they preach? Not a lot of loving thy neighbor going on, is there?"

"Ted, I don't know if you've read the Bible, but it speaks about this. In Matthew, chapter seven, Jesus warns, 'Beware of false prophets, which come to you in sheep's clothing, but inwardly they are ravening wolves.' A few verses later, He goes on to say, 'Not every one that saith unto me, Lord, Lord, shall enter into the kingdom of heaven; but he that doeth the will of my Father which is in heaven.'"

Ted's eyes appear to be glued to my lips as I speak, and the other two men stand frozen in silence. *Lord, please open their hearts and minds. Please speak through me and help them to hear your words.*

"See, Ted, God tells us in His Word that people are going claim to be Christians that aren't. But you can tell who the real children of God are by their fruit, the ones who are doing the will of God. Sure, Christians are going to make mistakes and sin and mess up, but not intentionally over and over. True followers of Christ desire to be like Jesus." I lower my voice as tears pool in my eyes. "If you think

8236

that creating a world without God is going to make things better, you might want to think again. All humans are innately sinful. Violence and evil won't go away. It'll get worse."

The man with red hair grunts, and in a fit of anger, he wraps his hand in my hair and yanks, snapping my head backward. "Why are you being nice to her, Ted? She's one of them. Listen at her, quoting scripture like she's better than us."

"Yeah, I know," Ted mumbles.

"I'm not..." He jerks my hair again, making my neck pop.

Agent Morgan strides back from the closet carrying my overnight bag. "I was trying to choose some clothes, but I found this bag that was already packed, toothbrush and all."

A stream trickles down the side of my face toward my ear as my head is pulled backward. *Steve made me pack a bag, so I'd be ready when I went into labor. Steve, where are you? I need you.*

"Let's move," Agent Morgan orders.

Ted turns and plods toward the door, and Agent Morgan follows with the strap of my small duffel bag across his shoulder.

The red-haired man yells at Ted. "Hey, Doc. I thought you were supposed to sedate her."

"Not until we get to the plane." He glances over his shoulder. "Do you really want to have to carry a pregnant woman?"

"Let go. I got her," the blond ponytail guy barks to the bearded man pulling my hair.

"I didn't hear anybody put you in charge." He lets go with a wad of my hair still attached to his fingers. He takes a step and scowls at me with narrowed eyes and his nose crinkled in disgust. "You make me sick," he snarls through one side of his mouth, and then as he walks away... he spits... on me.

My body is paralyzed. *I can't breathe.* I inhale but only get a tiny bit of air. "Get it off," I mumble. "I have to get it off." I squeeze my eyes closed. *It's only on my shirt. Please... I have to get a clean shirt.*

"Move your legs, lady." The man behind me shoves my arms into my back, thrusting me forward.

I can't make my legs move, and I tumble onto my knees. The man is still holding my arms, and I scream as pain tears through my shoulders from my wrists being wrenched over my head behind me.

Ted, Agent Morgan, and the other man dart back into the room.

"I thought you had her," the red-bearded man scowls.

"I did until you spit on her," the man holding me shoots back.

"Please let me change my shirt... please," I beg.

Agent Morgan strides over. "Let go of her," he orders the blonde-haired man. "Go find her shoes," he barks after the man as he reaches down and pulls me up.

"Please," I whisper, "let me change my shirt."

"No," Agent Morgan snaps. "You have wasted enough of our time. It's your own fault these guys are even here. Now, move!" he yells in a voice loud enough to be a drill sergeant and jerks me forward by my left arm.

The other men go on in front of us. Using my one free hand, I hold my shirt out, so it doesn't touch my skin, and then on quaking legs, I falter from the room beside Agent Morgan. My tingling feet drag across the floor, and I fear my shaking knees are going to collapse.

Use your sword, Ellie, I remind myself. *Use your sword. 'Though I walk in the midst of trouble, thou wilt revive me: thou shalt stretch forth thine hand against the wrath of mine enemies, and thy right hand shall save me.'* A stab pierces through my chest into my soul. *The baby's room.* I know I shouldn't look. It will only make the hurt worse, but I can't help but peer in as I walk by. The room is barely illuminated by the light from the living room that is trickling down the hall and through the doorway. *Steve worked so hard... the train, the wardrobe, the bassinet..., and our son will never get... the bassinet.* A small hump, covered by a blanket, sticks up over the edge. I look straight ahead, and my shaking legs quicken their pace. *Please don't make a sound... please, and whatever you do, don't rock.*

CHAPTER TWENTY

I n the backseat of the black sedan, I sit frozen with my fingers entwined in the hem of my shirt and my hands resting on my knees to keep the fabric stretched out away from me and slightly lifted. I can't let the spot with the man's saliva touch my skin. And as I sit in my obsessive-compulsive state of paralysis, I pray. I pray non-stop, without ceasing, trying not to let the 'what ifs' take control. I pray that Steve and my family and my friends haven't been harmed. I pray that God will lead me to them. I pray that God will protect my son and that He won't let these people take him from me. And I pray for my captors whose anger and hurt have blinded them from the true love of Christ.

As I pray, thoughts flash through my head like pages in a scrapbook... finding Eileen and meeting Steve and stopping President Denali and witnessing Gerald and Teresa accept Christ. All these memories of everything I've been through and the memories of what my family and friends have been through with me give me strength because I have no doubts that God will work this out for His good. '*In every thing give thanks.*'

I keep praying. *Father, I am thankful that my baby is okay. I am thankful that I have not been hurt. I am thankful that the saliva only went on my shirt. I am thankful that I am riding with Agent Morgan and Ted instead of those other two men because if the blond guy with the ponytail and the bearded man had gotten their way, I would be riding with them, probably being tortured right now.*

Back at the house, the two insisted that I ride with them and Ted, and then before Agent Morgan or Ted got a word in, they got into an all-out brawl over who would be sitting in the backseat with me. For a moment, it was more like a circus act than a kidnapping. The bearded man shoved the blond guy, and then the blonde guy punched the bearded man in the nose. Thankfully, their ringleader, Agent Morgan, stepped in and ordered Ted to ride with me in the backseat of his sedan. They got into their car and followed without another word. Neither one seems to trust the other, and needless to say, I am terrified of them both. After the spitting incident, I couldn't imagine having to ride in a car with either of them, much less having to share a seat.

We've been driving for about ten minutes. The sun hasn't risen yet, so darkness still shrouds our whereabouts, and from my position in the back, I have no idea which direction we have traveled. However, I have noticed the outline of some pretty expensive homes as we pass.

Out of the corner of my eye, I catch sight of Ted staring at my trembling fingers holding my shirt. I still can't process that he is involved in all of this and that he has been using Eileen. He seemed so sincere, but I guess if Satan can disguise himself as an angel of light, then Ted could put one over on us.

The car comes to a gentle stop beside the door of a huge metal barn.

Agent Morgan's eyes appear in the rearview mirror. "Get her inside and on the plane. I'll get the bags and make sure Frank and Milo understand the rules."

Ted nods and steps from the car, tossing a backpack over one shoulder. In a few seconds, my door opens, and he reaches for my hand to help me out. I ignore the gesture and get out on my own, using caution not to let any slack give in my shirt. As I stand, I survey the area, trying to make out anything I can, but the barn in front of me is it. A faint silhouette of a weathervane rests on the peak.

As Ted slides the door of the barn wide enough for us to pass through, the light from the inside makes me cower. Once my eyes adjust, I realize it's not a barn. It's a hangar.

"Walk fast," Ted utters in an undertone as he strides toward the steps that are folded down from the opening on the side of the minia-ture sleek black jet sitting in the middle of the spotless concrete floor. The dark tint makes the three windows along each side and the wind-shield blend with the paint. The only markings on the entire plane are the letters 'A.M.' printed in red near the rear tail fin.

As I try to keep up with Ted's long strides, my heart sinks when a row of vehicles along the far wall catches my eye. All of them are covered with large tarps, so I can't see them. But one is extremely small, the exact size of my dad's HydroMini. And the one on the end has the same rounded shape as the 'Bug' missing from our garage.

Ted stops at the bottom of the stairs and lets me go in front. The cabin is smaller than I expect. An opening to my left leads into the cockpit, a small bathroom is right in front of me, a refrigerator is tucked under a two-foot countertop next to the bathroom, and to my right is an aisleway between four seats leading to a bench-style row in the back. The first two seats are facing forward, and the second two seats are flipped backward, facing a full row of three along the back.

Ted jerks open the refrigerator and pulls out a bottle of water. Then he drops the backpack on the first seat and pulls out a large men's sweatshirt. "How fast can you change your shirt?" he asks as he takes the lid off the water.

"Fast. I promise," I answer.

He holds out the sweatshirt to me with his right hand and pours the bottle of water all over the front of the shirt I am wearing with his left.

I grab the sweatshirt from his hand and dash into the bathroom. It's not easy for a pregnant woman to change in an airplane bathroom, but I'm so thankful for the shirt that the small space is not an issue.

I step out of the bathroom just as the sound of Agent Morgan's voice approaches the opening to the plane.

Ted points to the seat in the back on the right. "Go sit back there and buckle up."

"Hey, Doc," Agent Morgan appears at the top of the steps, "I couldn't find your bag."

"Sorry, I have it. I don't trust anyone else with my things," Ted moves his eyes toward one of the windows, "especially those two out there."

Agent Morgan tilts his head back and forth as if to signal his understanding but then drops his head to Ted's large backpack. "Is that all you brought? You do understand that you are staying there, right?"

"Yes. I know the plan. I've never been one to overpack." Ted shrugs. "It's just stuff to have to keep up with and carry around."

"Alright then." Agent Morgan steps to the doorway of the cockpit and glances back at me. "She under control?" he asks as if it's not obvious.

"Yeah. I had to give her a shirt to change into." Ted points at me. "I let her have a bottle of water, and her hands were shaking so bad that she spilled it."

Agent Morgan shakes his head. "I'm sure she would have been fine, but whatever. I'm going to fire up the plane and get us out on the runway. Frank and Milo have some boxes of supplies to load in the cargo area, and then we'll take off." He hits a button to fold up the steps that form the door and disappears into the cockpit.

Ted sits in the front seat and tucks his backpack underneath. A moment passes, and the plane starts to taxi forward.

I can't contain my curiosity. "Why did you give me the shirt?" I whisper.

"Because if I didn't, the stress of that spit on your shirt was going to cause me to have to deliver that baby in the middle of the flight," he answers in a dry tone without turning around. "Not the ideal situation for a premature birth."

As the plane exits the building, I notice the dark sky is barely starting to lighten. Agent Morgan steps back to the door and lets the steps back down. Thumping and rattling echo up from beneath the plane. The cargo area must be right under these seats because the floor vibrates with the noise.

"Ted, I'm going to check our flight path and notify our destination that we're departing. Close the door when Frank and Milo get on and let me know we are clear for takeoff."

"Sure thing," Ted replies, staring out the window by his seat.

I bite my bottom lip, contemplating how to get Ted to talk, but I don't have much time before Frank and Milo get on. "Ted, could you at least tell me if Steve and the others are okay?"

He doesn't answer or even acknowledge that I spoke.

I try again. "Please. My husband, my parents, Eileen, my best friends. Everyone that's close to me is gone. I can't take it. I need to know."

"He still doesn't move."

"Please." My voice cracks. "Are they alive?" The question comes out through a whimper, and I'm not sure he could even make out what I said.

Ted turns around, and his hollow eyes meet mine. "It's time to be quiet. Not another word unless you want to ride in the cargo area." His tone is harsh, but as he is speaking, he slides his right hand up by the side of his face, appearing to scratch his head, but instead, he points one finger, taps it to his ear, and rolls his eyes upward. Then, he turns back around with a hard jerk and continues to peer out the window.

Pretty sure of the meaning of his gesture, I let my gaze shift toward the ceiling. A large speaker is mounted above the cockpit door. I thought it would be for the pilot to communicate with the cabin, but maybe it allows the pilot to listen to the cabin as well.

I'm not sure which is Milo, and which is Frank, but the red-bearded man leaps through the door without even using the steps. Sweat beads cover his forehead, and he is gasping for breath. He stands by the door, stretching his neck as if he is looking for something.

"Is there a problem, Milo?" Ted asks.

Milo. Blonde ponytail is Frank.

"Problem? There is some kind of wild animal out there." He leans his head through the opening. "Frank? You okay, Frank?"

A thud jars my seat, and then Milo backs away from the door as Frank clomps up the steps.

"You left the cargo hold open. What, did you expect gravity to hold the stuff inside?" Frank stomps past and sits on the front seat opposite Ted.

"There was something out there. You didn't hear it?" his voice quivers.

"Yeah. I heard you running instead of helping. I had to put the wheel dolly back in the building and close up the hold." Frank pushes forward to the edge of his seat and takes a water bottle out of the small refrigerator.

Ted stands and sidles over to close the door. "What exactly did you hear, Milo?"

"I don't know. I'm a city boy. It was a wolf or a bear or a lion or something bad that eats people." His words run together as one side of his face doesn't move.

Ted cracks the door to the cockpit. "We're all here and set."

Before Ted gets the door closed, Frank yells, "Be sure and tell him to alert the authorities. There is a lion on the loose right here in the hills of Fairfax." He laughs and hooks his seatbelt.

"Wild animals escape from the zoo all the time. Do you not watch the news or read now and then?" Milo retorts.

"Well, you're safe now. You better take a seat. The plane's taking off." Ted tosses his hand, gesturing to the seat behind Frank that faces the back of the cabin. At least it's on the opposite side of the plane and not directly in front of me.

With his face contorted in a snarl, Milo moves toward the seat but stops when his eyes fall on me. "I thought you were going to sedate her. She's not even restrained," he barks in disgust. "And you gave her a clean shirt." Milo looks back over his shoulder at Ted. "Whose side are you on anyway?"

"She's not bothering anyone or doing anything to warrant re-straining her. It's a long flight." Ted lets out an exhausted sigh.

"I'll take care of her." Milo steps in my direction.

Ted leaps to his feet. "Just sit over there behind Frank and leave her alone."

Milo pulls out a small .22 semi-automatic pistol from his jeans pocket. "I knew by the way you were being all nice back at her house that you were a traitor."

"Milo, I'm not a traitor. I'm doing my job. It's my responsibility to make sure she delivers a healthy baby. If she's stressed out about spit on her shirt and tied up for hours on end, her blood pressure is going to shoot up from the stress, and I will be trying to deliver a preemie while flying over the ocean." Ted slides out a .45 caliber pistol from beneath his shirt. "Now sit, unless you want to take responsibility for our mission failing."

"Enough," Agent Morgan booms through the speaker. "Put the guns away. This is a three-and-a-half-hour flight. Sit down and relax."

Milo slips his gun back into his pocket but waits for Ted to do the same before he moves to his seat. One click and then another reverberates through the cabin as Ted and Milo fasten their seatbelts.

The plane lifts from the ground, and all I know is I'm headed somewhere across the ocean. I close my eyes and wring my hands together. *God is in control. God is in control. God is in control. God is in control. God is in control. God is in control. God is in control.*

CHAPTER TWENTY-ONE

A jolt knocks me sideways in my seat, and Milo cries out to God when his head cracks against the window, which is ironic considering the purpose of his mission. Of course, he also vocalized his fear of leaving me unrestrained and unsedated and then went right to sleep only a few feet away from me.

"Buckle up." Agent Morgan's voice roars through the speaker. "That little bounce was only a sample of what's ahead."

Frank starts digging in the compartment under his seat and comes up with a vomit bag. The skin on his face is pale and pasty.

"You okay?" Ted asks, glancing in Frank's direction.

"I hate flying," Frank mumbles, pulling his seatbelt across his lap. "I have a fear of heights, and I get motion sickness." He presses his head back against his seat.

"Close your eyes," Ted suggests, "and take slow, steady—"

The plane drops, thrusting my heart right out of my chest. I grip the edge of the seat with both hands just as the plane bounces back up like a rocket taking off. Even with my seatbelt on, the laws of motion manage to lift me a tiny bit off of my seat. I turn loose of the seat with one hand with the intention of pressing it against my stomach, but the plane drops again, forcing me to grab back onto it. The plane lifts and drops over and over as if it is attached to a bungee cord that lets it hit the pavement below before pulling back up.

Frank is heaving, and Milo is whimpering like a frightened cat.

The plane jerks and flips sideways.

I once read that mosquitoes beat their wings over three hundred times per second. My heart rate now exceeds that. A tear streams down my cheek.

"We're gonna crash," Milo squeals three octaves higher than his normal voice. The part of his face without the scars is scrunched up, and the skin on that side matches his red beard. "I don't wanna die. I don't wanna die."

Another jolt jars the plane and vibrates through my body. Every muscle in my stomach tightens. I double over, gritting my teeth so I don't scream. Still clutching the seat with one hand, I let go with the other and wrap my arm around my torso as if that will help. *Please, Lord, don't let me go into labor. Please, not here, with them. I want Steve to be with me. Please.* My eyes fill with water, and I sink my fingernails into the leather upholstery.

"Doc. Doc," Milo yells, apparently noticing my position. "Something's happening to the woman."

Ted looks back over his shoulder. "No. Not now," he mutters. "Ellie," he speaks louder, "breathe. Take slow, deep breaths."

I jerk my head in a fast, half-hearted nod and then pull air in through my nose and push it slowly through my mouth in the same way I would if I were on my morning run. *That's it. Run with endurance. Breathe slow and deep. In. Out.* The cramp diminishes, and with my right hand resting on the top of my stomach, I sit up and press my head against the pillowy cushion of the headrest. My eyes are closed, but I hear Ted's sigh of relief.

The plane ride smooths out, and I imagine I'm floating on a cloud. Then the plane drops fast like a roller coaster, dips back up, and shimmies side to side as if the back is fishtailing. The pain shoots in lines like long fingers reaching around my sides to my belly button. This time I scream before I can stop myself.

With the plane still lurching and bouncing, a ratcheting sound comes from the direction of Ted's seat, where he has taken off his seatbelt. A second later, he is crawling down the small aisle toward me. "Ellie, it's going to be okay." He climbs into the seat straight across from me and snaps the belt. "Breathe. Remember to breathe." He reaches out his hand. "Here. Squeeze my hand..., oh, I forgot." He bends his elbow. "My arm. Is that okay? Can you squeeze my arm?"

I'm a little baffled as to how he knows about my hand phobia. *Maybe I told him about my OCD at the hospital.* Another sharp pain zaps the confusion from my mind, and I grasp onto his arm.

"Breathe, Ellie. Slow and steady," he almost whispers. "Close your eyes. Pretend you are somewhere else."

Tears run like waterfalls down my cheeks. "I need my husband. Please. I need him here with me." I lower my voice. "Why? Why would you do this?" I pat my stomach. "This is a baby, a tiny, helpless baby. Do you really have this much hate built up inside?"

"That shirt you're wearing," Ted leans his head closer to me, "my father gave me that shirt. It was the only thing I brought with me that was big enough to fit over your pregnant stomach."

I look down at the black sweatshirt. A mountain scene covers the front with *Great Smoky Mountains National Park* printed above it.

"He was a doctor too. He had to speak at a conference in Gatlinburg and brought that back to me. I think he felt bad that he had to miss one of my games. That was the week before he died. At least he got to see one more game... the night of the wreck." Ted turns and gazes out the window.

I realize in the midst of his words that my pain disappeared along with the turbulence.

"You asked why? Because I want to make things better. I want to make a difference in the world. My dad shouldn't have died."

"No, Ted. You're right. He shouldn't have." I loosen my grip on his arm but leave my hand there. "I'm reminded of the story of Saul. He arrested Christians and had them killed. He even watched a man named Stephen get stoned to death. At the time, Saul thought he was doing the right thing. He thought he was making a difference. But then one day, God stopped Saul in his tracks, and Saul saw the light. He was a changed man. From that point on, he went by the name, Paul, and he made a real difference in the world. He spread the Gospel, started churches, led people to Christ, mentored new believers, and wrote half the books in the New Testament. Paul realized that life on earth is temporary, and what matters is where we will spend eternity. He dedicated his life to telling people about Jesus so they would spend eternity in Heaven because the alternative is hell. See Ted, evil existed then, and evil exists now. The devil roams the earth, trying to keep people from knowing God because he doesn't want anyone to accept Jesus and spend eternity in Heaven. In 2 Corinthians 4:4, we are told that 'the God of this world,' that is Satan, 'hath blinded the minds of those that believe not,' and 2 Peter 5:8 warns that the 'devil, as a roaring lion, walketh about, seeking whom he may devour.' If you want to make a difference, be like Paul and look beyond life in this world."

"It seems your contractions have stopped." He unstraps his seatbelt and moves back to his seat in the front.

Milo's eyes follow Ted back to his seat, and his body language tells me it's a good thing he's afraid to take his seatbelt off. His jawline is hardened with his chin jutting out, and he has his hands clenched into tight fists.

"We are about to start our descension," Agent Morgan announces. "Be prepared for a few more bumps."

Lord, thank you for not letting me go into labor. I have no idea where I'm going or what I'm about to face, but I know you're with me. You are in control. Let Your Spirit guide me.

The sky has lightened. I lean toward the window, hoping to figure out where we are as the plane moves beneath the clouds, but the solid blanket of treetops below gives no clue, at least, not until we descend into a small clearing in the middle of tall, towering trees, some with large green leaves and some with fronds. And still, I only know it's somewhere tropical.

The plane bounces twice, with the thump of the front wheel making contact with the ground, followed by the back wheels. The clearing must be small because the plane screeches to a quick halt, flinging my upper body forward, and then slams me back against the seat.

I swallow hard, trying not to anticipate what's going to happen next. The plane engine shuts off, but no one moves. Frank groans, seeming to not be over his motion sickness, and Milo mutters something about still being alive.

After a couple of minutes, Agent Morgan steps out of the cockpit and scratches his head. "Frank, you don't look so hot," he comments in a cold tone as he pushes the button to lower the door. "Ted, get her off the plane. He's waiting."

Ted lifts his backpack as he stands and tosses one strap over his left shoulder with a bit more force than necessary. He twists at his waist, keeping his left hand on the strap of the backpack, and eyes me with lifted brows. "You coming?"

With trembling fingers, I press the button to release my seatbelt. *Father, please help me. I'm scared.* My legs tingle as my heart pumps harder and harder. As I stand, the baby presses on my bladder. "I-I need the restroom. It can't wait."

"Hurry up." Ted gestures to the bathroom.

"There's no time now. I told you he's waiting," Agent Morgan objects.

"It's your call," Ted argues, "but she's pregnant. She won't be able to hold it."

Agent Morgan stomps his foot. "You've got one minute," he snaps at me.

I dart past Agent Morgan in fear that I'm not going to make it and slam the door harder than I intend. Moving as fast as I can, I take care of business in record time, pump soap in my hand, rub as I count to seven over and over seven times, rinse, and dash out the door without drying. Ted takes my arm without a word.

We step off the plane into a tropical paradise. It's exactly how I would picture the Garden of Eden with fruit trees, large bright flowers, gentle rolling blue waves, and the snake.

CHAPTER TWENTY-TWO

A sudden calm falls over me. Bright radiating light pours down on my face, and fresh air fills my lungs. The breeze off of the water swirls around my body, and I'm weightless. I'm standing in the presence of evil, and I'm weightless and free. A voice booming inside my head overwhelms me with an unexplainable peace. I know it's the voice of God because I've heard it before. *Don't be afraid. I will never leave you nor forsake you. My spirit dwells inside you. You have my seal. He cannot touch you.* The same voice I heard during the reprimanding at the facility. The voice that made the darkness, the whispers, the hands, the screams, the sounds of torture, and all of the horror fade away.

Ted releases my arm and steps aside as the man emerges from the line of trees. I know who he is because he looks almost exactly as he did in the video at the training facility. Of course, he isn't wearing a suit or sitting behind his desk singing a ridiculous song. He's wearing long khaki shorts with an untucked white button-up shirt that intensifies his tropical-tanned skin. A long strand of leather cord is tied around his head, holding his combover in place, but a few strands of his unnaturally black hair have worked loose and are blowing in the breeze.

As he steps closer, I note his eyes. I don't remember them being so dark. They're not hollow like Ted's. They're black, so black that the centers of his eyes are a solid circle with no pupil.

"We finally meet face to face," he says with a smirk on his face.

Father, help me be strong. I stare back at him without blinking or batting an eye.

"It's about time, don't you think?" He stops a couple of feet away, towering over me.

Looking straight up, I don't respond. His stature is much greater than I realized. Steve and Teresa must have gotten their height from Cynthia.

"Tell me something," he continues. "How does it feel?"

Lord, please don't let my voice crack. "How does what feel?" I muse.

"Thinking you defeated me. Thinking you saved the world. Thinking you married the man of your dreams. Thinking your God was going to protect you." His lips form a lop-sided grin. "How does it feel to discover that none of it's true?" He holds his arms out from his sides. "I'm alive. The current population is still going to be destroyed. Your husband has deceived you. And as soon as your baby is born, you are going to die," he sneers. "Of course, I imagine at this point, you are welcoming death. I mean, you're all alone. What reason do you have to live?"

"I wouldn't send out invitations for your victory party just yet," I assert with a hint of sarcasm.

"Excuse me?" he challenges, tilting his head and narrowing his eyes.

"You can't win a battle that's already been won," I reply with a smile.

"In case you haven't noticed," he chuckles, "the odds are so far in my favor, I'm pretty sure my victory is in the bag."

"I concur. My situation seems a little bleak. But... Jesus said I'd have trouble. Of course, you know the Bible pretty well. I'm sure you remember when he said, '... In the world ye shall have tribulation: but be of good cheer; I have overcome the world.'" I shrug. "So, you see, it doesn't matter what you do. My Father has already won. And as far as me, in the words of Paul, '... to live is Christ, to die is gain.'"

"Quite the dreamer, aren't you? Well, we'll see, won't we?" He rolls his eyes to the side. "Actually, you won't be here to see it, but it's going to be great. Me, my son, and my grandson ruling the world... a world that has no idea who God is, and no one left to tell anyone about Him."

I watch his face light up as he describes his version of a perfect world. "I'm sorry," I blurt out. "I'm so sorry."

"Oh, honey. It's a little late for sorry. You and all your so-called brothers and sisters have had more than ample opportunity to change the world, but you haven't. I've watched churchgoers lie, cheat, steal, and some have even killed. And then, they get up the next day proclaiming 'Jesus, Jesus.'" He takes another step toward me, invading my personal space with his toes only a foot from mine. "Look at poor Ted over there." He nods his head toward Ted, who is waiting under a banana tree clinging to his backpack. "His daddy was taken from him by a drunk driver, and do you know who that drunk driver was? He was a pastor."

I take a deep breath. *Lord, let my words speak Your Truth.* "First, I wasn't seeking any sort of forgiveness from you. When I said, 'I'm sorry,' I meant I'm sorry that your only hope is invested in this world. Because no matter what you do, the things of this world are only temporary. And I am sorry people have hurt you to the point that you have lost your faith and turned from God. I'm sorry that you had to witness your grandfather hurting your grandmother."

His face twists and contorts in a grimace, and he opens his mouth to speak, but I cut him off.

"No." I hold out my hand. "If you are planning to take my life, then I'm entitled to some last words. And I have a few things to say regarding your misinformed and misled opinions. First, no one is perfect. Otherwise, Jesus wouldn't have had to die. So, yes, even Christians mess up. And second, while the enemy is running rampant in this world, many false prophets are going to come forward claiming to be followers of Christ. Isaiah 29:13 says, 'Wherefore the Lord said, Forasmuch as this people draw near me with their mouth, and with their lips do honor me, but have removed their heart far from me.'" I pull in a quick breath and continue before he stops me. "Saying that I'm a Christian doesn't make me a Christian any more than saying I'm a doctor makes me a doctor. I am a Christian because I believe Jesus died for me, I have accepted his sacrifice, and I have asked him to come into my heart because I want to live my life for Him. In Luke chapter six, Jesus tells us that 'a good tree bringeth not forth corrupt fruit, neither do a corrupt tree bringeth forth good fruit. For every tree is known by his own fruit. For of thorns men do not gather figs, nor of a bramble bush gather they grapes.'" I gaze into his black eyes. "But the devil is sneaky and deceptive, and he wants to tarnish the name of Jesus. Where true believers want to lead people to Christ, the devil will use hypocrisy to push people away from the love of Jesus." I clasp my hands together on top of my stomach in an effort to disguise the tremors running through my body. "Mr. Denali, I don't blame you for being angry about what your grandfather did to your grandmother. I don't blame you for wanting to prevent anyone from having to suffer like she did. But let me ask you a question. Was your grandmother a Christian?"

His eyes widen.

I don't know if he is in shock at my brazenness or if I might have hit a nerve, so I keep pressing. "From what I read in her obituary, I believe she had a great love for Jesus, and I bet she produced some really good fruit. I imagine she entered right into the presence of Jesus. You think that getting rid of all who proclaim the name of Jesus will rid the world of people like your grandfather, but instead, you are ridding the world of people like your grandmother. The devil will continue to walk upon this earth until the day of judgment when he is cast into the lake of fire. I believe it is 1 Peter 5:8 that says our 'adversary the devil, as a roaring lion, walketh about, seeking whom he may devour.'" I need to take another breath, but I don't want to lose my opportunity to finish. "Mr. Denali, don't you want to see your grandmother again? It's not too late. Not yet. Remember the man who was crucified on the cross next to Jesus? He believed right before he died, and Jesus said, 'Today thou shalt be with me in paradise.' Don't let the sins of your grandfather destroy your eternity. This perfect world you think you are creating, in the scheme of eternity, will only be like the blink of an eye. And then it's either Heaven or hell. God gives us the choice... live forever with Him... no more pain... no more hurt... or live forever away from Him in unrelentless torture. Think about it. Your grandmother wouldn't want you to give up Heaven because of the pain she suffered on earth."

Pulsing veins protrude from his forehead, and heat floods his face. "Enough," he screams, then lowers his voice and grumbles through bared teeth. "Not another word. Ted, get her out of my sight. A shelter for the birth has been constructed at the end of that dirt path. Keep her there and let her wallow in her loneliness until it's time." He points to one of the several paths leading off the clearing where the plane is sitting. "You are not to leave her. Is that clear?"

"Yes, Sir. The details of my assignment were straightforward. And as I noted, her due date is still several weeks away."

"I'm not an idiot, Doctor. I'm fully aware of the date my grand-child has been predicted to enter the world. And for your sake, you better hope that he is strong and healthy upon delivery."

Ted takes my arm but looks up at Dennis Denali. "I can understand you being upset with her but keep your attitude in check. I'm on your team in case you forgot."

Denali presses his lips together and strokes his chin. "Hmm. It seems you have forgotten your place and who you are speaking to, young man. You do understand that I will eventually be ruling the entire world. Royalty is not even a strong enough word to describe my presence," he barks. "I am granting you one do-over. Don't blow it."

Ted's lips part open, but I nudge him on toward the trail in fear that the situation is about to get out of control. We walk in silence down the sandy path scattered with loose shells and stones. The ache in my chest grows more intense with each step because with each step the realization that Steve and the others aren't here sinks a little deeper into my brain. And I'm afraid to think about what has happened to them if they aren't here. No, I'm not afraid to think about it. I can't. Because if I do, I might break.

Sweat runs from my forehead, burning my eyes as more sweat beads trickle off of my nose. At least the excess sweat camouflages the tears flowing down my cheeks, but between the tropical temperatures and the stress spiking my blood pressure, this heavy, black sweatshirt needs to go, or I'm going to have a heat stroke. The funny thing is, a few hours ago before I got on that plane, I was wishing I had been allowed to go back for my coat.

I stop short as a structure comes into view. "Is that it?" I question as I try to process what it is.

Ted tilts his head. "I'm not sure what else it could be." He strides toward it, pulling me with him until we reach the door.

The outside of the shelter is scrap fragments of metal and wood pieced together. The door is rectangular but with all of the corners rounded and a circular handle in the center.

My chin drops. "This is made from military ships and airplane parts." I look at Ted. "Where are we? And don't say a tropical island. I mean, exactly, where are we?"

"For the security of the mission, I was told that we were going to an undisclosed location where we would be protected until it was safe to re-enter and start our new society," he replies.

"Let me get this straight." I roll my eyes, glaring at him in my peripheral vision. "You joined a group that wants to let the people of the world destroy each other so they can start their own new world without any knowledge of God. You abduct a pregnant woman and board a plane with no idea where it's going so you can deliver the baby, give it to your new supreme leader, and then let the woman be killed. And you are doing all of this because something bad happened to you, and you have decided that you want to blame all Christians for your misfortune." I turn my head so that I am facing him head-on. "Am I understanding correctly?"

He drops his head. "I suppose that is somewhat accurate."

I turn back to the door, twist the circle in the center, and push it open. As I step inside, I notice the interior is one large room created from more ship and airplane parts. A rack with two cots, probably from a Navy ship, lines one wall. A compact toilet and a sink are stuck in the back underneath a porthole with a wraparound pull curtain as the only privacy. On the wall across from the bunk beds is a small refrigerator with a microwave on top. My curiosity peaks, and I take the few steps across the small room to the porthole and peer out. The back of the shelter is not that far from the ocean, and large pipes are running on top of the ground from the back of the shelter out into the water. Two large solar panels sit to the right, out to the side of the pipes. Those two would be enough to power the microwave, the refrigerator, and the tiny lightbulb in the center of the room.

I stare through the porthole out at the enormous crashing waves. My mind wanders back to that evening in the kitchen. We had just arrived home that morning after stopping Dr. Eckert from using his mind-control tactics. Agent Morgan stopped by to update us on the investigation. He said the guards in the facility had turned out to be clones of a group of Navy Seals that had never made it home. Of course, I have to wonder if anything he told us was true. It makes me sick to think about how much we trusted him. But as I move my eyes off the water and to the porthole that I am looking through, I have to wonder if that part was true. My theory has a lot of holes, but between the missing ship of Navy Seals and the toy airplane in the box with the recording of young Dennis's voice, I have a hunch about where we are.

I amble over, drop down on the edge of the cot, and press my fingers to my temples. "I think I know where we are. I just don't know how he's doing it."

"So," Ted sits beside me, "where do you think we are?"

"An island somewhere in the Bermuda Triangle." I keep my eyes glued on his face to catch his reaction. "Also known as the devil's triangle," I add.

He stares back at me in silence as if he's processing my theory. Just as he opens his mouth to speak, the door bursts open.

Two boxes fly through the air and skitter across the floor as an out-of-breath Milo darts in and slams the door behind him. "It's back. It followed us."

"What's back?" Ted asks.

"The wild animal. Whatever it is, it's angry." He steps sideways and peeps out another porthole by the door.

"Are you talking about the animal you heard before we flew across the ocean?" Ted questions with sarcasm in his tone.

"Yes. Yes, I am. And I do realize that we flew across the ocean." He presses his forehead against the small window, still trying to scan the area. "It must have stowed away in the cargo area when I left it open." He pulls out his small .22 pistol. "Well, my hands aren't full anymore, and it's not dark like it was when we left. I'll take care of whatever it is."

Ted stands to his feet. "Well, with that little .22 pistol, you better be a good shot."

"You know, I have had it with you and your little goody-two-shoes attitude." Milo moves toward him, stopping with his face only a foot away from Ted's. "You think that because you're a doctor, this mission won't survive without you. But I see you for who you are. You're a traitor. You've been chatting online like you're one of us, saying how you hate the hypocrites and you're all ready to make the world a better place. But you've done nothing but take her side. I heard you listening to her and soaking up her religious jargon on the plane. I'm no fool."

"Milo, she was having contractions on the plane. I thought the stress of the extreme turbulence was causing her to go into labor." Ted pinches the bridge of his nose. "That's why I'm here. Remember. To make sure she delivers a healthy baby."

"I don't get what's so special about that baby anyway. It's part of her, and she's one of them," he barks, waving the gun around by his side.

Ted sighs, still pinching the bridge of his nose. "The baby boy is Mr. Denali's grandson, and he will be intercepted before he ever hears a word about Jesus."

"I really don't think we need anything that's part of her in our new world." Milo takes a step toward me and presses the tip of the gun to the top of my stomach.

Lord, please. Please. No. Help me. I hold my breath. Every fiber of every muscle in my body is paralyzed. I'm cornered sitting on this cot. I roll my eyes down, focusing on his index finger that is resting on the trigger.

"Think about what you're doing. If you hurt that baby, or her for that matter, before the baby is born, he will kill you," Ted's voice quavers. "Now, put the gun down." He reaches out for the gun with a trembling hand and takes a bold step toward Milo.

Milo twists, thrusting his left arm upward to block Ted's hand, and the gun fires.

Chapter Twenty-Three

A bloodcurdling scream erupts from my mouth as Ted collapses on the floor.

"Milo." Frank's voice filters from somewhere outside in the distance. "What happened?" he yells, sounding closer.

Milo presses the tip of the gun to my head. "Not a sound. Do you understand me? I will come back and kill you," he murmurs. He bends down and slips Ted's .45 caliber pistol from beneath his shirt, and then turns and opens the door. "It's fine," he yells back. "A giant rat got in the shelter. It's dead now." He shuts the door behind him. A few seconds pass, the door rattles and shakes, and then his pounding steps fade down the trail.

I drop to my knees on the floor next to Ted. He's lying on his side with his knees pulled up toward his chest. Blood seeps from beneath his arms that are wrapped around his abdomen.

Lord, let him be alive. Please, let him be alive. "Ted. Talk to me, Ted," I utter in panic.

"L-let m-me be."

I rip the white sheet from the bottom bunk. "Pressure. We have to apply pressure." I wad the sheet, trying to wedge it under his arms.

He lifts one arm at a time, grabbing the sheet and pulling it to his torso.

Medical bag. He must have something in that backpack. I scan the room. *By the door.* I crawl to the door, grab his backpack, and unzip pocket after pocket. They're all filled with clothes and cosmetics except for the largest compartment in the back. I yank out a black pouch and pull the zipper that runs around three sides. It folds open like a book. Inside, a stethoscope, sphygmomanometer, tweezers, syringes, scalpels, and various other tools and supplies are neatly organized with small hook and loop fasteners. *Rubber gloves.* I slip them on, and sliding the pouch with me, I scoot back to Ted's side.

"Ted, I found your medical bag." I lay my hand on his shoulder. "Tell me what to do."

"Just leave me alone." Groaning, he pulls his arms tighter and presses his eyelids closed.

"Ted, please. Trust me," I plead. "My mother has been a nurse in the emergency room for as long as I can remember, and I spent a year in nursing school before I changed my major. I don't know how to help you, but you can tell me what to do. It's going to be alright."

"N-no. I-I would need surgery." His barely audible voice is wobbly and brittle.

"Ted, no. We can fix it."

"It hit my intestines." He opens his eyes and stares up at me. "I need y-you u-uhh to l-listen... to me. Y-you're strong. Y-you never uhh n-needed b-bed rest. I put a d-drug," he gasps for breath, "i-in your drink at d-dinner t-to..."

"You gave me something at dinner that night at my parents to make it look like I was going into premature labor," I finish for him, "so I would have to go on bed rest."

He gives a slight nod.

I look away for a second to regroup and then gaze back down at him. "I know you were listening to me on the plane, and you heard my conversation with Mr. Denali." I blink, but the tears burst out anyway. "Ted, Jesus loves you so much that He suffered an excruciating death so you could spend forever in Heaven with Him. He took the punishment for all of our sins so that we wouldn't have to take the punishment and endure eternal torture in hell." I lay my gloved hand on his. "That man who got drunk and chose to get behind the wheel of a car, he made a really, really bad choice. I don't know anything about him other than he did something the Bible says not to do, and I heard Mr. Denali mention that the man was a pastor. I don't know if it was the first time the man had decided to drink and drive or if he made a habit of going against God's Word. But, if he proclaimed to be a Christian and was intentionally sinning, that is hypocrisy, and Jesus spoke out about the scribes and Pharisees who were hypocrites. He said in Matthew 23:33, 'Ye serpents, ye generation of vipers, how can ye escape the damnation of hell?' But, Ted, that is for God to decide. He is the judge." I let out a deep breath searching for the right words. *Please speak through me, Lord.*

"Look, Ted. I know that man's bad choice took your father's life. And I don't blame you for being angry at that man. You're human with human emotions. But your anger hasn't hurt that man. It has only hurt you. You have let it build and build to the point that you want to destroy all Christians for what one man did. You want to rid the world of the opportunity to get to know Jesus and have a relationship with him. God gives us the free will to choose Him and accept His free gift of salvation. But you want to take that choice away. You want to doom the world to hell because of your anger with one person. Ted, let go of the anger. The Father is waiting with open arms to embrace you if you will let Him. He wants you with Him. Don't turn your back on the sacrifice Jesus made for you."

Tears drip from his eyes to the floor. "Ellie, will you get my backpack?"

I slide across the floor far enough to snag the backpack and tug it to me.

"R-reach down to the bottom." He pauses. "Th-There's a-a rip in the l-lining."

I move my hand down between the clothes and glide my fingertips back and forth across the thin nylon fabric until my pinky snags a hole. I wiggle my fingers through the opening and pull out a small, clear plastic bag with a cross necklace.

"W-would you take it out for me?" he whispers.

I take the chain from the bag, unsure what to do with it because his hands are pressed tight to his stomach.

"It was my d-dad's. I-It has J-John 3:16 on the back." His words slur together as he turns his face toward the floor. "Please put it on me."

"Okay." With trembling hands, I work one end of the chain under his neck on the floor and hook the latch. "So, your dad... he was..."

"Yeah." Ted's body quivers and chill bumps cover his arms. "H-he knew Jesus. H-he was the real deal, g-gen-g-genuine like y-you and y-your f-f-family. Truly loved J-Jesus. B-being with your f-family rem-reminded m-me of h-him."

I pull the blanket from the bed and drape it over him. "Ted..."

"I-I used to know J-Jesus t-too," he stammers through chattering teeth. "I-I was s-so m-mad wh-when D-Dad... I-I blamed God. D-Dad w-would be s-s-so ashamed of m-me."

"No, Ted. He'd want you to ask God to forgive you. He'd want to know that you are going to be in Heaven with him."

His back shakes with sobs. "God, please forgive m-me. I-I-I'm so s-sorry." He snivels. "Y-you d-died for me, a-and I-I t-turned my b-back on you. I-I m-mocked y-you. P-Please f-forgive me. Please t-take m-me b-back. Please be m-my s-savior." He opens his eyes and tries to tilt his head up toward me. "I'm sorry, E-Ellie. P-Please t-tell Eileen, I-I'm s-sorry. I-I d-did really like h-her. T-Tell her sh-she w-was special to m-me. Th-that wasn't a l-lie. F-forgive m-m..." His voice trails off.

"Ted."

His eyes go still.

No. Please. "Ted," I whimper. "Ted, don't." My shoulders shudder as my eyes take in the sight of his lifeless body. I lift my hand and rake my fingers over his eyes to close them. "I forgive you," I whisper. Biting my quivering lips together, I peel off the gloves as I push to my feet and let them fall to the floor.

The walls of the small room begin to press in on me. Either that or I really am smothering. I step to the door and push on the handle, but it doesn't budge. My shoulders fall, and I drag my feet over to the cot. Grasping the mattress, I lower myself to my knees and drop my head. *Dear Heavenly Father. Thank you. Thank you for protecting my son from Milo. Thank you for giving Ted a new heart before it was too late. Thank you for letting me hear your voice and giving me the courage to face Dennis Denali.* I swallow the acid rising in my throat at the thought of being on this island with him. *Lord, things aren't looking good, and I'm scared. I want to have courage like I imagine Shadrach, Meschach, and Abednego had when they were thrown into the furnace, but I'm struggling a bit with that. I know that for you nothing is impossible. And I also believe that I would not be in this place, in this situation, if you weren't going to use it for your good. Father, you have always been with me, and I know you are with me now.* I sniffle and swipe the back of my hand across my cheek. *I will accept whatever outcome you allow, but Father, I beg you to please protect my baby and let Steve and my family and friends be alright. Please stop Dennis Denali and Agent Morgan and whoever else is involved, and don't let them hurt anyone else. And Lord, please hold me. Hold me in your arms because I can't stop shaking. I love you, Father. In the Holy and Precious Name of Jesus. Amen.*

I roll onto the bottom bunk. I can't bear to look at Ted on the floor, so I curl up on my side, facing the wall. Hugging the pillow to my chest, I think of my husband, and I weep. I think of my parents and my sister, and I weep more. I think of Alice, Gerald, Cynthia, Dukakis, and Teresa, and then Kate and Ted, and the flood keeps coming.

As all their faces sweep through my head, I drift back in time to when Eileen disappeared. I missed her so much. I hadn't just lost a sister. I had lost my best friend too. Guilt consumed me because I had forgotten to meet her for lunch the day she vanished. I remember I would lie on my bed like I am right now and cry for hours, sometimes singing through the tears.

All of a sudden, the melody plays in my head, and I start to sing in a hushed voice.

"So much love crushed beneath so much pain,
Behind my eyes, tears hide like clouds full of rain.
When the cloud bursts and the river overflows,
I gasp for air beneath the flood, and no one knows... no
one knows.

Gazing through the darkness, I beg and plead,
Hoping to hear the voice I so desperately need.
But instead, whispers invade and turn to shouts ringing
in my ear.
You're all alone... all alone... is all that I hear.

The pain, the agony, the despair,
It feels like too much to bear.
But then, I think of the rejection and the scars on His

hands,
And I curl up in the arms of the One who understands.

I cling to Him and His promise of the coming day,
When I will have no more tears, and the pain will go
away.
I'm not alone... I'm not alone.
He will never leave me. I'm not alone."

A knock on the window makes my heart turn a somersault. *Please don't be Milo.* I roll over to get off the bed, but the cot is so small, I fall to the floor. Another thump bounces me to my feet in an instant, in spite of my large belly. As I step toward it, the small porthole above the toilet swings into the room. I dig my heels in to stop myself. *No one could fit through that window. I am safer at a distance,* I tell myself. And then his face appears in the window opening. He climbs through and leaps into my arms, holding the bear by one arm.

"How did you?" I whisper as I gaze at the bear dangling in the air. "The wild animal?"

Spencer's mouth spreads into a toothy grin as he nods.

I can't help but hug him with all my might. When I finally release him, he whines and points to the bear, so I put him on the bed, trying to block his view of Ted. Spencer unzips the back of the bear and holds it open for me to look inside.

My chin almost hits my chest. "My Bible. You brought my Bible," I utter in disbelief.

He claps his hands and then points for me to keep looking.

I lean my head over and peer in. "And peanut butter cups," I touch my hand to my chest, "lots of peanut butter cups."

His body quivers with excitement as he smiles from ear to ear, and then he holds up one finger and reaches his other hand down deep inside the bear. It takes him a second to dig through all of the peanut butter cups, but when he pulls his little hand out, he is clutching Steve's phone.

Chapter Twenty-Four

My excitement over the phone was short-lived. I don't know why I thought there would be a phone signal on a deserted island in the middle of the Atlantic, but Spencer was so proud when he gave it to me that I poked at the screen and didn't let on. I found an opportunity while Spencer was tearing into a peanut butter cup to reach down and pull the blanket over Ted's head, so now he is completely covered. I'm still trying to figure out what to do because, in this tropical temperature, it probably won't be long before the body attracts flies and starts to smell, and in my present state, I can't move that much weight. And even if I could, where would I move it to? I'm locked in.

I'm not being insensitive because the body lying on the floor is only a shell so to speak. Ted is in Heaven now, probably already reunited with his dad. I can't help but smile at that thought.

I watch Spencer scarf down the peanut butter cup and realize that neither of us has had food or drink. I use the rail of the top bunk to pull myself up off the cot and plod over to the refrigerator. *Great. It's empty.* In the middle of letting out a long, frustrated sigh, my eyes fall on the two boxes Milo brought in. I use my foot to slide them over to the cot one at a time, where I can sit and open them.

Spencer helps me rip open the top of the first one. The excitement written on his face and the gusto he uses to tear into it reminds me of a child with a package on Christmas morning. The first box turns out to be bottles of water. I expect Spencer's excitement to die, but he claps his hands as if he has discovered a gold mine. I suppose if you're thirsty enough, water is a gold mine. Spencer opens a bottle and guzzles while I open the second one. It's full of imperishable canned foods and healthy snacks.

I grab a bottle of water and a bag of trail mix that, as luck would have it, contains dried bananas. Spencer grabs my hand because he knows that's what we do before we eat, and as I say the blessing, I am in awe of how many things pour through my mind to give thanks for. *My baby's okay... I have food, water, and shelter... I have Spencer... my Bible... and I'm not alone.*

As we sit on the bottom bunk sharing the trail mix, I pick out the peanuts, Spencer picks out the banana chips, and we split the raisins and pumpkin seeds. When we finish, I open my Bible to the twenty-third Psalm and read aloud. I know Spencer doesn't understand what I'm reading, but he still stares at me as if he's hanging on my every word.

We curl up on the bottom bunk, and he snuggles close to me. The poor little thing is exhausted. I can't imagine the ride he had in the cargo area with all that turbulence, but God took care of him and brought him to me. I rub my hand up and down his furry back, knowing I need rest too. I close my eyes, trying to clear my mind and force myself to relax, but the adrenaline flowing through my body won't allow it.

As I lie with my arm draped across Spencer, the whispers creep in, and the eerie silence in the room makes it hard to drown them out. *Steve's gone. Your family and friends... gone. He took them one by one and left you... alone... pregnant and alone with nothing but a monkey, and God let it happen.* I press my hand to my forehead. *No. Stop.* "Satan, get away from me," I mouth the words in an undertone. "For the Lord thy God is with thee whithersoever thou goest. For the Lord thy God is with thee whithersoever thou goest. For the Lord thy God is with thee whithersoever thou goest. For the Lord thy God is with thee whithersoever thou goest. For the Lord thy God is with thee whithersoever thou goest. For the Lord thy God is with thee whithersoever thou goest. For the Lord thy God is with thee whithersoever thou goest."

You are mine. You belong to me. I will never leave you nor forsake you. You will never be alone. His loud but comforting voice erupts in my mind and peace flows over me. I know God is with me, but I'm also aware that, until my race is finished, the devil will keep trying to break my focus.

I open my Bible to Isaiah 54 and read to myself. I get to the last verse of the chapter and repeat it over and over in my mind, letting its truth soak into the depths of my soul. '*No weapon that is formed against thee shall prosper; and every tongue that shall rise against thee in judgment thou shalt condemn. This is the heritage of the servants of the Lord, and their righteousness is of me, saith the Lord.*'

The room begins to darken as night settles in, and while I'm not that little girl afraid of the dark anymore, I need the light right now. Keeping my eyes fixed on the string dangling by the tiny bulb in the center of the room, I move my legs in a gentle motion toward the edge of the cot, so I don't wake Spencer. My legs are elevated in mid-air when a man's cough and stomping footsteps make me jump, startling Spencer from his sleep. I roll off the bed and push to my feet. Panic floods through my body as the footfalls grow louder. With my heart beating as if I have just run a marathon, I scan the room, searching

for anything to use as a weapon. *Wait, Spencer. I need to hide Spencer.*
I turn back around, but Spencer is squeezing through the porthole,
pulling the teddy bear behind him. *No. No.* I want to yell for him, but
whoever it is will hear me. *The medical bag... the scalpel.* It's not much,
but it's better than nothing.

I step over Ted, scoop up the medical bag in one hand and his
backpack with the other, and as I stuff it all in the refrigerator to hide
it, I remove the scalpel and press the button on the side to extend the
blade. I can't do anything about the body, but I might need the stuff
in the bags. I have a hunch that it's Milo coming back to finish what
he started anyway. I move to the door, clutching the scalpel in a reverse
grip by my shoulder, and tuck myself as close to the wall as I can, which,
with my stomach, isn't that close.

Holding my breath, I try to discern how far away he is by the sound
of his coughing, but the bear growls and everything stills.

A few seconds pass. "I've got a gun," Milo shouts in a quavering
voice.

Is he moving again? Where is he?

"I mean it. I'll use this thing." His voice is closer.

The bear growls again, and the rhythm of running, pounding
boots fade into the distance.

Before I make it across the room, Spencer is crawling back through
the window with the teddy bear. As I grab him up in my left arm, he
points toward the front of the shelter in the direction the man ran,
covers his mouth, and quivers all over with laughter. Shaking my head,
the sudden urge to go to the bathroom hits me. Rushing to make it in
time, I pull the string to a bulb that barely illuminates a foot diameter
around it, traipse to the cot and put Spencer down, retract the blade
as I stick the scalpel under the mattress, and dash back over to the
toilet only to realize I have no light whatsoever when I pull the curtain
closed.

After using the bathroom and washing my hands seven times in
the dark, I open the curtain and let the light that almost amounts to

the glow of one Christmas tree bulb guide me to the bed. Spencer is already fast asleep using the whole pillow. Letting out a tired, exasperated groan, I reach up and get the pillow from the top when a sharp stabbing pain through my stomach folds me in half. *No. Not now. Not yet.* My knees tremble, and dropping the pillow, I grasp onto the edge of the bunk to keep from falling and wrap my right arm around my stomach. *Please make it stop. Please, Lord, help me. Not now. Lord, please not now.*

After a minute, the pain stops, and I drop onto the edge of the mattress, burying my face in my hands. *Thank you, Lord. Thank you.* I pick up the pillow and curl up on my side in the tiny space Spencer has left me.

"Not yet, baby boy, not yet. I need you to hold on a little bit longer," I whisper as I rub my stomach, and then I sing to him softly, more for my sake than his. "Jesus loves me. This I know, for the Bible tells me so. Little ones to Him belong; They are weak, but He is strong. Yes, Jesus loves me. Yes, Jesus loves me. Yes, Jesus loves me. The Bible tells me so."

My heavy eyelids fall.

"Ellie. Ellie, wake up."

I blink. The silhouette of his face is only a few inches from mine. I don't bother to move. A tear rolls from my eye and soaks into my pillow with all the others that have fallen tonight.

Pain flowing from my back to my stomach has yanked me from the horrors of my nightmares a few times already, and I've cried myself back to sleep. But this isn't a nightmare. It's a dream. Then again, maybe it is a nightmare because the torture is going to be excruciating when I wake up and realize this isn't real and never will be.

"Ellie, are you okay?" he whispers.

I lift my hand, longing to touch his face. "Steve, I miss you so bad. I need you here with me."

"I am here." He takes my lifted hand in his and pulls it to his lips. "It's alright now. We're going to get you out of this place. Are you able to walk?"

His hand... his touch... his voice... it's so real. Another pain twists my face into a grimace, and I clench my hands into fists. *My hand is squeezing his. I'm not asleep, and this isn't a dream. He's really here.* I bolt upright in spite of the pain and throw my arms around him. "You're here. You're really here. How did you get in? I couldn't get the door to budge."

"A stick was jammed through that spinning handle on the door." His strong arms pull me tight.

"I didn't know what happened to you. I was so scared." My words pour out in his ear as I press my cheek to his.

"It seems we were deceived by a couple of people. Those sleeping tablets apparently had nothing to do with your health and well-being." He draws his head back and glances at the lump on the floor. "I can't imagine what you've had to go through."

I swallow hard. "His job was to deliver the baby, but one of the men thought he was being too nice to me and kept giving him trouble. Then the man pressed his gun to my stomach. Ted intervened, and...," my voice trails off as I look down at the blanket covering his body. "He had a lot of anger. So much so, that it had consumed him. It was ruling his life." I pause. "But he prayed before he died, and his heart was sincere. I felt it." I tighten my grip on Steve's hand and gaze at him. In the dim light, he's barely more than a shadow. "Where have you been? How did you find me?"

"It's a long story, but after you took the pills and went to bed, I read a bit of that journal. Then Agent Morgan showed up. I assumed that since I had talked to him on the phone, he must have some information about your dad or Alice, so of course, I gave Herb the okay to let him in. He forced me to shut all the security and bots down. He said he'd kill you if I didn't. And then two more guys showed up."

"But Claude and Waves should have... before..." I'm so confused that I can't get out what I'm trying to say, but Steve seems to understand anyway.

"Morgan is... well, was on the safe list. I fixed that. But, as much as they appear to think like real people, they're robots. Their personalities are programmed using complex algorithms that make them seem human, but for security purposes, the safe list is hard-programmed. I was so worried about an accident with one of their weapons that... well, it's spilled milk now, right?" He rises to his feet. "Oh, and I found you through the GPS chip I have on my phone. That was brilliant, by the way. How did you bring it with you without them knowing?"

"I didn't. Spencer did." I turn and look back at him as the little monkey's back rises and falls in his sleep. "He's amazing. Somehow, he managed to be a stowaway. He must have sneaked into the cargo area when they were loading supplies."

He walks over to the porthole by the door. "We need to figure out how to get you out of here. Do you have any idea how many goons are on this island?"

"No. I have no idea what's even here. I would assume your father's shelter is a bit nicer than this one though."

He turns with wide eyes. "My father. You've seen him?"

"Yes. He was waiting when I got off the plane."

"I can't believe he's alive." He runs his hand over the top of his head and sighs.

"Who did you think was behind this?" I raise one eyebrow.

"I was starting to think it was possible, but then when Agent Morgan showed up, ultimate confusion set in. Honestly, I don't have a clue how he's tied up in this."

"He's Damon Sivers... and Damien Seaver... and probably a bunch of names that we don't know about." I bite my bottom lip as I watch Steve's mouth drop open.

"I can't wait to hear how you figured that out." He steps back over beside me. "So, my father is here, and the guy that shot Ted. How many others are here that you know of?" His tone gains urgency.

"Agent Morgan and one other guy. But," I lift my shoulders, "there could be a lot more. I walked off the plane to face your father and then straight down the path to this shelter. And look at it." I swing my hand in a circle. "It's airplane and ship parts. Someone had to put this together. And where are the people that were on the ship and the plane? Do you remember the guards that were at the complex? I have no idea if he was telling the truth, but that night in our kitchen, Agent Morgan said those guards were clones of some Navy Seals that never made it home."

Steve buries his face in his hands, takes a deep breath in, and then looks up. "Okay, I have my gun, but just in case, you need some kind of weapon."

I lean over and slide the scalpel from beneath the mattress.

He rolls his eyes. "Well, I guess it's something."

"I hid Ted's backpack in the refrigerator with his medical bag, but Milo took his gun." I tilt my head, noticing some kind of harness on his shoulders. "What are those straps for?"

"It's a parachute harness. Alice couldn't find a spot to land the plane without us being noticed, so I jumped."

I gasp. "You jumped from an airplane to get to me?"

He stretches his neck, lifting his head higher. Pride beams from his face. "Of course, I did."

I wrap my arms around his neck. "And Alice is okay...? What about...?"

"All safe and accounted for," he answers before I finish the question. "I'm not sure why they were keeping us alive, but we were all locked up in some old, condemned building. I was scared because Alice was the only one who wasn't there, but then Carlton showed up. He had been worried about your mom and Eileen staying alone, so he went back to check and saw your mom's SUV pull out of the driveway, followed by a van. But as it turned out, Alice was being kept in another room. She said she heard them mumble something about her being the mastermind of the group, so they were isolating her."

I nod. "Yeah, well she is."

Steve pulls out a small phone and glances at it. "Get Spencer and let's go. Alice says she sees the other plane and for us to go past it to the beach. She is going to sit down long enough for us to get on."

"How do you have a signal?" I glance over at the screen.

"I don't. These are connected sort of like walkie-talkies... the same way that Waves and Claude can send messages to each other."

I lean over and lift Spencer. "Come on, little guy."

Yawning, he rubs his eyes. The second he moves his hands from his face, he squeals and then leaps from my arms onto Steve's head.

"Shhh." Steve puts one finger to his lips.

Spencer kisses the top of Steve's head, jumps back onto the bunk, and grabs the bear. I hold out my Bible, and he tucks it inside with the peanut butter cups and the phone. Steve grips his .45 caliber pistol and motions. Taking Spencer's hand in mine, I grip the scalpel in the other hand and follow him to the door.

He freezes for a moment with his hand on the door and then turns around. "Ellie, when we went back to the house to look for you, we found the photos in the basement and that bag. It sort of looked like... I mean, did you think I...?"

"Not for a second," I say, staring straight into his eyes.

"Why? I have to admit... they had made it look pretty incriminating."

"Yeah. The devil tried to get in my head, and even Agent Morgan tried to convince me that you had played me all along, but I know you. We've been through too much together," I curve up one side of my mouth, "and you have never given me one smidgen of a reason to ever doubt your love or devotion to me."

He nods with a smile. "Stay behind me," his tone switches back to a sense of urgency.

He cracks the door open, and the pain hits. I lean over and hold my breath, wishing I could hide it. I don't want Steve to have more to worry about. He steps outside, but my legs won't move. He reaches back, and when I'm not there, he turns around and darts back through the door.

"Oh, no. You're in labor, aren't you?" His voice trembles. "How long have you been having contractions?"

"They started about the time it got dark," I utter and straighten as the cramping subsides. "I'm not sure that it's labor because it's only happening about every twenty to thirty minutes." I nudge his arm. "Come on. Let's go, so we make it to the plane before it happens again."

Steve half-nods with frown lines extending from his mouth. Lifting his gun, he goes out the door... again. And this time, Spencer and I are right behind him.

"Wait," Steve says in a hushed tone. He steps back to the door, lifts a stick from the ground, and jams it through the handle. He veers into the trees, moving along the edge of the path in the cover of the forest.

We only make it a few steps when a light appears, bouncing down the trail. Steve freezes, twists sideways, and puts his hand on my shoulder. Shielding me, he guides us at the speed of a sloth deeper into the trees. Spencer jerks his hand from my grip and creeps back toward the trail.

Steve's shoulders deflate. He shakes his head and pulls me behind a curtain of vines.

The teddy bear growls.

"Oh, brother," Steve whispers.

"I'm not afraid this time. I got my flashlight," Milo retorts, shining the light into the trees. The beam filters through the vines, but the leaves are too thick for us to be seen.

Leaves rustle near the trail, and a gun fires.

Spencer. No. I bite my lip, reminding myself not to scream, but a whimper still escapes.

Steve grips my arm tighter.

The bear growls again, sounding further from us and closer to the trail. I let out a shallow breath, knowing the danger isn't over, but at least Spencer isn't shot. Rapid footsteps pound against the ground and dwindle away as something moves through the muck of the forest floor toward us. Steve holds onto me, keeping me behind the vines, and slowly shifts so his body is between me and whatever's coming. I rest my left hand on his back and keep the scalpel in my right, hanging at my side.

As the sound gets closer, Steve lifts his gun. His body blocks my view, but the sudden swooshing of the vines rubbing together makes my heart plummet like a lead brick dropped from the top of a building. And as my heart is dropping, the vibration of the bullet leaving Steve's gun flows through him and tingles the palm of my hand. Something falls to the ground with a thud, and the blast from the shot pierces through my eardrums.

"Come on. We have to move fast," he rattles off as he pulls out the little phone and shines it on the ground.

My breath leaves me as the faint glow moves across the body. The red spot on the front of Frank's shirt is spreading and growing bigger by the millisecond. His mouth hangs open, and a semi-automatic with a suppressor lies inches from his fingertips. I press my lips together, hoping the gagging sensation will pass.

Stuffing the phone back in his pocket, Steve leans over and scoops up the gun. "Here, get rid of the scalpel and take this." He holds out his gun to me.

I retract the scalpel blade, slide it into my pajama pants pocket, and take Steve's pistol. Both of us now brandishing guns, we take off toward the edge of the trail. Just as we get to the line of trees that borders the path, a tiny hand snags my pinky finger. *Thank you, Lord.* I cast a quick glance down at the little monkey running beside me with his other hand wrapped around the teddy bear's throat.

Steve keeps in the line of trees as we move along the trail. The moon disappears, and a water droplet lands on my cheek.

"Frank!"

Steve comes to an instant halt as Milo's voice echoes down the trail.

"Frank, come on. The plane's here."

"No," Steve mutters under his breath as he pulls out the phone and types something. A second later, he flips the screen toward me.

> It's another plane. Stay back. We r still in air.

Steve slides the device back into his pocket as the beam from Milo's flashlight flickers down the trail.

"Frank. Let's go. I can't escort the whole crew to the lab by myself." Milo stops about twenty feet from us, turning in a circle with his flashlight.

In the shroud of the leaves, I squeeze Spencer's hand, hoping he doesn't use the teddy bear again, and at the same time, I try not to breathe.

"I don't know my way around this place," Milo whines as he turns and stomps back up the trail. The sprinkle bursts into a sudden pelting downpour. "Great," he yells. "Just great!"

Steve leans his head close to mine. "Are you okay?"

"Fine," I mutter. "Let's try to see what this other plane is about."

We plod through the umbrella of trees as the rain pounds on the path. Milo's light comes into view, and Steve throws out his arm in front of me, signaling me to stop. Keeping our bodies behind a towering trunk, we watch from the darkness of the forest as Agent Morgan charges toward Milo from the other direction.

"Milo, where's Frank?" he roars over the sound of the rain.

"Can't find him, sir." Milo shines his light in Agent Morgan's face, causing him to thrust his arm up to shield his eyes.

"Rrrrr." Agent Morgan's frustration is obvious. "Naval Commander Jones is waiting. Escort him and his crew to the lab. I'll deal with Frank." He disappears from Milo's stream of light.

No. Not again. I let go of Spencer's hand and lean against the tree, digging my nails into the bark, but no matter how hard I fight it, the cramp pulls my upper body over.

Steve's palm presses on my back. "Ellie. Try to relax."

"Drop the gun, Mr. Denali, or I will shoot."

A small beam illuminates behind me as Steve's gun falls next to my shoe.

"Well, well. It appears we're about to have a baby," he boasts in a sarcastic tone. "And since it seems that your doctor has had a mishap, we best get you to the lab."

He doesn't know I have a gun. Maybe I can... No, I can't. He has his gun aimed at Steve.

"Now, Ellie. Stop milking it. It's been more than a minute. Your contraction is over. Stand up, and let's get moving."

I twist my body as I rise and slip the gun into my pocket in one solid motion.

"Very good. Now both of you, keep your hands out to your sides." Keeping his gun trained on Steve, he leans in with his lips close to my face. "You think you're a slick one, don't you?"

His hot, rancid breath hits me in the face, and the smell of rotten eggs burns my nose.

He slides his left hand into my pocket and removes the gun. "You can't deceive the deceiver," he hisses and then shifts back to his position behind us. "Walk straight out onto the path," he orders.

Chapter Twenty-Five

With Agent Morgan on our heels dictating every footfall, we veer onto path after path, twisting and turning like a snake through the thick, plush mass of green leaves. The rain is slacking off, and the clouds are breaking as the first rays of the sun pop over the horizon.

My mouth is so dry that my tongue keeps sticking to the inside of my cheeks. Normally, I would be complaining, but thirst seems to be the least of my concerns right now. Agent Morgan's gun is so close to our backs that it has actually poked me a few times, and as much as I have been trying to convince myself otherwise, I can't deny it any longer. I am in the early stages of labor, which shouldn't be taking place for another four weeks. On top of that, I have no idea what happened to Spencer or if Alice and the others are still safe on the plane.

A clearing appears through the trees ahead, and as we near the opening, an enormous metal building comes into view. With its rounded arch design that is probably meant to withstand strong winds and possibly hurricanes, it has the shape and appearance of a metal can that has been cut in half, except this metal can is around a hundred feet long and thirty feet wide. Obviously, it was constructed and engineered with a much larger budget than the shelter I was given.

Agent Morgan nudges us toward a set of double metal doors centered on the front.

"I wouldn't get all worked up about what you see in here." Chuckling, he reaches around us and presses his thumb to a circle in the center of the knob. It glows red, and he turns the handle. "Neither of you is going to live long enough to worry about it."

I step into the building first, and the sight is breathtaking, in the literal sense. My airway constricts along with every other muscle in my body. Prickles run down my spine as if someone is poking needles into my flesh, and a sharp pain stabs like an ice pick into the upper right side of my chest.

Steve gasps behind me. I wish I could turn around, bury my face in his chest, and erase this image from my mind. Rows of glass cylinders standing upright and stacked two high, one on top of the other, fill the building as far as I can see. And inside each cylinder is a person, suspended and frozen in a solid tube of ice. Some are wearing military uniforms, but most have on a one-piece unitard similar to those we had to wear when we were lied to and forced to return to the facility for so-called testing.

"That way." Agent Morgan gestures with the tip of the gun to a narrow aisle running toward the back of the building between the left wall and the first row of tubes.

As we start down the aisle, a rough, deep male voice filters through a door in the wall on our left. I slow my steps, faking a cramp in my stomach so I can listen.

"I need to get the plane back. When will the funds be deposited?"

"Sorry." Another man replies. "You must have misunderstood."

"No. The assignment was clear. Upon delivery of a crew that is at least twenty-five percent female, my payment would be deposited."

"Yes, that part is correct. But you're not leaving. From the moment you land on this island, you become the property of Mr. Denali."

"Mr. Denali, are you talking about Pres..."

The tip of the gun digs into the back of my skull. "Move. It's not time for another contraction," Agent Morgan bellows with his lips only a foot from my ear.

We lumber all the way to the end of the aisle to another large doorway. Agent Morgan presses his thumb to the center of the knob. The door opens into a laboratory with various high-tech screens and equipment lining the perimeter. A few empty tubes stand in the center, and multiple doors leading out of the room are mingled in the midst of all the technology.

A man with bushy black hair with wide streaks of gray running through it steps from the door in the center of the back wall. His stature is so small that his white lab coat almost drags the floor. His skin is pale, strangely pale to be on a tropical island, and he is wearing black square-rimmed glasses that cover most of the upper part of his head. As he moves closer, I notice that his square glasses are only frames with no lenses.

"Sir," the man adjusts the glasses frames on his nose, "what brings you to the lab? It must be of utmost importance for you to venture all the way down here."

"Yes, Dr. Oglethorpe." Agent Morgan stays behind Steve and me as he speaks. "Highest importance at the moment."

Dr. Oglethorpe focuses on my stomach. "Um-hmm. I am guessing this is the grandchild we have been preparing for."

"You got it. The doctor assigned to the woman has had a tragic accident, and the woman is in labor," Agent Morgan explains in a dry tone. "I am going to need you to take over."

"Me," Dr. Oglethorpe snickers. "You are aware that I am a genetic physicist. I create people in test tubes. I don't remove them from other people." The doctor's face takes on a serious expression as he stares at Agent Morgan. "Are you aware of where that baby will be exiting her body?"

"I am fully aware," Agent Morgan snaps. "But if that bothers you, just cut her open. It doesn't matter because we will be letting her expire after anyway. Just make sure and get the blood sample first."

"Very well, sir," Dr. Oglethorpe utters in a submissive tone.

"I'm going to take care of the man. If I were you, I would keep my weapon in hand, loaded, and aimed. She may be pregnant, but she's still a special agent for the FBI with extensive fight training under her belt."

The man fumbles in the giant pocket on the front of his coat and pulls out a military M17 pistol. His trembling hand extends, and even looking down the barrel of a gun, I'm not able to stay upright. The pain flows from my back around my sides and contracts in the lower part of my abdomen. I press my knees together, trying to stay on my feet as the cramping gets stronger.

Agent Morgan walks Steve toward the door. "Alert me when we have a baby."

"Y-yes, sir." Dr. Oglethorpe gawks at me, looking like he has added those googly eyes on springs to his glasses' frames.

Hunched over with my arms hugging my stomach, I grit my teeth to endure the agony. Not the agony of physical pain, but the agony of my heart breaking as I watch my husband being taken from me, and for the second time in twenty-four hours, having to wonder if I will ever get to see him again.

CHAPTER TWENTY-SIX

Milo never brought my bag from the plane, so tropical temperatures or not, I am still wearing Ted's large, black sweatshirt. However, considering the frigid temperatures inside this lab, which I assume are because of the cryonics, a long-sleeved shirt would be nice if it wasn't soaking wet from the rain.

Dr. Oglethorpe follows me into a small room with a bed no larger than a stretcher. My heart is still pounding out of my chest from Dr. Oglethorpe's little mishap. I'm not sure why anyone would allow this man to have a gun. He was using the M17 to point to the door he wanted me to go through, but his finger was trembling on the trigger. The gun went off, shattering one of those glass tubes into a million pieces, and since no one came to check, I am led to believe that this lab is either soundproof or his misfires happen a lot. That being said, I need to get away from Dr. Oglethorpe before his finger slips again, but at the same time, I fear making any abrupt movements, especially right now with the barrel against my lower back.

With slow gentle steps, I cross the room to the narrow hard plastic bed. It has no adjustments, no pillow, no blankets or sheets, and no padding. And instead of side rails, it has a flat steel bar running the length of it on both sides.

"Lie down," he mumbles in a weak, timid voice.

"I need to turn around to get on the table." I keep my volume low, being careful not to alarm him. "I can't with the gun pressed so tight to my back."

"Oh," he mutters, "and the pressure from the barrel disappears."

I turn and almost bump the tip of the gun with my bulging belly.

He pulls his arm back a few inches but holds his stance as if his feet are glued to the floor.

With my eyes fixed on the unsteady tip of the M17, I wiggle up onto the bed, roll back on one elbow, and lower myself until my head touches the plastic.

"Place your arms on the bars." He reaches beneath the bed and pulls out yellow nylon straps with locking hooks on the ends.

Tears pool in my eyes. If he straps my arms, I won't get out of here alive. *Please help me, Lord.*

"How far apart are the contractions?" he asks as he tries to hold the gun and untangle the straps at the same time.

"Still about twenty minutes." I lift my head to watch what he's doing, tucking my hands close to my body. "I'm pretty sure we still have quite a while. You know, I'm not supposed to lie flat on my back for long periods of time. It reduces blood circulation to the baby."

The end of the strap slips from his hand and the hook clanks against the concrete floor. His shoulders slump, and he exhales with a long, drawn-out groan. "How exactly are you supposed to lay then?" he huffs.

"On my side," I reply.

"Fine, lay on your side." His words muffle as he strains to snatch the strap from the floor without taking his aim off of me. His efforts fail, and he pauses for a second with his body bent to the side. Then, in a quick jerk, he dips, taking the M17 just below the table.

Sliding my hand in my pocket, I push up on my elbow and roll from the table onto his back, knocking all the air from his body. He keeps his footing and shifts his weight to toss me off, but the fingers of my left hand are digging into his shoulder holding on. In one swift motion, I pull the scalpel from my pocket with my right hand and extend the blade with my thumb as I thrust it into the arm with the gun. The M17 drops. He twists with all his might, knocking me off. My spine collides with the hard floor, but adrenaline blocks the pain and springs me right back into motion. At the same instant that he reaches across his body to pull the tiny knife from his arm, I swing both of my legs around. With his face twisted in a grimace from the pain of the blade slipping from his skin, his feet fly out from under him. The back of Dr. Oglethorpe's head ricochets off the floor.

I crawl on my knees across the floor and grab the gun. Aiming it at him, I lean over beside his still unconscious body, press my fingers to the side of his neck, and breathe a sigh of relief at the pulsing sensation against my fingertips.

My eyes scan the room, searching for anything that will restrain him if he wakes up. *The yellow strap.* I stretch with my left arm and snag the hook with my pinky. Knowing I don't have a choice because I need both hands, I lay the gun to the side within my reach but out of Dr. Oglethorpe's and tie the strap around his wrists. Moving the gun with me, I slide down to his feet and knot the strings of his patent leather shoes together. In a single motion, I snatch up the M17 and push to my feet.

Clutching the handle of the gun in my hand, I rest my finger on the trigger and dart to the door. *I can do all things through Christ which strengtheneth me.* I shift my eyes upward. *Please, give me strength and guide me, Lord. Please help me to find Steve before it's too late.* I suck a slow deep breath in through my mouth and step from the room, knowing that no matter what happens, God is with me.

Since I have no idea how long I have before another contraction hits, I move with fast, long strides around the empty tubes, trying to avoid the broken glass while already contemplating what to do about the thumb pad on the door leading out of here. As I approach the door, I send up a *thank you* because the door doesn't have a thumb pad on this side, which makes sense that they would only want to keep people out. But then I think of Dr. Oglethorpe with that gun, and I could see a need to keep him contained.

I crack the door, listening for any movement or voices, and then inch it open bit by bit just in case the door squeaks or creaks. *Show me the way, Lord.* Sticking my head through the opening, I peer both ways, step out, and head back down the same aisle that Agent Morgan brought us. I'm not sure where to begin, but my gut tells me Steve is in this building somewhere. If Morgan was going to kill him right away, he would have shot him back in the forest.

I pause as I pass each door and listen, but only silence shouts that Steve isn't there. Even the room where I heard the men talking earlier is now quiet. I pivot down the next aisle between the first two rows of tubes. I can't handle looking at their faces, but my peripheral vision picks up enough to know that all of the tubes are inhabited. At the end of the row, I realize that I am at the back of the building by the laboratory where I started, so I turn and ease along the back toward the other side of the building.

A few more closed doors scatter the back wall, but no voices penetrate through. I near the last row of tubes on the opposite side, and another contraction announces itself in my lower back. I drag my feet a few steps down the aisle and press my body in the indention between two of the cylinders, trying to keep my body out of sight until the pain passes, but the tightening of my stomach muscles still pulls my upper body to my knees. A tear drips from my cheek and splatters on the concrete by my foot. I press my lips together, determined not to make a sound, but the clacking of hard shoes against the concrete tells me it's too late to worry about it. I shove my hand with the gun in my pocket, pulling the long sweatshirt down to cover it.

From my bent position, my lungs fill with air when he rounds the corner. I raise my upper body a few inches, but the pain from my contracting muscles won't let me go any farther.

"Ellie, I was coming to find you. What are you doing out here?" Steve puts his hand under my arm and leans over me.

I roll my eyes up at him. "You're okay," I whisper. "You're really okay."

"I'm fine." He tugs at my arm and points to the door a few steps away at the end of the row. "Come on, let's go in there until you feel better."

I nod in agreement, knowing that we're sitting ducks out here.

I don't pay attention as he opens the door, but as we pass through, I notice a thumb pad by the casing. The room doesn't appear to be in use. A small empty desk sits along one wall, and one of those tiny beds is pushed against another. He helps me up onto the bed, and then he rolls the desk chair over beside me.

"Where did you get those clothes?" I ask, staring at the blue polo and long olive-green shorts."

"My clothes were soaked, so Morgan gave me dry ones."

I crinkle my forehead as I wonder why I wasn't given dry clothes.

"He didn't want me to be dripping wet when I talked to my father."

"You talked to your dad?" I reach out and touch his shoulder.

"Yeah, I did. And I'm glad. He's not at all as I imagined he would be."

The pain is gone, so I push myself up and sit on the side of the little bed. "It's good that you have closure now." I press on his shoulder as I slide off the bed and stand. "The contraction is over. We better get going. I don't know how long Oglethorpe will be knocked out."

"Ellie, we can't."

I peer down at him in the chair. "I don't understand."

"My father is my flesh and blood. I'm not leaving him."

I peel my chin off my chest. "Your opinion of him changed that much in five minutes?"

"I know it sounds crazy, but he has good intentions. He's not the evil person you think."

"I'm about to give birth to our child, and it's not going to happen on this island." My heart is speeding out of control. "What did he do, hypnotize you? You realize that he is going to kill me after I have this baby, right?" I walk to the door.

He leaps from the chair and grabs my arm. "Ellie, you're not looking at the big picture," he says a bit too loud and then lowers his volume. "He is my father. You wouldn't abandon your father either. And in case you've forgotten, your dad isn't a saint. He wrote a letter asking my father to take you to his training facility and make you part of his army." He squeezes my arm as he rants.

"My dad did that because he thought he was protecting me, and you know it."

He laughs. "Do you really believe that, Ellie?"

I lean back against the door and stuff my hands into my pockets. I gaze into his eyes, into his dark brown eyes, into the eyes of a man who is supposed to be my husband, into the eyes of the man who is supposed to stand by me and love me as Christ loved the church. "Never forget," I utter.

"Never forget what?" He narrows his eyes back at me.

"I'm sorry, but I'm leaving." As I start to turn, his hand flies to his waistband. I don't have time to slip my hand from my pocket and aim, so I shift the handle down in my baggy pajama pocket, angling the barrel up, and pull the trigger.

He falls to the floor, and the blast echoes in my ears... a sound that I fear I will never be able to silence.

CHAPTER TWENTY-SEVEN

I crack the door, and without looking back, I pull it open and take a step from the room with my gun aimed in front of me, hoping that somehow this whole scene will vanish from my brain. I know I didn't have a choice. He was going for his gun.

"Ellie." An arm flings around my shoulders in a half-embrace as she brandishes her gun with the other. "Oh, Praise the Lord, you're okay." She catches the door before it closes all the way, pushes it open, and steps in the doorway, pulling me with her, but I hold my stance just outside the room. "Oh. Oh no. Ellie, I'm so sorry." Tears flood into Alice's eyes.

Before I get a word out, Waves rounds the corner from the end aisle. A low squeal escapes as he stops at the door opening and his glowing eyes fall on the body lying on the floor in a pool of blood.

His metal hand flings upward to cover his mouth, and his entire body quivers.

"It's not him," I utter.

"What?" Lines form in the middle of Alice's forehead.

"That's not him," I repeat a bit louder.

"Oh." Waves takes his hand down. "That explains it."

"Explains what?" Alice and I ask in unison.

"Why, there is a guy that looks just like him strapped to a table in one of those rooms around the corner."

"Waves, hurry," I urge. "Show me." I take off in the direction that Waves came from.

Alice is right on my heels, and Waves speeds up, taking the lead. He turns down the last aisle between a row of cylinders and the opposite wall that I haven't seen yet. As we approach, a man's voice coming from inside the room ahead makes me slow my step.

Waves locks his wheels and spins around. "Someone is in there," he says in a hushed tone, which is a struggle for Waves. His volume doesn't go that low. He turns his head to the side and points to the cylinders. "Hide behind those ice people."

"How are we supposed to get behind them?" I roll my eyes to my stomach and then to the few inches separating the cylinders.

Waves grabs onto one of the cylinders and slides it out about a foot. The one on top of it starts to sway. Alice waves her hand, trying to get his attention as she steps back, pulling me with her, but he doesn't notice her. He is too busy bopping his head side to side like he does when he is singing, and his focus is only on the bottom tube. He slides it a few more inches. The top cylinder comes toppling down, barely missing him by what seems like only millimeters, and collides with the floor right in front of his wheeled feet, shaking the entire building.

Alice thinks fast as usual. "Hurry," she whispers, nudging me through the opening and behind the next stack just as the door swings open.

"What happened?" A man's voice barks, the same one we heard as we approached the room.

"Earthquake," Waves yells. "I'm still sensing seismic activity. Proceed to the center of the building immediately."

Silence fills the air.

"Move now! The seismic waves are gaining frequency," Waves shouts.

Running feet pound on the concrete, fading as the man gets farther away.

Alice and I step out, and I look at Waves, shaking my head in disbelief.

"What? I encountered a lot of strange noises when I came through that jungle of trees searching for you." He rolls to the door. "Now, I'm running low on darts." He presses his finger to the thumbprint pad. The lock clicks.

"How did you do that?" I know it's Waves, but after the cloning thing, my trust level and my nerves are on edge.

"Oh," he glances back at the tube. "I can't really detect seismic activity."

"Not that. The thumbprint." I grit my teeth in frustration.

"A new software update. I can access the code on all the latest models and align the magnets inside my fingertips to match it." He presses on the handle and pushes the door open.

One look and I forget about the thumb pad. My jaw drops like a heavy brick, pulling my mouth open, and I gasp, taking in every ounce of air in the room. Steve is lying unconscious on a tiny, hard gurney-type bed. One of those huge, vertical cylinders filled with liquid stands next to the bed, and the lid is open at a ninety-degree angle with two huge hoses attached to the top of it. On the other side of the bed are the same two machines that we found in the lab at President Denali's training facility. Two anti-freeze canisters sit in a metal basket that is strapped to the side of one of the machines, and a large bag with a printed symbol that looks like a blood droplet is hanging from a hook at the top of the other machine.

The whole scene fills me with a sense of déjà vu, reminding me of when Steve and I found Alice sedated with all of this same setup. The only difference is we got to Alice before the process had started. Tears pool in my eyes, and the bitter taste of acid erupts in my mouth. The tubes are attached to Steve's arms, a humming noise is coming from the machines, and a few drops of blood are already in the bag. Steve's nose is covered with a small clear mask, and a hose is running into his mouth.

"Alice," I cry out with my eyes trained on the laptop that is open on the small table at the foot of the bed. The words, TASK IN PROGRESS, are illuminated in bold blue letters in the center of the screen with a progress indicator below it. "It's only at one percent. Do something? Can you hack that computer?"

Without a word, Alice steps around me, wedges up behind the bed, and pulls the plug from the wall. The humming of the machines stops, and the computer beeps with an error message flashing on the screen.

I snap from my frozen state of panic, stuff the gun in my pocket, and pull the tubes with tiny needles from his arms.

"How do we wake him?" Alice asks.

"I don't know. When it happened to you, Steve carried you back to his office and waited for the sedative to wear off." I press my fingers to his wrist. "His pulse is strong." Filled with hesitation, I reach for the mask, questioning whether I should remove it, but I continue when I remember the plug disabled all of the machines along with any oxygen that would have been flowing through it.

I peer down at his pale face, which is always so bronze and full of life. Even his lips have a bluish tint. Gripping his hand, I close my eyes. *Lord, I know we don't have much time, and we can't carry him. Please let him wake up. Show us what to do. Please,* my bottom lip trembles, *don't let me lose him.*

I lift my eyes, and Alice has a phone in her hand like the one Steve had earlier.

"What are you doing?" I pull the neck of my shirt up and wipe the moisture from my cheek.

"I forgot to send Gerald a message letting him know that I found you." She tilts her head back and forth as she types. "Of course, it isn't as if I've had a grand opportunity to send him one either, but I still feel guilty. I can't believe he agreed to let us separate to look for you."

"Where is Gerald... where is everyone else?"

"When Steve stopped answering, Gerald, your dad, Waves, Claude, and I got off the plane to find you guys. Since we need the plane to get home, we didn't want to leave it on the ground where it could get destroyed or tampered with. On top of that, we thought it would be too conspicuous if we all got off, so everyone else is on the plane in the air, circling the island."

My eyes widen. "If you're here, who's flying the plane?"

"Your mother."

I start to voice my concern, but another contraction interrupts my train of thought. I grit my teeth and lean my elbows on the edge of the bed, keeping my hand on Steve's.

"Ellie, are you in labor?" Alice's pitch rises two octaves.

I nod through the pain. "M-My con-contractions are f-far apart though."

I take a few deep breaths, and Steve's finger wiggles against my hand just as the pain subsides.

"Steve, honey, can you hear me?" I squeeze his hand.

His lips part open a tiny bit, and he mumbles.

"I know you're weak, but please," I plead, "I need you to wake up. We have to get out of here."

His eyelids open slowly, and he squints, probably from the bright light above him. He blinks a few times until his eyes are completely open, but his skin is still so pallid. He stares up at me. "I-I'm sorry," he mouths as the sound cuts in and out.

I gaze down into his deep brown eyes, the eyes that were gazing down at me after I woke up in President Denali's facility. "Never forget."

His eyes burn into mine. "The Lord thy God is with thee whithersoever thou goest," he whispers, his voice hoarse and raspy.

Thank you, Lord. The corners of my lips curve into a smile. "I love you."

The door rattles.

"Get down behind the bed," Waves says, grabbing up the clear mask and strapping it across his face.

I dart up by Steve's head. "Close your eyes," I whisper and then dip down beside Alice just as the door swings open.

"What's going on?"

Oh no. Dr. Oglethorpe.

"Keep the door closed. I've been ordered to decontaminate this room." Waves adds distress to his mechanical voice. "You are going to need to shower immediately."

"Why?" Dr. Oglethorpe exclaims. "What contamination?"

"The man had missile mites on his shirt." Waves keeps his dramatic tone.

"Missile mites? What's that?" Dr. Oglethorpe questions.

"You don't know? They are known to carry pseudosillogism disease. It's highly contagious and fatal." Waves raises his volume. "Hurry. Go shower and burn your clothes."

"The man was in my lab. What am I going to do?" His voice fades away, and the door clanks shut.

After a minute, I grab the metal bar on the side of the bed and pull myself up. The door opens again. It's too late for me, but I hold my hand back, signaling Alice to stay down.

"This area is contam—" Waves stops and lifts his hand at the sight of the gun, but it's too late to shoot the dart.

Dennis Denali pulls the trigger.

Waves' battery compartment shatters, and he goes still.

I bite my lower lip to keep it from quivering.

"That hunk of metal was a nuisance when he worked in my facility too," he laughs. "Not anymore." He turns his eyes toward me. "It seems you have a talent for escaping. Of course, if I had capable help, this wouldn't be a problem, and I wouldn't have to be in here taking care of you myself. But that's the reason you and your little crew aren't dead yet, isn't it? Well, you're a little more frustrating than the rest. If it weren't for my grandchild inside you, I doubt I would bother with you."

"What do you mean 'that's the reason' we aren't dead? What is it that you wouldn't bother with?" I ask without flinching.

"Could you imagine if I could create my new world with skilled people filled with the same motivation and determination as your little army? Look at what your little group has been capable of. It's uncanny." He takes a step closer. "I might not be able to make you all forget God, but I can create duplicates with the same DNA. The only difference between them and your army is that they will be my creation, and I will be the only leader they will ever know."

He glances down at Steve on the bed in front of me. "It appears Dr. Canton has my son prepared for preservation. You know, when making copies, it's always a good practice to keep the original." He lifts one eyebrow and smirks.

I roll my eyes. *Does he hear the words coming out of his mouth?*

"Well, I'm sure Dr. Canton will be back in a moment to finish. As for you, you get to come with me. I'm actually really excited. Rumor has it that my grandson should be here by tomorrow. Of course, I'm aware that I don't look old enough to be a grandfather," he babbles. "Oh, that reminds me, I've been told that you have a gun, an M17 specifically. You can just pass that on to me now. You won't be needing it."

"I lost it." With my lower body still hidden by the small bed, I slide the gun from my pocket and hold it behind my back, hoping Alice will take the hint. I can't aim it at Denali now with his gun fixed on me, and a shot fired from my pocket like before would only hit Steve from where I'm standing.

"Is that the best story the infamous Ellie Hatcher Denali can come up with?" He lifts one eyebrow.

"I was walking by those tubes, a contraction hit, I dropped it, and it slid under one of them. I can show you if you want." I rattle off without a stutter or hesitation as Alice slips the gun from my hand. I hold my hands out to my sides and step out from behind the bed. "No gun. Feel free to check my pockets."

"Fine," he grumbles, grabbing my wrist. He tugs me through the door with the tip of the gun inches from my head. "Any idea what happened?" He nods toward the cracked tube lying on its side." You look a little small to have caused this much damage."

"No. I overheard a man's voice say something about an earthquake or seismic activity though."

"Sounds like something Oglethorpe would come up with," he mutters under his breath as he guides me out of the metal building.

Chapter Twenty-Eight

Once we are outside the building, he clutches my wrist tighter and quickens his pace as he takes off down a different trail than the one Agent Morgan brought us on. This trail is much narrower and is completely covered and hidden by a thick canopy of trees.

We walk quite a long way. Well, he walks fast, and with his death grip on my wrist, I am almost in a jog to keep from falling. It seems as if we have walked miles, but I'm guessing it has been more like a quarter mile. The pain creeps around from my lower back, and my heels dig in.

"C-Con-traction," I mutter through heavy breaths as I hunch over.

"Toughen up," he orders in a cold, uncaring tone. "Let's go."

He yanks on my wrist, almost ripping my arm from the socket, and I tumble forward. My kneecap collides hard with the ground, and a sharp stone jabs into the palm of my free hand as I attempt to keep from face-planting. I try to get my footing, but between the cramping muscles in my stomach and him pulling my arm, I manage only to snag and rip the leg of my pajama pants on a root.

He blows out hard through flared nostrils and shoves the gun into the waistband of his shorts. "I'm sick and tired of games." He grabs my other wrist, twists me backward, and drags me down the path. My feet bounce over roots and rocks. One of my shoes catches on something and slides from my foot.

Tears stream from my eyes, but I refuse to make a sound. I refuse to give him the satisfaction of hearing me cry. I only wish I could wipe my eyes and hold back the rest that are trying to burst out. *Father, please give me strength. I know he isn't going to kill me yet, but please let him stop. Give me the strength to endure the pain.*

The crash of breaking waves gets louder, and the trees open to a blue sky and white wispy clouds. The rough, jarring ground beneath me changes to scorching, powdery sand, charring the exposed raw flesh on my heel left by the rugged trail.

A moment later, we veer back into the trees. My hair bounces in my eyes, but as I twist my head, I make out a small yellow house. It appears to be one level with a straw-thatched roof and a small straw-covered awning on the front.

He pulls me up onto a roughhewn lumber porch and through the wooden slab door into what I guess is supposed to be a living room. It's not a place that I would ever envision Dennis Denali living, but one glance around the room, and I know it can only belong to him. A single chair sits in the middle of the room, facing a giant high-gloss photograph of himself.

He drags me past a small eating table with two chairs and into a tiny, dark room with no windows that might be six feet by eight feet if I round up... a lot. A miniature cot with a thin mattress is pushed against the wall.

He lets go of my arms, letting me fall to the floor. "Don't even think of trying to escape. You're under my watch now," he says in a harsh tone. "And in case you haven't looked around, this is an island. You have nowhere to go." He steps toward the door.

"Who is going to help me deliver this baby? I need a doctor," I utter in desperation.

He turns and glares at me. His eyes are so black, and barely any white is visible. "Your mom's a nurse, and I understand you spent a little time in nursing school. You figure it out."

"Do you have one rational cell left in your brain? I can't deliver a baby in this room by myself. There aren't even any towels or water." Words are coming out of my mouth before I even realize what I'm saying.

His jaw hardens. "For your information, I'm the only one left in this world with any rational brain cells. And I suggest that you show me a little more respect. Your life is in my hands. I decide how long you live, and I get to choose the moment you die." He emphasizes the word 'I' as he speaks.

"I don't think so," I respond, shaking my head. "My life is in the hands of God. Job 12:10 says, 'In whose hand is the soul of every living thing, and the breath of all mankind.' He already knows the moment I will die, and I'm not afraid. As Paul said to the Philippians, 'For me to live is Christ, and to die is gain,' because the second that my earthly body dies, I will enter into the presence of God."

"You are delusional. I hope that isn't part of your genetics, or cloning you is going to be a complete waste." He stomps out and slams the door behind him, leaving me in a dark, windowless room.

I don't bother to move. I curl up in a ball right where I am on the floor. I don't sob. I just let the tears stream in gentle rivers down my face and drop onto the hard planks beneath me.

So much love crushed beneath so much pain,
Behind my eyes, tears hide like clouds full of rain.

When the cloud bursts and the river overflows,
I gasp for air beneath the flood, and no one knows... no
one knows.

Gazing through the darkness, I beg and plead,
Hoping to hear the voice I so desperately need.
But instead, whispers invade and turn to shouts ringing
in my ear.
You're all alone... all alone... is all that I hear.

The pain, the agony, the despair,
It feels like too much to bear.
But then, I think of the rejection and the scars on His
hands,
And I curl up in the arms of the One who understands.

I cling to Him and His promise of the coming day,
When I will have no more tears, and the pain will go
away.
I'm not alone... I'm not alone.
He will never leave me. I'm not alone.

My nose pours, but I don't have the desire to sniffle or even wipe it. *Father, the words of that song echo from the depths of my heart. I cling to you. I know I'm not alone.* I close my eyes and see Steve lying on that bed with those tubes running from his arms. *Father, I pray that Steve is okay and that he and Alice get out of that building safely. I pray that you would protect my dad and Gerald wherever they are in this place and take care of everyone on the plane.* I swallow hard. *Lord, I'm tired, so tired and broken. I have no fight left in me. So, if it's my time, I'm ready. I'm ready to be with you, Father. But for my son, I'm afraid. I know that I'm not supposed to be afraid, but this is my baby... Your baby... a tiny life that you have created inside of me... a life you created for your purpose. Please give me strength, Lord. Help me fight for this child. Let my son have the chance to know you and to have a relationship with you. Please, Lord.*

Another contraction comes and goes. I think they're getting closer together. Other than gritting my teeth through the pain, I lie on the floor in a vegetative state... not moving, not thinking... just existing. Another contraction comes and then another with less and less time between each one.

As I lie on the floor, a strange warmth builds inside me. It's as if God is mending my broken pieces back together. The words of Isaiah 40:31 flow into my mind, and I recite them aloud. "But they that wait upon the Lord shall renew their strength; they shall mount up with wings as eagles; they shall run and not be weary; and they shall walk, and not faint." I push myself up and wipe my face with my shirt. Determination pulses through me. "I can do all things through Christ which strengtheneth me." I don't need to say it seven times. It's written in my heart. Whatever comes, I'm ready.

Chapter Twenty-Nine

I sit on the edge of the cot, rocking back and forth. I think the contractions are about five minutes apart now. I've been trying to count in order to time them, but a rattle that resembles a chewing noise on the roof right above me keeps distracting me, causing me to lose my spot. I don't know much about island life, but I imagine a giant bird up there picking the straw from the roof and having a feast. Considering my situation, I probably should be using my mind for more productive things, but the image of the bird eating the roof makes me smile.

A moment later, a loud crunch sends dust falling from the ceiling, and a minuscule chunk of the roof rips off, letting in a tiny stream of light. I push to my feet, and with my eyes fixed on the tiny opening, another chunk disappears, followed by another, and another. Light floods into the room as the hole gets bigger and bigger. With my hand pressed against my chest, I stare with my mouth agape, and then I start to cackle. Through the hole in the roof are all of these tiny monkeys with yellow fur mingled with specks of green. Their small hands are hard at work ripping away the straw, and the mixture of the highs and lows in their screams makes it sound like they are laughing hysterically.

My eyes widen as I catch sight of one larger monkey in the middle of the troop that doesn't match the others. He has black fur, and an enormous teddy bear rests on his back with its arms tied around the monkey's neck. *Oh, Spencer. You never stop bringing sunshine into my life.*

Denali thrusts the door open, sending it crashing back against the wall. He steps in with his pistol aimed out in front of him. "I thought I warned you not to try your escape antics...," he fumes but his volume fades as his head tilts upward. "What on earth is going on? What are those little nuisances doing to my house?" he yells. He lifts the gun and fires a shot through the open roof.

The monkeys scatter. He lowers his gun and turns toward me with a scowl on his face. "Did you have anything to do with this?"

I let out a sigh and shake my head in disbelief. "Yes. I summonsed a troop of monkeys from a dark room with no windows to come and rip the roof off of your house. Seriously?"

As I finish my sarcasm, something flies through the roof and slaps into the side of Denali's cheek. I glance upward just in time to see the hole surrounded by little monkeys barraging him with handfuls of poop. I move my eyes back to Denali and bite my lips together, trying to hold in the guffaw of laughter that is trying to explode as I watch him get pelted by a hailstorm of feces. He lifts his gun and fires again, but the monkeys have already disappeared.

He reaches up with his fingers and wipes away the poop hanging from his eyelashes, and then with gritted teeth, he glares at me as if he has death lasers attached to his eyes.

Somehow, I manage to hold a serious expression. "There are many devices in a man's heart; nevertheless the counsel of the Lord, that shall stand."

"You always come up with a way to quote the Bible, don't you?" The barrel of the pistol presses against the end of my nose. "If it weren't for my grandson, I—"

He appears through the doorway behind Denali. "Put the gun down."

My eyes water. *He's okay.*

Denali lowers the gun to my stomach as he turns to face Steve. "I don't think so. If you shoot me, I pull the trigger, and they both die."

Frown lines crease around Steve's mouth. "How did you get here? How did you become this full of hatred that you would plot to murder innocent people... even your own family? I'm your son, and you were about to freeze me like a popsicle. Why? Are you that hungry for fame and power? Where has all of it gotten you? Look around. You're living in a shack on an unknown island in the middle of the Bermuda Triangle."

As Steve rants, I realize this is the first time he has talked to his father... that he remembers anyway.

Steve points as he continues. "For crying out loud, you are threatening to shoot your unborn grandchild."

"If you would stop fighting against me, and let me be, I am trying to save my grandson before you all have a chance to ruin him. That boy won't be lied to about how much God loves him. You want to know how I got here?" he screams. "As a kid, I was told over and over how much God loved me. I believed it for a while. But then I started realizing that one of the people telling me that God loved me was the one hurting her. Time after time, I heard her screams and listened to her excuses about the bruises. And then one day, he hit her so hard, she didn't wake up. I lost the most precious person in the world to me. So, either God didn't love me, or he loved my bully of a grandfather more. And as for my situation, this island is only temporary. Damien promised that we would rid the world of God and soon I would be ruling the world. He has it all mapped out. Everything is going as planned. Just because I am a little off the radar doesn't mean that I'm not keeping tabs on the plan. You all might have stopped Eckert and a couple of major catastrophes, but the aftereffects are playing out like a charm. The people are rising against the government and authority and destroying each other in the process. And when the United States falls, so will the rest of the world. Right into my hands." He howls in a menacing laugh. "Dennis Denali will hold the whole world in his hands."

Steve's eyes glimmer with moisture. "I'm sorry about your grandmother. I really am. But you can't blame God for the choices your grandfather made. God doesn't force us to love Him or follow His commands. But He loves us so much that He gave His one and only son so that we could have the choice. If God forced your grandfather's actions, then where would our choice be to follow Jesus and live for Him? Where would our choice be to accept His free gift of salvation? Ellie and I saw the obituary. It said my great-grandmother had extraordinary faith. I think God loved her so much that He took her to be with Him, to be in a place where she would cry no more tears and feel no more pain. And I'm not sure if you've actually read the entire Bible, but you won't be holding the whole world in your hands. News flash, God wins."

Denali's face reddens to the point it looks as if blood might seep through his skin. In a swift motion, he swings the gun toward Steve.

But the second the tip of the pistol leaves my stomach, Steve fires the M17.

The blast must be deafening, but only silence surrounds me as I gape down at my worst nightmare in a pool of blood... at the hole through his chest where his heart should have been.

I grab my stomach and fold over. Steve's arms wrap around me, and he lowers me to the cot, kissing my forehead over and over.

The sound of speeding footfalls pounds toward the room. Steve aims his gun as Alice pops through the doorway aiming hers. They both lower their guns, and Dad and Gerald appear behind her just as Steve pulls my head over against his chest.

Alice stares at the body on the floor. "Jillian messaged. Morgan took off on his plane. I'm going to go call for help." Alice turns and walks from the room past my dad in the doorway with Gerald behind her.

Dad stands frozen with his gaze fixed on the scene. As he uses his knuckle to wipe beneath his eyes, he whispers, "Thank you, Lord." Then, he takes a step and disappears back through the house.

Steve lifts my hand, turning it over in his, inspecting the dried blood mixed with dirt and grit around the gash. "I'm so sorry, Ellie. You knew he was alive, and I didn't listen. I didn't listen, and I almost lost you." Moisture gathers in the corners of his eyes.

"You didn't lose me." I touch his chin with the tip of my index finger. "It all played out exactly as God planned." I clutch my stomach with one hand and squeeze his knee with the other.

"Ellie, your contractions are pretty close together."

"How close?" Mom jogs through the door.

"I don't know, Jillian," Steve answers. "I didn't think to time it. Maybe three minutes."

"Mom, I thought you were flying the plane," I mutter in a strained voice.

"Alice told me you were in labor, so Herb moved into the cockpit." Mom is surveying the room as she speaks.

Steve jumps up. "What do you mean Herb is flying the plane?"

"He said he knew how." Mom shrugs and pulls my hair behind my head. "Ellie, are you having to fight the urge to push?"

I peer up at my mom without answering.

"Yeah, I could see it in your eyes." She tries to hide the worry in her voice. "We aren't going to be able to make it home, but it'll be okay."

"Well, well, well."

No. Not now. I gulp. Milo.

He aims his gun back and forth between the three of us. "Looks like I'll be taking over, and I won't be needing any baby to help me rule the worl..." His words cut off as he falls forward on top of Denali with a dart protruding out of the back of his neck."

"Yay. I've been dying to try out these tranquilizer darts," Herb says, wheeling right over the top of the bodies on the floor. "I brought towels and water."

"Thank you, Herb, but who's flying the plane?" Mom questions with wide eyes.

"Oh, don't worry. Spencer took over." Herb extends his arms, holding the towels.

"What?" Mom and Steve shout at the same time.

"Just kidding. I thought we could all use a bit of lighthearted humor." A mechanical laugh shakes his bowtie. "Miss Alice said it was okay to keep the plane on the ground since Morgan is gone. Gerald, Dukakis, and Carlton are on guard though."

Mom helps me lie down on the mattress. "Breathe, honey. Take deep breaths."

"We have a slight problem." Alice's voice flows from the door. "How long before we can take off?"

"Not sure," Mom replies without taking her focus off of me.

"What kind of problem?" Steve asks in a deflated tone.

"The grand island of Dennis Denali is a volcano... an active volcano... and it's about to get real active." Alice leans against the casing. "I managed to tap into Denali's private satellite internet connection, and I've notified the authorities. A military aircraft carrier isn't far from here, and they also have some jets in route to try and get the cryogenic tubes with the missing military personnel."

"Alice," Mom yells, "guard the door. I'm about to be a grandmother."

Steve darts to my side. He takes one of the towels and wipes the sweat and tears from my face, and then he lifts my hand, intertwining his fingers with mine. I gaze up into his deep brown eyes, and even though this isn't the setting I had in mind for the birth of our child, I have never felt more blessed.

"Alright, sweetheart," Mom says in that calm, comforting voice of hers, "it's time to push."

Gritting my teeth, I squeeze Steve's hand, tightening my grip like a vise as the pain worsens. I know I should probably let up, but he'll survive a few fingernail indentions on the back of his hand.

As we sit on the plane waiting to take off, I stare down in wonder at the little life in my arms. He's four weeks early, and even though he is small, he appears to be as healthy and strong as he would be if I carried him full term. *God is so good*, I think to myself as my husband gazes over my shoulder, and I soak up his warm breath against my cheek.

"I know we came up with a lot of ideas, but we've never officially decided on a name." Steve leans his head against mine.

"Yeah. Somehow, none of the names we chose seem to fit. What do you think of Kade Christian?" I cast my eyes over to get his reaction.

"Kade Christian," he says as if he is checking out the sound of it.

"Kade in memory of Kate, and Christian because I hope he will always keep Christ at the center of his life."

"It's perfect," he utters with a slight crack in his voice. "It's perfect."

Alice appears in the doorway of the cockpit. "Plane's ready for takeoff, and from the looks of the smoke out there, we need to move. Is everyone here?"

"Dukakis is still loading the monkeys in the cargo area, and Claude isn't here. I'll do a roll call to check everyone else," Herb answers. "Attention everyone," he announces, "I'm doing a roll call." He pauses, and the lights in his eyes blink on and off a few times. "Alright, I have a mental list pulled up. Steve?"

Silence fills the plane.

"It seems we may not understand how roll call works. When I call out your name, you say 'here'. Let's try it again. Steve."

"Couldn't you just look around... oh, never mind." Steve sighs. "Here."

"Very good. Ellie."

"Here," I say, trying not to laugh.

"Teresa."

"Here."

"Cynthia."

"Here."

"Eileen... Eileen."

"Oh, sorry. I was gawking at the baby. Here."

"Jillian."

"Right here, Herb." Mom waves her hand.

"Tom."

"Yep, over here."

"Good, good. Carlton."

"Here."

"Alice."

"Well, you know I'm here."

"Gerald."

"He's in the cockpit," Alice answers.

"Herb."

"Here," he answers himself.

"Spencer."

Dad points out the window. "He's helping Dukakis."

"Wonderful." Herb spins his head to Alice. "We just need Dukakis, Spencer, and Claude."

Dukakis steps up into the plane carrying Spencer and the teddy bear. "Wow, that's a lot of little green monkeys, and they are a bit on the rowdy side. Are you sure Wildlife Resources will be there as soon as we land to take care of them?"

"That's what they told me," Alice assures. "And an ambulance will be waiting to transport Ellie and the baby to the hospital."

Dukakis sits and puts Spencer in the seat beside him. His little monkey butt barely touches the seat before he has his hand stuck down in the back of the teddy bear. Two seconds later, Dukakis and Spencer both have their mouths stuffed with peanut butter cups.

A loud clinking and clanking noise pulls all of our eyes to the doorway as metal beats against the stairs.

Claude, with his metal body blackened from the smoke, rolls backward onto the plane, pulling Waves aboard. "No man left behind." Claude lets go, and Waves collides with the floor.

"You pulled him all the way across the island?" Steve questions. "I could have built another one just like him."

"An artist can try to paint the same picture twice, but it will never be identical." Claude leans over and tousles the red mohawk on top of Waves' head. "There is only one Waves."

Alice glances out as she pushes the button to close the door. "We have to move now. Buckle up."

A moment later, the plane lifts into the sky. I peer down through the window just before we pass above the clouds, and it's as if time stops as I process the scene. I'm on a plane somewhere in a place that has been endowed with the name, the Devil's Triangle. And how ironic it is that this island belonging to a man who wanted to rid the world of God is now a glowing lake of fire surrounded by an enormous ocean. *'These things I have spoken unto you that in me ye might have peace. In the world ye shall have tribulation: but be of good cheer; I have overcome the world.' John 16:33. God's Word. Truth.*

CHAPTER THIRTY

The den is packed. It's the only room in our house that's big enough for everyone to gather. Steve sat up the tables and chairs again, and Herb prepared brunch with bagels, muffins, juice, and coffee for the big event. And since I'm nursing, Herb is still forcing me to drink decaf.

After the news reports came out and people realized that they had acted as puppets following along just as Dennis Denali had planned, some of the violence died down. A few more candidates stepped up seeking the role of president of the United States, but Cynthia won by a landslide.

Of course, the speech she gave to announce her candidacy was powerful, and the fact that she was part of the group that stopped Eckert worked in her favor. But the media coverage after Alice landed the plane and Cynthia stepped off sealed the election. The EMTs barely got through all the cameras to get Kade and me on the stretcher.

Kade and I only had to stay at the hospital overnight. All the doctors stared in bewilderment at the little five-pound-four-ounce guy, with his head full of hair and his brown eyes open wide, taking in the world. Everyone questioned how his lungs could be so strong and how he could be so healthy, considering his arrival was a month early, the length of time that I had been without proper food and water, and the environment in which he was birthed. But the answer was simple... God.

Kade is in the nursery now. Yes, he's healthy, but I'm still a mother hen—an obsessive-compulsive mother hen. Too many people are in this room, carrying too many germs for a premature baby to be exposed to. But, oh, as I move my eyes around this room, how I praise God to have these people back. Dad has his arm around Mom's shoulders as Mom is checking off the wedding to-do list with Alice and Gerald one last time. Eileen and Carlton are making small talk in the corner, but from the look in their eyes, I believe the connection between those two is anything but small. Waves is making his way around the room, giving a detailed account of how he was shot and left for dead. Right now, he is doing a complete, dramatic reenactment for Dukakis and Teresa. And Spencer is here on my lap. He's a bit jealous, so every second that I'm not holding Kade, I'm holding Spencer.

"Alright," Steve calls from the front of the room. "It's time."

Silence fills the room as all our eyes fix on the screen for Cynthia's inaugural address.

"Fellow Americans, today is a celebration because today we embark on a new journey. Today marks a new beginning, a new chance to unite, go back to our roots, and rebuild our country on the foundation laid for us by our forefathers. I know that this new journey may not be easy. The circle of trust has been broken. The

wounds left by my predecessors are still mending. You
have been lied to, tricked, deceived, and manipulated.
You have lost all confidence in the leadership of our
country, and on top of that, you now fear technology
and social media. And I don't blame you. I am in the
same boat as you, my friends. My late husband and your
previous president plotted to kill you. Ha. He froze me
in a giant test tube. Talk about breaking the circle of
trust. When he failed at poisoning you, he devised a new
plan to make you kill each other. Then, he created a
social media site to lure hurting people. He preyed upon
their weaknesses and, little by little, turned this group
against Christians by posting material containing some
tragic sin committed by someone proclaiming to be a
follower of Jesus. You know how it works. A million
wonderful things can happen, but it's the one bad thing
everyone hears about and remembers. His goal was to
create a world without God. He even bribed high-rank-
ing military officials into surrendering some of our own
soldiers to be part of his new planned society. But as
evil as Dennis Denali was, our downfall did not begin
with him. When we take away the right to hang the Ten
Commandments on our walls, when we take away the
right to openly pray to our Creator, when we eliminate
Creation being taught in our schools along with evolu-
tion, we are taking away the opportunity and the choice
for people to believe in and know God. We are taking
away the religious freedom our country was founded
upon. I say founded upon because it is God who grants
us religious freedom. He does not force Himself upon
us. He gives us the free will... the freedom to choose to
follow Him. Ladies and gentlemen, I ask you to join
me in going back to our roots. Let's restore religious

freedom. Let's give people their right to choose God, to get to know Him the way our forefathers did. Fellow citizens, as long as we live, we will always encounter evil. No matter your beliefs, there will be people consumed with hate. As you are aware, my late husband was not alone in his plot, and this cohort of his is still at large. He is somewhere out there 'going to and fro in the earth, and walking up and down on it,' and now that Dennis Denali is gone, this cohort of his is seeking someone else 'to devour.' So, friends, protect your mind. Don't let anger turn to hate. Don't use social media to tear each other down. Instead, let it be a tool to inspire, encourage, and build one another up. Let's use it to connect and unite. And let's go back to being the 'one nation under God' that we used to be. Thank you."

Cynthia's face disappears from the giant screen on the wall, and the room erupts in happy tears and joyful cheers because, finally, our country has a leader who isn't afraid to take a stand for God.

CHAPTER THIRTY-ONE

Standing outside the church, I watch as secret service men scour the area.

Dad steps up beside me. "It kind of has this feeling of déjà vu, doesn't it? You and I, standing outside this church."

"Yes. Yes, it does. Except for the Secret Service, and I'm not the one in the wedding dress this time," I say with a hint of laughter. "But, hey, you're still walking the bride down the aisle."

Dad smiles. "I know since Alice's dad isn't living, she didn't have anyone to give her away. But words can't express how much it meant that she asked me. I've messed up so many times and made so many mistakes. The fact that she would still ask me to fill in for her father...," a drop of water forms in the corner of his eye, "well, I'm speechless."

"Oh, Daddy, we all mess up. And Alice knows that every mistake you made was never with any ill intent. Your actions were motivated by love."

I notice Dad's eyes trained on Carlton and Eileen clutching each other's hands as they walk into the church.

"They make a nice couple, don't they?" I ask, wondering if he approves of his baby girl having another man in her life besides him.

"Yes, they do." He shakes his head. "It's not easy for a dad. My instinct is to shelter you girls. But as I couldn't have asked God to have given you any better of a man than Steve, I believe the same of Carlton. I just hope they aren't rushing things. They've seen each other every day since we got back from that island."

"I'm relieved that the thing with Ted didn't leave scars. She's been through enough. Honestly, I hesitated to even tell her about Ted's involvement in all of this, but it wouldn't have been right to keep it from her. But as for her and Carlton, I wouldn't worry. They both have strong faith. God will lead them." I watch as Dukakis stops in front of the church door, pops a whole peanut butter cup in his mouth, and then steps inside. "Speaking of new relationships, Dukakis finally got the nerve to ask Cynthia on a real date. Because of the death threats, two secret service men sat at the next table, but it's nice to finally see those two connecting."

Dad grumbles. "Death threats. Unbelievable."

"For the most part, Cynthia's inaugural address was welcomed and embraced, but as she stated in her speech, there will always be those that allow themselves to be consumed by hate."

"Speaking of threats," Dad leans in closer, "do you know if there are any leads on Morgan," he rolls his eyes, "or Seaver or whoever he is?"

"Not that I'm aware of. I find it odd that no one can even figure out what his birth name is. It's like he is this phantom that repeats the same cycle over and over. He pops up wearing a halo, spins an evil web, and disappears into thin air." I take a deep breath and let it out slowly.

"It is frightening how many times he came into my home—how I trusted him."

"Ellie, 2 Corinthians 11:14 says, '... for Satan himself is transformed into an angel of light.' " Dad rests his hand on my shoulder. "That's why we need to put on our armor and keep our swords sharpened."

I nod. "You know, Dad, all of this has made me realize how important it is to make sure I'm bearing good fruit. My life is a witness for Jesus. It's easy to say I'm a Christian and that I love Jesus, but my actions tell the truth. The things I do can lead someone to Christ or turn that person away from Him. I pray my actions tell His Truth."

Steve steps up beside me. "Your knight in shining armor awaits."

"I better not keep my escort waiting. I love you, Daddy."

"I love you too, sweetheart." Dad leans in and kisses my cheek.

I take Steve's arm and slightly lift my dress as he leads me to the door.

"Did you make sure the rings were tightly fastened to the pillow?" I ask.

"Don't worry. Spencer won't lose them," he smiles. "He made it across the ocean with your Bible, didn't he?"

"Yeah. He's a pretty special monkey."

Steve laughs. "Have you seen your mother?"

"No. Why?" I lift one eyebrow.

"Well, let me just say, we may have trouble getting our baby back after the wedding. She has completely forgotten about being the wedding coordinator. She doesn't even seem to know anyone else is at the wedding besides Kade."

I shrug. "It's her first grandchild. What do you expect?"

The music starts.

"I guess that means it's time for the matron of honor and the best man to make their grand entrance," he says, reaching for the knob. He pauses as he starts to turn it. "Ellie, I've been wondering about something."

"What?" I turn my face toward him.

"When you shot my clone, how were you so sure that it wasn't me?"

I crack a smile. "Let's just say that God's Word truly is 'a discerner of the thoughts and intents of the heart.'"

He narrows his eyes and tilts his head.

"Never forget," I say, squeezing his arm.

"Aaah," he nods, opening the door, and as we take a step in, he whispers, "'For the Lord thy God is with thee whithersoever thou goest.'"

The End

ACKNOWLEDGMENTS

T hank you to my wonderful husband and best friend, Steve, for always being there to pick me up when I get discouraged and for not minding all those hours I spend in front of my computer.

Thank you to my two amazing children, Landon and Layna, for encouraging me to write and telling all your friends about my books.

Thank you to my mother, Carolyn Bryant, for all the time spent proofreading. (Just when she thought she was finished, she would get to start all over again.)

Thank you to all those who read my two novels, shared my social media posts, and helped me launch my books. I cannot express how much I appreciate all that you have done to encourage and support me.

And most of all, I thank my Heavenly Father for allowing me to do something I love and for putting a message on my heart to share. I thank Him for all the wonderful people He has brought into my life to support and encourage me. I thank Him for always being there to listen and wanting to know me... personally. Without Him, I could do nothing. All Praise and Glory to God!

BIBLIOGRAPHY

Although this is a work of fiction, the following is a listing of sources used in researching the historical matter referred to in the fictitious speech contained in chapter six of this novel.

"Constitution of the United States." Document, 1787. "The Constitution of the United States: A Transcription." National Archives. Accessed February 15, 2024. https://www.archives.gov/founding-docs/constitution-tran-script?_ga=2.35909734.717796534.1707876338-1916224300.1705805194.

"Declaration of Independence." Document, 1776. "Declaration of Independence: A Transcription." National Archives. Accessed February 15, 2024. https://www.archives.gov/founding-docs/declaration-transcript?_ga=2.114474049.717796534.1707876338-1916224300.1705805194.

Duché, Reverend Jacob. "First Prayer of the Continental Congress." Prayer, 1774. "First Prayer of the Continental Congress, 1774," Office of the Chaplain, United States House of Representatives.

Chaplain.house.gov. Accessed February 15, 2024. https://chaplain.house.gov/archive/continental.htm

Reagan, Ronald. "Remarks at an Ecumenical Prayer Breakfast." Speech, Dallas, Texas, August 23, 1984. "Remarks at an Ecumenical Prayer Breakfast in Dallas, Texas," Ronald Reagan Presidential Library & Museum. Reaganlibrary.gov. Accessed February 15, 2024. https://www.reaganlibrary.gov/archives/speech/remarks-ecumenical-prayer-breakfast-dallas-texas.

"Samuel Adams." *American Eloquence, Volume I, Studies In American Political History.* 1630. Project Gutenberg. Updated November 15, 2012. Www.gutenberg.org. Accessed February 15, 2024. https://www.gutenberg.org/files/15391/15391-h/15391-h.htm#link2H_4_0007.

Washington, George. "Thanksgiving Proclamation of 1789." Proclamation, 1789. George Washington's Mount Vernon. Accessed February 15, 2024. https://www.mountvernon.org/education/primary-source-collections/primary-source-collections/article/thanksgiving-proclamation-of-1789/.

Winthrop, John. "A Model of Christian Charity". Sermon, December 31, 1630. Teaching American History. Teachingamericanhistory.org. Accessed February 16, 2024. https://teachingamericanhistory.org/document/a-model-of-christian-charity-2/.

ABOUT THE AUTHOR

F. D. Adkins is a Christian fiction author and freelance writer. She hopes to pass along the comfort that comes from having a personal relationship with Jesus while offering her readers a brief escape from life's struggles through an action-packed story full of suspense, twists, turns, love, and a few laughs. In other words, her passion is sharing her faith through fiction.

Her previous novels in the TRUTH trilogy include the Christian Suspense Thrillers, *TRUTH IN THE NAME* and *TRUTH IN THE WORD*. In May 2023, Book One, TRUTH IN THE NAME received third place in the Selah Awards in the category of 'First Novel.' She has had freelance articles published in *FOCUS ON THE FAMILY* magazine and *FAITH ON EVERY CORNER* magazine. In addition, F. D. Adkins posts every Monday to a faith blog on her website.

She has been married to the man of her dreams and her best friend for 25 years. She loves spending time with her family, reading, writing, and always enjoys a good cup of coffee. She also has a soft spot in her heart for all animals, especially dogs.

She lives in South Carolina with her husband, Steve, their two children, Landon and Layna, and their dog, Lucy.

IN MEMORY OF

LUCY ANGEL ADKINS

NOT A WORD OF THIS NOVEL WAS WRITTEN
WITHOUT YOU (LITERALLY) BY MY SIDE.
A MEMBER OF OUR FAMILY FOR ALMOST 14 YEARS AND THE
GREATEST FRIEND A PERSON COULD EVER ASK FOR...
YOU WILL FOREVER BE IN MY HEART.
SEPTEMBER 8, 2010 – JANUARY 8, 2024